R.D. Shah spent his formative years in the north west of England before attending Rugby School in Warwickshire. At seventeen he attained his private pilot's licence in Florida and shortly after attended the University of Miami where he studied motion picture & psychology before returning to the UK to work in television & leisure. He has travelled extensively throughout Europe, Russia and the Americas. R.D. holds a scuba diving licence, which he gained along the shores of the Hawaiian island of Kauai. All this experience has prepared him for a career in writing. He lives in Wiltshire with his wife and young daughter.

Also by R.D. Shah

The Harker Chronicles

Relics
The 4th Secret
The Last Judgement
The Dark Temple
The Shadow Conspiracy

The Disavowed

Project Icarus

R.D. SHAH
PROJECT ICARUS

CANELO

First published in the United Kingdom in 2021 by

Canelo
Unit 9, 5th Floor
Cargo Works, 1–2 Hatfields
London, SE1 9PG
United Kingdom

A CIP catalogue record for this book is available from the British Library.

Print ISBN 978 1 80032 530 2
Ebook ISBN 978 1 80032 529 6

Look for more great books at www.canelo.co

Printed and bound in Great Britain by Clays Ltd, Elcograf S.p.A.

1

To James. For all the times I was there and all the times I wasn't.

Prologue

Another volley of silver flashes lit up the night sky, illuminating the black Jaguar I-Pace as it drew closer to the German Chancellery located in the very heart of Berlin. UK ambassador David Breams leant forward and gazed out of the passenger side window as a horde of enthusiastic reporters continued snapping pictures and bustling for a good spot behind the blue separation banners.

Even after all these years of diplomatic service he still found it absurd that such an announcement could cause this intense interest, but it flattered him nonetheless, and a haughty smile spread across his face. In days gone by, the simple welcoming of a new ambassador to his role would have enticed only a few uninspired reporters to the scene, but these days, in the era of twenty-four-hour rolling news, one couldn't burp in public without attracting a media swarm, all salivating at the chance to ruin a public official's reputation.

Breams expelled a satisfied sigh and stretched back in his seat, the grey leather creaking beneath him. They were already ten minutes late because some idiot had screwed up the schedule, but even this blunder did little to dampen his enthusiasm. This was a momentous occasion for him personally, and one he had been privately coveting for many years. Still, someone would pay for that mistake, of that he would make sure.

In the seat next to him, a grey-haired man raised his eyebrows cheerfully, then proceeded to rub his palm firmly along his thigh, flattening the small wrinkle which had developed along his charcoal, pinstriped suit trousers. "You deserve this, David," the man said graciously, "your work for the party and the country has been exemplary, and the PM feels the same way."

"I appreciate that, Jacob, and thank you for your support. I doubt I could have got here without it."

"Utter tripe, my friend," Jacob said, maintaining his perfected politician's smile for the cameras as the Jaguar began grinding to a slow halt upon the asphalt driveway. "You've earned this off your own merit, so for God's sake, enjoy it."

Breams's nostrils flared slightly with pride as a blonde doorman dressed in a long black overcoat and blue cravat strode over to the passenger side and grasped the handle. "Yes, Home Secretary. I will."

The Home Secretary nodded in approval, but still sensing some anxiety he gently patted the ambassador on his forearm. "Remember, David, all our dreams can come true, if we have the courage to pursue them… and pursue them you have."

The adage appeared to bolster Breams's demeanour, and his shoulders relaxed a little. "Who said that, Churchill?"

"No," the Home Secretary said, "it was Walt Disney, so enjoy yourself. That's an order!"

The door swung open, bathing the Jaguar's interior in a crescendo of dazzling flashes, and Ambassador Breams stepped out onto the red carpet before offering a tight-lipped smile to the eager press.

He didn't want to look smug.

Breams remained there, somewhat stiffly, until the Home Secretary had joined him, and then they began to march up the tethered walkway side by side, in unison, towards a man standing patiently at the far end.

"Does your appointment signal even closer relations with Germany, Ambassador?" shouted one of the waiting photographers before he was sucked back into the frenzied pack, to be replaced by a female reporter literally hurling her microphone towards him.

"Who will you be supporting in the European cup final, Manchester United or Liverpool?"

The question was obviously a joke and Breams stopped for a moment. "Neither of them," he said, smiling like a Cheshire cat. "I'm a Tottenham Hotspur supporter."

The off-the-cuff remark received a few chuckles from the crowd and after a polite nod the ambassador continued calmly up the red carpet to the grey-suited man with short blonde hair who greeted them warmly.

"Chancellor Schenk, it's good to see you again," Jacob said cordially, "and thank you for meeting us here today. I apologise for the delay."

The Chancellor was already shaking his head. "Not a problem, although another few minutes and we were about to call it off and go for dinner."

All three men laughed jovially as the Chancellor now extended his open palm towards Breams. "It's a pleasure to see you, Secretary Ryan, and of course Ambassador Breams."

Breams took the Chancellor's hand and shook it firmly. "The pleasure is all mine, Chancellor."

The three men stood posed for a moment as the flashes intensified and, once satisfied the photo opportunity had been milked to the max, the Chancellor retrieved his hand and proceeded to usher his two guests inside and through the impressive entrance of the Federal Chancellery building.

Built at the end of the twentieth century, the Federal Chancellery building, or 'Bundeskanzleramt', as it was known, had been built to house the various German governmental institutions following the relocation of the German capital from Bonn to Berlin at the end of the Cold War. It also housed the Chancellor's main office, and was within a stone's throw of the Reichstag, the seat of German Parliament and the world-famous Brandenburg Gate. In humble comparison to the domed Reichstag building, the Chancellery itself was not that impressive, with a white, two-storey building at its centre flanked by long rectangle corridors on either side, but it offered a style of symmetry that expressed the perfection at the heart of Germany's soul. As with cars and industry, the country's architecture offered something different, and while Breams followed behind the two leaders he found his thoughts drawn to the top of the building. On the roof above, numerous pear trees had been planted, each one symbolising a different German leader, and with the latest polls out that morning, Breams wondered if Chancellor Schenk's leaves had perhaps wilted of late. Of course by the end of the week they would no doubt be flourishing once again. Such was politics... and the polls.

The inside of the Chancellery felt like a hospital, and exuded cleanliness. With numerous floors on either side, all painted in a dazzling white, it was an assault on one's senses, akin to being caught in a blizzard. For a moment Breams felt snow-blind, the media's camera flashes only adding to the intensity.

4

"Gentlemen," Schenk declared as they reached a set of open white double doors, before pointing inside towards two microphone-adorned podiums, which faced a crowd of eager reporters all sat impatiently on black plastic chairs. It was a tight fit, with attendees sat shoulder to shoulder, and the numerous secret service guards lining the room's edges looked particularly concerned and hampered by the number of hot, sweaty bodies that had been squeezed in for the press conference.

The three men made their way inside, with Schenk and Breams taking the central podiums. Secretary Ryan stood off to the side as the Chancellor raised his hands pacifyingly and the room rapidly descended into silence. Not until he was satisfied did the German leader begin to speak, in English.

"Thank you all for being here today. I would personally like to extend my gratitude to Home Secretary Ryan for the drive he has displayed in the organisation for this occasion. As you all know, this type of event is not in line with the usual protocol between countries, but since the United Kingdom has left the European Union, and given the strong, unyielding bond we have with them, it seemed suitable for us on the continent to show our continuing friendship and the ties that bind us as nations…"

As the German Chancellor continued to reel off his prepared speech, Breams found himself slipping off into something of a daze. At first he put it down to low blood sugar, having not eaten all day but, as his mind began to slip deeper into an ever-developing trance, the reasons seemed more immaterial with every passing second. Even the invasive camera flashes began to melt away into the background, and a single idea came to the forefront of his mind. An idea that not only seemed highly rational, but necessary. In fact, it was without doubt the most important idea he had ever had. It sent a wave of euphoria rippling through his body, and he wiggled his fingers lightly, the tips tingling pleasurably.

Beside him the German Chancellor was coming to the end of his short introduction and as yet another flurry of flashes flickered unyieldingly he returned his attention back to the task in hand.

"...and despite some lone voices within the press who have tried to insinuate that there is a great division between Great Britain and the European Union, I am here today to assure you that our countries are closer than ever before, with a vested national interest in each other's success. With that in mind, allow me to introduce you to the incoming UK ambassador, David Breams."

Ambassador Breams cheerfully grasped at the stationary microphone with all the zeal of a nightclub singer and gazed out across the crowd before him. He waited for a few seconds, allowing the crowd to settle, all the while biting his cheek in an attempt to stem the building excitement that was now filling every part of his body.

"Thank you, Chancellor Schenk, and may I begin by saying how proud and honoured I am to have been chosen to act as the diplomatic link between our two great nations. As many newspapers have recently written, it is a link that goes much deeper than simply title. My father was born here in Berlin, no more than a mile from where we now stand..." Breams paused, then gave a gentle, disbelieving shake of his head as a proud smile crept across his face. "When he sought refuge in Great Britain as a Jewish refugee at the beginning of the war, he often felt that his ties with his homeland had been cut permanently. But if he had been told that eighty years later his grandson would return as ambassador to the country he loved, to play his part in maintaining the crucial connection between our two great nations… well, to say it would have warmed his heart and his soul would be an understatement. So, it is with thoughts of him that I thank you for my welcome, and on behalf of the British government, I say to you that we look forward to continuing our robust relationship, which has lasted for so many years. I'll leave you with this one thought that I know my grandfather would have shared. As individual countries we are strong, but together we are unshakable."

At first there was dead silence, but as Chancellor Schenk raised his hands and began to clap, the rest of the delegation did likewise and Breams stepped back from the podium, nodding gratefully as even a few of the press corps now put their hands together. There was nothing sweeter than basking in the glow of appreciation and he lapped it up for a few moments, allowing it to engulf him like the warmth from an open hearth. Then, as the sound began to fade, he moved back to the microphone and smiled once more. "And with those words having been said… Let's get this party started."

With his left hand, Breams reached into the inside pocket of his Savile Row suit, pulled out a black Walther 9mm handgun, pointed it directly at Chancellor Schenk's forehead and squeezed the trigger.

Every single person in the room flinched in unison as Schenk's head violently snapped backwards like a Pez dispenser, spraying blood across his closest advisors, who stood there, rigid with shock, as the German leader collapsed backwards to the floor with a thud. Still grinning gleefully, Breams now swung his weapon towards the press corps and began unloading his weapon indiscriminately, one of the bullets catching a first-row reporter in the jaw and sending bone and cartilage flying into the eyes of her nearest colleague, blinding him instantly.

Screaming erupted throughout the room as reporters dived for cover, and as Breams swung the gun towards the Chancellor's entourage, the sound of a short burst of machine gun fire thundered deafeningly throughout the room. Ambassador David Breams was sent plummeting backwards to the floor in a crumpled heap. With his chest riddled with bullet wounds, each haemorrhaging crimson bloodstains across his white shirt, the ambassador's head rotated in jerks as his muscles spasmed uncontrollably. His dulling eyes locked on to the secret service agent pointing an MP5 at him, as behind him Home Secretary Ryan was being rushed off stage by his security detail, all shielding him with their bodies. Next to him officials were rushing over to the lifeless body of Chancellor Schenk and attempting pointlessly to stem the flow of blood with their own suit jackets, as a few of the more seasoned journalists raised their cameras and began snapping off shots.

The still twitching body of David Breams was for the final time lit up in the bright magnesium glow of camera flashes as the ambassador's pupils began to widen and his body started to bleed out. He gazed into the horrified faces of the crowd, who were staring at him in disgust, and only one thought came to mind.

What the hell was wrong with these people!

Chapter 1

Shimmering street lamps lit up passers-by as dusk swiftly fell across the city on that chilly spring evening. In the distance London Bridge sparkled its lights and busy shoppers hurried their way across it as beneath a tour boat lazily sailed past along the Thames on its final trip of the day. On the far side City Hall sloped to one side, its neo-futuristic design looking like a silver fingertip decked with solar panels. Across the famous river stood a line of seven-foot plastic domes filled with small groups, all enjoying a meal. The Coppa Club was as famous for its excellent Italian cuisine as it was its location and each plastic bubble, or igloo, as they were known, seated seven guests and offered a unique dining experience for the tourist masses who descended upon the capital all year round.

It was a busy night, and even though all of the igloos were occupied by happy patrons, there was one that appeared to be creating more commotion than all the others combined. Inside, a tall man wearing a garish, floral green jumper, rose to his feet and held up his champagne flute.

"Welcome everyone... except Bill," the man said, raising his glass towards a man with short ginger hair wearing a worn blue Adidas tracksuit, "for almost forgetting to book this dinner, and the even worse crime of attending it so underdressed."

The other guests followed in raising their glasses momentarily, with Bill holding his higher than everyone else.

"What can I say, Peter, I'm a slave to fashion," Bill remarked, his Liverpudlian accent heavy and his tone smug and uncaring.

The host's eyes drooped and he lowered his glass slightly, peering over the rim towards the party's worst-dressed guest. "Yes, quite, Bill, I just wasn't aware 'Hobo' was in vogue this year."

Laughs erupted around the table and Bill offered a sarcastic smile and a dismissive swipe of his hand as Peter continued with his welcome.

"Seriously, it's good to see you all looking so well given the train wreck of events over the past few years. I can say from the heart that I am so happy to have the family together again."

All the guests offered a nod of approval except one, a woman with short blonde hair wearing a black business suit with a white shirt buttoned up to the top. "If you mean a bunch of strangers thrown together by fate then sure… family."

"Now Abi," Peter replied, raising his chin, "no matter the roads that led us here, we are all part of the same clan. Whether by fortune or misfortune, you represent some of the last alumni to graduate from Strawberry Field children's home, and that bond is as indelible as blood itself. No one gets to choose their family, and we are no different."

Abi allowed herself a small yet content smile, and she was joined by Peter.

"I may be getting ancient, but when I say this, I say it from the heart. I have been proud and lucky to be your mentor from the time I set eyes on all of you."

"Tyrant is more like it, Peter," suggested a man with brown hair; he wore a silver suit and red tie, and sat directly to the host's left.

Peter craned his neck towards the man and he grinned mockingly. "Well, some were more of a pain in the arse than others, Trevor 'I enjoy joyriding' Roper."

"Never convicted," Trevor replied, raising his finger straight up in the air and puffing out his chest proudly.

The group now broke into laughter as Peter shook his head in mild despair and he waited for it to die down before continuing with his welcome speech.

"Well, despite any 'entanglements' your formative years at Strawberry Field generated, I say again how proud you have all made me. And always remember, you may not share the same name…"

The whole group now erupted in unison with the same dreary, monotone, "…but we share the same spirit."

Again the igloo was filled with laughter and Peter dropped back into his seat with the look of a father giving in to his children's impudence.

"Yes, yes, very funny. Let's all take the piss out of the man who raised you."

Abi reached over and gently slapped the cloth-covered tabletop before him.

"You know how we really feel about you."

Peter offered a humorous shrug and his shoulders slouched. "Yeah, that's the problem."

All the guests, including Peter, now descended into a final chorus of laughter, and as it began to die out it was

Trevor who stood up and raised his own glass of bubbling champagne, signalling quiet.

"Before we settle down and get to catching up, there is something else I want to say. I know I ain't been to one of these dinners in a few years now, and I've not spoken to any of you since then… much to the betterment of my mental health."

Around the table eyes rolled in their sockets as Trevor comically shrugged it off, enjoying his joke. He then gazed down at the attractive brunette sat next to him, dripping in Cartier jewellery, from the emerald-encrusted necklace hanging around her neck to the oversized diamond ring on her index finger. "I wanna say thank you for allowing me to bring my wife, Debbie. I know these events are usually just us, but it shows a lot of respect, you know."

Abi, among others, was already shaking her head at Trevor's arrogant tone, but the synchronised gesture was ignored and he carried on regardless.

"I know you all think I can be a bit aloof at times, but just to prove I still think about you all I wanna say congratulations." Trevor now turned his attention to the man sitting opposite, the only person whose demeanour had been subdued throughout the short speeches.

"I wanna propose a toast to Ethan. You may 'ave forgotten but I 'aven't. Today is his birthday, and even though we're on opposite sides, I just wanna offer him congratulations on this special day. I don't know if the world is a better place with him in it, but like Peter said, we all share the same spirit."

At thirty-three years old Ethan Munroe didn't have exactly what you'd call an intimidating presence, but his piercing dark brown eyes alone expressed more menace than any physical presence could. He wasn't thickset, although his slim, athletic build and wide shoulders bolstered his five-foot-ten frame with the density of a boxer: solid yet flexible. He stared over at his toastmaster and offered a forced smile.

Munroe, like all the others sat at the table, with the exception of Trevor's wife Debbie, had grown up together at Strawberry Field children's home in the suburbs of Woolton in Liverpool. By the time he arrived, at the age of four, the children's home had already become somewhat famous by association to John Lennon, who had grown up nearby and whose famous Beatles track 'Strawberry Fields Forever' had put the place on the map. Like many of the kids Munroe had no recollection of his own parents, having been abandoned before his long-term memory had really formed, and with only snippets of recall from times past he had, over the years, formed a bond with the others, but none more than Peter Devon. As the overseer of the home, they had many names for Devon, but the one which had stuck was 'the mole', for the man's uncanny ability to pop up just as they were in the middle of doing something they shouldn't have been doing. At sixteen Munroe had, as he saw it, made the great escape to join the army. He left the graffitied gates of Strawberry Field, thanks to the numerous Beatles fans who continually sought to show their loyalty through artwork, and began a regimented life in the military.

There he stayed, working his way up through the ranks before, after thirteen years of service, he got out. He had his reasons, none that he cared to dwell upon, and he quickly integrated back into civilian life and undertook a course in criminal justice at Oxford University. Within a year he had graduated with an MSc in Criminal Justice and immediately entered the Metropolitan

Police. Within two years, and thanks mainly to the Direct Entry Initiative, he had made superintendent, and given his past military experience had taken the track towards crisis negotiation, which he discovered was where his real talents lay. Three years in and his experience was vast, having been involved with incidents from domestic situations to a terrorist negotiation a year earlier where a young man had taken a family hostage and threatened to blow himself up. As it turned out the only weapon the desperate man had on him was a large carving knife, and the bomb vest was nothing more than silver-painted carboard toilet rolls sellotaped together with coiled piano wire. Regardless, he had negotiated the release of the hostages – unharmed, although understandably terrified by the ordeal – along with the perpetrator himself. Mental illness and Jihad websites did not mix well.

There were many of his Strawberry Field 'alumni', as Peter put it, that were curious about how he had climbed the Met ranks so quickly, but that was another story entirely, and one for his consumption only. Besides, they probably wouldn't have believed him anyway.

And then there was Trevor Roper. The two had spent many years together at Strawberry, but each had taken very different paths. While Munroe was getting pummelled on an assault course by unyielding combat instructors Trevor was ingratiating himself into the criminal fraternity. Munroe chose not to know exactly what the man did for a 'living'; he had always kept his distance and, so far, their paths had never crossed. He wanted to know as little about the life of his old acquaintance as possible, and given the idiotic smiling face of his, which was now staring at him, it was obvious Trevor felt likewise.

"Happy birthday, mate."

Trevor's eyes widened, waiting for a response, but there appeared little appetite for it among the other guests. In fact it wasn't until Munroe raised his glass that the others followed suit.

"Thanks, Trevor," Munroe said as the others chimed in, all in a somewhat conciliatory tone, and once a sip was taken the rumble of independent conversation between guests began to flow again, leaving Trevor looking sour-faced. He sat down and then leant over to Devon. "Jesus... who died?"

If anybody else heard the comment they certainly didn't acknowledge it, and Peter replied in a hushed voice, "His wife and daughter."

The look of contempt on Trevor's face disintegrated in an instant.

"They got caught in a terrorist attack, car bomb... Five years ago today."

"Jesus Christ," Trevor replied, now looking genuinely guilty.

"Ethan walked away with barely a scratch. He got lucky, if you can call it that."

Trevor now glanced over to find Munroe staring at him, his face bearing no shred of malice.

"It's all right, you didn't know," Munroe said above everyone else's chatter. They could of course all hear him in this small domed dining room but none, understand-ably, wanted to join in.

Trevor gave a sorrowful look, or at least the best he was capable of. "I'm sorry, Ethan. They were lovely."

Trevor had barely known them, he'd only met them once, but Munroe nodded courteously and retreated back to his thoughts before Abi touched him on his forearm.

"Forget him," she said, moving closer. She, like almost everyone there, knew of the tragedy but unlike the others she was usually the one to bring it up. "How are you doing, Ethan?"

Munroe shook his head wearily. "Sometimes it seems like a never-ending black hole and I'm scrambling to get out of it. Just can't move on."

"Jesus, Ethan, you really are in a bad place, aren't you?"

Munroe necked the last of his champagne and nodded grimly. "I know it's been a few years now, Abi, but every time I see light at the end of the tunnel it seems to crumble and close in on me."

Abi was now looking as depressed as he felt and without hesitation Munroe switched gear and returned to her question.

"But, despite all my doom and gloom, I'm actually doing OK. Just not good when dwelling on it, you know." Munroe reached over and squeezed her arm. "It's really good to see you, though, and doing so well."

This attempt to change the subject was completely ignored by Abi. Instead she moved in closer and began to nibble at her bottom lip. "So, are you involved in any interesting cases at the moment?" she probed, allowing her morbid curiosity to get the better of her, as was usually the case.

Abi was a decent sort, but she could be a dark one at the best of times, and her curiosity for all things murder was legendary.

"No, not really," Munroe lied, "things have been pretty quiet recently." He could see Abi was beginning to chew at the bit, and before long she'd be looking to extract every last foul detail of each case he'd worked on. The more gruesome the better. "If you don't mind, Abi, I'm going to get a bit of fresh air. I'll be back."

She gave his arm another squeeze. "If you want to talk, I'll be right here," she said as he got up from his seat. "And if you want to give me some of the grisly details of any of the investigations you're involved in, then I'm here too."

Munroe shot her a knowing look, and with that her expression morphed into the look of an innocent angel. "Thanks, Abi," he said, and with a glance at Devon he made his way out of the igloo's curved doorway and into the cold night air outside. Usually when someone wants to leave the room for a breather, they can relax the moment the door closes behind them. But all the igloos were see-through, so Munroe calmly made his way to the railings, leant against them and looked out across the dark, rippling dark water.

After losing his family he had thrown himself into the job, and that's where he had stayed. Like an alcoholic into a whisky bottle he had sunk himself into his work, but having to meet up with his 'old family' and bring up the tragedy again was something he could have done without. Like ripping off a plaster for a wound that wouldn't heal. Painful and unproductive.

The deeper into his work he ground himself the less he'd think about that terrible night, and perhaps a few days would pass without him waking up from a nightmare, soaked in a cold sweat and crying like a baby.

Pathetic.

He had survived, and it was this fact that had dominated his dreams more than anything else. His yeaning to see his wife and daughter again was tearing him up, but the guilt that engulfed his waking moments was worse. To have survived with little more than a concussion and bruising, and the knowledge that he wasn't able to protect the ones he loved when they needed him most – that was the bitterest pill to swallow.

The sound of the igloo opening and closing behind him whisked him away from such thoughts, and Munroe turned to see Devon sauntering towards him. He was the closest thing to a father he had ever had, if you didn't count the army, and it made him smile to see how agile the man still was, even at the age of sixty-five.

"Yes, I know you're fine, Ethan, but it's getting a bit stuffy in there and I get the feeling Trevor and his wife are about to engage in a good old-fashioned family tiff."

Munroe looked over his friend's shoulder to see the couple glaring at one another as Abi stared at them nosily with what could have been a smirk.

"I think Debbie feels that her husband has embarrassed her with his birthday toast."

"Believe me," Munroe said, turning back towards the waterline, "he doesn't need me to embarrass himself."

"Quite the truth. Trevor says things that would make a chimpanzee blush at the best of times."

They both let out a laugh as Devon now joined him at the railings. "I can only imagine how tough a year it's been for you Ethan… and I know you don't want to talk about it, so I will say only this…"

Munroe knew what was coming… the pep talk… but even though he could do without it right at this moment there was something about the very act that he found comforting, so he kept his mouth shut and allowed the older man to say his piece.

"I don't know if I've ever told you, but the first time I ever set eyes upon you, how old were you, four? I saw in your eyes a resilience that I'd not seen before, or since.

You were small and fragile, yes, but there was a determination in your eyes that made me know that whatever life threw at you, you'd always come back stronger." Devon double-tapped his finger on the metal railing like a judge preparing his final statement. "And over the years you've proved me right, time and time again."

The silence which ensued wasn't uncomfortable, but rather one of apprehension for Munroe. He wasn't a fan of the old man getting soppy, but he knew it was coming, as it always did, from a good place and he stayed silent.

"I suppose what I'm trying to say is that I am always here when you need me, and that, well, I'm very proud of you, boy."

"Oh God, Peter, you're not going to cry, are you?"

"Oh, shut up, Munroe," he said with a smirk. "Always the smart arse."

Munroe was now grinning as well. Devon now raised his chin stoically, as he always did when he was about to recite a quote.

"Always remember, as Sir Francis Drake once said, 'Greatness from humble beginnings.'"

"From small beginnings, not humble," Munroe replied, shaking his head. "You're memory's going, old-timer."

Devon's eyes widened and he raised his eyebrows. "Really! Well I'm not too old to take you out, boy."

They both laughed again and Devon punched Munroe gently on the shoulder as a voice called out from behind them.

"Mr Ethan Munroe?"

Munroe turned to see one of the waiters that had served them their drinks on arrival holding a cordless landline phone in his left hand.

"Yes."

"There's a call for you, sir. Extremely important."

Munroe reached over and took the phone from the waiter's outstretched hand. "Who is it?"

"The police," the waiter said with a blank expression.

"Thank you," Munroe replied, and then stared back with the same blank expression. After a few moments the waiter got the message and with a small bow he turned around and headed back in to the Coppa Club's main building.

Devon stayed where he was as Munroe placed the receiver to his ear. "Superintendent Munroe."

"Ethan, why aren't you answering your mobile?"

Munroe knew the voice instantly. It was the head of the Met's hostage negotiation team and his superior. Mike Regis was a firm but fair man who valued competency above all else, and tonight he sounded really pissed off.

"I'm at a dinner. I told you about it. My phone's turned off," Munroe said quickly. "What's up?"

As always Regis went straight to the point. "There's a situation developing. Barricading of a house with two hostages, believed armed. I need you on this."

"Any information?"

There was an unusual pause and then Regis came back on the line sounding almost flustered, again unusual.

"A patrol saw a man dumping a body from the boot of his car underneath Blackfriars Bridge. The suspect drove off and they tailed him to a house in Kilburn. The suspect crashed his car and scooped two pedestrians off the street after he bailed. Mother and child. He dragged them inside at knife point. They've been holed up for the last fifteen minutes."

"Mike, it'll take me over thirty minutes to get there, don't we have someone closer?"

If anyone had overheard the conversation they might have thought Munroe was trying to pass the buck, but when it came to this type of situation the sooner a negotiator was on site the better.

"I'm on my way right now, but I'm in Brighton. It'll take me at least forty-five to get there."

"Brighton? I thought you were at HQ tonight?"

"You thought wrong, Ethan, and yes, I do have other people, but that's not the issue."

"Then what is?" Munroe said, but even before Regis replied he knew what the answer would be. It didn't make an ounce of sense and had never happened before but somehow, he just knew.

"The hostage taker, Ethan. We've got a landline to him but he only answered once and says he won't pick up the phone again until we do as he asks."

"What's he asking?"

"He's not asking, he's demanding."

They were going around in circles. "So what the hell is he demanding, Mike?"

There was a slight pause, and then Regis came back on the line, and this time he shouted. "You! He's demanding to see you… and only you."

Chapter 2

A light fog had descended upon the small London cul-de-sac as Munroe approached the two uniformed policemen manning the residential entrance. He'd left his black BMW 330e on the kerb and had walked the last fifty metres deliberately. Keeping calm was of the essence in a situation of this type and pulling right up outside the house would do no good. Besides, if the suspect was expecting him to show up, he didn't want to announce it until he had more information.

"Sorry, sir, but you're going to have to turn back," one of the officers said with a raised hand, and Munroe retrieved his identification from his jacket pocket and hung it in front of him.

"Superintendent Munroe. I'm expected."

The officer, a young man in his twenties, dutifully stood to one side. "Go on ahead, sir, they're waiting for you."

"Cheers lads." He proceeded calmly over to the two policemen waiting by the two Land Rover Discoveries whose flickering blue and red lights were illuminating the residence in question. The nearest policeman, an older-looking man with a greying moustache and ruddy complexion, heard the footsteps and turned around to face Munroe.

"Sergeant Brian Howell," the officer announced, introducing himself with a swift handshake. "You the negotiator?"

"Superintendent Ethan Munroe."

Howell was already eyeing Munroe's black, knee-length Roma overcoat, which covered a white-collared shirt along with a perfectly ironed red tie.

"Catch you in the middle of something?"

"Only my birthday dinner," Munroe replied with a shrug.

"Well, happy birthday, Superintendent."

"Thanks." He turned his attention to the house with all its curtains drawn closed. "What's the situation?"

"We've got a middle-aged Caucasian holding a young girl hostage."

"How about the mother?"

"The mother's not in there, the suspect threw her out before he holed up. It's just the girl."

Munroe's eyes narrowed as he contemplated the act. Two hostages were always better than one, unless there was a reason for it.

"Is he armed?"

"No sign of a firearm, but he came to the window holding a knife and he says he's armed. I've got two blue berets covering the back and two to the sides of us covering the front."

Munroe glanced from left to right to see the familiar sight of two armed men crouching semi-prone behind the opposing neighbouring fences, dressed in full tactical gear with helmets and holding SIG716 assault rifles aimed towards the house. The term 'blue berets' was police slang for the SCO19 armed response unit and it surprised him because these boys and girls were usually only called upon in the direst of circumstances.

"It's a bit heavy, isn't it?" Munroe noted, turning his attention back to Howell. "Why not the regular armed response unit?"

Sergeant Howell looked uneasy and he offered a shake of his head. "You know this spate of murders over the past six months, the pregnant woman over in Whitehall and that man they found chopped up under London Bridge?"

Munroe knew the case – who didn't, it had been in all the papers. Five grisly murders, almost one a month, and all in a different 'style'. If it hadn't been for the killer's message, written in blood at every scene, they might never have been connected. The finger-painted note was always the same: his name, his signature.

"*Icarus*," Munroe mouthed softly to himself.

"Yep. We think so," Howell said, taking a deep uncomfortable breath. "A squad car caught him in the act, still signing his name. The woman was already dead and he took off in his vehicle with them in pursuit. He crashed his car just a road over from here and broke into this house after he got cornered."

"Was anyone else in the house?" Munroe questioned, staring at the windows for any sign of movement.

"No, the mother *was* inside but he threw her out and locked himself in." Howell motioned back up the street. "We've got her with a counselling team up the road… she's in a hell of a state."

Munroe looked po-faced. "So would you be, Sergeant."

Howell only offered a nod of his head as Munroe surveyed the windows once more. Still no movement, no shadows, nothing. "Tell your men to turn off the blues, will you. There's no reason to make him more nervous than he already is."

Without hesitation Howell reached in through the open window of his vehicle and clicked a switch before turning his attention to the other policeman standing by the other Discovery and waving his hand downwards. "Shut it off."

In an instant they were all thrown into a dim light as the street bulbs above bathed them in a yellow glow. As a mild breeze drifted through the cul-de-sac, creating slow-moving swirls of fog across the darkened terrace house, Munroe caught sight of an eye poking out from behind the downstairs curtain. It remained there for a second before disappearing as quickly as it had appeared.

"Are we linked up to the house?" Munroe asked, before removing his overcoat and gently laying it across the Land Rover's bonnet.

"We are," Howell said, unclipping a mobile phone from his belt and handing it over, "but he only answered once and that was to give us a demand... said not to call back until we 'made good' or he'd kill the girl."

"And the demand was for me?" Munroe said, lighting up the screen of the Samsung Galaxy S20 with his thumb.

Howell appeared bothered by it and his lips tightened. "Well, Superintendent, yes. He asked for you."

"It's all right, Sergeant," Munroe said, preparing to press the call icon. "And call me Ethan."

Howell gave a strained smile. "Brian."

"What's the girl's name, Brian?"

"Stacy Wells."

"How old?"

"Six."

"Mother's name?"

"Sarah."

Munroe quickly digested the information, then placed the mobile to his ear and listened as it began to dial. "Please stay silent, Brian, and let's see what's going on, shall we?"

Ring ring, ring ring, ring ring.

The line connected in silence except for the sound of steadied breathing against the receiver, and Munroe held off for a few seconds before beginning to talk.

"Is this Icarus?" he said in a comforting tone, taking a big chance on using the name this man had apparently bestowed upon himself. On the other end the breathing now withered into a soft cry as the voice of a young girl replied.

"No, this is Stacy."

The little girl's voice was subdued and it was clear from the whimpers that she was doing her best not to cry.

"Hi, Stacy, my name is Ethan, and I'm here to help you get back to your mummy. Are you all right?"

"Yes," the soft voice replied as Munroe continued.

"That's good to hear. Stacy, is there a man with you?"

"Yes. He's standing next to me."

"OK, thank you, Stacy. May I speak with him?"

There was a pause. Munroe focused his eyes on the curtained downstairs window, but there was still no movement as the girl came back on the line.

"He says you have to come inside if you want to talk."

The answer was ominous, because this killer already knew who he was. Hell, he'd asked for him personally, and that suggested to him that the man had an axe to grind and to play this out on his terms was a dangerous path to go down. The whole point of a negotiator was to make the man feel like he was in control, gain trust in order to find resolution without anyone getting hurt, but him being the centre of 'Icarus's' attention could act a stressor and that could place the girl in danger... as well as himself.

"I understand, Stacy. You're being very brave. Could you please ask the man if I can just hear his voice, so I know whom I'm speaking to?"

The line fell silent again. There was a slapping sound and muffled cry before Stacy returned to the line, her voice now wavering, clearly fighting back tears.

"He says... if you don't come inside to talk then he'll... he'll cut my throat."

The little girl now began to sob and at the downstairs window the curtain was pulled back, revealing Stacy's face, one side of her cheek red from a slap, a large hand gripping her blonde hair tightly as the other held a serrated kitchen knife tightly to her throat. To the left, one of the blue berets was already readying his assault rifle, but it was a dangerous shot to take, the angle all wrong, and the officer glanced over at Munroe, who shook his head subtly. With a confirming nod the officer pulled back and resumed his earlier position.

Usually an armed officer would never take such a chance, but with the man inside considered a known serial killer whose gruesome crimes were splashed over all the papers, the blue berets were showing an uncharacteristically agitated state of mind.

"Stacy. Can you hear me?" Munroe asked and the curtain slowly fell back closed before he could hear a light sobbing on the line once more.

"He says he won't give you another chance."

The demand was finite, and as Munroe pushed the mute button and considered his options he could already see Howell slowly shaking his head from the corner of his eye.

"You can't go in there, Ethan," Howell ordered in nothing less than a growl. "I'd rather breach the house. The men are already in place and waiting to go with a plan to enter from the back."

"Do you have the house plan?"

Howell offered a single nod before producing a hand-drawn layout of the lower floor from his trouser pocket. He held it below the car's window so as not to be seen from the house. "The mother drew it."

Munroe scanned the image and then pointed at the page.

"Do they know if the back door's locked?"

"One of our men did a soft check. It's locked and bolted from the inside but at least there's a chance… If you go in then I have two potential deaths on my hands."

Even before he replied Munroe knew what he was going to do. The only words he needed to speak now were to convince Howell, who would undoubtedly take the fallout for such a risky decision. "Given that we know this man has no issues with taking a life, I'll tell you how it's going to go. A forced entry from the rear will take at least six to ten seconds to reach the front room. That's more than enough time for him to slit that girl's throat before your men subdue him. If they come from the front, it will take less time, but we have no idea if it's barricaded. Either way the girl dies." Munroe lifted his shoulders and loosened his muscles as Howell remained silent. He too knew the odds of success.

"We have no idea what this man wants. If he's rational or on the brink of mental breakdown… He's under a lot of pressure. The only thing we know for sure is that he wants to speak with me… so let's give him what he wants."

Howell stood motionless and unblinking while Munroe stared at him, his head lowered slightly, looking ready to go. Seconds passed before the sergeant's shoulders began to sag.

"This is so beyond my remit that if it goes wrong my career is over," Howell said, his cheeks beginning to flush, though not out of embarrassment. "And more importantly, I could have two dead people on my conscience."

"If this goes wrong then that little girl's life is over, guaranteed," Munroe replied, softly tapping the mobile still held in his hand. "What's one more life to a man that we believe has already killed five?"

Howell considered his options for a few more seconds and then, with one last glare, he gave a stiff nod. "OK, Ethan, we'll do it your way, but take this." He reached in through the car window and unlocked a small grey case sitting on the passenger seat. The top popped open; nestled within a cut-out in the foam interior sat a small earpiece, which the sergeant retrieved and then passed over to Munroe. "It's one way, so we'll hear everything that's going on," Howell explained as Munroe turned away from the house and slipped the tiny radio into his ear, as deep as it would go. "If I hear even the slightest hint of a threat, we breach. Understood?"

Munroe gave a firm nod as Howell continued with his stipulations. "I can't give you a firearm, so you're on your own the moment you step inside, but we'll be listening."

"I understand." He reached into his pocket and offered Howell a glimpse of a black metal switchblade handle. "Just in case."

Howell turned his head at the illegal item. "I didn't see that," he said sternly, grabbing a walkie-talkie which he placed to his ear. "Hold your positions. The negotiator is entering the house. Stand by for a full breach on my command."

As soon as the order had been given Munroe was back on the mobile, his voice still calm and comforting even though his stomach was beginning to twist with the usual feeling of controlled apprehension. "Stacy, can you hear me?"

"Yes, Ethan," came the reply. Any signs of sobbing had now ceased.

This was one tough little girl.

"Can you tell the man I'm coming in unarmed, and to unlock the front door."

Without a reply the line abruptly cut off and, after adjusting the switchblade in his pocket for easy access, Munroe stepped out from behind the Land Rover and began to walk slowly forward towards the darkened doorway with his hands held upwards.

The front door was only twenty metres away but it felt like an eternity. The fog was beginning to clear, the thick wisps becoming mist, and as he approached the green wooden door the sound of a lock unclicking could be heard. He stopped at the entrance and with one final glance back at Howell, who was wide-eyed and understandably looking extremely out of his comfort zone, Munroe turned the knob and pushed back the door before then cautiously making his way inside.

The air was humid and Munroe looked down at a radiator that had been knocked or kicked from its position, creating a hot wet puddle beneath where the pipe had been cracked. He felt the fine vapours lapping against his trousers as he moved to one side to avoid the dampness. The hallway was dim, lit only by the ambient light coming from the first doorway on the left which was ajar only a fraction, and Munroe surveyed his surroundings for any sign of a threat. Against the left-hand wall stood a glossy wood side table on top of which was a blue plastic bowl with flowery patterns, filled with darkened petals of potpourri. To his right a coat rack hung from the wall holding a light green anorak and a child's pink plastic raincoat with the image of a white unicorn on the back and silver lettering beneath reading 'Lil' Princess'. The hallway was typical of any family house in the UK, with two muddy pairs of wellington boots positioned neatly underneath the coat rack, but the smeared mark on the floral wallpaper beyond transformed the home into something far more insidious.

Munroe stared at the bloody handprint and noted the size. *Icarus was a big lad*.

"Hello. I'm inside," Munroe called out, but instead of a reply he was greeted by the sound of scraping coming from the nearest room, like an object being dragged heavily across paintwork, and a sharp object at that. "I'm closing the door behind me." He shut it with a hefty thud just to confirm his actions. He then slowly began to make his way forward, his steps heavy on the grey carpet informing those ahead of his approach. As he moved closer towards the partially open doorway and the subdued grainy light shining around its edges he heard a whimper from somewhere inside.

Munroe halted and then stood motionless in the hallway, the air stifling, but with no further sounds he continued with the last few steps and then paused to call out once more. "I'm at the doorway. May I come in?"

There was a creak from inside, as if someone was shifting their weight, but no response. Munroe stood by the edge of the door and with one hand nudged it open.

Inch by inch the door gently swung open on its well-oiled hinges until it came to a stop against the black rubber stopper screwed into the green carpet floor and Munroe got his first look at the chaotic mess that was the Wells's front living room.

To the left was an open doorway that, by the plans he had seen, led to the kitchen. A two-seat dark blue leather sofa had been jammed into the opening, preventing easy access. On the opposite wall an armchair had been flipped upside down, now resting against the drawn curtain of the main window. In the corner next to it, part of the carpet had been pulled up and what appeared to be knife marks had been cut into the wood flooring beneath. A forty-inch plasma screen was attached to the wall opposite. A circular crack expanded outwards from its centre, clearly made by a heavy blow, and the hazy white static offered the only light in the room. In front of it the silhouette of a large man stood, wearing jeans and a T-shirt and slowly swaying from side to side. On the wall next to him jagged words had been cut into the plaster, *Never Forget*, and *Betrayal* underneath that. Below the scrawled words a single triangle had been carved, no doubt by the kitchen knife currently being pressed against the young girl's throat as she was held firmly in his clutches.

The man raised the knife and used it to wave Munroe forward, the white of his teeth flickering from the flashing static of the plasma screen. "We've been waiting for you, Ethan. Come in and join the family."

Chapter 3

"Icarus?" Munroe said, as the kitchen knife now returned to the young girl's throat. "Thank you for meeting with me."

Icarus offered no reply and only continued to sway from left to right while the knife stayed stationary against Stacy's thin white neck. Munroe turned his attention towards the girl.

"Hi Stacy, how are you doing there, little one?"

Stacy opened her mouth, but before she could utter a word the knife pressed even tighter as Icarus began to speak.

"We've been playing."

The killer's voice was soft, with a strong Scottish accent, maybe Edinburgh. He released his hand from the girl's shoulder and pointed to a makeshift den built from the sofa's cushions. "Just to pass the time."

The backlight from the television made it difficult to get a clear view of the man, and apart from the outline of long, scraggly hair hanging down the killer's cheeks his face was clouded by shadows.

"I got here as soon as I could, Icarus. May I call you Icarus?" Munroe raised his palms slightly and moved out of the hallway so his whole body was visible, showing that he had nothing to hide. It was odd because the movement caused no reaction from the killer; he continued to sway left to right before giving a slow nod.

"OK, Icarus, is there anything you need? Food or drink?"

Icarus gently shook his head. "I have everything I need now that you're here."

To say there was an air of menace in his answer was a huge understatement, and sensing something was looming Munroe calmly turned his attention to the young girl, his priorities now taking charge.

"Hi Stacy, you OK there?"

Stacy gave a tearful nod.

"You're very brave, Stacy, and I'm here to get everyone out safely." Munroe looked up at the knife-wielding killer. "Both of you. So if you agree, then perhaps Stacy could play in the fort while we talk a little. I'd like to know what I can do for you."

The repeated mentioning of the young girl's name was deliberate on Munroe's part. If Icarus could see her as a person and not just a bargaining chip then he might be less inclined to do something stupid. That was the theory, anyway, but given this man was an experienced killer with five, potentially more, gruesome murders under his belt, then it probably wouldn't count for much.

Icarus looked down at Stacy and then he released his grip and pushed her in the direction of the makeshift den.

"Thank you," Munroe said gratefully, and he motioned to the box of cushions. "Go on, Stacy, that's a good girl."

Stacy did as she was told and, her body rigid, stepped over to the den, pulled herself inside and sat down with crossed legs, her mouth quivering and her tear-strewn red eyes full of terror.

With the hostage now at a distance, Munroe turned his full attention to the silhouette of Icarus, who still had the kitchen knife held tightly in his hand, pointed in Munroe's direction.

"It would be nice if I could see who I'm talking to." He motioned to the light switch next to him, but the answer came with a swift shake of Icarus's head.

"No, I don't think I'll be lighting up any silhouettes for the nice men with guns outside." Icarus instead reached down to a white china table lamp lying on its side. He scooped it off the floor with his free hand and, with his knife still raised, placed it on the top of the sofa barricading the door. He then clicked the white switch on the cable and as the light illuminated the corner of the room Munroe got his first good look at the killer. "Like what you see, Superintendent?"

Icarus raised his head and then craned it in an arc, offering a clear view of his face. Best guess the man was in his late thirties, with a short stubble of black beard growth and lifeless black eyes. His straight dark brown hair, greasy, hung to his shoulders, and dark rings of fatigue were visible beneath his eyes. A jagged two-inch scratch mark ran down the man's right cheek and a smudging of dried blood surrounded it. He lifted his hand to the wound and sniggered. "Mothers, heh, protective to the end." Icarus's eyes drooped and he gave a shrug. "Still, there are far more agonising things that can happen to a person, but I think you already know that, or you wouldn't be here, would you?"

The killer's direct reference to his previous victims was unnerving, because rarely did such men freely admit or allude to their crimes. Certainly not during a hostage situation like this. Sure, he had already appeared to acknowledge the name Icarus, but still.

"I'm not here to judge you, Icarus, I only want to get you and Stacy out of this situation safely. I don't want to see you hurt any more than her. I'm sure you have good reasons for the mistakes you've made…"

Icarus ejected a condescending snort and smiled to reveal a perfect set of bright white teeth. "How very slimy of you, Superintendent, but I wasn't referring to my history… I was referring to yours."

Munroe was now looking confused. "My history?"

Icarus now continued with a smirk, evidently enjoying Munroe's puzzled reaction. "The horrific death of your wife and," he glanced down at Stacy before resuming his stare, "and young daughter."

The atmosphere immediately changed as Munroe felt the warmth of anger building in his chest.

"Such a terrible fate, and to know your little Lucy died in such a cruel way." Icarus's lips pursed together condescendingly. "Just tragic… truly tragic."

Munroe could feel his expression beginning to slip and his emotions becoming more evident with every passing moment, but he composed himself. He wasn't about to allow this psychopath to goad him with his own misfortune.

"I'm impressed, Icarus, you know a lot about me. You have me at a disadvantage."

Icarus's face now lit up excitedly at his guest's honest assessment. "Oh, I had you at a disadvantage the moment you set foot through the door, and as for knowing you… I've known about you for a long time, which makes things difficult."

Munroe watched as Icarus's knife began to shake awkwardly. His grip around the handle tightened and he reached up with his free hand and began to rub at his forehead as if attempting to dispel a sudden headache.

"Confliction is not in my nature, yet I feel it stabbing behind my eyeballs like hot needles. It hurts to resist, like a story already told and unable to be rewritten."

Whatever mental issues Icarus had they were quickly unravelling into a spiralling descent and Munroe was now, very slowly, moving his right hand towards his trouser pocket and the switchblade hidden there. He was within inches of its tip when Icarus suddenly bolted upright and the shaking knife in his hand became rigid once again. His eyes widened and focused on Munroe before he casually took a single step forward and studied his face, his eyes squinting in curiosity.

"Yes," the killer said, moving his head slowly from side to side in order to get a full look at Munroe's features. "I see the similarities. They're somewhat hidden, but they are there."

Munroe's controlled his breathing as he'd been trained to do, and gently rested his forefinger on the edge of his pocket. "What do you see?" he asked as Icarus straightened up and glared at him with both his eyebrows raised, his eyes becoming dull and emotionless.

"I see destiny, Ethan Munroe." The killer's head now lolled to one side and his body began to tense up. "Destiny... denied."

The kitchen knife was thrust forward with such speed that Munroe's hand was forced to retreat from his pocket and with open palms he slammed down hard against Icarus's wrist, sending the blade to one side as the killer let out a deep growl. From the den Stacy shrieked in terror as

Munroe locked his shoulders and slammed Icarus's hand against the wall, but the collision did little to loosen the killer's grip on the knife. For a second time Munroe slammed the knife against the wall, this time putting a hole in the plasterboard, sending white powder into the air. As he prepared for a third slam he felt Icarus's knee jam forcefully into his groin and with a pained groan he instinctively fell to his knees.

With watering eyes he looked up to see the killer's arms raised above him, the glinting kitchen knife already plunging down towards his chest. Munroe thrust both his hands upwards and latched on to the knife's handle, bringing the blade to a full stop just inches from his face. Icarus applied all his weight from above, pushing down on the knife, the tip quivering wildly against the pressure.

"Run, Stacy," Munroe gasped, but fear had the girl glued to the spot. She only wrapped her arms around her knees and curled up in a ball while in the kitchen the sound of heavy thuds against the back door echoed into the living room as the blue berets attempted their breach.

Munroe stared up at the killer's eyes, which were now blazing with rage as they both pushed against one another, the knife still wavering in the middle. Suddenly the tension eased for a split second as Icarus shifted his weight backwards, preparing for one final downward push. It was at that moment that Munroe seized his chance. In a single move he twisted the killer's wrist in on itself, revolved around the joint so the knife was facing just off to the right and with a spin of his shoulders rotated Icarus's weakened grip hard to the left, feeling the wrist bone give way.

Icarus yelped in pain and instinctively dropped the knife and fell onto one knee as Munroe applied even more pressure to the near broken joints. After one final excruciatingly painful twist Munroe leapt to his feet and grasped his own right wrist. Icarus, his face full of agony, only managed to partially turn his face upwards before Munroe slammed his elbow in an arc-shaped blow across the killer's jaw, sending him slamming into the plasterboard, knocking him out cold.

Munroe kicked the knife away just as the crashing sound of the kitchen door giving way could be heard, and then he leapt over to Stacy and grasped her tightly to his chest with one arm and raised the other high up in the air. "Don't shoot, don't shoot!" he shouted as two of the blue berets ploughed into the living room. The first aimed at them and then scanned the room before shouting, "Suspect is down and secured." Holding the muzzle of the SIG716 assault rifle at Icarus's unconscious body, the second beret knelt on the killer's back and handcuffed him from behind.

The entire entry had taken less than fifteen seconds by Munroe's figuring, and as the officers continued to secure the area he stood up and allowed the girl to cling to him with both her arms and legs.

"It's all over, Stacy. You're safe now," was all he said before getting a satisfied nod from the nearest blue beret and then, with the young girl still clamped around his waist, Munroe led her out of the back entrance whose door was lying splintered on the kitchen floor.

The air was like ice against his neck. He only now realised how hot he was, and as he made his way around to the front of the house he was greeted by a green and yellow suited paramedic who tried to softly prise the young girl from him. The attempt was in vain, her grip nothing short of vicelike. Munroe got down on one knee and looked down towards her face, still buried in his chest. "You did

39

great, Stacy. You were very brave... now how about we get you back to your mummy?"

The mere mention of the girl's mother had her immediately looking up at him through red eyes, and although clearly in shock she managed a nod.

"Now you go with the paramedic and she'll take you to her right now, OK sweetheart?"

Without any further encouragement Stacy released her grip and with a trembling hand grasped the paramedic's before being led away to an undoubtedly grateful mother.

Munroe stood back up and remained motionless until they were out of sight, and then leant back against the cold house wall and allowed himself a well-earned deep breath, giving the adrenalin in his veins a chance to subside. He looked down at the gash across his knuckles where he had collided with the plasterboard and rubbed at it. The wound felt numb but in twenty minutes it would be aching like hell and as he continued to catch his breath the thought of Stacy no longer occupied his mind. Only one thing did: Icarus, and his obsession with Munroe and his family.

Who the hell was this man?

His mind was swimming with questions when from the corner of his eye the shadow of a figure appeared in the side alleyway and he stood back up to see the face of someone he knew well.

"Ethan, are you all right?" Mike Regis, head of the Met's hostage negotiations department, reached over and grabbed Munroe by the shoulders. In his forties, Regis was a small man whose five-foot-five height and tubby girth made him look far fatter than he actually was. With deep crow's feet running from the corner of his eyes, a bald head and crooked teeth the man looked as dodgy as they came and anyone who was honest with themselves would cross to the other side of the street on seeing him. In truth he was one of the most decent and honest men Munroe knew; the saying 'don't judge a book by its cover' was conceived precisely for people like Regis.

"I'm fine, Mike. Just a scraped knuckle. Did you have any idea this guy was the serial killer everyone's been looking for?"

"The information was limited. I had no idea until I got here a few minutes ago. I swear."

Regis looked down at the minor scratch, and then after a relieved sigh his expression turned to one of anger, although his tone was measured and calm, as always. The four horsemen of the apocalypse could have come riding over the horizon and Regis would still sound composed, as if sweet-talking his own mother. "Regardless, that was unbelievably foolish, Ethan."

Munroe was already shaking his head. "I know you're right, but there wasn't much of an option left to me, and if I hadn't gone in that little girl would be dead right now."

Regis looked entirely unpersuaded by the argument and it was he who was now shaking his head. "Maybe so, but what you just did was totally irresponsible."

"How much did you hear?" Munroe asked, still catching his breath.

"Everything. I arrived just as you were walking in the front door."

"Then you heard what he said about Lucy?"

Regis may have been a hostage negotiator, trained to keep the truth to himself, but to his friends and co-workers he was an open book, and because of the man's long pause Munroe was now eyeing him with suspicion. "What do you know, Mike?"

"Not now, Ethan," Regis replied, looking hesitant. "There'll be time for that later on."

Oh, he definitely knew something, and Munroe moved closer to his boss with an unyielding stare.

"Time for what?"

A few awkward seconds passed as Regis mulled over whether to impart what he knew. As Munroe bore down on him with accusing eyes he finally relented, placing his hands on his hips.

"They did a check on the suspect's car while I was on my way over and got an address. Officers are already on site."

"What did they find?"

"Well, they've only just got there, but they did find something taped to the front door."

Before Munroe could ask Regis pulled out his iPhone and began scrolling.

"One of the boys recognised it and sent it directly to me." Regis passed over the mobile and Munroe felt his heart sink as he looked down at the screen and the picture on it. It was of a grey door with a black iron handle and silver letterbox and above them a photograph had been taped to the door. A photograph of Munroe's dead wife and daughter with their arms around each other.

Munroe let his hand drop to his side. He felt as if the wind had been knocked out of him as Regis plucked the mobile from his palm and then switched it off. "Whatever this Icarus arsehole was up to, it would appear that he knew he'd be caught tonight."

Munroe was already heading back into the house and Regis immediately grabbed his arm and held it securely.

"Not now, Ethan, that's an order. He'll be questioned when he gets back to the station and then we can go from there, but not here and certainly not now, given what just happened."

Munroe genuinely considered pushing Regis to the ground and stampeding in, but Regis was right, now wasn't the time. But it didn't mean he was just going to slink off and go home. "OK, but I'm going to the address right now. You coming?"

Regis looked relieved and he let go of Munroe's arm. "Do you know the kind of hoops we're going to have to jump through in explaining your actions here tonight? The lack of procedure, putting your own life at risk and possibly others..."

Munroe pulled out his car keys and let them dangle from his fingers. "Is that a yes?"

Regis stared at the keys for a moment and then focused back on Munroe. "Of course it is, but we'll take my car."

Munroe was already heading back to the front of the house as Regis reluctantly followed. "Sure. But I'm driving."

Chapter 4

The village of Brooks Green was a small slice of English country life just south-west of London. A leafy hamlet with only sparse residences and farmland, where almost everyone knew one another. In these green pastures the only scent of a crime came in the form of a cow making its great escape from its grassy enclosure or a local teen who had consumed one too many pints… but not tonight.

Munroe steered Regis's silver Mondeo Zetec across the uneven threshold of Orchard Farm's entrance and proceeded steadily towards the collection of police cars parked on its driveway. The farmhouse could have been a National Trust building given its timeworn red brick-work, and the attached stable house looked as if a mere nudge could have brought the whole thing down in a pile of rubble.

Munroe came to a stop within inches of the nearest yellow and blue Vauxhall, which given its age was likely from the local constabulary, and then he stepped out onto the muddy driveway and swiftly headed towards the ageing farmhouse with Regis in hot pursuit.

"Take it easy, Ethan," Regis ordered, slightly concerned by Munroe's withdrawn demeanour during the drive over. "We shouldn't even be here."

Munroe glanced back and gave him an expression-less glare. "I just want to look around, Mike, and we're involved if you say we are."

Regis looked accepting and he zipped his mouth shut as Munroe reached the already open doorway, pausing to note the picture of his family still pinned to the door. He gazed upon their faces for a few moments, his breathing measured, and then he glanced back at Regis. "We're involved."

Munroe stepped into the brightly lit hallway and surveyed the open plan interior. In the room to his left a large empty fire grate full of ashes was the central point of what appeared to be the lounge. There was no carpet, only grey tiles with a large, red Persian rug taking up most of the room. The fine wooden coffee table in the middle looked out of place, as did the two red leather wingback armchairs facing the open hearth, and the lilac-painted plaster walls held paintings of Paris, Rome and Berlin. The view of the room was only possible due to the wall, or lack of it, separating it from the hallway. Three dark wooden beams ran from ceiling to the floor with large gaps in between, giving one the impression of it being either stylish or unfinished.

Munroe turned his attention to the left and the small kitchen running off from the hallway. Its chipped green wall tiling, stone slabbed floor and basic gas grill cooker and single washbasin suggested an owner with little to no interest when it came to cuisine, and the steel microwave on the counter cemented that fact.

Further up the hallway a staircase draped in green carpet led up to the first floor. Munroe focused on the open doorway at the end through which a young policewoman with curly blonde hair appeared, heading over to the new arrivals with a look of concern.

"I'm sorry, gentlemen, but this is an active crime scene. I'm going to have to ask you to leave."

"It's not a problem, Constable," Regis replied, slipping past Munroe and retrieving his badge which he hung in front of her. "Superintendents Regis and Munroe."

Munroe offered a courteous smile to the young policewoman and quickly glanced around the hallway. "Who's in charge, Constable?"

"It's Dawkins, sir," she introduced and then gave a light shrug, "and I am. DC is on their way."

"Good. And how much do you know?"

"Not a lot, sir. Info was pretty thin. Murder suspect and we're to secure his premises."

By her tone the woman was undoubtedly confident, but the look in her eyes was one of unease. Hardly surprising given the lack of information she'd been given. It was enough to make anyone feel like a third wheel.

"The good old lines of communication," Munroe replied, and received a flicker of agreement from the policewoman.

"That's why they call us mushrooms, sir."

The reference had Munroe smiling. "Kept in the dark and fed bullshit. I remember, I was a mushroom once."

"Weren't we all," Regis added, dropping the badge back in his pocket.

The constable now appeared to relax as Munroe continued, "Then let me to bring you up to speed. The suspect is believed to have been involved in five murders or more. We took him into custody tonight and as such this house will need to be gone over with a fine-tooth comb."

The mention of the number made Constable Dawkins look uneasy, and she quietly muttered one word, a word that in the modern vernacular could change the atmosphere quicker than someone farting at the dinner table. "Serial?"

"We believe so… a bad one," Munroe replied before checking himself. "Not that there are any good ones, but I need you to move all the officers out of the house and contact HQ to make sure they're sending a forensics unit. We know what communication's like."

Constable Dawkins was already nodding before he finished his sentence. "Of course, sir, immediately. I'll have us patrol the front entrance. Quiet village like this is sure to notice a police presence soon."

"Good thinking, Constable, quick as you can."

Within twenty seconds the five police officers on site were all outside, making their way up to the property's front entrance, leaving just Munroe and Regis alone in the now silent farmhouse.

"How about you do the first floor and I take the ground?" Munroe said, pointing upstairs.

Regis replied with a light nod but he looked unsure. "And what exactly are we looking for, Ethan?"

Munroe motioned to the picture of his family, taped to the front door. "Not sure, but Icarus wanted me here for a reason, even if he did just try to kill me. So like I said, let's take a look."

He knew that Regis would always support him, even if it wasn't exactly procedure, but that was because the head of hostage negotiation knew Munroe would never ask him to cross the line. Sure, some lines were OK, but not the kind you couldn't come back from.

"OK, I'll meet you back here in five."

With a nod Regis made his way upstairs while Munroe headed towards the open doorway at the far end of the hall, pausing for a moment before taking a step inside. The sight that greeted him was far less mundane than the rest of the house, perhaps even impressive. It must have been used as a dining room. A rectangular dining table ran the length of the room, with a total of six chairs sat around it, two along each side and one at either end. A creaseless white silk tablecloth covered it and five of the places had been set with ornate gold-rimmed china plates and silver cutlery laid out for a three-course meal. The starter, judging by the knife, was to be fish. Fine, sparkling crystal wine glasses with hollowed-out stems were placed on the right, just above the knife tips, and a rolled crimson red napkin held by a gold ring holder had been placed at an angle across each of the plates.

Who's coming for dinner?

In the left-hand corner a pre-war drinks cabinet in a half-globe had been rolled back to reveal bottles of vodka and pear schnapps waiting for consumption, and in the right-hand corner was placed a more modern electric hostess for keeping food warm before service.

The room was void of wallpaper, instead having been covered with cedarwood panels that had been lacquered for a darker colour. Brass uplighters, maybe French, lit up the ceiling, adding a cosy or gloomy atmosphere, depending on one's taste, to the whole room.

Munroe said nothing and immediately made his way to the hostess. He gently slid its top open, but whatever he expected to find was not there and he was met instead by empty grill trays.

It was only now as he turned around that he noticed the anomaly that he had missed upon entering, and he took a few steps towards the curiosity, the set placing at the head of the table. While all the other placings looked fit for royalty, the head looked anything but. A cheap, scratched blue plastic plate sat between a white plastic fork and knife, and where the crystal wine glass should have been stood instead a single cracked, transparent plastic glass with a stem.

The full meaning of this was lost on Munroe; the only thing he was sure of was that the person who laid this table had placed a setting for an unwanted dinner guest. But why?

Munroe now turned his attention to the only other opening in the room, a thick wooden door with red hinge bolts at its edges and a round cast iron handle that would have looked more appropriate in a castle. Munroe moved over to it and twisted the handle.

Locked.

He pressed his palms against the door and lowered his ear to its surface and held his breath, listening for any sign of movement, but there was nothing except a kind of low-level humming. Any other place he would have assumed it was the boiler turning over, or maybe a washing machine or dryer in its final stages, but given the owner of this place was the suspect in five murders, all kinds of gruesome possibilities instead came to mind.

Munroe pulled his head back from the door and reached up to the top of the doorframe and ran his finger along it but found only dust, which descended slowly to the floor below. He tapped his palm against the door mindfully before turning his attention to the splendour of the table settings, and it was then that something caught his eye. It was nothing more than a glint of light coming from just underneath the cheap plastic dinner plate, but he immediately moved over to it and gently nudged it aside to reveal the object.

The small brass Yale key glinted under the light of the nearest wall lamp which reflected its light off the ceiling and down onto the dinner place below. The key had been perfectly positioned so the glint of the key could only be seen when one was located next to the door. With his forefinger Munroe guided it off the table. He then moved back to the door, slid it into the lock and with a turn it clicked open.

Munroe had always had a strong sixth sense when navigating the world around him. It was nothing supernatural, as some believe, but rather an acute awareness of his surroundings that began with a tingling in his chest and cheeks. It had served him well in the military and more so as a hostage negotiator, and as he grasped the door handle he could feel that same tingling begin to well up inside him.

Still holding the handle, Munroe positioned himself back towards the hinges of the doorway and then with his left hand pressed flat against the door's surface he turned the handle and slowly began to pull it open, using the resistance as steady leverage. It was then he heard a click.

The gunshot blast sent the door slamming back into Munroe's shoulder hard as a plume of smoke erupted from the now open doorway. The noise was deafening and he winced as he pushed his body back against the wall, instinctively thrusting his foot against the door, sending it hurtling back into its frame. The door didn't slam shut but instead bounced off the now bent locking mechanism, which had been hit during the impact, and slowly swung back towards him before finally coming to a stop.

Munroe's ears were ringing but he could hear the heavy scuffling overhead as Regis tore down the landing to investigate. He pulled off his jacket and threw it across the open gap in the door but nothing happened, no second shot, just silence. Trusting his instinct, Munroe grasped the door handle, pulled it back towards himself and cautiously leant around it to get a better look and saw what he'd expected to see.

The nut-brown wooden handle of a sawn-off shotgun had been clamped between the jaws of a metal vice which was bolted to the inside wall. The barrel had been positioned directly at anyone entering and a filament line, probably from a fishing rod, had been set up to engage the triggers once the door was opened. Apart from this deadly mousetrap there was only an empty cupboard, and Munroe had already reached over and released the barrel to reveal two spent cartridges as Regis poked his head around from the entrance of the hallway.

"You all right?"

"I'm fine," Munroe said, motioning towards the empty cupboard. "Our man had the door booby-trapped with a sawn-off. Don't worry, it's spent."

Regis, looking startled, entered the room fully. He had only just reached the cupboard to see for himself when the farmhouse's front door burst open and Constable Dawkins, followed by two more uniformed officers, swept into the hallway.

"Its's all over, Constable, the owner set a booby trap," Regis yelled with his hands raised calmingly. "Everyone back outside, please. Stay by the main entrance. If the neighbours weren't curious, they will be now."

Constable Dawkins looked pumped and ready to go but she immediately offered a nod, and after exhaling a deep breath she ushered the other two police officers back out of the front door, leaving the two men alone once more.

"Christ," Regis said, rubbing the top of his head reassuringly. "Why would he want you here just to have your head blown off by a shotgun?"

This was the same question Munroe was asking himself. "I don't know, but back at the house Icarus said something about being conflicted. Just before he attacked me. Something about not being in his nature."

Regis looked unimpressed by the insight. "Replace 'nature' with 'in his right mind' and it makes more sense."

"Perhaps," Munroe replied, but he was now clearly more interested in the empty cupboard, and Regis also began staring awkwardly inside.

"Why the hell would anyone set that up in an empty cupboard?"

Munroe reached over and ran his palm against the nearest inside wall before moving on to the back. "Because it's *not* empty. Feel that."

Regis reached inside and pressed his hand against the back wall.

"The sides are cold but the back wall is warm… There's something behind it."

Munroe bent down on his haunches and rubbed at the wood tiled flooring with his fingers. "There are scratch marks," he said with curiosity, and then stood back up and placed his hands back against the inner wall. "This opens outwards. Stand back, will you."

Regis seemed more than happy to pull back into the dining room as Munroe probed the back wall with his palms laid upon it, and after a firm push it fell inwards a few centimetres before swinging forwards towards him, revealing a hidden door.

Turning back Munroe waved his hand at Regis. "Shift it, will you. I don't fancy taking a shell in the face if he's booby-trapped this one as well."

Regis needed no further encouragement and he moved off to one side. Munroe followed suit and then, gripping the top corner of the door, he gave it a pull. The whole frame swung back effortlessly on well-oiled hinges, allowing Munroe to peer into the darkness. A draught of warm air swept past them both, filled with the sweet scent of flower petals, and as Munroe's eyes adjusted to the gloom he began to make out a single set of wooden stairs leading downwards into the depths of the farmhouse's foundations.

"Wait here," Regis ordered gruffly as he headed back into the hallway. "I'd rather have Dawkins stationed up here, just in case."

Munroe gave little more than a casual nod as Regis took off. Regardless of the order, he pulled out his iPhone, lit up the torch and began to make his way downwards into the sickly sweet depths of Orchard Farm.

The steps underneath him were solid, well-constructed and despite the eerie nature of this hidden hideaway Munroe felt no fear but rather apprehension. Apprehension of walking straight into another booby trap and taking a bullet to the chest, or even some machete sling-trap. These were the things that concerned him and as he reached the final step he felt a shiver of relief wash over him.

The picture of his family pinned to the front door and Icarus's knowledge of them still had him riled. What the hell did a psychopathic murderer have to do with his wife and child? Whatever it was he was going to find out, even if it meant beating it out of the man. Violence was not a natural state for Munroe, but he was more than capable of wielding it when the situation arose. But as he swept his torchlight across the room in front of him his welling anger began to dissolve and was replaced with a disconcerting feeling in the pit of his stomach.

The room looked more like a morgue than a farm basement, with glossy grey tiles covering the floor, all the way up the walls to the ceiling. In the middle an uncomfortable-looking steel chair had been bolted to the floor and as he moved his torch over to the left towards it the silhouetted outline of something huge loomed out of the darkness. But as he reached it his torch gave out.

"Shit." How was it that his phone always seemed to die on him just when he needed it the most?

He was still cursing this act of sod's law when off to his left something flickered into life. Two orange balls of light that appeared to pulsate in tandem stared back at him, and for the first time Munroe felt the familiar warm feeling of panic attempting to hijack his senses. He buried it immediately and instead looked to the wall nearest him. The only light available was coming from the dining room at the top of the stairs, but after a few moments of sliding his palm back and forth he hit upon what he'd been looking for. A switch.

With a single click, the tubed lighting above flickered into life and the room lit up in a yellow hue, revealing not some terrible demon with glowing eyes but instead something far more unnerving as far as he was concerned.

The furnace looked for all intents and purposes like a huge oven encased in polished metal with two small round glass peepholes which were emitting the orange glow he had seen. But that's where the similarities to any cooking apparatus ended, because at ten feet tall and eight feet wide this was no chef's equipment but something far more disturbing. It was a cremator... still lit. And as Munroe scanned the rest of the room it suddenly seemed the most inoffensive thing down here. Cages, four of them and big enough to house a single person. Each had thick padlocks on them and although empty they all displayed dark stains and marks that he cared not to imagine how they got there.

"A sadist's playroom," he said quietly and with disgust, and as he took note of the various knives, screwdrivers and drills hung from a work rack above the cages he could only guess how terrifying these 'decorations' must have been to anyone unfortunate enough to have found themselves locked up down here. There was also a wall cabinet that was gaining his interest as heavy footsteps on the stairs drew his attention; he turned to see Regis rushing down them only to come to a stiff halt as he saw the offerings of a sick mind laid out in the room before him.

"Oh God," Regis said, jogging down the final few steps to join Munroe. "Is that a cremator?"

Munroe gave a slow nod and then began to make his way over to the bolted metal chair facing the cages. "Icarus has been a busy boy," he said, tapping the back of it with a closed fist, "and with front row seats... Who is this guy, Mike?"

"I have no idea, but I can tell you *what* he is... A seriously disturbed individual."

"That's not what I meant. I meant, why does a man who enjoys showing off his work need a crematorium that's big enough to turn a coachload of people to dust?" Munroe turned his attention back to the white cabinet with glass doors, and one of the bottles sitting on the shelf inside that he had noticed before Regis entered. "And how about that?"

Munroe walked over to the cabinet and pulled open the door before pointing to a glass bottle with a label covering it in large, bold printed lettering. "That's scopolamine, if the label's correct. And this one is amobarbital and Christ, he's even got 3-quinuclidinyl."

If Regis knew what Munroe was getting at he certainly wasn't showing it, and he was now looking at his colleague with great scepticism. "I don't know what's weirder, Ethan. Icarus's basement or your knowledge of medicine."

Munroe ignored the comment and instead tapped at the nearest glass bottle. "They're truth serums, Mike. This is very specific stuff. So, like I said, who is this guy, and what the hell has it got to do with my family?"

Regis didn't have an answer and Munroe knew it. The question was rhetorical, but none of this felt right and his antennae were setting off alarm bells.

"I have to speak with him."

"No, you *want* to speak with him, there's a difference."

Munroe could see the worry in his superior's face. This was all becoming very personal – it wasn't how one conducted an investigation. But regardless of Icarus's knowledge of his family he couldn't help but feel he needed to be involved. It was almost like a calling from a silent voice, familiar, like a kind of déjà vu.

Munroe stood up straight and took a deep breath. "I'm not angry, Mike, I'm calm," he said, raising his hand up momentarily to show he didn't have the shakes. "But I can't help but think that shotgun up there was meant for me, like the photo on the front door. Whatever game this Icarus is playing, he appears to have factored me into it.

So," Munroe took a step forward and shrugged, "let's find out what it is."

A few moments passed as Regis considered it and then finally he gave a nod. "OK, but we're not even going to try and go in the interview room. We can watch and supply questions."

"Good. So, where is he?"

"He was taken to Charing Cross, but he's being moved to Walworth Police Station in the next hour. If we get going we can probably follow the transfer van after it sets off. But we do things my way, no ifs or buts. You're very close to this, Ethan. Last thing we need is it interfering with the case."

It was exactly what Munroe wanted to hear, and he was already heading back up the stairs as Regis called after him.

"You said those truth serums were specific. Why do I get the feeling you know more than you're letting on?"

Munroe didn't feel like making wild allegations with such little proof on hand but considering the leeway his boss was giving him he knew the least he could do was throw him a bone. He came back down the stairs, not wanting any of the constables upstairs to hear him. "Look, I don't know anything for sure, but when I see this place and the drugs, I don't see a serial killer's lair or playroom."

"So then, what do you see?"

"I see something I've seen before, but not for a long time," Munroe replied, feeling vulnerable at even having to admit he knew these things. "I see a wet room, Mike. Interrogation and elimination. And a professional one."

Regis was now staring at him suspiciously, and even though Munroe wasn't looking at him directly he could feel the man's eyes burning into the side of his face. As he looked anywhere but towards Regis he noticed a line on the far wall. It was easy to miss, just a thin gap, and Munroe walked over and ran his fingers over it. "Our boy's got a thing for secret doorways," was all he said as Regis ambled over to join him. "See that gap, the craftsmanship is solid but you can just see it there."

As Regis squinted his eyes and moved closer for a better examination, Munroe placed his shoulder against the wall and then pushed his weight against it. An entire section of the wall swung outwards, revealing a shiny metal door with a heavy-duty plastic handle attached to it.

"Same as upstairs," Regis noted, and he took a step back as Munroe clutched the handle. After glancing at Regis, who was warily keeping his distance, he gave it a gentle tug and it swung back, releasing a cloud of icy mist into the air.

"It's a walk-in freezer," Munroe said as he reached into the darkness and grasped the dangling piece of string which was the only thing visible. He gave it a firm tug and with a click a bulb overhead lit up the interior. What they saw had Regis jerking backwards with his hand across his mouth. "Fuck me."

Suspended from the ceiling, three bodies hung from meat hooks, their skin frozen with an icy sheen as white frost covered their hair, making each corpse appear older than it was. There were two men dangling stiffly either side of a woman, all naked, each with grey frozen eyes which stared at Munroe, as if they were positioned to do so at anyone opening the door. The bodies themselves were horrifying enough, but what caused Regis to turn away and gag were the limbs missing from both the men, and the fact that the woman's eyelids had been removed at some stage along with her lips, revealing the white enamel of her teeth. Both men were missing a leg, and one had a hand removed at the wrist, but what really got Munroe's attention was the stitch work that had sewn up each of the wounds. As he moved in to take a closer look the true horror of what had happened now became apparent.

"There's healing around the stitching."

"What does that mean?" asked Regis, his face becoming whiter by the minute.

"It means that after their limbs were cut off and stitched back up... they were still alive."

Chapter 5

"So who've we got back there, Sarge?"

"What! Jesus, you really are a mushroom, Constable Pendrew."

"I only just got on shift when they assigned me to drive."

Sergeant Richard Mills stared at the young officer with unease as the windowless Ford police van passed Parliament Square and went on towards the silhouette of Big Ben towering high in the night sky. In front of them two motorcycle cops with blue lights flashing were ensuring a straight run with no delay as behind an unmarked Land Rover with four heavyset men wearing plain clothes stayed within eight metres of the van's bumper at all times.

"Don't usually get an armed response unit for transfers," Pendrew added, glancing back at the 4x4 in his wing mirror.

"Don't usually transfer killers with such notoriety."

The young driver's eyes widened. "Who is it?"

"Icarus."

"The serial killer?"

"Apparently," Mills said, returning his attention to the road. "Someone leaked it to the press so we're moving him to a more secure location."

"Bloody hell. Been front page in the tabloids for months. My girlfriend's parents actually cancelled a trip down here to see us because of that bastard."

"Yeah, well be prepared to read about him a lot more in the coming weeks. Now keep your eyes on the road, Constable."

Pendrew offered a respectful nod as he steered the van left past the Houses of Parliament and down Victoria Embankment along the edge of the River Thames. "What does he look like?"

Mills could hardly blame the young officer for being curious. Most people expected those who committed terrible crimes to look like monsters, but this could not have been further from the truth. "He looks just like anyone else, son. They always do. It's how these people go unnoticed for so long. Hell, he could even look like you, Pendrew. That would be one ugly bastard, a real monster. Now keep your eyes on the road."

Pendrew shot Mills a sarcastic smile. The roads were pretty clear and within minutes they were turning onto Waterloo Bridge leading into south London. As they passed the halfway point and the two motorcycles sped up towards the upcoming junction it was the young driver who saw it first.

"What's that?" he said, pointing to a black minivan parked up on the kerb with its side door slid open. As something poked out from the dark interior, the officer's question was answered.

The first bullet caught the constable squarely through the neck, splitting his larynx in two and spraying blood across the windshield in a single burst. As he gripped his throat with one hand he managed to keep his other on the wheel. At the same moment a six-wheel truck came surging towards them from the left and screeched to a juddering stop just metres from the oncoming motorcycles. The lead rider had no time to react and collided head-on into the side of the truck's main cabin with a dull thud, while the other skidded onto its side, sending the bike sliding underneath the truck and its rider slamming hard into its thick rubber wheel.

Back in the cabin of the Transit van Mills was wrestling with the wheel as Pendrew instinctively clutched at his neck with both hands, trying in vain to stem the discharge of blood streaming down his chest. As the young officer continued to choke on his own fluids, Mills lifted his left foot and jammed it down hard onto the brake, bringing the van to a screaming halt at an angle, halfway across the road.

That's when the sound of automatic weapons shattered the night air.

"Jesus Christ," Mills yelled as a cascade of bullets smashed through the windscreen and thudded into Pendrew's chest in a spectacle of ripped fabric and blood, sending the sergeant ducking down into the footwell as low as he could go. In the back, the sound of his prisoner hitting the floor could be heard, and then all fell silent except for the blaring of the van's horn as Pendrew lay spread out across the steering wheel.

Mills reached up and pushed the dead officer back into his seat and then poked his head over the dashboard to see the truck driver up ahead exit the cabin, pull a pistol from his jacket and pump two slugs into both downed motorcycle drivers, each to the face. The gunman was then joined by three others, all dressed in the same beige Kevlar protective gear and equipped with AK-47s with extended clips, which they raised in the van's direction before beginning to advance.

From somewhere behind Mills the sound of additional machine gun fire began to flare up in short bursts and realising the armed response unit were retaliating, he made the decision to move. He released the passenger door handle and with a nudge opened it a crack before sliding down onto the tarmac outside and then pressed his body against the van, manoeuvring himself towards the back end, the angle allowing him cover if he needed it. And he did.

The sound of automatic gunfire once again blazed away, but as Mills stole a look around the corner of the van what he saw made no sense. Of the four armed response unit one was lying in a pool of blood, splayed out a few metres from his position, while the others were using the Land Rover for cover as they fired from behind. The perplexing thing was not *that* they were firing – it was *where* they were firing. All three men were shooting timed bursts directly up into the air, and as Mill's gaze followed their arc he felt a downforce of wind attempting to crush him back to the ground, and through wincing eyes he saw it. The sleek black helicopter hovered silently about fifty metres up in the air. There was no sound except for the expulsion of air underneath it and an extremely light buzzing from the rotors. It just hung there as sparks riddled its black canopy from the bullets being fired up at it. It had no markings and was painted such a dark black it was difficult to even make out its shape against the night sky.

The sparks continued as more bullets ricocheted off the surface of the helicopter, and then from its nearest side a rectangular compartment slid open and the automated muzzle of a thick 50-calibre appeared... and that's when the real shooting started.

—

Munroe was already turning onto Victoria Embankment when he heard the sound of automatic gunfire, and from his position the flashing of muzzles dancing in the dim light could be seen over Waterloo Bridge. Within seconds the Mondeo Zetec's engine was pushed to its maximum performance as Munroe tore down the road towards the firefight.

There were no complaints from Regis. Instead he jabbed a number into his mobile and did what he did best. Gave orders.

"This is Superintendent Mike Regis, we have shots fired on Waterloo Bridge. Attending scene. Possible officers down. We need armed backup ASAP. Repeat, armed backup now."

Even though Munroe was aware of the conversation going on in the seat beside him his mind was locked on the bridge. He was already weighing up and countering what came next, but it wasn't so much a decision as a checklist. The reason that military training is so repetitive is to ensure that when entering combat a soldier's procedure is second nature, like a reflex. But with his own training, ground assessment and quick independent decision-making were key, the additional layers that would make the difference between success and failure. He wasn't considering how to approach, that part for him *was* the reflex. No, he was already calculating the way through.

As they approached the bridge the sight of all four armed officers was clear, their bodies lying motionless around the Land Rover which had been completely torn up by heavy-calibre ammunition, although Munroe couldn't see such a weapon in sight. The entire bonnet and engine had been destroyed, and it was only then that he noticed the jet-black helicopter hanging in the sky just off the side of the bridge. There was no familiar hum of an engine or rotor blades and below four masked men wearing protective gear were in the process of dragging a man from the back of a windowless police van.

Icarus.

Further back Munroe could see an older man in police uniform crouched behind the wreck of the Land Rover, surrounded by the fallen bodies of the armed response unit.

"Get ready to duck and roll," Munroe ordered as Regis, still with his phone clamped to his ear, looked at him in total confusion.

"What?"

Munroe brought the Mondeo to a screeching halt just at the bridge's entrance, and before Regis even knew what was being asked of him his seatbelt was unclicked and Munroe reached over, flung open the door and with a solid push shoved the chief hostage negotiator out of the car and onto the tarmac outside.

The Mondeo took off at high speed, leaving Regis looking in complete shock as the dust from the tires washed over him. He uttered the only words that came to mind.

"What the fuck!"

Munroe switched off his lights and then flicked the engine to electrical. The car went silent. As he approached the mangled Land Rover the four gunmen were already leading Icarus back to the helicopter, which was now descending onto the bridge itself. Three landing gears popped out and it landed gracefully on the tarmac as a side door slid open and waited as the gunmen and Icarus headed towards it.

Munroe brought the Mondeo to an abrupt halt and jumped out to join the older uniformed officer squatting behind the Land Rover.

The movement must have caught the attention of the nearest gunman, and he raised his black Colt M3A1 SOPMOD rifle and began firing towards the Mondeo, shattering its windscreen and popping the nearest tire with a loud bang.

"What's your name?" Munroe shouted over the gunfire, grabbing the M6A2 tan carbine lying next to the nearest body.

"Mills," came the reply.

"Are you hit?"

"No, just shaken."

"Good, stay here. Support's on the way."

With barely a nod Munroe was pushing forward, using the back of the police van for cover, which he reached in seconds as more bullets struck against its metalwork. It was no more than suppression fire, but it was doing the job. He backtracked around to the other side and then he held up the carbine to his chest, took a deep breath to steady himself, and leant out, took aim and fired off a single shot.

The nearest gunman dropped to the ground like a dead weight, the bullet having missed his back armour and found its mark right at the base of his skull. Munroe pulled back to his cover position as the bombardment of bullets against the van started up again.

Up ahead Icarus was already being bundled into the helicopter, followed by the others, who began to jump inside, each lending supporting fire as they moved, keeping Munroe pinned behind the van until the final gunman turned and boarded through the tight opening in the helicopter.

The break in firing was seized upon immediately and Munroe once again leant out and managed to clip the last gunman in the back of the knee, sending him sprawling inside as the helicopter rose quietly upwards.

Through the carbine's scope Munroe had a perfect head shot of Icarus, but the killer did something that caused him to pause for just a millisecond. It was enough for him to lose the shot, and the helicopter's side door slid shut as it continued to gain height.

Icarus had winked at him! The bastard had actually winked at him.

Munroe wasn't exactly sure what had thrown him off. Perhaps in that millisecond he had admired the brazen lack of care Icarus had shown in the face of death. It could also have been that to kill him there and then would have constituted cold-blooded murder on his part, and in a moment based on instinct perhaps his moral shell had got the better of him.

Up above the helicopter was putting more distance between them. Munroe came out of cover and raised his carbine once more but it was pointless and besides, a stray bullet in a city of 9 million could land anywhere.

"Shit." With the flashing of police lights now approaching the exit of Waterloo Bridge he lowered the muzzle and rushed over to the body of the gunman. He knelt down and grasped the neckline of the balaclava before ripping it off.

The man with blonde hair stared up at him with lifeless eyes. Munroe dug his forefinger in to his neck but there was no sign of a beat, and with that realisation he expelled a long, frustrated sigh. He laid the carbine on the ground, kicked it away and then rubbed at his ears, which were still ringing from the gunfire.

The helicopter was unlike anything he had ever seen before, and the almost silent running of the engine was remarkable. Sure, he'd seen adverts for near-silent helicopters passed around military circles, but they always turned out to be bullshit. Whatever or whoever these people were he had no idea, but they were professional, with a level of tech even the Americans didn't have, so far as he knew. There was only one thing Munroe knew for sure, and it concerned Icarus. The man wasn't just your average serial killer, if there was such a thing, he was something else entirely. The real question was what.

Now Munroe began to consider his options. What had just transpired would be just a matter of course if this was a movie but, in the real world, picking up a loaded weapon and killing a man in public had consequences. Even if it was in self-defence.

"What the hell was that, Ethan?" Munroe turned around to see Regis, his face flushed and judging him warily.

"Sorry to boot you out the car, Mike, but I couldn't risk you getting hurt."

Munroe's response received a blank look from Regis, who briefly glanced down at the carbine Munroe had kicked away before looking back at him nervously.

"Me! Forget about me. You just shot a man. You're a hostage negotiator, not a fucking killer." Regis was looking at him with not only contempt but accusation. "Who the fuck are you?"

Before Munroe could answer the sound of someone clearing her throat behind him caused him to turn around and he found himself face to face with a stocky red-haired woman in a long overcoat, shadowed by two beefy-looking men in identical charcoal suits. "Someone would like to speak with you, Mr Munroe, and time is of the essence. So chop-chop."

It wasn't a refusal, but Munroe stood there for a moment, unsure of what to make of the three goons standing in front of him, not to mention where the hell they had appeared from. Sensing his hesitation, the woman casually grasped the edge of her jacket. "We can do this the easy way, Ethan," she said, pulling back her coat to reveal the Ministry of Defence ID card attached to her belt, "or the hard way."

Munroe wasn't exactly sure, but he had a rough idea what these people were, and he managed a courteous smile as he glanced down at the dead body beneath him. "Easy way every time, ma'am. Please, lead the way."

Chapter 6

"Just up here." The redhead directed Munroe up the long gangway to the top deck of HMS *Belfast*. Built to serve in World War Two, the light cruiser warship had served with distinction throughout the Korean War until being taken out of service in 1967. By 1971 it had ended up a symbolic museum piece after being permanently docked on the river Thames, within shouting distance of Tower Bridge. Munroe had taken the tour some years before and as he stepped onto the deck he could make out the flashing emergency lights from the police presence attending the clear-up on Waterloo Bridge in the distance.

"If you'll just wait here, sir," the redhead said, and began heading away, towards the bow of the ship.

"You really don't need to leave the chaperones," Munroe said, and glanced over at the two suited goons waiting either side of the gangway who, like his host, had not uttered a word during the short drive over.

"I know I don't," came the reply, and without even looking back at him she casually disappeared out of sight.

Munroe looked over at the two suits and offered them an impatient smile, but with not even an inkling of a response he turned to the railings, grasped the edges and looked out across the river. Whoever these people were they were unquestionably government-connected, because no one just gets pulled away from a crime scene, especially a shooting incident near Parliament, without even the mildest complaint from the local authorities. No, this... they... was something else entirely.

Munroe allowed his shoulders to sag against the ship's steel railings. He could see the Coppa Club from here, and the domed igloo he'd been having dinner in only hours earlier. Of course it was now empty, but the lights were still on, and his mind began to wander among the multitude of unanswered questions fettering his thoughts.

"I've heard the food's good at the Coppa, Captain Munroe. I'm certain this birthday will be one of your more memorable ones."

Munroe stood back up straight and slowly turned to face the newcomer. The man standing before him offered a dry smile and Munroe replied with a curt nod. He'd not been greeted by his military rank in some years and it immediately generated a more formal dynamic between the two of them, as Munroe instinctively stiffened in his stance.

"Memorable, yes. But not for the food."

Wearing a tight-fitting black suit and a loose-hanging black, knee-length overcoat the man offered little more than a forced smile before taking a few steps forward and resting one arm on the metal railing next to Munroe. At a guess the man was in his early fifties, with a full head of short, greying hair and deep wrinkle lines extending around his eyes and forehead. Either a sign of bad genes, or a man whose life had been spent under pressure and the weight of responsibility. His appearance was compounded further by a thin scar that ran from just below the man's left eye all the way across to his sideburn, causing a small indent encroaching into the hairline.

"I'm not one for food myself. I don't have an adventurous palate. It's more of a sustenance kind of thing for me," the man continued as Munroe eyed him blankly. "My mother couldn't cook for shit, so growing up I never developed a love of food. Her every-night lasagne was like digging your teeth into wet cardboard."

The man now glanced back at the redhead who had driven Munroe here and who was leaning casually against the opposite railing. "How about you. Your mother any good at cooking?"

The woman barely registered the comment. "I wouldn't know, sir, my father did all the cooking in our house, and he could screw up a boiled egg."

The man turned his attention back to Munroe. "Ah, the modern age."

The man was most likely intelligence-connected, and not part of the forces. Military men of all ranks were prone to getting to the point within seconds, whereas intelligence agents had a habit of skirting around a conversation, probing with what seemed like vague banter until they saw an opening to drop some unpleasant truth that would prompt the answer they wanted to hear. It was a tried and tested tactic that left the target feeling off-guard and potentially pliable, but for Munroe it was simply frustrating, and given the current situation he was in no mood to play.

"So we all had shitty dinners growing up. I'll store that little nugget of information under the file heading 'things no one gives a fuck about.'"

The man's expression remained unchanged as Munroe threw caution to the wind. "Waterloo Bridge just saw one of the most audacious and brazen military actions on UK soil in recent years, and only metres from the centre of

British power. An action that rescued one of the sickest serial killers the UK has ever seen. Seven officers were killed, and I'm responsible for shooting dead one of the attackers, and then you whisk me away without even a word to the authorities. So, how about we put aside the psych 101 bullshit and you tell me what's on your mind."

The man stood silently for a few moments and then a thin smile emerged across his lips. "They were right about you, Captain Munroe. You are obnoxiously direct... for a military man."

"I'm not a military man anymore. I'm a superintendent in the Met."

"Not that bright though," the man replied, his smile evaporating. "Just because you play in civilian clothes... Please!"

The older man motioned to the redhead with a flick of his finger and the woman dutifully stepped forward a few paces, eyeing Munroe contemptuously.

"Ethan Munroe. Arrived age four at the Strawberry Field children's home in Liverpool. Age sixteen applied and accepted into the British Army. Royal Marines by seventeen. Age twenty applied and accepted into the Special Boat Service. Served in Iraq and Afghanistan with distinction before being reassigned to the SAS aged twenty-five, which is no mean feat. Four years of special operations, counterterrorism in Iraq and Afghanistan including distinction for operations during the Boko Haram insurgency in Nigeria. I won't even mention the medals and decorations, because your head's big enough, Munroe." The redhead paused to glare at him again before continuing. "Aged twenty-nine, abruptly quit the Special Air Service, rank captain, before entering the Metropolitan police at age thirty, ending up in the hostage division, rank superintendent, where he's remained for the past three years." She gave a sarcastic smirk. "If he's not military through and through, sir, then I don't know who is."

The older man now took over the conversation without even pausing. "And then, aged thirty-five, you met me. That's quite a winding career path you've taken, Ethan, and to throw it all in the crapper to join the police... Now that's a question."

"If you know that much then you know why," Munroe replied, staying calm. There was nothing in his record to be ashamed about, with the exception of quitting the military. "It's all in my dossier, which clearly you've read."

The older man was already nodding. "I have, and I'm not sure whether to applaud you or chastise you."

"Neither. You don't know me," Munroe replied sharply, and he nodded in the direction of the red-haired woman. "Now, why don't you and Harley Quinn over there tell me what's going on. And you can begin with names."

The abrupt dig received no reaction, but after a few seconds the man started to nod and a genuine smile erupted across his face. "Boris Humperdinck, and that's Doris Delaney," he said, flicking his finger over at the redhead.

"Doris and Boris? What're your real names."

"Get to know us better and maybe you'll find out. But for now I'm Boris and she's Doris."

Surreal? Sure, but Munroe glossed over it, not wanting to waste any more time. "OK... Boris. So now the little sideshow is behind us, why don't you tell me why I'm on the deck of HMS *Belfast* instead of being debriefed back at Waterloo Bridge."

For the first time since arriving Boris looked serious. "I'm assuming you know the name David Breams."

Munroe was almost insulted. "Who doesn't. The British ambassador who had a psychotic breakdown. Murdered the German Chancellor before turning the gun on himself two months ago."

"And?"

"And, if the papers are to be believed, Breams had an inoperable brain tumour he told no one about. It's widely accepted that the condition destroyed his faculties, which resulted in a psychotic episode that almost destroyed Anglo–German relations in one short moment of insanity."

Boris's eyes narrowed. "Detailed like a historian, but what if I told you that the brain tumour was only a cover story, something to blame his actions on? What if I told you we have no idea why the man did what he did?"

Munroe pondered the information for a moment, "Then I'd say you'd better get to work."

"We are," Doris interrupted, reaching into her coat to retrieve a small photograph which she passed over to Munroe. "Because the last call David Breams received, just before his inauguration, was from an unknown mobile phone, a phone that was discovered in this house less than forty-five minutes ago."

Munroe held up the picture in front of him and he finally began to understand what was going on. It was a picture of same house he had visited just hours earlier. The house of a serial killer.

Munroe blew a long breath as Doris took back the photograph and slipped it inside her coat pocket.

"Only one call was made from it before the battery was taken out," Doris informed him, now looking at Munroe with genuine concern, "and that same person appears to have an infatuation with you, Captain Munroe. Or should I say, with your dead wife and child."

The careless mention of Munroe's family caused him to glare at the redhead. "Easy, *Doris*," he growled. "Show some respect."

Doris looked unperturbed and shrugged. "You have to admit, it's odd, is it not?"

They locked eyes with one another in an unyielding stare. It was Boris who sought to referee. "I think what my colleague means is that there are things going on here which we are in the dark about, and you appear to be in a position, especially given your history, to help us as well as yourself."

"And how would I be helping myself, Boris?"

"You can't expect me to believe you don't want to know why this maniac has an infatuation with you and your family?"

Of course Munroe wanted to know, but there was too much about these people he didn't trust. And more than that, he had made a promise to himself that he would never go back into military life in any capacity. It was a promise he wanted to keep. "And what if I say no?"

Boris smiled, one of his eyebrows slightly raised. "You won't... but we can always drop you back at Waterloo Bridge to go through your debrief, followed by months of hearings. And how you will emerge from that is in the hands of the gods."

It was a thinly veiled threat, but it wasn't because of this that Munroe had already made up his mind. Like Boris had said, why the infatuation? And that he did need to know.

"If I say yes then there are some ground rules. If you can't get past them then forget it, I walk."

The obstinate look now plastered across Boris's face told Munroe that this was a man who didn't care for deals. It was a one-way street only for him, but regardless, he did nod lightly.

"Depends what they are. Try me."

Munroe's shoulders loosened and he folded his arms boldly to show there would be no leeway given on his part. "Firstly, I want to know who you are, what division? Secondly, I'm not military anymore, I work autonomously. And thirdly, I want to know everything you and the redhead over there aren't telling me. They've only just begun trawling through Icarus's house and there's no way in that short time you could have recovered and analysed his mobile phone. You already knew about him and what you were looking for."

Although Boris was still expressionless, he did let slip the beginnings of a smile as Munroe continued.

"And don't play me as naïve, because if you are what I think you are then honesty isn't a natural part of your trade. Be honest with me and I'll be honest with you."

"And what trade would that be?"

"Not trade, but tradecraft… you're a spook."

"We prefer the term 'intelligence officers'," Doris replied, "but you're not far off."

Munroe returned a knowing smile of his own. "Then you'd better bring it into focus for me."

Boris remained motionless, but behind those dark brown eyes he was calculating a response, and after a few seconds he reached up and gently pulled at his left earlobe. "Very well, Ethan. That seems reasonable, but only if you commit right now."

Munroe said nothing for a moment as he looked back and forth between the pair, sizing them up. Eventually he gave a slow nod. "Consider me committed."

"Good," Boris replied and his whole body jerked upright like a burst of electricity had just rippled right through him. "Let's take your second one first, shall we? We are not military, as you've already alluded to, so there's no problem there, and although you'll have no leash as such you will report to me."

Munroe's eyes tightened and Boris noted it straight away.

"Temporarily, until we part ways."

With no complaint from Munroe, Boris continued. "As for how much we know, yes, you're correct. Icarus has been on our radar for some time, but not because of his killings." Boris reached inside his jacket pocket and pulled out a small photo which he displayed in front of Munroe. It was in high resolution and it showed the man known as Icarus in a smart grey suit making his way down the steps of a building Munroe knew well.

"The Ministry of Defence."

"It was taken over a year ago, and it wasn't the first time he was seen entering and leaving either, although despite our best efforts we haven't been able to ascertain who he was meeting with."

Curiosity now gripped Munroe and his eyebrow raised slightly at the unpalatable suggestion being offered. "You think he's one of ours!"

Boris's expressionless stare answered the question and Munroe's head tilted back slightly in surprise. He knew damn well how the government worked. The different layers of reality that existed. On its surface the rule of law was absolute and rigid when dealing with society.

It created certainty and stability for the citizens who lived in it, and rightly so. But there was a deeper layer, unspoken, unacknowledged, where 'nothing was ever off the table'. What needed to be done would be done when protecting a nation, just as long as it remained in the deepest crevices of the intelligence world. But the use of a serial killer! Their mindset was usually chaotic, unpredictable and always self-serving. You'd have to be crazy to place any kind of trust or responsibility in a person like that... unless...

"Icarus isn't a serial killer, is he?" Munroe stated coldly, as Boris continued to stare, clearly wanting to see how much Munroe could discern with this fresh information. "Who were his victims?"

"You know who his victims were," Boris replied casually, "they've been on the front pages of the newspapers for months."

"I mean... who were they really?"

"Three of them were just regular people, simply going about their daily lives."

"And the other two?"

"That's the problem, Ethan. The other two were MI6 agents."

Munroe rubbed his chin thoughtfully before settling upon the obvious conclusion. "You think the other three were just a distraction, like chaff in the wind."

"Maybe," Doris chimed in, taking a step closer. "The targeted assassination of two MI6 agents, lost in the media frenzy around a serial killer's victims."

Munroe was already doubtful and he shook his head, unconvinced. "But MI6 would know, two of their agents murdered. GCHQ would be all over it."

"One would think so," Boris replied, his voice strained, "but there's been no investigation. No one has even flagged it."

Boris and Doris's assessment seemed improbable but certainly not illogical, and it in turn led to a far more disturbing problem. "You think someone in MI6 is targeting its own agents? Why?"

"We don't know," Boris replied bluntly, "but we need to find out. There was also another contact on the mobile we found at Icarus's house. A Mr Tobias Kessler, home address in France, near Bordeaux. Usually I would have one of our own take a look, but seeing as you've been pulled into this investigation unwittingly, and given the bizarre connection with the passing of your family, I suspect you would cause more problems being on the outside of this than you will be on the inside. And I know you can keep things hush-hush. So, with that in mind, I would like you to pay Mr Kessler a visit, see what you can dig up. He may be no one but, then again, maybe not. We don't know. You can contact me here." Boris passed over a handwritten number on a scrap of paper. "I'll have a package waiting for you on your arrival, and as of this moment you have licence to kill status reinstated. Given your extensive background it won't have been the first time, but don't abuse it. You *will* be held responsible for your actions."

Licence to kill was nothing new to Munroe, but allowing it on Western soil was a rarity. Whoever Boris was he had a lot of pull, or at least was pretending to.

"Seeing what happened here tonight, and the helicopter equipped with silent technology that we don't even possess, I would say it goes a hell of a lot deeper than just one rogue MI6 agent," Boris said sternly. "This Kessler chap is probably a dead end, but given how little we know I want all the boxes ticked."

In Munroe's experience the eating of one of your own within the intelligence community was rare. It did happen from time to time, but only after serious consideration and never without the go-ahead from the top brass. Add the helicopter, and such an audacious breakout back on Waterloo Bridge, and this amounted to something else entirely. Something professional, something specialised, operating within the top tier of military capabilities. For the moment he was at a loss, but there was a question that could and needed to be answered. "So Boris, who are you exactly? MI5, MI6?"

Whether it was because Munroe looked so curious, or just that he enjoyed playing the mystery man, Boris gave a grin and glanced over at Doris. "Neither. We work for a different department. One that keeps us off the usual books... DS5. And just so we're clear from the outset, that designation is never to be repeated outside of us three. I'm placing a lot of faith in you, Ethan. I don't just approach anyone with such information or tasks, but given your background, and your involvement, I'm prepared to trust you and give you a shot. Just remember, mentioning it to anyone outside of DS5 will get you a military court hearing. And that's a promise."

"DS5?" Munroe was racking his brain, but it didn't sound familiar. "Never heard of it."

"Not a bad thing either," Boris replied gingerly. "Our scope deals in the areas of certain international affairs on behalf of the UK government."

There is no more pungent smell than that of bullshit, and Munroe's nose was now filled with it. "That's as vague as a fart in the wind," Munroe said, now more concerned about who these people were rather than the tale they'd been spinning him. "Have an ID or credentials?"

Boris said nothing, but Doris handed him an iPhone, whereupon he tapped in a number and placed it to his ear, waiting for an answer which was quickly forthcoming. "I'm here with Ethan Munroe, sir."

The other side of the conversation was inaudible to Munroe but after a few moments the mobile was passed over to him. "Hello."

"Captain Munroe?"

The voice was familiar, although Munroe couldn't quite place it. "Speaking."

"Captain Munroe, this is Jacob Ryan, Home Secretary. Pleasure to meet you. I'm sorry it has to be under such dire circumstances. I hope that Mr McCitrick has brought you up to speed."

Munroe glanced over at 'Boris' and grinned. "McCitrick! Yes, sir. He has."

"Good, then I don't need to tell you how sensitive this is. Your offer to help in this matter on behalf of Her Majesty's government is greatly appreciated, and of course comes under the Official Secrets Act."

"I understand, Minister."

"Excellent. Mr McCitrick has my full confidence in this matter and he reports directly to me, and me only."

"Thank you for the clarification, sir."

"No, thank you, Captain, and godspeed. I look forward to receiving your report."

The line then went dead and Munroe passed the phone back into Doris's waiting palm. She pocketed it before outstretching her hand. "Jaqueline Sloan, but you can call me Jax." Munroe shook her hand tightly and offered a mutual nod of respect as she continued, "Captain with the Royal Marines. Those are my credentials."

Munroe now turned to 'Boris', who didn't offer a handshake.

"John McCitrick, and that phone call you just took… they're my credentials."

Chapter 7

The lone figure of a decrepit old man slowly made his way up the dirt road as a solitary street lamp flickered overhead, sending shadows across the cracked pink plaster of a small building opposite. With little more than a shuffle the man took a few more steps and came to a stop next to the street lamp, and with his eyes wincing looked up at the twinkling bulb and gave a disappointed shake of his head. Placing his black leather suitcase on the ground next to him he then slid his shirt sleeve up to the elbow and raised his quivering hand upwards before bringing it down against the pole with a thud. Up above the light bulb ceased its flickering and the man pulled his shirt sleeve back down, picked up his suitcase and once more began slowly walking down the street to the last building on it.

He was within metres of the doorway when behind him the street lamp began flickering once again, and the old man merely flipped his free hand downwards in annoyance. It was a strange reversal of mind, he thought, that the older he got, the more the small things bothered him, rather than the big things.

With a few more steps he reached the front door of a respectable-looking white bungalow, and pulled a key from his pocket which he slipped into the lock and turned. With a well-oiled click the door swung open and the old men entered the darkness and placed his bag down on the floor before reaching over to one side and pressing the light switch.

The front room was lit up by an overhead light and lining its walls were a series of small wall lamps covered by frosted glass, illuminating the room with a cosy hue. The old man closed the door behind him and made his way to the central coffee table opposite a thirty-inch plasma TV, and plopped his bag onto the clean, grey leather couch in front of it. He raised his arms outwards and stretched his back shakily, raising his head upwards, and with a satisfied yawn made his way towards the darkness of the kitchen opposite. He gently pressed the inside light switch with his forefinger and looked downwards with a wince as his eyes adjusted to the glare.

"Hola, Senhor Ferreira."

The old man jerked backwards uncomfortably as he turned to see a man sitting at his extended oak leaf kitchen table, slouching back on the furthest chair. "I hope I didn't scare you."

"That's exactly what you meant to do, idiot," Ferreira berated in a heavy Portuguese accent. "I told you never to come unannounced."

His guest's mischievous smile told him all he needed to know as the man sat upright in the chair and tucked his purple short-sleeve shirt tightly into the top of his jeans.

"I'm afraid time is of the essence, and I didn't want to hang around outside to be mistaken for a burglar by one of your neighbours."

Ferreira looked puzzled by the response and he picked up two whisky glasses off the counter and placed one on either side of the kitchen table. He then pulled a bottle of Macallan single malt Scotch whisky from the polished wall rack and began unscrewing the cap before pouring a shot into his guest's glass until the man tapped its rim.

"And what's so important to bring you all the way out here?" Ferreira asked gently as he began to pour his own glass.

"Icarus."

Ferreira stopped pouring and left the whisky bottle hovering over his glass apprehensively for a few moments before continuing to top up his glass. "What news?"

The man waited for his host to place the cap back on the bottle and take a seat before raising his glass. "Thanks to him our timeline has changed. We must proceed now."

The guest's voice had an Eastern European twinge to it, putting a heavy emphasis on the word 'proceed', and although Ferreira looked uncomfortable at the news he still raised his glass dutifully before taking a deep sip, almost polishing off the drink in one gulp.

"But my work isn't finished," he replied, flinching at the sharp bite of his whisky. "The new batch is proving far more impressive than the last."

The guest took another, smaller sip from his glass and offered an affable smile. "Your work, your results, have been more than anyone could have hoped for, Senhor Ferreira. It has been the cornerstone of everything we have sought to build, but we all knew this day would come. And it's a day we should be proud and welcoming of."

Ferreira looked sceptical and he leant forward with both elbows on the table's lacquered surface, his hands clasping one another tightly as if in prayer. "If I could have just another few short years, then the results it would yield would be the ultimate accomplishment, and—"

The guest sternly flicked his finger towards Ferreira, silencing the older man instantly. "Your work has been accomplished, and now it is time to move forward. It's time your dedication was rewarded."

"But the work is my reward," Ferreira spluttered excitedly, still not quite ready to concede.

"Where we are going there will be much more for you to do... but this part of the adventure is now over."

Ferreira's excited expression began to melt and after a few moments of staring into empty space he slowly began to nod his head. "I understand. How long do we have?"

The guest pushed his chair back and stood up. He then moved over to Ferreira, grasped his underarm and gently pulled the man to his feet. "Soon. Within the next twenty-four hours. I will take care of the logistics. But I need all of the data, everything, backups as well. There must be zero chance of any record falling into the wrong hands."

Ferreira gave a short nod and he stood up and made his way into the front room with his guest in tow. He knelt down by the nearest electricity outlet, pulled away the white plastic front cover and then poked his fingers inside and retrieved two blue memory cards. "Original and backup," he said, getting to his feet and passing them into his guest's waiting hand. "They contain everything, but there is also some documentation back at the office which will need to be destroyed." Ferreira pulled a bunch of keys from his pocket and wriggled off one of the Yale keys, which he also passed over. "This will let you in."

The guest smiled, then patted him on the back and began to make his way over to the front door. "Leave it to me. I will take care of that, and when I return we can run through your travel plans. I would begin packing though." The guest paused and turned back towards Ferreira. "Think of what is to come, Senhor."

"Yes, I know. But what of everything we will lose?"

The guest wagged his finger at this. "Not lose. Think of everything I will gain. Now come and see me off."

The guest ushered the old man towards him with a wave of his arm. As Ferreira passed by and reached for the front door handle he suddenly froze.

"Wait, what do you mean, 'I'?"

The thin metal wire of a garrotte was thrown around his neck and tightened with such speed that it had already sliced a centimetre into his wrinkled flesh before he had time to react. As it sunk deeper, Ferreira scratched at his throat in vain, blood now dripping from the thin wound, and he forced out his last words in a gurgle as the wire reached his trachea and carved through like a hot knife through wax. "Hans... Why?"

Hans Bauer stared downwards at the old man, now crumpling to his knees, his expression cold and unforgiving as he pulled tighter on the garotte handles. Blood was now pouring down Ferreira's neck as the wire cut through both carotid arteries and the assault continued until he felt the metal grinding against the front of the old man's spine. Bauer, still pulling tightly, dipped his head towards Ferreira's ear and whispered, "All good things must come to an end... and your journey ends here."

Only now did Bauer ease his grip and uncoil the garrotte, having to dislodge it from Ferreira's throat with a hard tug, sending the old man to the floor with a dull thud. He then reached over and opened the front door to reveal two men wearing black balaclavas, plastic hospital shoe coverings and blue latex gloves over their clothes.

The two men said nothing and with a nod from Bauer they closed the door and began unwrapping a green tarpaulin from a bag. The body was already being rolled into the plastic sheeting as Bauer sauntered back to the kitchen where he picked up the two whisky glasses, gave them a quick wash in the sink and, using a nearby dish-cloth, held them up to the light checking for fingerprints before placing them back on the counter. "Just in case." He then returned to the front room and watched as the body of Ferreira was packed tightly in the tarpaulin with plastic zip ties at both ends.

"Dispose of the body as agreed. I don't want it ever found," Bauer said coldly before tapping the closest man to him on the shoulder. "I will see you when you're finished. There is much still to be done."

Chapter 8

The sky was clear as sunrise broke, and although unusually overcast the white cliffs of Dover could be seen off in the distance as the man slammed his axe into the thick chunk of wood, splitting it in half with a hefty whack. Leaning the axe against a small pile of logs, Michael Hanks reached down to pick up four of the pieces and proceeded to slip them underneath his arm before raising his head skywards, breathing in the fresh, salty air. Content, he headed back towards the small French villa and made his way inside, dropping his gatherings beside the open hearth full of burning red embers.

The front room looked like something out of the 1940s, with a worn olive green couch placed in front of the hearth on a bare wooden floor. No paintings or ornaments graced the room and the cracked pink plastered walls only added to the already dull ambience.

"He's awake and ready for you, sir. I'll be up here if you need me."

Hanks gave a simple nod and then slipped off his grey knitted skullcap, which he dropped onto the armrest of the couch. He then headed past the waiting man and slowly down the tight staircase to the basement below. Each step produced a squeaking sound of strained wood. He came to a stop at the last, whereupon he looked over to the solitary man in handcuffs, seated on a metal chair, shirtless and barefoot in the centre of a dank empty room, staring blankly at the concrete floor. Above him a sturdy nylon climbing rope had been run between the man's bound hands overhead to a series of discoloured steel water pipes that ran the length of the room, juddering rhythmically as they transported their contents to the boiler somewhere up above.

"You've put us in a real bind, Icarus," Hanks said glumly. He hopped off the last step and strolled over until he was just a few feet away. "You've made a lot of people very unhappy and put the whole project in jeopardy. Timelines have had to change, and you know how sensitive it is."

Icarus emitted a contemptuous laugh before looking up to face his captor. "Just doing what I needed to do."

Hanks's eyes dulled and he shook his head melodramatically. "No, what you were meant to do was exactly as you were told. But now I'm wondering if you were ever even capable of obeying orders. Perhaps we misidentified your potential for such things. You wouldn't be the first. Would you?"

This last sentence garnered a devilish look from Icarus, and although his lips tightened in anger he remained silent as the man gazed upon him as if he was a curiosity to be observed.

"If I didn't know better I would think you wanted to be caught. Have you been feeling left out… did you want us to rescue you, forcing us to reveal ourselves?"

Hanks leant down to him with both hands in his pockets and his eyes full of unease. "Or was it something more, something closer to your heart. In some twisted, sick way do you see Ethan Munroe as… a brother in arms?"

Icarus suddenly looked dejected, and his nostrils flared as his emotions momentarily got the better of him.

"Jesus Christ. You do, don't you? You insane son of a bitch."

Hanks stood back up, pulled his hands from his pockets and clapped them together as he let out a deep bellow of a laugh, and then without hesitation his expression turned sour and hateful as he slapped Icarus across the face hard with the back of his hand. "You fucked up, son. You fucked up royally."

Icarus barely winced, his split lip trailing a thin drop of blood down his chin while Hanks massaged his striking hand.

"My daddy was a hunter. He bred coonhounds for the chase. Tough little bastards those dogs, and fearless to a fault, but the real key is in the breeding. You get the right match, the right genetics, and the offspring are pure gold. Strong, fearless and loyal to their masters. Not a thing they won't do when told to. But in any litter there's always one that has all those qualities, and yet there's just something not right. Can't say if it's the ass end of inbreeding but when they look at you there's something… not all there. Something going on behind those eyes that's unquantifiable, leery, mistrustful. And you have no choice but to put that puppy to sleep." Hanks now glanced up at the ceiling as if searching for some reasoning. "I love animals and I don't like doing it. Hell, I'm a vegetarian. But it has to be done, for the greater good."

He gazed back down at Icarus, who was now staring at him menacingly, and lifted up his coat to reveal a black SIG Sauer P320 poking out from beneath his belt. "But I want to give you a chance, son." Hanks lowered his coat to conceal the gun. "Yes, you've caused us a lot a lot of trouble, but it's not what we do know that concerns us so much as what we don't. If you hadn't been caught then we wouldn't be having this conversation. Hell, we probably would have left you to your own devices, but bringing this Ethan Munroe into the fray and getting arrested, well, we need to know what you've been saying, and to who."

Icarus continued to stare up at his captor with resentment. He knew the real reason why they had brought him here but he remained silent as Hanks continued, now trying to sound ever friendlier. Good cop and bad cop all rolled into one.

"Personally I don't believe you let slip any of our arrangements or names, but Mr Bauer and the top honchos aren't as convinced given your rogue behaviour of late. Can't say I blame them, but with so much at stake it's hardly surprising." Hanks got down on one knee and looked up at Icarus. "If you did run your mouth then tell me exactly what you said and it's a problem that can be dealt with. Do this and I promise you I will release those cuffs and send you on your merry way. With the proviso," Hanks raised his finger in the air, "that you stay underground just for the next few days, until the event has taken place. After that, things are going to change and you can come along for the ride, which I know you want to. But, if you have said something to the authorities during your arrest and you don't tell me, then there's nothing I can do for you."

Icarus thought about it for a moment and then he smiled. "Whether I told anyone anything or not you're going to kill me regardless, but if I escape then I'm free anyway."

Hanks was already beginning to laugh even before Icarus finished his sentence, and he stood back up and took a few steps backwards before raising his hands in the air. "And where would you go, friend? We were able to arrange your audacious escape from custody within only a few hours of a heads-up. Imagine if we had the whole lot of us tracking you down. And you're forgetting, son – in under a couple of days' time, when the big show's over, it'll free everyone up and they'll rain down on you with full force. There wouldn't be a rock you could hide under. But no point in daydreaming. You're here, with us, and that ain't changing anytime soon."

Hanks stepped back and hovered over Icarus like a predator eyeing its prey. "Don't you see, this is your only chance for redemption, and if you don't tell me what I need to know then you know what comes next. It won't matter how tough you think you are, there's only so much a human being can take. We'll break you. The only question is how long it'll take."

Hanks again got down on his knees, his face displaying genuine empathy. "You've done so much for us. Why throw it all away for reasons I can't even grasp? It'd be a damn shame, and when we're so close as well. Now, all I need to know is, did you tell anyone anything about what we've got planned in London? Simple as that. Or," Hanks licked his lips, "we're going to have to work on you."

The threat barely registered and Icarus continued to stare at his captor with contempt. "You better get started then."

Hanks looked down at the ground and sighed deeply, before getting to his feet and heading back over to the stairwell. "Davies, get down here!" The sound of heavy footsteps made their way across the floor above them and then down the stairs to where Hanks was waiting.

"It's going to be the hard way," Hanks said, pointing over to Icarus, who was now just staring at the filthy basement floor. "I'd suggest starting with cutting before you bother with truth serum. Soften him up a bit. Start with the toes and work your way up to the fingers. I'd leave his testicles for later in case we need to deliver some electric shock therapy."

Davies was a short man with blonde hair poking out the sides of a plain blue baseball cap, and despite his stature his forearms looked powerful. After a slap on the shoulder from Hanks he made his way over to their seated hostage, whereupon he dropped a thick leather wrap held in his hand to the floor. He then knelt down and unrolled it to reveal a number of metal instruments including a scalpel, hammer, flat head screwdriver and a pair of blue-handled pliers.

Hanks gave a limp-wristed salute. "What a goddamn waste," he muttered, before heading up the stairs. He barked a couple of orders to someone and then left via the front door, slamming it in his wake, leaving Icarus alone in the company of the smiling Davies, who was already tapping the point of the scalpel to gauge how sharp it was.

"I don't usually enjoy this type of work. There's no sport in it," he said in a thick Louisiana accent, and pulled back his jacket to reveal a Glock handgun sticking out of his belt. "Prefer the hunt myself, but I intend to make an exception in your case."

Icarus remained motionless as Davies stood back up and slapped both his hands on the sides of his waist in frustration. "Shit. I need to get some towels to stem the blood. Sit tight, I'll be right back. Don't worry, I won't forget about you."

Davies had barely managed to turn back towards the stairwell before Icarus jumped upwards and in one effort grabbed the pipes above with both hands and twisted his waist to wrap both thighs tightly around the man's neck. He then he swivelled his contorted body as the crack of snapped bones rippled through his muscles. "I'll happily forget about you," Icarus whispered in a growl, as both of Davies's thick arms dropped limply to his side and there he hung for a few moments before, after one final sharp squeeze, just to be sure, Icarus loosened his grip and gently lowered the man to the floor.

Upstairs nothing stirred. Icarus stretched out his legs and with his toes latched on to the dropped scalpel, limberly retrieving it and flinging it into his lap. Within moments he had cut through the nylon restraints and he immediately set about undressing Davies. Once dressed in the man's attire he slipped the Glock under his belt and with the scalpel hidden up his sleeve he put on the cap, pulling the visor down over his forehead, providing cover for his face.

The guard upstairs barely registered the man entering the room, and as Icarus looked down and played with his pockets as if searching for something he spoke out in near perfect mimicry of Davies's voice, the cap's visor concealing his face. "I'm going to need some towels. You got any?"

Without pause the guard shifted off the sofa and walked over to a cupboard on the opposite side of the room and began pulling out the bottom drawer before reaching inside and retrieving a stack of three white fluffy towels. "If you need more I'll have to go out," was all he managed before an arm slid around his neck and the blade of a scalpel pressed against his carotid artery.

"Only speak if spoken to. Understand?"

"Yes," the guard replied, his whole body stiffening as Icarus reached around with his free hand and pulled the handgun sticking out of his waist holster and stuck it in to the back of his own trousers.

"How many men outside?"

The guard hesitated, and it was only after the scalpel began cutting deeper into his neck that he replied.

"Six, including me. Two armed with shotguns at the main gate and three with machine guns patrolling."

"Same people who brought me here?"

"No, you were dropped off."

"And the helicopter?"

The man managed a jerky shake of his head, his face turning paler by the second. "Dropped you off and left."

"It was a short trip, are we in Calais?"

The man closed his eyes and nodded.

"Quickest exit away from the main gate?"

The man resisted an answer but as the scalpel was dug in deeper and blood began to trickle down his neck there came not only a distressed groan but a quick reply. "There's a path running along the cliff at the back of this building. Brings you out onto the road leading into town. But there's a guard positioned there."

"Good," Icarus replied, coming to the end of his questioning. "And who did they have looking for me?"

"Everyone."

Icarus continued to hold the scalpel at the man's neck. Sensing what was about to happen the guard said in nothing more than a whisper, "I don't want to die."

Icarus pulled the Glock from his belt and leant in closer so his lips were only centimetres from the guard's ear. "Then today is your lucky day. But if I find you've lied to me, then I will be back, and I promise I will carve you up, real slow."

Icarus slammed the butt of the Glock down hard against the guard's head, sending him to the floor, and then he slipped the scalpel into his back pocket and with his cap pulled down he moved to the window and peeked outside. The guard had been honest with him and Icarus found himself looking at the edge of the coastline no more than fifty metres away, the rippling blue waters of the English Channel beyond. Far off to the left he could see the two guards patrolling a set of rusting gates leading to what looked like open farmland, and to his right a man in jeans and a black windbreaker holding an MP5 machine gun walking towards the building.

Icarus ducked down onto his haunches and peered out from his hiding spot as the guard slowly made his way past the building, scanning the area as he went, and then walked on towards the main gate and the two other guards with shotguns.

Icarus waited until he reached them and with one final scan he moved over to the door, pulling it open just an inch and checking that the coast was clear. He then placed the gun in his jacket pocket and swiftly exited, immediately making his way around the side of the house and then beyond towards the cliff edge. He didn't run, nor did he creep, but calmly walked towards the gated path leading on to a dense leafy forest. A guard wearing a thick grey sweater and jeans looked out to the forest, his back turned to Icarus, an automatic MP5 resting in his hands. The guard never even heard the footsteps as Icarus approached and slammed the butt of his gun across the back of the man's head, sending him to the ground in a crumpled heap. He reached down and picked up the machine gun before throwing it over the cliff and then began to pick up speed, darting deeper into the dark recess of the forest and beyond until he was out of sight.

It would be almost an hour before Hanks discovered the unconscious bodies of the guards along with Davies's cold corpse, and as they scoured the property and soon after began to pull out of the area, they never once noticed the pair of cold eyes watching their every move from deep in the treeline, already calculating his next course of action.

Chapter 9

The hot sun overhead was stifling as Munroe slammed the door of the silver Renault Clio shut and made his way along the short dirt path leading up to the impressive red brick chateau at its end. The wooden storm shutters were all closed and with no car out front the residence looked empty. With the neck of his coat clutched in his hand and his tie hanging loosely he probably looked like a lost tourist or a salesman concluding the last visit of the day. Reaching the front door, he gently pressed the green buzzer at the side.

After departing from the deck of the HMS *Belfast* with nothing more than a polite wave from John McCitrick, Captain Sloan, or Jax as she preferred, had driven him to Heathrow airport where he would catch a flight to Bordeaux and then on a few miles west to Lège-Cap-Ferret, a town on the east coast peninsula. They had barely spoken during the drive. The only full sentences she had offered him were as he was getting out of the car. "Call me when you've done some digging. There's a rental car waiting under your name and a key to an airport lock box in the glove compartment. You'll find a handgun inside." As the car had begun to pull away she had barked one last order through the open window. "And don't go waving it around like an idiot."

It was clear Captain Sloan had little time for people in general, and he was no exception. She was a woman of few words and he had no problem with that. It was a luxury not afforded to him on the flight over. The passenger next to him, a French man on his way home after a business trip, had attempted to force him into conversation multiple times. When the man had finally got around to trying to pique his interest in a timeshare in Paris, Munroe had simply said no politely before admitting he he'd been suffering from a severe bout of flu and breaking into a series of deep, bellowing coughs. His little act had done the trick and the man said not another word, leaning as far away as possible in the direction of the window for the entire flight.

After picking up the rental car he had spent the drive mulling over what McCitrick had told him. Munroe was having a hard time squaring the focused assassination of two MI6 officers with the man who carried it out. Icarus was a mystery to him and, rogue agent or not, something, no everything, felt wrong, and it unnerved him. In the shadowy world of espionage you take out targets and blame it on something or someone else. You never drew attention to it, as Icarus had seemed so keen to do.

Munroe waited at the front door of the chateau for a few moments before taking a step backwards and inspecting the windows for any sign of movement. There was none, so he reached over and pressed the buzzer again. This time there was a response. There was the sound of a lock unclicking and then the plain wooden door opened a quarter of the way, revealing the unsure face of an old man with curly white hair and moustache.

"Mr Kessler, Tobias Kessler?"

"Yes," said the man, peering gingerly from side to side to see if anyone else was there.

"My name is Ethan Munroe, and I was hoping to speak with you about a mutual acquaintance of ours."

Most likely Mr Kessler had no idea someone he knew was the media-famed serial killer known as Icarus. Munroe reached into his back pocket as the man frowned; without knowing the murderer's true identity a photo would have to suffice.

"And who would that be?"

Munroe held a close-up photo of Icarus leaving the Ministry of Defence. "Him."

Kessler squinted at the image, and suddenly his unsure expression melted away and he smiled with a nod. "Oh, David. How is the boy? Keeping out of trouble I hope."

There was genuine sincerity in Kessler's voice and Munroe offered an appreciating smile. "You know David."

The old man now opened the door fully and while nodding agreeably he ushered Munroe inside with a wave. "Please come in. Any friend of David's is welcome in my house."

With a polite nod Munroe obliged and stepped inside as Kessler closed the door behind him. The open hallway was as big as most people's front rooms, with more rooms opening up on either side and leading to a single staircase at the end which curled around on itself to the floor above. The walls were pasted in embossed white wallpaper on which hung a collection of oil paintings showing various scenes from French life. None were particularly notable. On the left hung a brass-coloured coat rack and apart from the antique-looking side table sat upon the thick navy carpet the rest of the space was empty.

"Please, this way," Kessler said, leading Munroe into the front living room. "Can I get you a drink?"

"Thank you, but no," he replied as he followed the man inside. As Kessler began to talk his voice faded out for a moment as the intense décor of the living room made its impact. Every space on all the dark wood-panelled walls was occupied by a hunter's trophy: deer, caribou, zebra and even an alligator with its jaws wide open, teeth bleached white. Above the unused fireplace hung the stuffed, snarling face of a black jaguar, but it was not these oddities that stood out the most. The glass coffee table placed between two yellow fabric sofas was resting on four deer antlers, substituting for legs, and the old-fashioned tubular TV in the corner had been inserted inside a mismatch of carved animal femurs, constituting its casing.

"It's quite a collection, is it not?" Kessler said as Munroe returned to his senses.

"That's for sure. I don't think I've ever seen such an assortment before."

"I can believe that," the older man stated proudly, surveying the oddity that was his front living room. "Do you hunt?"

"I've been known to," Munroe replied, once again surveying the room and for a moment becoming trans-fixed by the sight. "But they're not the kind of trophies I'd care to hang on my wall."

Kessler's eyes lit up. "Interesting. You must be a small game man. Is that how you met David?"

The mention of Icarus returned Munroe's focus to him and he faced the old man with interest. "It was, as it happens. In fact that's the reason I'm here you see. I've been working overseas for the past few years and lost track of him. You know how it is."

Kessler nodded his head, his eyebrows raised. "Oh, I do. Happens to the best of us. Of course at my age it's usually due to death."

There was a candour to Kessler that Munroe liked, and apart from the oddity of his decorative choices he seemed like a lonely old man with a hobby that had, or should have, died a death long ago.

"If you're sure you wouldn't like a drink then you won't mind if I finish mine."

"Please, of course."

Kessler slowly made his way over to side table next to a yellow sofa and picked up a glass tumbler full of what looked like either water or neat vodka. Judging by the man's trailing aroma it was the latter.

"So, you're seeking to rekindle your relationship with David?" Kessler said, and pointing to the framed photo on the side table next to the bone-encrusted TV. "He's a good boy. I knew his father, a hunter second to none."

Munroe moved over to the side table and picked up the frame. It showed the man known as Icarus kneeling above a downed elk carcass wearing a green hunter's jacket and pulling at its antlers so as to pose the carcass for the camera. Next to him knelt a slightly younger-looking Mr Kessler, smiling proudly like a Cheshire Cat.

"We felled that beast ten years ago," Kessler said, joining Munroe at the side table, "in the Czech Republic. It was the largest one we ever hunted. Took almost two days of tracking but we got it in the end, thanks to David."

Kessler raised his glass sloppily in a toast, sending a hefty splash all over Munroe's cheek and trickling down his neck. The old man was probably halfway through his daily drinking binge and Munroe jerked backwards as Kessler began to apologise.

"So sorry, Mr Munroe. My hands aren't what they used to be… and I don't get many visitors these days. Truth is, you're the first one I've had in weeks."

Munroe was already wiping the vodka from his face as Kessler pulled out a handkerchief and passed it over.

"Here, use this," the old man said, looking mightily embarrassed. "Please, keep it and don't worry, it's clean."

With a forced smile Munroe took the handkerchief and dabbed at his face as Kessler ambled back to the far sofa and lowered himself gently into it before placing his glass firmly back down on the side table next to him. "Please, take a seat," he said as Munroe accepted the offer and sat down opposite, dropping his coat on the cushion next to him. "I don't think I'm able to spill it on you from here."

Munroe expelled a courteous chuckle and mopped up the last drops. "Not a problem, and thanks for this," he said, stuffing the handkerchief into his front trouser pocket before sitting stiffly. "So, have you heard from David lately?"

Kessler looked somewhat ambivalent about the question and he rocked his head lightly from side to side. "Not for a few months, but that tends to be our normal routine. I know he's a busy man."

"What's he been up to?" Munroe asked, putting his hands together so as to appear as inoffensive as possible.

"He's still working in IT, but he was talking about getting out of the game and trying his hand at something else."

"Oh, and what's that?"

"I don't think he's decided, but he's looking around for new opportunities."

Kessler was now looking apprehensive and his eyes began to tighten curiously. "And what is it that you do, Mr Munroe?"

There was a hesitation in the older man's voice and Munroe merely smiled pleasantly. "I'm a corporate headhunter for a London firm. I track down the right person for the job." Munroe's reply was said in an ominous tone and he stared at Kessler sternly as the man licked his lips, his breathing now becoming heavier. "And I think I've found my man."

Kessler's eyes were now squinting intensely. "I'm not sure I like your attitude, Mr Munroe."

"And I don't think I like your bullshit, Mr Kessler," Munroe replied, and he slid his hand into his jacket pocket lying on the sofa beside him and pulled out a black SIG Sauer P320 handgun which he pointed directly at his host, resting it on his knee.

"What the hell are you doing?" Kessler erupted, and although shocked he remained where he sat, looking unintimidated by the barrel now pointed at his chest.

"I'm calling you out, Mr Kessler. Let's play a little game, shall we. It's called 'let's go around the room'."

Munroe motioned to the hallway. "On the side table there is a pile of envelopes I noticed on the way in, and the top one is addressed to someone with the first name 'David'. It also carries the address of a house I visited yesterday evening. A house of horrors, you might say."

Kessler looked unperturbed at whatever accusation was being made. "I offered to co-sign for David's house years ago. I still get redirected mail from the mortgage company."

Munroe ignored the excuse and continued motioning towards the hallway. "You said you haven't had any visitors in weeks, yet there's a brown leather jacket hanging on the rack that's way too big to be yours. It would drape over you like a robe."

Kessler was shaking his head in irritation. "It belongs to my neighbour, Jacques Demose, if you must know, and he left it here weeks ago, you fool."

Munroe stared at the older man now with nothing short of pure menace as he turned his attention to the side table next to the TV and nodded towards the drawer underneath it, and the thin piece of paper sticking out of it. "And why are you collecting newspaper clippings about a serial killer?"

Kessler's look of incensed innocence began to evaporate as he too looked over at the offending item. There was only one sheet and it appeared to have been stuffed inside in a rush, leaving just a few centimetres poking out. Munroe had noticed it after having the drink spilled on him. It was a newspaper clipping with only one word visible, part of the banner headline. 'Icarus.'

"For someone who knows little of his friend's activities you appear to follow his work closely."

Munroe now got to his feet and he moved to the hallway door where he poked his head out. Once satisfied it was clear turned his attention back to Kessler, who was looking not so much uncomfortable as angry. "Who else is in the house?" Munroe said in little more than a whisper, pushing the barrel of his gun closer towards Kessler.

"It's only us," Kessler replied softly through gritted teeth.

"Well I don't believe that." Munroe urged the older man to his feet with a flick of his gun. "Why don't we go take a look, and then we can have a good chat about what you do know."

As Kessler stood up something curious happened to Munroe, and he began to feel his knees weaken. Then his head began to swirl slightly, knocking him off balance, and suddenly it dawned on him. He thrust Kessler back into his seat with the butt of his gun and immediately reached for the glass tumbler on the side table and raised it to his nose. It was pure vodka, but there was another scent, almost undetectable. Something chemical.

"What's in this?" Munroe growled as he threw the glass to the floor, smashing it and sending shards everywhere.

"Don't worry, it's just something to make you a bit more comfortable," Kessler said, his lips now curling upwards sinisterly, and he stood up as Munroe staggered backwards and very slowly tugged away his gun with ease. "It's been seeping into your pores ever since I spilled it on you. But don't worry, it won't kill you." Kessler now looked over Munroe's shoulder and nodded. "He, on the other hand, is a different story entirely."

Munroe barely managed to turn his head before he felt a nylon cord thrust around his neck and then tighten. His head was swimming as the pressure intensified and it was at this point that instinct took over. Raising his left leg, he slammed it hard against Kessler's chest, sending the older man flying back into the sofa. The momentum thrust him backwards against his unseen attacker, pushing them both back into the hallway, landing hard on the floor. The jolt did little to loosen the grip around his throat and Munroe now slammed his elbow into the attacker's side and hip repeatedly. The firm stomach muscles felt like a man's and with this in mind he struggled to place his feet on the ground either side and then he arched his back and slammed his hips down hard into the person's groin.

The blow hit its mark and along with a pained groan the grip on the cord loosened around his neck. Munroe slid both palms through the opening and then pulled it over the top of his head. He flung himself off to one side and groggily got to his feet to face the unknown attacker. He'd been expecting the face of Icarus, but the man before him was nothing like him. Still lying on the floor, cupping his genitals, the man was muscular, with thick, defined arms sticking through a sleeveless black T-shirt, wearing black gloves and a blonde crew cut.

Munroe lurched forward and landed a heavy blow again in the man's groin with the heel of his boot, but as he went in for a second time the attacker grabbed his sole and twisted it, sending him twizzling to the floor with a hefty slam. The drug was now really kicking in and by the time Munroe had stumbled to his feet the blonde-haired attacker was on him. Munroe blocked two flailing haymakers with his forearms and managed to drive his heel into the side of the man's calf, putting him down on one knee, but 'Blondie' replied with an upwards punch to his ribs which sent him careening backwards and through the nearest doorway. Munroe slammed against the kitchen table, his head colliding with a brass cooking pot dangling from the overhanging partition, the blow dropping him face first to the surface. He looked back to see the attacker rushing him through the doorway. The kick he delivered to the chest had had less of an effect than he'd hoped for, his drug-laden muscles now stiffening, but it sent the man back a pace, giving him time to slip around the table, where he began retreating backwards slowly as Blondie advanced on him.

Judging by the growing numbness in his hands and the way his vision was wavering, everything seeming to be lit up intensely, it was a given that his body would succumb to unconsciousness at any moment. As the attacker began to move closer Munroe retrieved a final desperate note from his playbook.

And it was desperate.

He came to a stop at the end of the kitchen table and waited as the man paced towards him down the narrow walkway, the table on one side and the kitchen appliances on the other. Munroe began to look as if he was starting to cry in helplessness, and when the attacker was no less than a metre from him he flung up his arm, pointing behind him and shouting in a terrified, high-pitched voice, "Jesus Christ, look out!"

He couldn't believe it, but Blondie actually turned to look, and in that moment Munroe reached for the refrigerator handle next to him and flung it open with all his weight behind it. The timing was perfect, and it hit the man just as he turned back to face him, sending him down onto his hindquarters with a bone-crunching whack. Without missing a beat Munroe reached up and grabbed the nearest overhanging brass pot, and then with a full swing slammed it down on top of the man's head, sending him to the floor in a crumpled heap.

The blow had done its job and Blondie was out cold, blood running from his nose, but it was now Munroe who collapsed to the floor, his back slamming against the far cupboard as the heavy pot dropped with a clang between his legs on the white tiled floor.

"Impressive. You've got real stamina," Kessler congratulated as he appeared at the kitchen doorway, pointing

Munroe's own SIG Sauer P320 at him. "Most people go down in half that time."

Munroe was now unable to move his arms, which lay limply either side of him. As his vision began to fog over, and as the familiar serenity of deep sleep captured his senses, he heard a few final words.

"Well then, Mr Munroe. What exactly should we do with you?"

Chapter 10

The distant sound of slapping could be heard well before the stinging feeling of the blow, and Munroe woozily opened his bleary eyes just as another struck him across his right cheek.

"Good. Finally," Kessler said in exasperation. "Drugging you may have taken twice the time but waking you up has been almost intolerable."

Munroe had no idea how long he'd been out but given the view of a moonlit sky from the kitchen it had been some time. The muscles in his neck were sore from the attempted strangulation and as he looked past Kessler he could see the man who'd administered it. Blondie was leaning against the far kitchen wall, his bulging arms crossed, with a white plaster strip running across the bridge of his nose and two black bruises underneath each of his eyes, which were glaring at Munroe forebodingly.

"That looks painful," Munroe said with a slur as the numbness in his tongue began to subside, "you should get it looked at."

Blondie angrily unfolded his arms and took a step forward but Kessler put his arm out and tapped the muscular beast on the chest.

"No, Gustav. There'll be time for that later."

"Gustav!" Munroe said with a weary chuckle. "I had you pegged as a Barry or a Brian."

Kessler delivered another hard slap across Munroe's cheek and then shook his head in dismay. "For someone in such a precarious predicament I would have expected a bit more humility."

Munroe wrinkled his nose at the blow and attempted a smile, even though his lips were also still numb and his head was pounding. "That's the problem with expectations, they tend to let you down."

Kessler let out a short snort. "I don't like to be let down, Mr Munroe. But by the time I finish you'll be screaming like everyone else."

The word 'everyone' did not sit well, and Munroe struggled momentarily with the nylon rope binding his arms behind the back of the chair.

"It's quite tight, I assure you," Kessler noted as Munroe turned his attention to the cooking hob just feet away. It was an old gas stove and one of the burners was lit, its blue flame licking the glowing metal point of an ice pick which had been laid across it. "Cooking tonight? You really didn't have to go to the trouble on my account."

"Oh, but I do, Mr Munroe," Kessler growled, and he picked up a green ceramic plate off the kitchen counter and smashed it over Munroe's head, sending pieces tumbling down around him. "Consider that your entrée."

Kessler reached over and picked up the black wooden handle of the ice pick and held it to within inches of Munroe's face, the orange glow lighting up the droplets of sweat on his forehead. "I think we'll forgo another entrée, but the main will consist of the curdling of horrified screams as I slowly probe one of your testicles with this red-hot ice pick." Kessler moved the weapon nearer. "By the time I move on to the other one, you'll beg to lick my arsehole just to make me stop."

Munroe's expression remained calm yet resilient and he winced slightly. "Not really the meal I had in mind."

Kessler glared at him furiously and it looked as if he were about to jam the glowing point deep into Munroe's eye, but at the last moment he pulled back and returned the ice pick to the stove burner. "Enough of the games," he shouted, allowing Munroe's cavalier attitude to get the better of him, frustrated that his initial threats had failed. "Why have you come here, Mr Munroe. What is it you want?"

Finally they could talk, and even though Munroe knew he was playing a risky game the only card he held was information. If he gave it up straight away he'd be dead within minutes. "I want Icarus."

With closed eyes Kessler raised his face to the ceiling, his lips taut in a grimace. "Icarus, Icarus, Icarus. Hasn't that poor boy has suffered enough."

"Tell that to the people he butchered," Munroe replied, sending a line of drool onto his shirt as he grappled to gain control of his mouth due to the after-effects of the unknown drug he had been given.

Kessler raised his eyebrow uncaringly and slowly shook his head. "Oh please, Mr Munroe. Let's not bullshit each other. You're not here for those deaths."

Now it was Munroe who raised his eyebrows. "And how do you figure that?"

"Because that's a job for the police, and police don't swan into a foreign country and go waving guns at old men like me… No, you're something else entirely, and unless you tell me what that is, I am going to ask Gustav to begin breaking your fingers one by one."

Kessler flicked his hand towards Gustav, who was now smiling; he raised both his gigantic palms in the air and wiggled them slowly.

"We'll get to the ice pick later, I promise, but let's begin with some old-fashioned bone snapping."

If ever there were a time to let slip a morsel of information, now was that time, and as Gustav took a step forward Munroe gave a nod. "OK. You're right. I'm not here for all his victims. Just two of them."

Kessler signalled to Gustav and reluctantly the muscular henchman stopped within a foot of Munroe's chair. "Go on."

"Two of them were MI6 officers."

Kessler looked stunned, and his shoulders sagged. "How do you know that? Even if you're MI6, you shouldn't know that."

It was an odd reply, but before Munroe could say anything a wicked look emerged across Kessler's face. It wasn't one of fascination but rather exhilaration, and he moved close to Munroe and looked over at Gustav.

"Unless... Could we have a true believer? Here in this very kitchen?"

Munroe had no idea what the old man was talking about but he played it straight and stared unemotionally as Kessler craned his head closer.

"Could you be working for... DS5?"

Munroe continued to stare blankly but Kessler obviously saw something in his eyes, perhaps a flicker of recognition, and he laughed out loud and slapped his hands together as Gustav also let out a deep grunt of satisfaction.

Munroe wasn't sure exactly what his connection meant to these people, but whatever it was, it wasn't good. "Not *for* them, but I've had contact with them, and you should know, they'll be on their way as we speak."

His answer wasn't what Kessler had been hoping for and his excitement waned for a moment, but as he continued to stare at Munroe his smile returned.

"Oh, I doubt that, Mr Munroe. If they knew who I really was they would have sent a team instead of a hired lackey to do some of their legwork."

Kessler leant back against the kitchen table and folded his arms. "You have no idea of the fiery cauldron you've been dropped into. Do you? What are you, ex-special forces? That's usually the murky pool they dip into when they need a hired gun."

There were a lot of things that Munroe could have been concerned about at that moment. That he was tied to a chair at the mercy of Gustav. That he could be murdered at any minute, or that the ice pick on the stove was now red hot again. But what was top of his list was that this man appeared to know more about the organisation he was working for than he did.

None of this was lost on Kessler, who once more folded his arms together. "You, my friend, have found yourself in the middle of something very, how should I say, hush hush. Not just within Whitehall's corridors of power but globally. Very secretive, but I'm sure DS5 told you none of that."

Munroe said nothing as Kessler continued to speak, his voice wavering from time to time. He appeared to be taking great joy in illuminating everything Munroe didn't know.

"Icarus is but a pawn. A pawn within a much larger game. A chess match, if you like, that has been playing out for some years. We all have our parts to play, although young Icarus has taken it upon himself to try and shorten the game, and it's left a bitter taste in everyone's mouth."

"Can I ask you a question?" Munroe asked politely, and Kessler smugly replied with a nod.

"Of course, ask away."

"What the *fuck* are you talking about?"

Gustav sent a hard punch across Munroe's face, knocking him to one side as Kessler waved the blonde meathead off. "It's all right, Gustav. It can be frustrating being a lapdog and not in the know."

Kessler knelt down next to Munroe and rested his elbow upon the armrest. "Icarus is not his name, obviously, but it refers to something much bigger." The old man began to unbutton his white shirt all the way to the bottom, and then he slipped out his right arm and lifted it up in the air before pointing to a small, black tattoo on the underside of the skin. It was a maze within a triangle, and at its centre lay a red circle, thin lines running off it in all directions like the symbol of a dark sun. "There is only one way in, and once inside you never leave." Kessler sneered at Munroe's puzzled expression and he tapped the tattoo with his free finger. "And neither would you want to. Project Icarus represents the kind of true devotion that transcends time and can never be extinguished There are those who build for a better future and those who hope for it… We take it."

Munroe was struggling to fully grasp what the old man was alluding to. To him it sounded like any other terrorist organisation he'd come across. And there had been a few. But as he stared into Kessler's blue eyes he recognised something that all these people shared. It was the look, glassy wide eyes with an unshakeable stare. The look of a believer.

Kessler, still kneeling, slipped his shirt back on and began to button it up. "Of course no one gets the tattoos anymore, they're far too identifiable. A practice from a bygone age, but one that is soon to resurface in all its magnificence. As a kinsman of yours once wrote, 'Cry Havoc, and let slip the dogs of war'." Kessler looked up at the kitchen clock and then smiled ominously. "But I'm sure you can discuss it with your new friends."

"New friends?" Munroe replied as Gustav emitted a playful grunt.

"Yes, I called them just before you woke up. They should be here any minute. But I should warn you, they don't like to play as I do… they're far more serious."

Munroe thought about it for a second and then he gave a polite and accepting nod of his head. "Then I should thank you for giving me the time I needed."

A look of puzzlement fell across Kessler's face and he leant in closer. "For what?"

"For this."

Munroe pulled his hands free, grabbed the red-hot ice pick from the stove and jammed it between Gustav's ribs, sending the searing hot spike sizzling directly into his heart, which dropped the man to the floor like a sack of bricks. Kessler was already stumbling backwards as Munroe grabbed him by the hair and held him tightly in his grasp. "Piece of advice," he said, holding up a small shard of green ceramic plate between his fingers. "If you smash something over someone's head, make sure they don't catch any of it. Cuts through nylon easily." He threw the piece at Kessler's chest and tightened his grip. "And thanks for the information. A little bit vague, but I'll take it." With his left hand Munroe jerked Kessler forward, as his right fist slammed into the old man's face, crumpling his nose in one blow.

Kessler dropped to the floor in an unconscious heap as Munroe slid out of his chair and knelt beside him to pat down the old man's jacket. He quickly found the bulge he was looking for in the side pocket and retrieved his black SIG Sauer P320. "And I'll take that back, government property and all," Munroe whispered to himself as he grabbed Kessler's arm and hoisted the body onto his shoulders using a fireman's lift. "Now let's take a ride."

Munroe quick-stepped it back to the hallway and headed for the front door but he stopped within a few feet, realising there was one thing he'd forgotten. To his left in the front room his dark navy coat was still folded on the yellow sofa and he made a beeline for it, dropping Kessler down to the floor momentarily and slipping it on.

"I like this coat, and besides, it's got my driver's licence in it," Munroe justified to himself given the urgency of getting out of the house. He then picked his host up again and headed back towards the entrance, but he stopped dead in his tracks as the door handle began to turn.

Munroe froze, his gun raised, and watched as the door slowly swung open and a man in blue jeans wearing grey body armour over a navy T-shirt stepped inside. There was a moment of hesitation and then he turned to face the sight of Munroe, with Kessler flopped over his back, pointing his handgun directly at him. The man remained stationary – there was no twitching or jerking back in surprise but instead only a slow movement from the other side of his body as his left hand reached for something by his waist. Munroe shook his head warningly but the handgun was already being raised towards him and so he discharged two shots. The first clipped the man's neck but the second hit its intended mark just above the left eye, sending his assailant to the ground in a puff of red mist.

Munroe was already moving to the far side of the living room to find cover when he heard the familiar sound of a metal spring unloading and a grey canister flashbang dropped into the hallway, bouncing along the carpet before coming to a stop next to the dead body.

With his eyes clenched tightly shut Munroe turned his head, clutching Kessler's body close to one ear and raising his shooting hand to his other. Both rooms were lit up in a bright light as the canister erupted in a white flash and unleashing a deafening explosion, sending plumes of smoke outwards in every direction. Fortunately Munroe's reaction had softened most of the intended sensory overload and he looked back to the doorway to see two men pile through it holding M4 carbines with vertical grips, training their barrels around the hallway in arcs.

The first shot Munroe got off hit the closest attacker right in the forehead, sending him colliding backwards into the other one, knocking him off balance. His next shot merely winged the second man's shoulder as his assault rifle now began spraying bullets across the living room, sending trails of broken plaster into the air as they riddled the walls of the front room.

Munroe's final shot capped the man right through the throat and with blood gushing from the wound the attacker dropped his rifle and fell to the carpet in a writhing heap, clutching at his neck.

Before the attacker had even hit the floor, Munroe was already manoeuvring through the living room side door into a dining room and heading deeper towards the rear of the house when the bombardment of gunfire erupted all around him. The rouge-tinted china on the dining table began to explode around him as the barrage shredded everything it came into contact with and Munroe plunged to the floor, bringing Kessler slamming down on top of him. Inches above the mayhem continued as shots tore over both men, slamming into the walls and sending pieces of plasterboard down on top of them.

Munroe pressed his head to the floor and waited. If Kessler's friends had wanted him alive then their plans had changed and they had no misgivings about taking out the old man either.

The volleys above him abruptly ceased and Munroe could now hear the attack being focused on the other side of the house. He seized the moment and rushed to his feet, slung Kessler back over his shoulder and ran as fast as he could to the only visible way out, the large single window at the far end of the dining room. Above the intense sound of gunfire the shattering of glass was hardly audible as Munroe crashed through the window and landed with a hard thud on the lawn outside, with Kessler rolling off to one side. The nose of Munroe's gun had hit the ground barrel down, twisting his wrist painfully in the process, but after a quick shake to ensure no bones were broken he got to his feet to see the old man regaining consciousness, his eyelids beginning to flutter. One swift punch to the face and Kessler was once more out cold. Munroe heaved the old man back onto his shoulder again and, after quickly rotating his gun hand a few times just to shake off the stiffness, he made his way towards the waist-high wood-panelled fencing skirting the property and the row of conifers towering behind it.

Back at the house the gunfire was beginning to die down, and by the time he'd dumped Kessler's body over the fence and followed after it the commotion had stopped completely. With the old man back on his shoulders, Munroe pushed past the dense conifers until, on the other side, he found himself only a hundred metres from his rental car. Better still, there was no one guarding it.

Within seconds he had reached the silver Renault, unlocked the front passenger door and pushed Kessler inside. It was now he got his first clear look at the men undertaking the assault. Three tan Humvees were parked up in a line and six men, dressed identically to the others in jeans and grey chest body armour, were lined up outside the front entrance about to make a breach of the chateau. Everything from the trucks, weaponry and tactics screamed military, but the nearest HQ Munroe knew of was the NATO air base in Bordeaux-Mérignac, twenty miles away.

Munroe made his way to the driver's side and quietly slid into the leather seat as he felt an unsettling twitch in the depths of his stomach. With the high-tech rescue of Icarus back on Waterloo Bridge and now this crew of trained mercs, whoever was pulling the strings clearly had serious, professional backing.

He turned to the slumped body of Kessler, propped up in the seat, and then tapped the old man's leg. "You and I need to have a talk," Munroe whispered, waiting for the team to enter the house, and with the sound of flashbangs going off in the distance he turned on the engine and slowly drove away into the night.

Chapter 11

"So, I'm eleven years old and my parents are downstairs watching *Star Trek.*"

"*The Next Generation?*"

"Yeah, that's the one. Anyway, I sneak into their room and make my way over to this big old dressing table where my father used to keep his socks and, as quietly as I can, I pull open the top drawer and begin rummaging around. It takes me a few nervous seconds of scrambling around in the dark before I feel it, right at the back. A *Playboy*. I'd seen my father looking at it earlier that day and I just had to get my hands on it. Of course nowadays I wouldn't even bat an eyelid, but to a thirteen-year-old boy in the throes of puberty, it was like hitting the jackpot, hitting pay dirt. Anyway, so I get my hands on this 'jazz mag', right, and I sneak back to my room to check it out. Now I don't know whether my father had some sixth sense or what, but within minutes he bursts into the room and busts me ogling this full spread of Miss November and he goes ballistic. He snatches the magazine out of my hands and starts giving me this big lecture about how I'm too young to be looking at such things and how I should be ashamed of myself because women are not objects, which is a foolish point to make because it was his magazine, so I told him: 'Father, you bought this magazine, not me!'"

The storyteller took a deep breath and then exhaled with a knowing shake of his head. "Of course I knew the moment I said it I'd gone too far. You could see the sparks in his eyes flaming up. Sure enough, within seconds my father had slid off his belt, folded it in half and proceeded to give me five of the hardest slaps on the ass I've ever had. My cheeks were burning for hours. Anyway, my point is that corporal punishment is no way to treat your own child, and I never forgave him for it. I was his own blood, for Christ's sake. It's just heartless, mean. It's got no place in a modern society. Of course you have to teach your children the difference between right and wrong, but there are other ways of doing it without getting violent which are just as effective."

"OK. So how do you maintain discipline? For me shouting works. Put the fear of God into them."

The storyteller shook his head in disagreement. "No, there's a better way. We use the naughty step method."

"The naughty step?"

"Yeah, the naughty step. You telling me you've never heard of the naughty step? Everyone's heard of the naughty step."

"Well I haven't."

The storyteller looked dumbfounded, but with a disbelieving sigh he proceeded to explain. "OK, when your child does something wrong you give them a warning not to do it again, and if they do, then you place them in a designated area, like on a step or a chair, and that becomes your naughty step. Then you tell them they'll have to stay there for, let's say, five minutes. Then, when the time's up, you go back to them and ask for an apology. If they give you one then you give them a hug, say that's very grown up of you and, tada, they've learnt their lesson. If not then they have to stay there for another five minutes. And you keep doing it until they finally crack."

"And what if they don't want to stay on the naughty step?"

"Then you keep placing them back on the step and start the timer again. It's like breaking a horse in the old west. Repetition. You keep doing it until they apologise."

"And that works?"

"Oh, sure. Eventually. Think of it like a battle of wills. You may have to put them back on that step twenty or thirty times, if your child's really unruly, but if you stick to the process it becomes like second nature to them. The child realises that you're the boss, and if they don't want to end up on the naughty step then they better do as they're told. And it's all done without ever having to lay a hand on the ones you love. No violence, and you're a dad of the modern age... Perfect."

"I like that. I'm sold. Next time my boy plays up I'm going to try it. Yeah, the naughty step."

"Of course, not all kids are redeemable," the storyteller said gruffly as he gazed towards to the fragile-looking thirteen-year-old boy lying at his feet, tears still streaming from his puffy red eyes and down his cheeks, and over the silver duct tape wound tightly around his mouth. "Not these ones, for sure."

Both men now looked down the rows of brown wooden pews standing in the main hall of the church, dozens of people crowding its cold stone floor, each one of them hogtied. The sounds of quiet whimpering and the terror in each of their wide eyes had absolutely no effect on their captors.

"Are you sure that's all of them?"

"Yep, all sixty-eight. The whole commune."

"Good, then let's finish up."

Both men made their way to the church entrance and outside onto the village's main dirt street and into the refreshingly cold night air. Parked a few metres away were four black Range Rovers surrounded by a group of men in full camouflage fatigues, all armed with hefty FN P90 submachine guns.

They had already reached the men when a blue Porsche Cayenne pulled up next to the nearest Range Rover and from the passenger side Hans Bauer, wearing an expensive grey Armani suit, exited the vehicle and slowly made his way over to join them.

Noting the new arrival, the storyteller and his colleague moved back to either side of the church entrance and pushed the heavy set of wooden double doors shut, reducing the moans and terrified screams to nothing more than muffled background noise.

"Any problems, Hector?" Bauer asked, looking up at the church steeple.

"A few," Hector replied, flipping his finger towards two black ziplock body bags by the tires of the furthest Range Rover. "A few of the parents tried to stop us with shotguns, but it was taken care of."

Bauer looked over at the bags. "Take them to the crematorium and have them burnt. And retrieve the spent bullets once they're done."

"Of course, sir. I'll see to it."

Bauer began scanning the area until he saw the body of a man propped up next to the church's left wall; he had dark skin and wore torn jeans and a black Southern Comfort T-shirt. "Is that the frame?" he asked, and Hector replied with a nod.

"He's a local cartel man, low level. We grabbed him off the streets last night and one of the parents' shotguns was used on him. It'll look like a either a drug vendetta or a cartel warning. Whatever conclusion the authorities reach it'll be anything but us."

Bauer was now nodding his head. "Good, because in the next few hours the whole world is going to hell. Every government and intelligence agency in the western hemisphere will be out for blood and grasping at any leads they can find. Any and all ties that could link to us must be severed, and with Ferreira and his little experiments gone we remain insulated."

Hector was nodding sternly as Bauer glanced over at the locked church.

"Have you used enough gasoline?"

"More than enough, sir, and those stone walls will heat up and act like a pizza oven. There won't be much left."

Bauer stared up at the church steeple once more and then he began to make his way back to the Porsche, glancing back as he did so. "I want men here until it's all over. I don't want anyone making a miraculous escape, understood?"

"Yes, sir. Until the end." Hector watched as Bauer pulled open the car door, whereupon he paused. "And I want them burnt to a crisp. No evidence except for dental records."

"Yes, sir," Hector replied again, dutifully, and he continued to watch as Bauer ducked into the car only to reappear again a few moments later.

"Well… what are you waiting for?"

Hector swivelled on his heels and headed back to the church entrance and opened one of the doors just a crack. He reached into his top pocket and retrieved a red-tipped match which he cracked into life on the tip of his thumb-nail. With that he flicked the lit match inside and watched the line of petrol ignite and begin quickly travelling in a straight line towards the sixty-eight children, mothers and fathers all writhing in abject terror as their flaming harbinger of doom approached.

Hector took a final look and then slammed the door shut again and briskly made his way down the church steps and onto the main street. He walked towards the others as behind him the screams began to morph from terror into ones of scalding pain.

Within a minute most of the shrieking had stopped and had been replaced by the sound of roaring flames. As one stained-glass window blew outwards, sending a thick black torrent of smoke into the night air and upwards to the glittering stars above, Hector ordered all the men but two to take off. He took one final look at the pyre of flames twisting upwards into the sky and then got into the last jeep and wound down the window, sniffing the air. "Smells like roast beef," he said without any hint of emotion or care, before turning his attention to the other occupants. "I'm hungry. You boys fancy some dinner?"

Chapter 12

Munroe slid the white plastic tub of ice onto the bedside table, took a piece and popped it into his mouth before stepping out onto the balcony of the surprisingly impressive Best Western hotel. The streets of Bordeaux were, even at this early hour, beginning to ramp up for the day as delivery vans and early commuters started venturing out into the city, and he crushed the piece of cool ice between his teeth and took a moment to enjoy the scene. The sun would be up soon and already he could feel the change in the air as a gentle breeze blew over him. He closed his eyes and allowed the freezing, melted liquid to trickle down his throat. It felt invigorating. It was one of the few oddities he enjoyed even if, for most people, the thought of crunching ice was unappealing.

The drive from the chateau had only taken half an hour, and Kessler had been out for the count throughout. It wasn't until he pulled into the hotel's underground car park and then dragged the older man from the silver Renault that the moans had begun. In the guise of a chaperone for his drunk uncle, Munroe had checked in at reception, and after a quick back and forth with the night clerk, to explain the old man had fallen flat on his face, causing his bloody nose, the two had headed for the second floor and one of its rooms.

He stepped back into the room and closed the balcony doors as the sound of groaning started up again from the bathroom. He calmly strode over and pulled open the door.

Standing up from the toilet seat and with a white bedsheet tying his wrists to the shower rail, Kessler looked over with heavy eyes and grimaced.

"You've made a serious mistake." He flared his nostrils before recoiling at the sharp pain in his fractured nose, which had swollen up nicely. "You've killed us both."

Munroe said nothing but stepped over to Kessler's side, untied the bedsheet and sat the old man back down on top of the toilet seat before rebinding both his wrists. "Your mistake was drugging me back at your chateau, and anyway, I'm sure your friends wouldn't want to kill one of their own."

Kessler's eyes widened doubtfully. "My 'friends' don't like loose ends, and they'll consider me a liability... just like you."

Munroe didn't show it, but he was surprised at how well the old man was coping with all this, given that he must have been in his late seventies, and had been smacked around, knocked unconscious and restrained. Kessler had remained calm, collected and somewhat blasé in the way he spoke and it was this that made Munroe uneasy. "Then maybe we can help each other."

Kessler considered it for a moment, and then he began to nod his head. "Well, you could free me of this bedsheet and then blow your own brains out. That would help."

Munroe would have smiled, but he could tell the old man was deadly serious. "I don't think I can be that helpful, but you're right about being a liability." Munroe allowed his eyes to dull and he now looked anxious. "You were right, I am ex-special forces, and I'm not a member of this DS5 you mentioned, but I was asked to do some contract work for them."

"So you are a rent-a-cop," Kessler replied, taking a touch of enjoyment at the knowledge.

"Not quite, but something like that." Munroe tapped his forefinger gently against his thigh thoughtfully before bending down on one knee so he was at face height with the old man. "Your boy, Icarus, has taken an interest in me," Munroe said solemnly, "and in my wife and child, which is the reason I offered to track him down."

If Kessler knew anything he didn't show it, but he did look intrigued. "Did he hurt them in some way?"

Munroe allowed the question to linger and then after a light frustrated sigh he shook his head. "No, they were involved in a car bombing a few years back, but I found a picture of them on the door of his house."

"So you have been in contact with him, then."

Munroe offered a nod. "I was called to a hostage situation in London. Icarus asked for me by name. It ended peacefully and your man was taken into custody... but he escaped."

Kessler's lips flickered in amusement but he remained silent as Munroe explained further.

"The thing is, Mr Kessler, I've been calling my contact at DS5 for the past hour and I'm not getting any reply, which leads me to one of either two conclusions. One, they've no one manning the phones, which seems unlikely given it's a government agency, or two... for whatever reason, I've been cut loose, which means as a contractor I'm a party of one. Either way, I need to find out what the connection is between my family and your... madman."

Kessler sat there for a moment and scanned Munroe's face with the look of a judge, jury and executioner. His head tilted to one side and then his eyes tightened before flinching at the pain in his nose. "Icarus is no madman, of that you can be sure. He's as pure as the driven snow, and everything he does is calculated. And to correct you, he is not mine, or ours, but he is on a mission, and believe me when I tell you it is one that neither of us want to see accomplished."

Munroe was about to ask what, but he hesitated and allowed the old man to continue.

"Concerning your family, I can say that I know nothing. Whatever his business it's his alone, but what I can tell you is David, 'Icarus', is a man of sheer focus and determination. His talents lie in subterfuge, counter-surveillance, assassination, and if you took him into custody peacefully then it was only because he wanted you to. I should know, I trained him. In my younger days I tutored many from an early age before they entered the ranks, but no one like him. Despite what you may think of his crimes, I can assure you that when it comes to his skillset, he's about as good as it gets." Kessler paused and smiled smugly. "He was bred to be that way."

Munroe sat back on his haunches and gazed at the old man cynically. "Who the hell are you people?"

Kessler's smugness slowly evaporated and he stared at Munroe with a dynamism that had seemed lacking in the old man thus far. "We are Daedalus, Mr Munroe. Named after the fabled father of Icarus, who flew too close to the sun and melted his wings. It is a lesson that we have learnt from, and will not repeat."

"I don't know about that, Mr Kessler. Your boy Icarus appears to be singeing his own wings pretty well right about now. Going rogue and all."

Kessler looked untroubled by the assessment and he raised his eyebrows. "Perhaps, but setbacks do occur. The true measure of a person is how those issues are rectified, and that is something we are very good at, holding steady to the course laid out. Daedalus is the beginning of a new world. A far better world than the one so far constructed. There are few people who know our name, and I only tell you this because I see something in you. Something I've not seen in a while."

"And that is?"

"I see providence in you, Mr Munroe. I see a man capable of great things. I see someone who wants to belong to something, but hasn't yet found it. Tell me, were you abandoned as a child?"

Up until that point Munroe had been playing the game, but the question caught him off guard. "So you've seen my file, you do know who I am."

Kessler was already shaking his head. "On the contrary. Before you turned up at my door I had never seen or heard of you before, but you exude a certain self-belief, a self-reliance that usually comes from those who have experienced extreme adversity or abandonment. These experiences provide a strong motivating factor for instilling such traits for the man one becomes. It's no wonder you became what you are."

"And what's that?" Munroe asked, his eyes widening, sounding sincerely interested.

Kessler stared at him now without any malice or judgement. "You're a killer, Mr Munroe, as all special forces men should be. But not without good cause, and I sense in you it is the cause, the right cause, that you yearn for." Kessler leant closer towards him. "I can offer you that cause."

Munroe leant backwards and his mouth dropped open ever so slightly. He didn't trust the old boy one iota. There was something about Kessler that reeked of deceit, but it was underpinned with conviction and a belief that was absolute. Besides, some of what he was hearing resonated to Munroe's core. "You see a lot, Mr Kessler."

Kessler sat back upright. "It's what I do best," he said confidently, and if one set aside, in that moment, that he was sitting on a toilet seat, hands tied together with a bedsheet and with dried blood encrusting his nose, the man looked almost saintly. "And if you're willing, I'd like to offer you an opportunity. An interview of sorts. We need men of moral fibre and resilience. Even given the unfortunate start to our relationship, strong kinships have formed from far worse beginnings."

Munroe stood up and then looked down upon the old man blankly, his breathing becoming heavier. He took one last deep exhale and steadied himself. "You're asking me to betray the people I work for, to join a group I know nothing about, who protect a man like Icarus, and all based on the guess that I was an orphan!"

Kessler looked genuinely upset by the misinterpretation of his offer. "You said it yourself, DS5 have dropped you like a dead weight. They have betrayed you. It's their usual way of doing things. Believe me, I know them well, and it seems better than you do, especially that snake McCitrick."

Munroe looked surprised, and it was noted immediately by Kessler. "I wouldn't trust anything that passes between that man's lips. That's not even his real name,

didn't you notice? 'McCitrick'! Take out the 'C's...
Mitrick... My trick! He has a sense of humour, I'll give
him that, but make no mistake – he's a bullshit artist with
a bit of power and a questionable agenda. As for Icarus,
as you have already mentioned, he's gone rogue, and we
want him stopped as much as you do. The man he was,
the man I cared about, is long gone, and the man he has
become... the terrible things he's done..." Kessler looked
like he had a bad taste in his mouth. "Unforgivable."

Munroe looked puzzled and he gazed downwards to
the floor, contemplating the offer as Kessler continued.

"I can see the conflict playing out inside you, Mr
Munroe, but despite what you think you know, or don't,
could it be that you have found yourself on the wrong
side?"

"The wrong side of what?" Munroe snapped, and he
ran his fingers through his hair irritably. "I don't know
what fuck 'this' is."

Kessler raised his bound hands comfortingly. "I understand your frustration, but I've not lied to you since we
met. I said you had been dumped in the middle of something you had no idea of. What I'm offering you now is a
chance to know what is really going on and then... well,
then you can make up your own mind."

Munroe rubbed his forehead as Kessler waited patiently
for an answer. To say he was becoming torn about what
to do was an understatement. What did he actually know
about McCitrick and DS5? Nothing. And the Home
Secretary on the call could have been impersonated.
Christ, he'd never even met the man.

Munroe slammed his fist against the bathroom wall and
grunted. "OK, let's say, just for argument's sake, I consider
what you're saying is true. That I've been duped royally.

This DS5, whoever the fuck they are, will come after me with a vengeance. No loose ends and that. So what the fuck do you expect me to do?"

Kessler offered a friendly and supportive smile. "Undoing this bedsheet would be a good start, and then allow me to make a call and I can tell you everything about the situation you've found yourself tangled up in." Kessler gave a shake of his hands. "But I can't help you with Icarus's fascination with you or your family. As I said, I don't know anything about that, but when we find him, you will get your answers, of that you have my word."

The small bathroom fell into silence as Munroe contemplated his options and his eyes darted about the floor broodingly. To be so out of control in any situation was unsettling for him, not in his nature, and he fretted through taut lips as Kessler sought to reassure him further.

"If DS5 is at the heart of your concerns then it needn't be. In just under an hour they will no longer be a problem."

Munroe looked up and stared at the old man in shock. "What?"

Kessler looked confident and almost magnanimous seated upon the white porcelain toilet seat. "I can't give details, but let us say it's a venture that your Fawkes would have been proud of."

"Fawkes?" Munroe repeated as an icy realisation shot through his mind. "Guy Fawkes?"

Kessler only smiled. Munroe stood there totally stunned for a mere moment, then he rushed out of the bathroom and grabbed the iPhone lying on the bed. He tapped in a number and made his way back to the bathroom to find Kessler now looking unsure of himself.

"What are you doing?" he demanded as Munroe pulled the phone from his ear and attempted a redial.

"McCitrick, 'My Trick'. Not bad. Was that on the spur of the moment, or is it an inside joke for you lot?"

Kessler looked upset by the con played on him but then he clicked his head to one side, looking reverent. "You bullshit well, Mr Munroe. Not bad. I almost believed you were reconsidering your position."

Munroe held the phone to his ear and offered a forced smile. "Two rules to bullshitting, Mr Kessler. Firstly, always hide a lie between two truths, and secondly, when telling a lie, you have to make yourself believe it. The face can easily give away too much unintentional information. Either that or have a phenomenal flair for acting, which I do not."

Surprisingly, Kessler didn't look particularly annoyed, and he now began to smile. "I'm afraid you won't have the time," he said, watching Munroe pull the phone back from his ear after his second attempt and now noticing the 'no service' sign. "No service?" he muttered to himself as Kessler cleared his throat then tapped at a small scar on his forearm and the raised bulge underneath it. "It's a tracker implant. You were playing for information, and I for time. Call it a draw – we both got what we wanted, only you won't have time to tell your friends."

"They're blocking the signal," Munroe muttered under his breath, and he leapt across the bed to the side drawer, jerked it open and pulled out the black SIG Sauer P320.

That's when the explosions began.

Chapter 13

The door shattered inwards, sending smoke and wreckage hurtling across the room, just catching Munroe's back leg as he flung himself down by the side of the bed for cover. From underneath he had a direct line of sight to what had been a door moments earlier, and he watched as two pairs of boots swiftly filed inside. At the sound of Kessler yelling one of them turned and disappeared into the bathroom as the other slowly approached the far side of the bed. One of the terrace windows had been taken out due to the blast, blown onto the street outside, and as the boots got closer Munroe lay on his back and aimed his gun upwards, but low enough not to be seen over the top of the bed.

He wasn't taking any chances. He readied himself as the tip of a the M4 carbine passed into view, aiming at the window, followed by a man wearing the exact same outfit as the hit squad back at Kessler's chateau. The moment his balaclava-covered face became visible Munroe pulled the trigger, sending a single 19mm Parabellum bullet slicing through the man's chin and into his brain cavity, dropping him to floor. Munroe then turned his aim to the bathroom and from underneath the bed clipped the other armed goon in the ankle as he appeared to investigate. As the man fell to the floor in agony, Munroe saw the Kessler's shoes skip past him and outside into the corridor beyond.

With the attacker's head now clearly in sight, Munroe sent a single bullet straight through the gunman's forehead.

Munroe leapt up and seized the nearest assault rifle lying on the ground, whilst in the background he could hear Kessler barking orders to what must have been the rest of the team. His position in the small hotel bedroom was no place to make a last stand, so he turned to the wrecked window and unloaded a barrage of shots towards the hallway before leaping from the terrace and downwards to the street below.

Moments before the jump he had visualised the outlay he'd noted earlier when gazing out into the street and it proved accurate as he landed directly on top of the parked white 6 Series BMW below, crumpling the roof and sending him rolling off, down onto the tarmac street. If that wasn't enough to piss off the BMW's owner then what came next certainly would as the metallic thudding sound of bullets striking the hood and roof forced Munroe to hug the side of the driver's door. One of the bullets connected with the nearest wing mirror, sending shattered glass to the ground, and Munroe seized the largest, closest piece and positioned it to get a good glance at the person unloading his magazine. The man above was dressed identically to the others, as expected, but it was obvious to Munroe he wasn't committed to a simple spray and pray of the car below. He was delivering timed single shots to the BMW's roof so as to keep Munroe pinned down until his brethren made it downstairs to greet him.

This was no time for a waiting game and Munroe eased the carbine upwards as far as he could without offering an easy shot of himself and began firing indiscriminately towards the terrace. None of the shots connected, but they weren't meant to, and moments later he received the reply he had wanted. A barrage of bullets rained down on the car until they suddenly ceased. Munroe threw himself backwards onto the road and found himself staring up, as expected, to see his attacker changing his clip. A short volley of shots to the man's chest sent him careening back into the hotel room, and although not a kill shot due to the body armour it gave Munroe the window he needed. Leaping to his feet he dashed for the nearest side road opposite. Upon turning the corner the deafening sound of gunfire erupted again, sending pieces of the brick wall exploding behind him.

Munroe dashed up the side street, rubbing the rifle's frame with his shirt to rid any fingerprints, and then he clipped out the magazine and dumped the carbine in a green wheelie bin further up before turning onto the main street at the end. He hurried along it until the next road and took the first left whereupon he dropped the magazine over the wall of someone's residence and began scanning the parked cars. He made it about halfway down the road before coming to an abrupt stop next to a dark silver 1986 Porsche 911.

"Perfect." He slid off his coat and retrieved his handgun from his pocket. He then flopped the garment over the window with one hand and, holding the gun barrel, brought the butt of the gun down hard against the glass.

It only took one attempt to shatter the window and he opened the driver's door and threw his coat inside before kicking at the plate underneath the steering wheel until it broke off. Modern cars with security safety chips were a near impossibility to hotwire without the right equipment, but with an old model like this it was as easy as depressing a millennial. A few crossed wires and the sleek hum of the 911's engine purred into life, and Munroe pulled out and began steadily heading down the road towards a set of traffic lights. Dawn was already breaking, with most of the street lamps beginning to turn off, and by the time he reached the lights and came to a stop he was already jabbing the redial button on his mobile. This time the call clicked through and a single word was spoken.

"McCitrick."

Munroe began to open his mouth when in front of him a tan Humvee screeched to a halt and he found himself staring directly into the eyes of Tobias Kessler, as behind him a man wearing a balaclava was already raising his carbine through the passenger side window.

Munro dropped the phone, slammed the 911 in reverse, ducked down and hit the accelerator as bullets tore into the windshield. Using only his side mirror he sailed back down the street, clipping a white van and leaving a silver stripe down its side before he reached the crossroads. He bobbed back up and flung the steering wheel to one side, sending the 911 into a half pirouette before slamming the car into gear and accelerating off at high speed.

As Munroe sped down the one-way street, just missing an early morning delivery van, more bullets began hitting the boot. One hit the back window and, although remaining intact, the whole piece of glass shattered, making it impossible for him to see behind.

Munroe glanced at his wing mirror to see the Humvee in hot pursuit, and as he unleashed the power of the 911 he was surprised to see it keeping up. The vehicle must have been kitted out and loaded to keep the pace, but as he jammed the gearstick into fourth he began to pull away at high speed.

Munroe stretched over and probed his hand down towards the passenger side between the seat and the door, that black hole space where everything from keys to phones ends up. He felt the edge of his iPhone, which he managed to pinch with his fingers and retrieve. Up ahead was a roundabout and the mobile now began ringing. It was McCitrick.

Munroe was within centimetres of tapping the accept button when a thunderous high-pitched roar erupted from his right side and he turned to see another Humvee careening across the roundabout within metres of him. Munroe yanked on the handbrake and turned into the skid, bringing him parallel with the oncoming jeep, but it wasn't enough. The Humvee clipped his back fender and sent both spinning almost 360 degrees, locked together in a duet, the force of the impact sending his mobile flying. The crash smashed out the 911's passenger window and even before the two vehicles came to a screeching halt in the centre of the roadway Munroe had already pulled his gun from between his thighs and unloaded two well-placed shots into the Humvee next to him. The driver was hit in the head, immediately followed by the front passenger, but as the 911 slipped back into first gear and tore away the men in the rear of the jeep began firing, sending a line of bullet holes down the side of the 911.

In his wing mirror Munroe watched the passengers leap out of the Humvee and drag out the dead driver and front passenger as the other jeep carrying Kessler ploughed past them, back on Munroe's tail. Up ahead the road was already beginning to fill with the early morning commuters. Somewhere below him the mobile was ringing again but there was no time to search for it, and as he sped ahead his choices became limited. Either hit the sidewalk and slam through an old woman wearing a knitted crochet bobble hat, hunched over with a wheelie bag, or come to a screeching halt. Munroe took the third option and skidded left through the entrance of Bordeaux's Jardin Public and onto the white gravel walkway, beeping his horn as he went. A few joggers dove off to the grass as he zoomed through the lush green park and past an old-style carousel across the waterway to his right. The operators of the carousel flicked their heads towards him in surprise and watched as he sped past, sending up plumes of white dust from his wheels. Ten diving joggers, a stunned group of Tai Chi enthusiasts and a scrambling black Labrador later and Munroe was out of the park and back on the streets of Bordeaux, heading up Rue de la Course and into the north of the city.

The Humvee behind had now gapped the distance, having fared well on the park's gravel walkways, and again the sound of gunfire flared up, the focus now on the boot of Munroe's car where the 911's engine was being put through its paces. The road ahead was thankfully fairly empty, but Munroe swerved back and forth attempting to avoid taking a direct hit, and he only just missed a parked-up municipal police car which immediately took after him and was almost clipped by the chasing Humvee. Luckily for everyone involved it was a crappy Citroën Berlingo and, even if it could have kept up, its chase was cut short as one of the jeep's passengers leant out of the window and delivered a few shots to the police car's front wheels, bringing it to a tire-burning full stop.

Munroe was now accelerating ever faster and he glanced down to see his iPhone sliding around the passenger footwell. He lurched downwards and grabbed it before momentarily ducking down again as another round clipped his headrest, sending pieces of foam against the windshield like the feathers of an exploding chicken.

Kessler could have been lying about the Guy Fawkes remark, but it wasn't a chance Munroe was about to take. Given the audacious rescue of Icarus on Waterloo Bridge and the equipment they had used, anything was possible. The incident would have prompted tighter security around the centre of British power, but if his own experiences in the special forces had taught him anything, it was that there were no coincidences, and nothing was impossible if you had the sheer will and equipment to carry it out. If there was going to be an attack on Parliament they needed to know. And know now. How long had Kessler said... within the hour? And this jaunt through the streets of Bordeaux was making his window of opportunity narrower and narrower.

Munroe glanced down at the mobile and tapped the missed call symbol before looking back at the road. A cold bolt of fear ran through his body as he saw a yellow school bus with the red sign sticking out of its side reading 'Arrêt' just metres ahead. Munroe flung the 911 to the right, missing it by inches, and in that moment his perception melted into slow motion as he caught sight of a small brown-haired boy staring at the near miss with a look of absolute exhilaration on his face.

At least someone was enjoying the show.

With both hands on the wheel and the iPhone once more on the floor, the gunfire opened up again. Kessler's men were not only merciless, they were fucking reckless, and it only bolstered Munroe's belief that what Kessler had told him about the attack on Parliament was true. They were going above and beyond to stop him from telling anyone. Using automatic weapons in a popu-lated city during a high-speed pursuit was insane, as was taking out a police car. The French may have garnered

144

an unfair stereotype of surrendering easily since World War Two, but nothing could be further from the truth. When it came to gun crime or perceived terrorist attacks, the authorities came down fast and hard. There was no attempted soft negotiation as in the UK and the disabled police car's occupants, now a few miles back, would already have made the call. An armed squad would already be en route to intercept them.

Somewhere beneath his seat the phone was ringing again and unable to take his hands off the wheel Munroe chose to ignore it and focus all his attention on making his escape, but with the ever-increasing traffic on the road and the build-up of commuters it was going to be tough to outrun his pursuers. If he had enough time then sure, the 911 could take them easily, but that was the point, he didn't have the time. He needed to speak with McCitrick now.

Over the pounding grind of the Porsche's engine a serene calm descended over Munroe and he already knew what he was going to do before he even decided to attempt it. The idea was so brazen, so irresponsible that it went against all his training, but he knew he could pull it off… probably.

Munroe retrieved the gun from between his thighs and weighed it in his hands. At a guess there were four, maybe five rounds left in the clip, and he turned his attention back to the straight road which stretched on for roughly three quarters of a mile. He could see further up there was a break in the traffic, and he dropped the gun back in his lap, slammed back the gearstick and gave it all the 911 had to offer. If he could just put enough distance between the Humvee and himself he had a chance.

As he pushed the car faster, winding between vehicles, he never once let up on the accelerator. Then when he reached an empty space in the road, void of traffic and about fifty metres from the next set of traffic lights, he veered off to the right, padded down hard on the brakes and with the handbrake yanked upwards as far as it could go brought the 911 to a sideways stop. The rubber of the tires was still screeching to a halt in a cloud of black smoke as Munroe flung open the driver's side door and stepped out onto the street with his gun raised. He'd managed to put a good 200 metres between him and the Humvee. As it hurtled towards him, a carbine poked out of the back window and began firing.

The first barrage was well off target and hit the road beside him, but the second delivery was closer, one bullet grazing the back bumper of the 911. Despite the onslaught Munroe held firm, his aim unwavering, and as the Humvee closed in Munroe prepared to pull the trigger.

His first shot ricocheted off the bonnet but the second hit the windscreen. His perception now slowed and as he controlled the adrenalin spike already pumping through his veins, as experience had taught him to do, everything around him faded away; every sense in his body honed in on the target.

The next two shots were quick, tearing into the driver's head and body, sending the Humvee out of control; it careered to one side and up the sidewalk before slamming bonnet first into a concrete pavement bollard. There was no give and the impact flipped the vehicle upside down onto the tarmac, sparks flying from the sides of its roof until it ground to a full stop just metres from where he was standing.

Munroe let out a short, relieved sigh. He was a bloody good shot, if he did say so himself, but he'd got lucky and he knew it.

At a glance all the passengers now hanging from their seatbelts were either dead or out cold. He took a step towards the upturned wreck with his gun still raised, but the sound of police sirens in the distance made him reconsider, and he turned around and got back into the 911. He was aware of a few bystanders nearby gawping at what had just happened but he made no eye contact and reached over to the passenger's side for the umpteenth time and retrieved his iPhone. He was already returning McCitrick's call as he turned off the main street in the opposite direction of the wailing sirens, and now began to trek a route out of the city. He'd have to find a quiet backroad and dump the car before making it on foot to the nearest bus station. That was unless he could find another older model car in the process.

The phone connected and McCitrick came on the line, his voice intense. "What the hell's going on, Ethan?"

"I haven't got time to explain. You need to clear out Parliament, now."

There was a brief hesitation before the answer came. "Parliament! What are you talking about?"

"I've got information that an attack's going to happen at Parliament within the next forty minutes, maybe less."

"From who?"

"From the guy you sent me to check out. He's with a group called Daedalus. You probably know more about that than I do."

There was now a long pause and when McCitrick came back on he sounded monotone and cold.

"Are you sure about this?"

"Not a hundred per cent, but the armed men trying to kill me would suggest the information is solid."

There was now another pause. "OK, Ethan, I'll call it in as a potential bomb threat. The cabinet are arriving for an early morning emergency session as we speak. Most of them are already there."

"Then you better get your arse in gear," Munroe replied as he heard McCitrick barking orders to someone in the background before coming back on the line.

"How compromised are you?"

"Not sure. Still in the middle of it. I'll find somewhere safe to hole up and make my way back to the mainland. But McCitrick, I want some answers when I do. DS5 and everything else."

There was one final pause, followed by a cold reply. "Fine, but I'll call you."

The line went dead and Munroe dropped the phone into his lap. An attack on Parliament was something from the movies, and if it did occur it would be as outrageous as the time the IRA dropped a couple of mortar shells into Number Ten Downing Street's garden a few decades earlier. He was hoping it would turn out to be a wish on Kessler's part – the guy was a bullshit merchant, no doubt – but his gut told him the slip had been genuine. Either way, he wasn't about to be dragged further into this shitshow until he'd found out exactly what McCitrick wasn't telling him. He needed to know everything there was to know about DS5, Daedalus, the whole shebang – and all the dirt he suspected came with it.

Chapter 14

Home Secretary Jacob Ryan stepped from his black Jaguar XJ Sentinel, barely acknowledging the security guard opening the door. He was already running late and as he swiftly made his way across the drive towards the visitors' entrance of the Palace of Westminster, his mobile began to ring. Clutching his red formal brief binder in one hand he pulled the Samsung from his pocket and placed it to his ear, never slowing up his pace. "Ryan," he answered gruffly, almost dropping his binder in the process.

"Secretary… we have a… Westminster… communication dow… return to… we're on our…"

The line was crackling heavily and Ryan came to a stop and pressed the mobile closer to his ear. "McCitrick? You're cutting out, I can hardly hear you."

The line continued to fade in and out. "… urgent you… we have a… imminent."

It was the words 'urgent' and 'imminent' that had Ryan look over his shoulder, and he began to walk back towards the Jaguar before raising the mobile into the air and staring at the signal bar before returning it to his ear.

"Imminent what, John?" he replied, and the closer he got to his car the more the interference faded until, within feet of the vehicle, the line fully restored.

"Sir, can you hear me?"

"Loud and clear. This better be important, I'm already late," Ryan replied, rolling his eyes comically at his driver, who had exited the car upon his return and was standing dutifully waiting for any instructions to come his way.

"Sir, there's been a bomb threat. The hard-line communications have been cut and mobile coverage is down. Local uniforms are on the way to you now."

"On their way to me?" Ryan replied, puzzled but beginning to realise what was going on.

"Yes, sir. It's the Houses of Parliament."

Home Secretary Ryan allowed the phone to drop from his ear and gazed up towards the iconic, turreted tower of the Parliamentary Archives looming over the far end of the House of Commons as a feeling of panic washed over him.

"Peter, with me," he yelled to his driver before pulling open the driver's side door, hurling in his red brief bunder and then taking off like a maniac towards the visitors' entrance. "Bomb threat."

"Then we have to get you out of here, sir."

"Bollocks to that, no one's been told."

Peter continued voicing his concerns but Ryan ignored them and ran into Westminster Hall, barking orders at the posted security guard as he ran past. "Evacuate everyone, there's been a bomb threat."

The guard barely blinked before springing into action as Ryan sped onwards, sternly ordering the stunned groups of tourists making their own way inside as he ran: "Everyone out, now. There's been a bomb threat."

There was almost no reaction as people froze, and as Ryan hurried down the long, stone-slabbed hallway it was only Peter and the security guard now yelling behind him that caused the mass of people to start rumbling towards the exit.

Ryan slid around the corner to the left and he picked up his pace as he sprinted along the red and tan encaustic tiles of St Stephen's Hall, lined by stone statues of kings and politicians past, infused with light from the stained-glass windows and shiny brass chandeliers overhead. He leapt over the five broad stone steps at its end in one bound and finally came crashing through the entrance and into the central lobby, slipping on the shiny tiles underneath him and bringing himself to full stop against the central reception desk.

"Bomb, everyone out, now!" As he caught his breath the crowds of visitors remained still, stunned at the outburst, with the exception of a single man with his young son who immediately took off running back in the direction of where Ryan had arrived from. "Didn't you hear me?" he puffed. "There's a bomb in Parliament, get out, now!"

Within seconds the people nearest to the exits began to move forward and then, like a herd, everyone else followed, a slow walk turning into a mad dash.

All the parliamentary security guards took off in opposite directions, some towards the House of Lords and others towards the House of Commons chamber, where there was a full house.

From behind, Peter came piling in after him, skidding to a halt and grabbing the Home Secretary's shoulder, shouting something about protocol, but Ryan pushed him off and began running down the long hallway towards the chamber beyond. Peter was still yelling at him to stop but Ryan was now in full flight. To citizens of the UK these people were just politicians, but to him they were trusted colleagues and welcomed adversaries and he would do all he could to help.

He approached the first set of open double doors. The security officer ahead was just heaving open the inner set when the shockwave hit. Ryan was lifted off his feet and sent hurtling backwards to the floor as the explosion punched through the inner doors in a balloon of smoke, crushing the security officer behind them and sending wood and debris peppering the hallway.

The sounds of muffled cries for help were the first thing Ryan heard and he opened his eyes to see the blurred, faded sight of the crafted wooden ceiling timbers high above him. At first he thought his vision was damaged, but as he turned his head to one side he realised it was due to the air being filled with thick dust and smoke. His ears felt like someone had stuffed them with cotton wool and for the first few moments he had no idea how he got there, until he caught sight of Peter just off to his left, splayed out on the floor like the statue of David.

"Peter," he managed in a whisper before he propped himself up using his elbows, and it was now that he saw the devastation the explosion had caused. Both of the inner doors were missing, and the Commons chamber beyond was full of a thick fog as a dim flame, subdued by the smoke, flickered forebodingly.

With his head still swimming, Ryan slowly dragged himself up onto his feet and instinctively staggered over to Peter, where he knelt down with a shaky wobble and pressed his finger against the security guard's carotid artery. There was a pulse.

"I need help." His throat was dry and it came out in little more than a croak.

He swallowed a few times and then tried again. "I need some help here." This time his voice gained some traction and from somewhere in the lobby there now came other cries for help.

Ryan turned his head towards the Commons chamber and found himself gazing up the bronze statue of Winston Churchill next to the hollowed-out doorway, staring down at him with his usual expression of stern defiance. On sheer impulse the Home Secretary got to his feet. He stared into the dark abyss that had been the chamber moments earlier, and among the swirls and intermittent sparks of electricity igniting in the air there could be seen the outlines of people congregating near the demolished doorway. Ryan moved towards the opening as the first shadowy figure emerged and he raised out his hand supportively as the sounds of pained groans began to fill the hallway. He held it there, outstretched, as the first stumbling figure reached him and through the smoke a quivering bloody hand with two missing fingers clamped around his open palm.

–

The navy blue BMW 7 Series raced down Victoria Embankment without slowing as John McCitrick stared out of the passenger-side window at the smoke rising above the building tops, hovering over Parliament like a bad omen. He'd heard the explosion upon leaving the Ministry of Defence less than a quarter of a mile away and the smoke only confirmed what had happened. "Move it," he growled to the driver, who to his credit was traversing the busy embankment road like a professional slalom skier and even passing on the wrong side of the road to avoid the white bollards.

"Well at least Big Ben's still standing."

"Shut up, you tool," McCitrick barked, already repositioning his gun holster on his hip as the BMW screeched around the corner and approached Parliament's car parks. The fact that communication to Parliament security had been impossible due to the lines being dead showed that whatever had happened was highly organised. Even the localised mobile coverage had gone black, and that was no easy thing to pull off... not at all.

"Pull up here," he said, pointing to the visitors' entrance where dozens of people were sitting and lying as a number of police in hi-vis yellow jackets tried to get a handle on the chaos which was unfolding.

"Whereabouts, sir?"

"Where do you think, you twat?" he snapped, pointing to the smoke billowing from the visitors' entrance.

As the driver endeavoured to manoeuvre through the onlookers, McCitrick could see people still staggering from entrance. *Jesus* he thought, *it had gone off inside, possibly near the Commons itself.*

"This'll do." As the car came to a halt he pushed open the passenger door and got out, turning briefly to his driver. "Get out and do some good," was all he said before hurrying towards the smoke.

There were people everywhere covered in black and grey soot. Some sat nursing their wounds, others stood motionless staring back at the mayhem, wide-eyed and still in shock.

One woman was crouched down and gently shaking her baby, whose face was covered in the same grey soot, calling out for help. As a policeman approached McCitrick he pulled out a Home Office identification card and held it in front of him.

"That child needs help. First priority," he said, pointing to the woman and her motionless baby.

The officer briefly inspected the ID and with a simple nod moved over to the distraught mother as McCitrick headed straight for the visitors' entrance, barely taking note of the people taking photos on their mobile phones, a number even documenting their own tribulations, probably to be uploaded later to TikTok or Instagram. The scene was bloody and harrowing, but as McCitrick approached the still smoking entrance he saw something that stopped him in his tracks.

Home Secretary Jacob Ryan staggered from the doorway, his clothes singed black, a deep cut across his cheek dripping blood, holding the still body of a young girl, maybe ten years old, with blonde hair.

"Sir!" McCitrick rushed over to meet him as Ryan moved to a clear side of the gravel and placed the girl down on the ground. He then pulled off his suit jacket and began to administer CPR. McCitrick knelt down at his side and attempted to take over, but Ryan didn't even register who he was and just pushed him away roughly. "Give her room!" he shouted and continued alternating between blowing air into her lungs while pinching her nose and then counting off the compressions to her chest.

Behind them a black-haired woman appeared from the crowd, her clothes and face covered in grey soot. "Lucy!" the woman cried out, dropping to her knees next to the girl, and although tears began to flow she stayed back while Ryan continued his CPR.

"C'mon, c'mon," Ryan spat as he repeated the process like a man possessed and then, like that, the young girl's body shuddered and she thrust upwards in a fit of coughing and clasped at her chest.

"That's it, breathe slowly," Ryan said, supporting her as she regained full consciousness. He leant back as the mother pushed in and held the girl in her arms.

Ryan stared at the two in relief, and then he rubbed the mother's shoulder and stood back up to see a number of phones being pointed at him.

McCitrick tried to pull him away from the lenses, but Ryan jerked his arm away roughly.

The Home Secretary was still in shock.

"Sir, it's me, McCitrick," he said softly, and as he looked towards him there was a flicker of recognition in Ryan's eyes.

"John. What happened?"

"You've been in a bomb attack, sir," McCitrick answered, not sure how together, or untogether, Ryan was at that very moment.

"I know that," he replied angrily, still getting his bearings. Then he gazed forward, suddenly becoming sombre. "They got all of them, John."

"The cabinet? The bomb went off in the Commons itself?"

Ryan gave a weary nod. "I was metres from the door... and the carnage. Some are alive but... Jesus."

It was impossible to tell who had been killed, that would come later, but as McCitrick turned to see firemen now rushing inside he focused on the moment and the way forward. Ryan was in no good state, but the man needed to know. "Ethan Munroe alerted us to the attack, but the timeframe was too small. We just didn't have time to react fast enough."

Ryan placed his hand on McCitrick's shoulder to steady himself. "Last minute or not, he saved some lives today."

"Yes, sir, he did. Just not enough. But there's something else. He knows who carried it out."

Ryan's eyes instantly blazed with interest. "Who?"

McCitrick hesitated and then he said it, softly. "Daedalus, sir. It was Daedalus."

Ryan looked dumbfounded. "What? They'd be committing suicide, sticking their head so far above the parapet."

"You'd think so, but it was them. Or at the very least they were involved and knew about it."

Ryan took a step backwards and glanced over at the scores of injured people littering the car park. His head swayed slowly from side to side and when he returned to face McCitrick he was seething.

"This game stops now, John. Do you understand me? No ifs, no buts, no quarter given. Bring everyone together. The whole of DS5."

McCitrick knew what was being asked of him, but he felt duty bound to clarify the order.

"'*Everyone*', sir?"

Ryan's chest heaved, his face reddening, and he didn't so much growl his response as yell it. "EVERYONE!"

Chapter 15

Michael Hanks shifted uncomfortably in his first-class seat as he tapped away at his iPhone. His failure in allowing Icarus to escape after such a brazen operation to rescue him was something he'd not yet had to face up to with the Daedalus high command. Failures and setbacks were tolerated if justified, but to have the man in his custody only for him to slip through his fingers was frankly unforgivable. Flying back to the US was the right thing to do, and he was not about to compound his blunder by contacting them directly on an unsecured line. Especially considering the entire Western intelligence apparatus would be scouring communications chatter so soon after the attack on Parliament. Two fuck-ups like that in less than twenty-four hours and he would find himself on the end of a long rope. His team had spent hours combing the port city of Calais for that shit Icarus, with no success. What did he expect? The assassin was trained too well to be caught, and with safehouses and stashes all over the world he was probably halfway to God knows where by now.

Hanks knew the only way to redeem himself in the eyes of his seniors was to capture the psychopath, and even then he would still have Bauer to contend with for the mess he'd made.

Hans Bauer.

Hanks wasn't sure who was more dangerous, Icarus or Bauer. Bauer could be brutal, even by his own standards, but he was competent, and if a job was given to him it always got done to the letter of the instruction. Hanks was now hoping that the instruction that had been given wasn't to make him pay for such a foolish mistake. To have Bauer as a colleague was fortuitous, but as an enemy… well, that was a death sentence.

"Excuse me, sir, but you'll have to turn off your phone during take-off." A blonde-haired stewardess leant over him, smiling pleasantly as she pointed at the mobile in his hand "You can turn it back on when the seatbelt sign turns off."

Hanks replied with a nod, but then realised she wasn't leaving until he complied. With a final tap to send his message he held in the power button. Only once the screen went black did she stand back up, satisfied.

"I wasn't sure I'd get a flight given the Parliament attack," Hanks said, hiding the smug pride he felt at knowing more about it than the authorities, let alone some air stewardess.

"I believe we are one of the last flights to leave. I'm told all further flights are being grounded. You've got good timing, sir."

Yes, Hanks thought, knowing how close the timing had been. Even with the search for Icarus he had made sure he was already boarding when the news began to pour in over the news channels.

"Just terrible," the stewardess went on, shaking her head solemnly, "but you can rest assured that this flight is safe and secure. We also have sky marshals on the plane for added security."

"I feel safer already," Hanks said as the stewardess smiled again. "You just never know who you're sat next to these days."

The stewardess patted him on the shoulder reassuringly and then headed down the cabin to help a young woman with her bag as Hanks settled back into his seat. He'd been coordinating tracking teams to find the tremendous thorn in his side that was Icarus, but as yet it had proved fruitless. Christ, the man was a ghost, and a dangerous killer. Hanks had no problem with torture or murder, hell, it was part of the trade, and he loved it, but not when it involved their own. Icarus might have been a psychotic cold-blooded killer, but he was *their* cold-blooded killer, and could the poor bastard really be blamed for turning on everyone given what had happened? Still, it was strange. He was so unlike the others.

Hanks settled into his seat. With some free time on his hands until he could turn his iPhone back on, he began to consider his story. Of course he would take the blame for the escape, but how it happened would go a long way to shifting some of the blame. Within seconds he had decided that Davies would be the fall guy. The man was dead, so what difference did it make? Hanks now set about concocting a reasonable tale. Perhaps Davies had made the mistake of loosening Icarus's bindings during the act of his torture, or perhaps his carelessness had allowed the assassin to escape. Either way he had some time to formulate the story, one that would present him in the best light possible, before reaching the US.

He allowed the worries and fears he had to wash from his mind. The Parliament attack had been a success, and plans were moving forward. Even though Icarus possessed cunning and great expertise it would count for little as the whole weight of Daedalus was now free to bear down on him. Something told him that he would be seeing the assassin very soon, and when the moment came he would deal with it personally, and this time swiftly.

Hanks closed his eyes and rested as the behind him more stewardesses swanned around, speaking to the other passengers reassuringly. None of them seemed to notice the man sat in the back row of first class. He raised his hand and immediately a male attendant moved over to him.

"Can I help with anything, sir?" he asked, smiling amiably.

"How long will the flight take?"

"Flight time to Atlanta should be just under nine hours, sir. Are you connecting from there?"

"Not sure yet," the man replied, smiling again. "I'm meeting an old friend."

"Sounds nice. Catching up?"

"Yes."

"Sounds like fun." With a final smile the attendant headed back towards the cabin as the man pulled a dark set of sunglasses from the leather case next to him and slipped them on before staring at the crown of Hanks's head, just visible over the top of his seat.

"Yes, it does. It really does."

Chapter 16

Munroe crunched the last piece of ice in his mouth and placed the empty glass down on the bar counter before calling over to the barman and tapping its rim. "Another glass of ice, please."

The white-shirted barman nodded and bent down, scooping another plastic shovel of ice cubes and lightly dumping them into Munroe's glass.

"Would you like a drink with that?"

It was the second time the bartender had asked the question, and Munroe just smiled and shook his head. He had been here for over half an hour and the fact he was only ordering free ice really seemed to bother the young Frenchman. He probably thought his patron was just another cheapskate, and Munroe now called him back over. "Give me an orange juice then."

The order received a polite smile and a within moments a slim-jim full of orange juice was pushed towards him on a single red napkin.

"Cheers," Munroe said, passing over a five-euro note. "Keep the change."

The barman pointed to the menu hanging above the bar's drinks rack. "It's six euros."

"In that case, here's a ten and I'll take the change."

The lost tip did little to dampen the barman's demeanour and he opened the till and placed a few coins down on the bar counter as Munroe turned his attention back to the flat screen mounted on the wall opposite. The news channels were full of the terrorist attack on Parliament and it was only now, six hours later, that an accurate picture of what had happened was emerging.

After getting clear of Bordeaux, Munroe had headed to the city of Nantes and its international airport. Far enough away to be clear of any more Daedalus entanglements, and close enough to make a quick exit out of the country. But en route he'd received a call from McCitrick. The conversation had been a morbid one, to say the least. Though they didn't yet know the full list of casualties, there was a high expectation that the Prime Minister and most of the cabinet had been killed in the blast. The news had hit Munroe like a blow to the face, and his initial reaction was to curse himself for not being able to report the threat sooner. But when he heard about the communications blackout preceding the attack it dampened some of the guilt he had felt. To pull off something like that was incredibly impressive, and he couldn't help but slightly admire the operation. To get an explosive device into the Houses of Parliament and also cut communications, stopping a response, was unheard of given the levels of protection. At first glance the Houses of Parliament were easy access and open to the public, but the reality was far from it. Bomb blast windows, scanning tech, mail checks and numerous layers of security made it one of the most secure locations in the country.

But not today.

The situation was still being assessed by MI5 and the intelligence services at GCHQ, but given they already knew Daedalus was involved, the '*who*' was taking 'a back seat', as McCitrick had put it. The DS5 head had rerouted

Munroe to Brest Bretagne international airport, located just off the tip of France's most north-westerly coastline, and told him only that they were sending him transport and to sit tight in the Concorde lounge. They would find him.

The change in destination had added an extra three hours on to his trip, and on arrival Munroe had done what anyone awaiting pickup would do. Find the nearest bar, dig in and watch the news.

"We've just received official confirmation that the Prime Minister was killed in today's attack. He was taken to the Royal London Hospital where, despite resuscitation attempts, he was pronounced dead." The BBC correspondent looked conflicted between the terrible news he was reporting and the thrill of such a huge story. "The Civil Contingencies Committee, COBRA, has convened an emergency session over the past five hours and as of now we can report the death toll at one hundred and forty. Of the twenty-three cabinet ministers, sixteen were among the dead, including the Prime Minister, the Chancellor of the Exchequer, the Secretary of State and the Foreign Secretary, who succumbed to his injuries less than an hour ago." His last sentence trailed off as the shock of what he was saying sank in, but he regained his composure moments later. "It is a truly dark day for the realm, and one that will be burnt into the minds of the British people and the United Kingdom for many years to come. Security at airports and other potential targets across the country is being tightened and we are awaiting a message from the government within the hour. Meanwhile, messages of support have been flooding in from world leaders across the globe..."

Munroe turned away from the TV and slid another ice cube into his mouth, crunching down on it as he instead watched the bustling passengers making their way back and forth. It was busy, and as he scanned the concourse someone caught his eye. A blonde woman in a grey turtleneck jumper with the sleeves rolled up was staring over at him. She immediately broke eye contact upon seeing him glancing at her, and moved off behind one of the round white support pillars and out of sight.

Munroe slowly swivelled off his bar stool and knelt down to retie his shoelace and surveyed the other passengers. Quickly he caught sight of a balding man in a green sleeveless aertex jumper and washed jeans, who was looking over at him from his magazine before his eyes darted back to the page.

He *was* being watched.

Munroe finished with his shoelace. He could see, using his peripheral vision, that the man hadn't moved, which he took as an indication he hadn't noticed him noticing them. He stood back up and popped one final ice cube in his mouth before nodding to the barman, who appeared relieved to see him go, and then he made his way nonchalantly out of the bar and up the concourse with all the other passengers. A few metres along he deliberately bumped into a man wearing an open shirt, white boat shoes and a pair of Mambo shorts. He turned around and apologised, just managing to catch a glimpse of the blonde woman and the bald guy again before he resumed his stroll up the concourse.

They were definitely following him, but Munroe continued to walk at a casual speed. Could they be McCitrick's? Unlikely, because why not just approach him? He was waiting for someone, after all. Daedalus? But how could that be? He hadn't been followed on the drive up, he was certain of that, and there was no way they could know he was here at the airport. Unless they were watching all the airports, which seemed a tough ask given the number of them in western France.

Munroe was already considering his next move when up ahead he saw a sign for the restrooms, and an image of Kessler sitting tied up on the toilet seat holding up his forearm smugly flickered through his mind.

Could he have been so careless?

Munroe's body had received multiple knocks and bruises during his escape from the hotel back in Bordeaux, and he'd not questioned any of the aches and pains he was feeling, but with this sudden realisation he began to subtly rub at the most tender parts of his body. He slid his hand down to his thigh and glided his palm across the bruise on his right thigh.

Nothing.

He moved his attention to the ache in his left shoulder and neck, but still nothing. Finally he slipped his hand across his stomach before coming to a stop on his right side, just above the hip. Now he felt it. A puncture mark, and something very small beneath the skin.

Cheeky bastard. Kessler, the sneaky little shit, had tagged him with a tracker. He must have done it back at the chateau, when he was out cold.

Suddenly things began to make sense. That's how they'd found him so quickly after he'd 'borrowed' the 911. At the time he'd thought it was blind luck, everyone gets lucky sometimes, but luck had nothing to do with it, and these two goons following him had now tracked him here!

The line that his special forces training had taught him ran through his mind, and he berated himself for not following it. 'There are no coincidences.'

Munroe made his way to the restroom sign and then headed inside without looking back to check if his pursuers were still following. He didn't need to. A public restroom, away from the hordes of other passengers, would be a perfect place for them to take him, and he was happy to oblige.

The restroom was large, with multiple cubicles along one side standing on a blue and white mosaic tile floor, and two large mirrors on the opposite side above the washbasins. He was about to check each stall when his mobile rang and he answered immediately in a hushed voice.

"Munroe."

"Ethan, your ride's waiting," McCitrick answered bluntly.

"Whereabouts? I'm at gate twelve, on the concourse."

"Go to gate fifteen. There's a familiar face. And pull the lead out, Ethan. You're on a tight schedule."

"That could be tough, I've picked up a tail. Two of them, actually."

There was a pause, and when McCitrick came back on he sounded as unconcerned as ever in that monotone voice of his. "Where are you exactly?"

"I'm in the restroom. Let me take care of this and I'll head to gate fifteen."

Munroe heard the restroom door swing open behind the privacy partition and he turned off the mobile, slipped it in his pocket and began washing his hands at the nearest basin just as the bald-headed man who'd been following him appeared.

His pursuer didn't skip a beat and made his way over to the washbasin a few down from Munroe, where he also began washing his hands.

Munroe looked over and smiled politely and the courtesy was returned, but as Munroe turned off the tap and began walking towards the hand dryer the bald man was already reaching into his pocket. Before he had a chance to retrieve anything, Munroe grabbed the man's wandering arm by the wrist and with his other hand slammed the front of his head against the washbasin, leaving a dark bloody smudge from the impact. The man pushed back up but Munroe focused on his wrist and he jerked it upwards to reveal a thin, hardened plastic spike with a wooden handle, no doubt designed to pass through the metal detectors at customs undetected.

"Christ, what is it with you people and ice picks?" was all Munroe managed to say as the bald man swung around and kneed him right in the groin. Thankfully he missed both of them, but the blow sent him down on one knee as the bald man now swivelled his wrist around and pulled away from Munroe's grip. The ice pick was now forced downwards as Munroe grabbed his wrist again and held, pushing against the wavering sharp end above him.

The bald man slammed a couple of kicks into Munroe's side in an attempt to weaken him, as the blonde-haired woman he had seen earlier now piled in through the bathroom door, and ran at his back with an identical plastic ice pick to the one that the bald man was using. Munroe glanced back and then in one swift motion he swivelled the bald man's hand with all his weight, sending him to the floor on his back. Still battling for control of the plastic ice pick he jumped from his kneeling position up onto one leg and with his other drove his boot into the chest of the woman, sending her flying backwards to the far wall.

It was a bad impact, her head slamming against the cement, and then she collapsed to the floor, leaving a bloody smear as her weapon rolled out of her hand and across the tiles.

Munroe now turned his attention to the bald man. He slammed the sole of his boot directly downwards into the man's groin, causing him to yelp in pain and drop the makeshift ice pick to the floor. Munroe yanked him to his feet and flung him against the basin, and as the man fell back towards him he landed a solid punch to the face, sending him crumpling to the floor.

Behind him the bathroom door flung open again and Munroe grabbed the plastic ice pick and turned to see a woman holding a black 9mm Glock directly at him. He froze.

Captain Jaqueline Sloan stared at him, eyes wide at the scene, and then she lowered her gun and turned to the collapsed blonde woman on the floor next to her, checking for a pulse.

"Dead." She stood up and gave Munroe her full attention as she blew a loose strand of red hair from her face. The two simply gave each other a friendly nod before Munroe grabbed the bald man under the arms and began dragging him towards the nearest cubicle. "Give me a hand, would you," Munroe asked, motioning his head towards the dead blonde.

Jax said nothing but did likewise, dragging the woman's body towards one of the cubicles before propping it up against the toilet. She then closed the door and joined Munroe as he perched the bald man on the toilet seat and began checking his pockets.

"Nothing," he said, and Jax, noting the man was still breathing, looked over at the plastic ice pick in Munroe's hand.

"What are you going to do?" She asked as Munroe looked at the man and then back at Jax. "Your mess, your call."

Munroe considered it for a moment before shaking his head. He wiped down the plastic ice pick using the front of the unconscious man's jacket and then tossed it into a silver waste bin next to the wall. "We'll leave him here. Let's go."

Munroe pulled the cubicle door closed and was about to follow when he called out after her. He'd almost forgotten. "Do you have anything sharp on you?"

Jax didn't even question the request and she pulled out a small pocket knife, which she unfolded and passed over to him.

Munroe pulled up his shirt and made a nick just above his hip. "This is how they found me," he said, wincing in discomfort as he picked at the small puncture wound, retrieving a little capsule no more than half a centimetre long and as thin as a pencil lead. "It's a tracker."

Jax looked at him in puzzlement as Munroe placed it on the basin counter and pulled out his iPhone.

"Long story. I'll bring you up to speed once we get out." He snapped off a few pictures of the tracker before dropping it down the plughole and washing the drops of blood away with the tap.

Jax only raised an eyebrow. "Amateurs," was all she said and headed to the bathroom's exit. Munroe couldn't tell if she meant him or the people who had put it in, but he swiftly followed her outside as she made her way along the concourse.

"I wasn't expecting you," Munroe said, actually glad to see her.

"Yeah, well I wasn't expecting *that*. You're lucky McCitrick called me or who knows what would have happened."

"Don't you worry yourself. I was doing just fine without you."

Jax looked unconvinced. "You mean like getting that tracker inserted into your body without realising it?"

"Didn't quite happen like that."

"No, never usually does."

Within a couple of minutes they were at gate fifteen and Munroe followed as Jax bypassed the reception area and, with no one batting an eyelid, they headed through into the connecting tunnel and then out of a service door leading down onto the central tarmac.

They were met by two Royal Marines dressed in fully military attire, minus the weapons, and with a nod from Jax they were escorted towards a grey Merlin Mk 2 helicopter whose rotors were already beginning to rotate.

"I could have taken a flight back to the UK, you know," Munroe said loudly as the roar of the helicopter engine increased, the downforce pushing against them.

"That would be pointless," Jax shouted as she climbed on board, then waited for Munroe and the soldiers to join her. As he sat down opposite, the door was slid shut behind him.

"And why would that be?"

"Because we're not going back to the UK."

Chapter 17

The sun was glorious and flooding the skies with its warm, yellow embrace as the Merlin Mk 2 helicopter skimmed above the thick layers of cloud. By the direction they'd been heading in for well over an hour Munroe knew roughly where they were, but their intended destination was still a mystery. Above the roar of the engines, which had hardly slowed since taking off, he leant forward towards Captain Sloan and spoke into the microphone of the headphone he'd been given shortly after take-off. "So, Jax, are you going to tell me where we're going or just keep me in suspense?"

It was the second time he'd asked after giving her a debrief on Kessler and his run-in with Daedalus. The first had ended with Sloan simply lifting a finger to her lips and, judging by the blank stare he received now, her discretion wasn't about to end any time soon.

"You're not much for small talk, are you, Captain?"

Jax pushed her own headset mic closer to her lips. "You've got a big mouth, Ethan."

Munroe smiled. At least she was talking. "So have you, when it suits you."

"Well it doesn't suit me now, so do us both a favour and shut up."

Munroe still hadn't decided whether Sloan was acting tough or was just cold as ice, and he now probed playfully. "You know we're on the same side, right?"

Sloan's unyielding stare continued and she sat back further in her seat. "That's still to be determined."

Her response was hardly unexpected. She was a woman in a man's army, and to thrive one needed to meet the bar, though to be fair that was the same whatever sex you were. The attitude in the military was one crafted from centuries of experience and centred around the need to follow orders and give no leeway. To be and act as tough as your teammates and hold that standard for the good of everyone. The group mentality needed no weak link in the chain. For special forces, a bit more free thought was welcomed – no, expected – but as he looked over at Sloan he couldn't quite gauge what side of the fence she landed on.

From the cockpit, one of the pilots reached back and tapped Sloan on the shoulder. He raised his index finger in the air and then clasped his hand into a fist.

"Your suspense is over, Ethan." The helicopter began to descend through the clouds, turning the view outside a foggy white, until moments later they broke through the bottom and down towards the foamy crests lapping across the dark blue waves below.

The seas were rough today, and as Munroe pulled himself closer to the window for a better look her got his answer.

HMS *Queen Elizabeth* sat proudly atop the waves like a shining monolith of grey steel. As the Merlin helicopter closed in on her, Munroe could already make out the row of F-35 Lightning II combat stealth jets lining the top deck. The aircraft carrier was the flagship of the Royal

Navy, and despite only recently being put into service it had already become a beacon for naval and national pride. Its size was second only to the Americans' Nimitz-class aircraft carrier, the most impressive naval ship on the planet, but regardless she was a sight to behold and the two unique separate command centres, the forward housing the bridge and the aft responsible for air operations, made her stand out from most traditional carriers.

"The *Queen Elizabeth*. Never seen her up close," Munroe remarked as Sloan glanced back at him.

"Well congratulations, because you're going to see a lot more of her."

The Merlin sank lower and as they approached the deck a ground crew with yellow hi-vis jackets and white helmets were already directing them to their landing spot.

Immediately after the Merlin gracefully landed it was lashed down. After the pilot was given an all-clear signal, the door was slid open by one of the Marines, and Munroe dropped his headset onto the seat and followed Sloan as she strode across the deck towards the towering command centre.

The upper deck was about 1,600 square feet and almost as long as three football fields. It had been a while since he'd found himself on an aircraft carrier and he stopped for a moment to inspect the row of F-35s. They were comparable only to the Americans' F-22 Raptors, to which they were almost identical in shape, and as he sniffed the salt spray in the air a mild wave of euphoria ran though him. It felt good.

Back in the saddle, he thought, unable to prevent the smile that was now etched across his face. He'd forgotten how much he'd missed this. The energy and excitement of the unknown, and the danger that came with it.

"Munroe!"

He looked over to see Sloan beckoning him with a sharp flick of her arm. She stood beside a tall man in his fifties, dressed in a blue naval jumpsuit, at the base of the looming aft command tower.

Munroe allowed himself a final sniff of the sea air before heading over to join her, as the rotors of the Merlin helicopter behind him ground down to a halt.

"Captain Markham, this is my colleague, Ethan Munroe," she announced as Munroe offered his hand, which was shook firmly by the captain.

"Welcome aboard the *Elizabeth*," Markham greeted him courteously. "I hope your ride was enjoyable."

"Long time since I flew in a Merlin. Appreciate the pickup," Munroe replied, nodding in the direction of the helicopter as the ground crew began the task of folding back the rotors in preparation for the elevator trip to the lower deck.

"You're welcome, Mr Munroe. But given that the whole country is on high alert, the government is in chaos, and we've been placed on a war footing, if you'll forgive me for being blunt, I'd like to know what the hell my visitors' business is when letting them aboard my ship. Especially at such short notice, and given the circumstances."

"We understand, Captain, and considering the attack on Parliament I think we're all on edge," Sloan interjected with an understanding curtness that appeared to calm Captain Markham slightly. "As I'm sure you're aware, the army has checkpoints all over London, and if my sources are correct what's left of Parliament is about to issue a nationwide curfew. We certainly don't want to add to your concerns or troubles, but the truth is we're not exactly sure why we're here either."

Judging by the captain's expression, it was clear he knew she was lying.

"Mmm. Really. I find that very hard to believe, but given the state of our national security at the moment, and the need now for cohesion, I suppose I have no option but to trust you, Captain Sloan. Very well, let's get you down there." With Sloan looking respectful, and Munroe behind her, they were quickly led into the command tower and deeper to the decks below.

"We were supposed to be setting a course for a NATO exercise in the South China Sea within the next few hours, but considering the terrorist attack at Westminster I'm unsure what our orders will be. The political chain of command is in a bad way and a breakdown in command means mistakes. Mistakes cost lives. Either way, I suspect yours will be a short visit unless you're intending to travel with us."

Captain Markham was doing his best to wheedle out any information about their visit, but Sloan kept her reply short.

"I doubt we'll be here that long, sir."

"Mmm," The captain murmured again as he raised his hand towards an open area at the bottom of the steps. "No time for a tour, but that's the galley, and the doors ahead take you to the main hangar."

"Impressive aircraft up top, sir," Munroe said, referring to the F-35 Lightning jets as Captain Markham guided them quickly down the next flight of metal steps.

"Hell of a fighter. We can hold thirty-six of them. Bloody shame we only bought twenty-one! That's the government for you. What's left of it anyway. Luckily there's another thirty on order, but it means we're travelling light at the moment."

Sloan said nothing but Munroe snorted at his honesty. "The only thing you can count on in the military is not having what you really need."

The comment brought a frustrated smile to the captain's face. "Don't I know it, son, today more than ever."

The lower deck they arrived on was lined by a main corridor and Captain Markham pointed to a closed oval doorway opposite. "Mr Munroe, you're in there, and Captain Sloan, you're a bit further down."

Sloan gave him a nod. "Catch you later," she said, and without any further explanation headed down the galley with Captain Markham in the lead.

The chain of command for the military was as essential as breathing, and the captain's assessment was absolutely correct. There had never been an attack like this before. Individual assassinations did and had occurred throughout history, but almost the entire political system in one shot! They were in uncharted waters, and as Munroe looked at the navy staff passing him by he saw an unease in their faces that he only now began to consider. With so much going on he'd hardly had time to truly appreciate the worldwide consequences, and a troubling feeling of uncertainty now ran through him as he stepped over to the doorway, turned the handle and let himself inside. The attack on Parliament was a game-changer, the UK's own 9/11, and even more worrying was that he had the feeling it was just the beginning. He was still in the dark… That had to change, right now.

The briefing room could have held forty people, at a squeeze, with four lines of plastic seats all facing one way and bolted to the floor. The walls were metal grey with protruding bulkheads every few metres, with a number of maps and various instruction signs attached to them.

"Ethan. You made it."

The deep, monotone voice was unmistakable and Munroe turned to see McCitrick with his arms folded, resting against a briefing table with a sixty-inch flat-screen monitor on the wall behind.

"Ahh, Boris," Munroe said lightly. McCitrick only stared at him blankly and pointed to a seat in the front row.

"I think we're past that, don't you? Please, have a seat."

Munroe didn't move immediately, waiting for a few moments and leaving McCitrick's hand hovering in the air before he finally walked over and sat down in the central front chair.

"Well, I agree we're past it, but have we reached the point yet?"

"And what point would that be, Ethan?"

"The point where you tell me what the fuck is going on, McCitrick. You send me into that crazy old bastard's house without so much as heads-up to the danger I was walking into... And then there's Daedalus... John!"

McCitrick looked entirely unfazed. He unfolded his arms and rested them either side of the table edge. "Firstly, it's McCitrick to you. Only old acquaintances and friends call me John, and we're neither. Secondly, the *point* is that half of Her Majesty's government has been wiped out in a single day, including the PM. COBRA is frantically attempting to ensure the continuity of a government for the whole of the nation, and it's just a matter of time before politicians begin making power grabs for the top spot. It's bloody chaos out there. But we can't let the people know that."

McCitrick now delivered a single jab with his finger in Munroe's direction. "And you're bitching about having to deal with some old man? Grow up, Ethan. This is a big boy's game. I thought you knew that."

The chew-out made no impact on Munroe and he jabbed his finger straight back towards McCitrick. "And it could have been a whole lot worse if I hadn't got you the information on the bomb."

"That's the only reason you're sitting here right now, and despite your whining – which, just so we're clear, I'm not interested in hearing about again – I want to make you an offer."

Munroe couldn't quite put his finger on it, but there was a steely resolve and determination that resonated from the man, and that Munroe did respect. "OK, McCitrick. What's the offer?"

McCitrick pushed himself off the table and picked up a silver TV remote from the side of the desk. "Usually I would never fast-track what I'm about to say, but given the bloody mess the country is in, and the weight being brought down on all of us, I'm making an exception. So screw the pleasantries and let's get straight to the point. The offer is to join us at DS5 – but before you even consider it, there are some things you should be aware of, so pay careful attention. The information I disclose here and now is not only above top secret, but the men and women under my command are sworn to secrecy on pain of death. It sounds medieval but, and I shit you not, once the offer is accepted, then that's it, you're in for life or until you retire, and even then never a word can be spoken about what it is we do. *Ever.* We recruit only from those in the special forces, and even then their talents and skills must be of the highest calibre."

McCitrick clicked the remote and the monitor lit up, showing footage from a colour CCTV camera of a man jumping from a balcony onto a car roof as someone above shot at him with a carbine. "I got this from our contact in France. Don't worry, it's the only copy."

Munroe sat up in his seat and watched the CCTV footage that had been spliced together from road cameras, showing his escape from the Humvees and ending with him exiting his car and bringing Kessler's Humvee to a crashing stop with only a few shots.

"Some might say that was a bloody foolish stunt," McCitrick said, pausing on a frame showing Munroe still aiming his weapon at the upturned vehicle. "I say it was a calculated action backed by years of military training and a lot of guts. Quite a move, Ethan, although I'm betting it was mostly instinctual. Still, it's a shame Kessler got away." The footage now skipped ahead, to after Munroe had driven off. Another Humvee appeared at the crash and two men pulled Tobias Kessler from the wreckage before driving off.

Munroe remained silent, quietly enjoying the rare opportunity to watch his own handiwork as McCitrick tapped on the remote once more, bringing up CCTV footage from inside the restrooms back at Brest airport.

"If the French public knew there were hidden security cameras in public airport toilets there'd be an uproar. Unfortunately 9/11 changed all that."

They both watched as his attackers were disarmed and subdued before Jax's arrival and then the aftermath as each body was hidden within the cubicles before he paused it on a still of Munroe gouging out the tracker from his waist.

"Again, good work, and realising you had a tracker on you shows an aptitude for thinking outside the box, which are the qualities we look for in our operatives." McCitrick fast-forwarded to another section of the tape showing Munroe standing over his bald attacker perched on the cubicle toilet with the ice pick in his hand and Jax at his side. "Why didn't you kill him, Ethan? Why leave any witnesses?"

The question drew a raised eyebrow from Munroe and he considered it before replying. "What would have been the point? Daedalus already knew I was there, and there was no need to take the man's life just for the sake of it."

McCitrick eyed him judgingly before finally nodding, clearly satisfied by the answer. "DS5 operatives mostly work alone, and it's not just their skills we rely on but their moral judgement out in the field, something you've shown you possess."

Jax had been testing him back in the restroom. In the heat of things she'd given him the option to kill the man, leaving it up to him to make the final decision. Clever.

McCitrick's little show was turning into an evaluation, and although he was keen to know what was on the end page of his speech, Munroe kept his mouth shut. Those dead at Parliament deserved that at least.

"We don't accept walk-ins here, Ethan, we work on crossed paths, a bit of destiny if you will. You can't climb the ladder to end up in DS5, you fall into it, and you have done just that. How's your history, Captain?"

McCitrick's reference to rank had Munroe sitting up sitting up straighter on pure reflex and he bobbed his head. "Military or cultural?"

"Global."

"Iraq or Korea?"

McCitrick gave a grim smile and he expelled a snort. "Oh, a bit further back than that. Do you know what the problem with world history is?"

"Yes," Munroe said, crossing his legs and getting comfortable for the lecture he knew was coming, "it's written by the winners."

"Exactly. Winner takes all, including the truth."

"Always been that way, always will."

"Yes, and the winners teach it to their children. A few generations in and it's gospel. I'm going to tell you a story. It's about a boy who was born into a broken home and grew up with all the pathology that such an environment instils. Insecurity, mistrust, resentment. But this little boy was different. This little boy was also born with an absolute belief in himself and a determination that most never learn to harness. As he grew his resentment focused into courage, and only when his world collapsed around him did those feelings manifest into a sheer hatred of those who, as he saw it, had betrayed him. It was this burning desire for revenge and power over these people that propelled him onwards towards fulfilling those twisted aspirations, and he managed it too, much to the misery of those he hated."

"It's a lovely fairy tale, but if you are referring to me then you're far off the mark. You should know, considering you have my entire history on hand. I've never had a desire for revenge or power," Munroe said, even though he wasn't entirely sure this Brothers Grimm story was directed at him. He watched as McCitrick's eyes widened at the suggestion.

"This isn't about you, Ethan, although your beginnings were vaguely similar. This is about a man becoming the very embodiment of the worst characteristics of humankind. The people he hated were not just a select few, but the world as a whole. It was a world he sought to change, and he came very close to pulling it off, too."

Munroe almost let slip a laugh as he finally realised who they were talking about, but the seriousness in McCitrick's expression restrained him. What the hell the man in question had to do with anything was a mystery. "Are we talking about... Adolf Hitler?"

McCitrick sat motionless on the edge of the table, his arms folded. "What would you say if I told you that the 'Führer' never died in his bunker underneath the war-torn streets of Berlin? What if I told you that he, and many of his high-ranking cronies, made it out alive and escaped justice?"

"I'd say you were crazy."

A menacing smile crept across McCitrick's face. "Then consider me admitted, because your view of world history is about to change... irrevocably."

Chapter 18

Munroe's first thought was that this was another test, one of his gullibility, but as he gazed at McCitrick and his stony expression he began to think better of it. "It sounds like you've been spending too much time on YouTube and going down the Alex Jones rabbit hole. Seventy-odd years of taught history, hundreds of historical books and countless scholars would disagree with you."

"True, but as I said, history is written by the victors. Everything else just bleeds off. Do you know how the greatest lies are forged and upheld, Ethan?"

"By hiding them between two truths," Munroe replied, and his assessment brought a taut smile to McCitrick's lips.

"Fifty million dead and the necessity of not giving millions of German troops a banner to flock to at the end of the war are pretty solid truths, wouldn't you say?"

"I would say so."

"Then let me disclose to you the reality you find yourself in. The truth that only the victors can offer." McCitrick raised the remote control towards the monitor and clicked.

The picture of an elderly gentleman wearing a light blue suit, perhaps in his eighties, standing over a birthday cake and surrounded by children appeared on the screen. With short black hair and deep wrinkles around his eyes and cheeks the man was smiling as he prepared to press a large cake knife into the icing. The clean-shaven man was so familiar, yet not, and at a glance it would have been easy to dismiss as an innocuous family photo.

"It's remarkable how the simple shaving of such an iconic moustache can be such an effective mask." McCitrick said as Munroe moved from his seat over to the table, transfixed by the photo. "He was eighty-three when this was taken, somewhere in Argentina. The exact location is unknown, but we do know he died nine years later, in 1981, at the ripe old age of ninety-two."

Munroe was now mesmerised and he stood there examining every wrinkle, every contour of the old man's face as McCitrick continued, his voice remaining calm and unwavering.

"It's hard to believe, isn't it, that the old bastard saw the advent of space travel, computers and the modern world that he indirectly helped create through his butchering and lust for world domination. And never has such a travesty of justice been so repellent, and unknown to the people of the globe."

Munroe still said nothing, continuing to study the image, until after a few more moments of near-hypnotic scrutinising he tore his gaze from the photo and turned towards McCitrick. "How?"

McCitrick pressed at the remote again and brought up a map of Europe displaying the last days of World War Two, the black swastika representing the last refuge of Nazi power in Berlin surrounded by the Soviets on one side and the Americans on the other. "Hitler's body was never found. It was said to have been burnt to a crisp on his orders. The leader of the Reich had no wish to end up like Mussolini, whose body was hung from a lamp post for show and beaten to a bloody pulp along with his mistress. The advancing Soviets got there first and took what was left, but Stalin insisted it wasn't Hitler. Allied high command believed it was a ruse to allow the Soviets to keep the war going, and in doing so snatch up more of Europe, which ultimately would have continued into the Pacific to make a land grab in Japan. No, the war in Europe had to end, and so his death was reported and concluded as suicide. Can you imagine, Ethan, if the German Army and all the devout Nazi believers had realised Hitler was still alive! With that kind of loyal fanaticism the war would have raged on. The German Army would never have surrendered in droves, as they did, and the world would have been set ablaze again for many years, with millions more dead. Far better to end it all with a single suicide, which many of his contemporaries likened to 'the breaking of a spell'."

Munroe was dumbstruck by the idea, but before he bombarded McCitrick with questions, he needed to know something. "Just so were clear, this isn't a test, is it? You're on the level."

McCitrick almost laughed out loud. "It's hard to digest, I know. I had the same reaction upon first hearing it. The wartime Allies bought into Hitler's death… Churchill, though, did not. Within days of Germany's surrender a covert team of British and American investigators were sent into the Führer's bunker, and what they found caused an emergency meeting between Churchill and President Harry Truman, which is how this whole thing of ours got off the ground."

"And that was?"

"They found a secret access hatch leading directly from Hitler's private room, via a network of tunnels, to the old U6 subway station, exiting next to Tempelhof airport. Back in 2015 a team of researchers had the same idea and actually found it using sonar equipment, but we made sure the news cycle moved on, quickly. Twenty-four-hour rolling news is a godsend for intelligence operations. But back then, it was concluded that this was how the little bastard escaped, and then went on to South America via U-boat. It soon became the perfect place for ex-war criminals, due to the Nazi leanings of Argentine President Juan Perón."

The admission caused Munroe to fall silent in shock for a moment while McCitrick stared at him, gauging his reactions. "So the stories are true." He'd heard the conspiracy theories over the years, and they were now confirmed as McCitrick gave a heavy nod of his head.

"There are still whole German communities deep within the Argentinian and Brazilian forests. The lasting legacy of their Nazi fathers. I've seen them with my own eyes. They have little to do with Daedalus, or not anymore, at any rate."

"So the internet gossip got it right," Munroe said, filled with fascination by the idea.

"Some of it, yes. Gossip is a hard thing to regulate, but easy to manipulate, and we've done a good job of it over the years. You see, Churchill recognised that if the world knew Hitler and his top Nazis had got out it would be nothing short of a worldwide beacon for far-right extremists and sympathisers, and after five years of war that had taken the world to the brink, he wasn't about to let it all resurface. And so an operation was put in place. One of the last things Churchill signed off on, which evolved into a secret charter between Great Britain, America and France. A clandestine organisation was formed to hunt, track and monitor any emergence of whatever the remaining Nazis might want to achieve."

"And that was?"

"Simple, and exactly what you'd think. A Fourth Reich, which would last for the thousand years Hitler had promised."

Munroe sat back down in his chair and exhaled a deep breath as he tried to take stock of the bombshell that had just dropped on him. It had been almost eighty years since the end of the war, and to think that the original Nazi clan had maintained a presence was difficult to comprehend. "Shouldn't you have taken care of it by now? You've had long enough."

McCitrick looked unoffended by the insinuation. He rested back down on the edge of the desk and leant forward. "You make it sound so easy. The war ended in the biggest displacement of human beings of the twentieth century. Possibly in the history of humankind. My predecessors had no idea the SS, knowing the war was lost back in 1943, had spent years cultivating the escape lines to South America. The huge amount of money they had stolen from Europe was used to create new lives and networks for those bastards and, from what we've learnt in the years since, they were planning this resurgence of Nazi doctrine long before the war ended. That's why there was no surrender until after Hitler's supposed death. Why the army, civilians, kids, pensioners, were all ordered to fight for every last metre of dirt. To give them time to fulfil their escape plans… and it worked a bloody treat."

"But so many of Hitler's inner circle were caught or died trying to escape," Munroe replied, instinctually wanting to push back against the tall tale he was hearing.

McCitrick on the other hand appeared to be enjoying this retelling, like a man who had bottled up secrets for years and could finally tell someone else what he knew. "Sure, many were caught, but look at who they were. In the final days of the war Hermann Goering demanded he take over from Hitler and then surrendered. Heinrich Himmler tried to make a deal with the Allies and subsequently committed suicide. These were the weak links in Hitler's inner circle, and he was more than happy to feed them to the dogs. A long time back we got our hands on one of the original insiders, an old man at the time but an SS general during the war who had escaped to Argentina. He told us that no one except Hitler and Martin Bormann, his personal secretary, knew the full picture of the escape plan. Hitler had been paranoid about being betrayed and considering the number of drugs he was on it's understandable, but he was proved right. Goering and Himmler went to their deaths never knowing they had an out, and if they'd held steady they would have escaped as well."

"How about Bormann? I read they found his bones during excavations under the Rhine a few years ago."

McCitrick laughed out loud sarcastically. "Yeah," he chuckled, "after almost a century, and among thousands of previously undiscovered war corpses, they just happen to come across the skeleton of one of the most famous war criminals ever. Hell of a coincidence, wouldn't you say? We pushed that story when interest in escaping Nazis caught the public's fascination back in the late nineties, and then had it confirmed a decade later when improved genetic testing became available, just so it seemed more plausible. It was total bullshit though. We caught Bormann back in the sixties and handed him over to Israel, on the express understanding he would be dealt with by a military tribunal, in secret. He was hung in 1968 after being convicted by a 'jury of his peers'." McCitrick sniffed at the idea. "In reality he didn't stand a chance, and good riddance, as far as I'm concerned."

"How about Goebbels, didn't he kill his children and then commit suicide with his wife in a final show of loyalty to his Führer?"

"Good old Joe Goebbels," McCitrick said, still smiling. "Hitler may have been a narcissistic psychopath with the morality of a serial killer, but he was a cunning little prick. He hand-picked individuals to double for him during the war, a safety precaution against all the Germans who had pegged him for the fruitcake that he was and wanted to see him dead. It was one of these doppelgangers that was used to take a bullet to the head in his apparent suicide. Which was another reason for having his body burnt. It must have been a good likeness, because when he was taken out to be cremated nobody noticed the switch, even his loyal Joseph Goebbels, who then committed suicide, never realised the switch had taken place." McCitrick pointed his finger towards his own forehead. "A gunshot to the head does wonders for the skin. It was Goebbels's act of sacrifice, even if it was done unknowingly, that cemented the belief that it was Hitler's crispy nugget in that shallow grave instead of the poor soul who took the bullet for him. Yes, the Grey Wolf was as cunning as he was insane."

"Grey Wolf?"

"It was Hitler's codename after the war, while in Argentina. Quite the ego for someone with more of a resemblance to a scurrying rat than the magnificent canine he named himself after."

Munroe took a moment to process the information. it was a lot to take in, and even though he could get on board with the historical rewrite he was struggling to be convinced by almost everything else. "OK, so the Nazi hierarchy escaped justice. A travesty, yes, and I can see why no one wanted to admit it publicly, but… That was over seventy years ago, and seeing as they haven't managed to take over the earth so far, why DS5?"

The question was asked bluntly, but McCitrick looked as if he'd been asked it many, many times before.

"That's the real question, isn't it. What relevance does a clandestine organisation, operating at the behest of the highest positions of political power in the Western world, have in the modern age?"

McCitrick shifted off the table and sat down in the seat next to Munroe and then rested his arm on the back of it. "Churchill wasn't just a remarkable orator, he was also blessed with tremendous foresight, which is why, I think, President Truman got on board with his idea in the first place. How do you plan for all eventualities about a threat that could rise up at any time, from anywhere, and compromise anyone – including those in power? That was the real concern."

"Difficult, but not impossible. Put too much power in one person's hands and it's open to corruptibility," Munroe replied, sounding vague because he wanted to hear it from McCitrick's own mouth and not dilute the conversation with his own theory.

"Precisely. There are few absolutes in life, but one is that power corrupts even the best-intentioned people. It's an unfortunate part of the human condition, which is why it's no coincidence that the most democratic countries in the world are the ones with the most checks and balances the higher up the totem pole you go. I believe it was Lincoln who said, 'If you want to test a man's character, give him power. Give a little power and you see the true mettle of a man.' This was something that Churchill also believed emphatically. He was a big fan of Lincoln."

McCitrick pulled out a pack of cherry cough drops. "Helped me quit smoking, been addicted to them ever since," he said, popping one into his mouth before continuing. "It was decided that a group would be set up, kept from the public, for the reasons I've already mentioned, with total authority coming from the Home Secretary and his or her opposite numbers in both America and France. The number of operatives would be small, for accountability reasons, and no other member of government would be aware of its existence. If a Nazi resurgence was ever to be attempted, then it was presumed infiltration of the Western political apparatus would be a given, and the top jobs would be the most coveted for anyone attempting a takeover from within. Each defence head, with access to military and influence beyond the country's borders, would be watched for any signs of Nazi re-emergence, as well as keep an eye on each other, like a safety net. The Fourth Reich may manage to acquire one of the positions, but all three at the same time? Extremely unlikely."

"And what if any of these positions, or any singular operatives, did become corrupted?" Munroe asked, already seeing the need for such safety valves.

"Back in the Forties, secret military courts had been set up during the war effort in both the UK and the US to deal with Axis spies, keeping trials from the public domain. These courts had the right to execute as well. They went on being used, if necessary, during the Cold

War. They've rarely been employed since, but the structure for them is there just in case it's ever needed. It was this instrument that was agreed on by the three leaders to deal with any infiltrations into western democracy, if and when, they occurred. It is this instrument of justice that applies to us as well, Ethan."

The idea was harsh, but Munroe knew the reality, and to him it was more than warranted.

"DS5 are a protective measure and although we've evolved over the decades – there were major changes in operations after 9/11 – the mandate still holds true. We watch, wait and intervene when the need arises. Given all the original Nazis died out long ago, the movement which they started and backed with stolen money from the people of Europe has morphed into something similar yet operationally very different... Daedalus. They are highly organised, well financed and over the decades have infiltrated many areas of industry and political life. Have no illusions, Ethan, these people aren't like the Taliban. They are near impossible to spot, having been born into their cover. They are highly motivated, highly trained and true believers in a Fourth Reich, and they will stop at nothing to make it happen. Their goal is long term, generations in the making, and they rarely stick their head above the parapet unless it's essential to advance their goal. Sometimes years can go by with nothing, not even a lead, and then they pop up again, and that's when we swoop. It's a game of chess. A long game – but the attack on Parliament changes everything. There's no reason to have committed it unless it's a stepping stone towards bigger things."

"Jesus," Munroe replied, unsure of what worried him more – the fact that Daedalus was out there, or that DS5 knew hardly anything about them. After over seventy years!

McCitrick must have sensed Munroe's concerns and he leant in closer, even though they were the only ones in the room. "Look, I know it might appear like we're in the dark, but I assure you there's a lot I'm not telling you, need-to-know information. What I can say is that we've had our suspicions about Icarus for months, and by killing two MI6 agents he stuck his neck out too far. He's Daedalus to the core, and we were hoping he'd lead us deeper into the furnace, but now he's gone rogue it's essential that we track him down. That's what I want you on."

"And how about his contact at the Ministry of Defence? The photo you showed me back in London appeared fairly conclusive that he has someone on the inside."

McCitrick looked unconcerned and he tapped Munroe on the shoulder. "It's in hand, you leave that to me. Right now, as I said, I want you on Icarus. He's the lead to follow. And we need him brought in."

Munroe had no issue with such an assignment – there was still too much he needed to know from the man about his family. But he was still trying to fathom DS5, an organisation that he was already being inducted into. "So essentially you're Nazi hunters."

McCitrick chuckled at the idea, for the first time looking almost embarrassed. "Something like that, but we're so much more. We also carry out operations through the Ministry of Defence. But yes, in a nutshell, you're correct. Our primary role *is* hunting Nazis – or Daedalus, as they've become."

Munroe didn't know whether to laugh or cry. The whole thing was surreal. And despite the idea of a Nazi group still attempting to act out the wishes of a thousand-year Reich at the behest of a dead man and his cronies, there was a more pertinent question on his mind. "Is this… DS5… legal? You are keeping it from the PM and the other two presidents, right?"

"Oh, it's legal. It's a bit rocky since the EU came into force, and as I mentioned the events of 9/11 have complicated things, but yes. We may be the most secretive organisation in the intelligence community, but we also have a presence everywhere within it and beyond. As for our place in the world, it's best put like this. There are many layers of security, intelligence and accountability in each of our governments but, from the position we work from, we can't even see those layers, let alone be bound by them. It's one of the reasons why DS5 operatives' moral virtues must be unimpeachable. Licence to kill is standard, and we have all and any equipment or resources needed to assist in our remit at our fingertips. And above all else, we take the heat for the government when needed. To put it bluntly, Ethan, we are unaccountable by all and only accountable to each other and the UK, US and French secretaries in charge." McCitrick now bit at his bottom lip. "It also means we're expendable."

"Expendable?" Munroe said. Even though he liked what he was hearing it put an uncomfortable twist on McCitrick's whole sales pitch.

"Yes, if need be. You remember your brief? 'For Queen and country', Ethan. Well, this is for 'humanity and world'. Doesn't get much bigger."

McCitrick stood and began heading to the exit. "Follow me, there's some people you should meet."

Munroe also got up, but he remained where he was, and when McCitrick reached the door he turned around and raised his eyebrows. "What?"

"Why the name, DS5?"

McCitrick smiled. "It's the Roman numeral for 5, 'V'. It's an acronym."

"For what?"

"Disavowed, Ethan. It stands for the Disavowed. Because that's exactly what we are."

Chapter 19

The group was small, amounting to eleven men and women including himself and McCitrick. As Munroe was led into the adjoining briefing room the sound of chatter fell silent and every one of the attendees stared over at the new arrival including Sloan, who made her way over to join them both.

"Apologies for giving you the bitchy treatment over the past few days, but you're not in until you're in. Know what I mean?"

Munroe nodded his head and shook her outstretched hand. "No complaints, Jax. Anyway, I've not *officially* accepted the position."

Sloan glanced over at McCitrick and rolled her eyes before slapping her palm down onto Munroe's shoulder. "Oh yes you have, Ethan. Welcome to the team."

Munroe didn't respond immediately, but then he nodded with content acceptance as McCitrick ushered him towards two people standing nearby, as the rest of the small crowd once more broke out in conversation.

"Each of the three countries in DS5's charter has three operatives and a section head. On top of that are each of the defence heads of those countries and on our side the Home Secretary. Fifteen people in all."

"Minus the politicians I only see eleven."

"The UK is… was… down by two," McCitrick said, gently patting Munroe on the back. "Now we're down by only one. The two MI6 agents Icarus killed. They were ours. C'mon, let me introduce you to some people, and don't get your nose bent out of joint if they're a bit hostile. New DS5 operatives don't usually enter the fray so quickly, and these people are only doing their job."

"And that is?"

"To be suspicious," McCitrick said under his breath, "just like I am."

Suspicious or not, the cavalier attitude on display of such monumental revelations was, to Munroe, somewhat jarring at first, but a part of him was loving it. His ambition for wanting to join the military's special services had always been about being the best he could be, pushing his abilities and seeing how far he could go, but the conservative decorum of such a life had never suited him very well. Here, though, was an organisation with inflexible moral demands, a place he could push his skills to their limits and be part of something that had worldwide implications.

"Colonel Anne Sinclair, US Sector Chief, and Colonel Jacques Remus, French Sector Chief. May I introduce Ethan Munroe, our newest recruit."

Sinclair was in her mid-forties with blonde hair, peppered with grey, and her green piercing eyes were accentuated by her pale white skin tone. She shook Munroe's hand, followed by Colonel Remus who, dressed in full military khaki, appeared far friendlier. He offered Munroe a smile and a firm handshake.

"Welcome," Remus said in a thick French accent, motioning towards McCitrick. "John tells us you're going to be a strong asset to the team. Too fast for my liking, but if John says he trusts you then I can live with it."

Munroe remained relaxed and calm. Rank had never bothered him. "Pleasure to meet you, Colonel, and good to be on board, although I'm still in the briefing stage. Over seventy years of new history is a lot to learn and process."

"Isn't it just, and call me Remus," the Frenchman said in a deep, husky voice. With his black, receding hairline and long face there was a look of Jean Reno, the French actor, about him. "We don't do rank at DS5, only respect for the chain of command, and as for processing, you better get your mind clear. With Parliament still smoking things are going to move fast."

Remus's blunt talk was appreciated by Munroe and he replied accordingly, wanting to show his best. "You can count on it, Remus. I'm ready to go as and when. Just give the word."

"Good," the Frenchman replied, displaying a satisfied smile.

"Unlike Remus here I like rank," Sinclair interrupted, staring at Munroe frostily. "You can call me Colonel Sinclair, and we should thank you for the intel on Daedalus's attack. It may have come too late, but the connection to Kessler is invaluable."

"Thank you, Colonel, but I'd say luck had a lot to do with it," Munroe replied, staying humble, but Sinclair was quick to admonish the idea.

"Bullshit. Luck had nothing to do with it. I like my people to be honest in their assessments. Do well and pat yourself on the back, screw up and be prepared to admit it and suffer the consequences. In our business we may have to lie to people about our intentions, but we don't lie to ourselves. Understand?"

"I understand," he replied, blank-faced. "In that case, yes, it was a remarkable piece of work and use of my skills, Colonel."

Sinclair stared at him for a moment coldly and her eyes tightened, but then a thin smile appeared on her lips and she expelled a deep laugh. "I've seen your record and your handling of Kessler. I've seen the CCTV footage. You're an experienced operator with a sharp mind, and that's exactly what we need, especially now, given the shitstorm at Westminster."

It was McCitrick who interrupted. "We all share gathered intel with one another. Nothing is held back, politics has no place in what we do. And command is shared equally between section heads. An order from any of these two is as good as coming from my own mouth."

For a clandestine military unit it was pretty liberal thinking, but Munroe approved, and after spending the last few years in the public sector the ethos was welcomed. "Good to know, sir. That's the way I like it."

The response drew a smile from Remus but it quickly faded. "Good, you'll fit right in, my friend. But don't fuck up or you will feel the full weight of my boots."

"Also good to know, Remus," Munroe replied as Remus now turned his attention to McCitrick and began speaking as if Munroe wasn't even there.

"I like him, John. But I don't like the circumstances around his leaving the military. Honourable discharge or not. Try that shit in my unit and I would have locked you up and thrown away the key. Permanently."

Munroe said nothing as McCitrick considered his reply, but surprisingly it was Sinclair who came to his defence.

"We've all fucked up at some point in our career, Remus. Even you. I've seen his record, just as you have, and that's the only blemish I could find. I can only speak for myself, but I'm only interested in what he brings to the table going forward."

"I agree," McCitrick added, and Munroe watched Remus share a gaze with the other two section heads. He found the whole discussion very strange. In the military this was the kind of conversation that would usually be held behind closed doors, but yet here they were, putting their cards on the table right in front of him. DS5 was just as McCitrick had told him it was. No bullshit, and everyone open to a fault. Everyone knew where everyone stood and the chain of command was the only thing sacrosanct… Munroe liked it.

"OK, Ethan," Remus said finally, turning his attention back to Munroe. "Let us see what you can do."

The other two heads nodded in agreement as Remus motioned to the others behind them, still in conversation among themselves. "Why don't you meet the others."

"Introductions will have to wait, I'm afraid," McCitrick said, glancing over at the three large monitors on the wall. "The three wise kings will be online any moment."

"Three 'wise' kings?" Munroe asked and received a forced smile from McCitrick.

"Just a nickname for the Defence and Home secretaries from each country. But don't let the 'king' part fool you. With the potential change of political guard we keep them in check as much as they do us. Now if you could give us a moment."

The three section heads filtered away from him and Munroe was left with Sloan, who had been listing to the whole conversation.

"They're a motley bunch," Sloan said, motioning to the small group of DS5 operatives chatting among themselves. "But once you get to know them you'll realise they're the best at what they do. Believe me. I'd rather have these lot watching my back than a brigade of regulars. And as for Remus, he's probably got more operational experience under his belt than everyone put together. He ran covert operations during the Bosnian War as a sniper and ran French special forces in Afghanistan and Iraq."

"How about Sinclair?"

"She's recent to DS5, about a year, but before she worked mainly in army intelligence. Tough old broad though, and with the resolve of a steel elephant."

"And McCitrick?"

They both looked over towards McCitrick, who was deep in discussion with the other colonels. "McCitrick's a bit of a mystery, even to me. He doesn't talk about his past much but he's ex-SBS. Honest and loyal to the core. One thing that I do know though, is don't cross him. He's had the ear of every Home Secretary since 1998, and should anyone betray DS5 it's McCitrick who pulls the trigger. No courts, no hearings, no bullshit. Honour and loyalty are everything in this unit. It's all we have to rely on, being completely outside the framework of the real world."

For the first time since being given the brief by McCitrick, Munroe found himself in awe of everything he was hearing and seeing as it began to sink in. He knew there were acknowledged operations and units working outside the government. Christ, he'd worked for many of them, but this was different. A small group with thousands of tonnes of weaponry and combat men and woman at their fingertips, and the resources of nations to use as they saw fit. Quite a responsibility and, as he saw it, the ultimate honour – to serve not just one's country but the world. And all this to kill Nazis. One of the most dangerous groups to ever have existed.

"So how about you, Captain Sloan. What's your story?" Munroe asked, curious as to how his new teammate had made it into the fold.

"I could ask you the same thing. Remus over there wasn't very impressed, although he can be like that with everyone from time to time. How did you get your honourable discharge?"

Munroe just stared at her, and after a few moments of uncomfortable silence he made a clicking sound from the side of his mouth. "Maybe when we get to know each other better."

Sloan didn't look offended; she just shrugged her shoulders. "Same for me then. A bit of mystery never hurt anyone."

They both smiled respectfully at one another as on the wall opposite the three separate flat-screen monitors lit up and Munroe found himself staring at the people known as 'the three kings'. On the left sat the French Minister for Armed Forces, in the middle the US Secretary of Defence, and on the right was the UK Home Secretary, Jacob Ryan.

With McCitrick, Remus and Sinclair standing at the front of the crowd they turned to face the screens and waited as the US Secretary spoke first.

"Thank you for gathering at such short notice, and especially Section Head McCitrick for organising it. You are all aware of the atrocities that have occurred in London earlier today, and as such I would now like to turn this meeting over to Secretary Ryan, who will speak on behalf of us all. I would also like to impress upon you that this brazen attack on British soil by Daedalus will not go unpunished, and as always is considered not just a national attack but an attack on the world as a whole."

"Thank you, Mr Secretary." Ryan shifted in his chair before resting both his elbows on the table in front of him, staring sombrely at them all. "When our three countries formed this charter over seventy years ago, it was in the hope of maintaining world peace after the horrors of World War Two. Our leaders made a solemn promise, not just to each to other but to the world, that the Nazi war machine would never again be allowed to roll. Our predecessors held true to that promise, and although the inhumane and sick ideals of Nazism have endured, it is us that has kept it at bay. Our remit of secrecy has made it a thankless job and, so far, never-ending, as the ground-work laid down by the Nazi hierarchy has morphed and evolved into the organisational cult we know as Daedalus. As they have evolved, so has DS5, and we have become a watchtower that strikes down this ideological scourge when it rears its ugly head. But as of today, that all changes. This attack on the very fabric of the Western political system, we believe, represents a sea change in their thinking, and what has remained for so long a secret cold war, a chess game of ideologies, has now become hot. They have changed the rules of the game, and we must respond in kind. From this moment going forward we will no longer defend the status quo, but take the fight to them. For far too long we have maintained a type of balance, only striking when necessary, but now we will dig them out and finally end what should have been concluded back in 1945. Your section heads will brief you on the various operations. But know that you have at this moment any resource, any department, any army, including NATO, to aid you. Revisit every lead we've ever had, any escapes we allowed to slip by, and any and all suspects, regardless of how unsure we are of their involvement. If they are a suspect, then bring them in for questioning. This game stops now. If not, then what will be next... the French Parliament, the White House? We know you will carry out your duties to the best of your abilities – and know that once our task is concluded, we can disband the charter that has kept the world safe for so many decades."

Ryan leant closer to the camera, the cut on his cheek from the bomb blast tied with fresh stiches. "This ends now, under our watch... and none too soon. Godspeed, ladies and gentlemen. The weight of history is on your shoulders. We know you will make the world proud."

With a nod from the other secretaries the screens went black, and as the group descended into the mumbling of conversation the three section heads huddled among themselves for a few minutes before moving to join their respective groups.

"Both of you, walk with me," McCitrick ordered, and he headed out of the briefing room with Munroe and Sloan on his tail. It wasn't until they reached the top deck that McCitrick began to speak again. He now pulled out his smartphone and held it out in front of him. "I received this just before you arrived. One of my contacts in Brazil found it on the victim of a massacre there."

McCitrick tapped the screen; it brought up a picture of a burnt hand, charred by flames, but it was the tattoo on the inside arm that aroused the curiosity of both Munroe and Sloan. The tattoo was a triangle with a maze lying within it, and Munroe recognised it immediately.

"Daedalus, it's their symbol. I saw it on Tobias Kessler's arm, but he said they don't mark themselves anymore."

"Well someone has, and considering it was found on the arm of a woman along with sixty-seven others who had been burnt alive in a commune church, I think it pertinent to take a look. Daedalus are covering their tracks, and I want you to find out why."

Munroe was about to ask a question but McCitrick raised a finger. "I don't know any more than that, but my man on the ground can give you all the information he has. And if you do come across any of Daedalus's people I want them brought in for questioning. Not on sight, do you understand? A lot of people died in the attack on Parliament and it's got the other countries worried. Who's next? If Daedalus are moving into their endgame then this could be the moment we've been anticipating for over seventy years."

Munroe needed no persuading. "We'll leave now."

McCitrick nodded and flicked his finger towards the waiting Merlin Mk 2 helicopter already spinning up its rotors. "That'll take you to back to Brest airport where you'll connect with a waiting C-130 Hercules with a care package on it, then on to Brazil. You'll refuel in mid-air." McCitrick passed over a set of plastic cards with both their names on. "You've got CIA, FBI and UN attaché identification, use them as and if needed."

Munroe and Sloan dropped the cards into their pockets and with barely a nod began heading towards the waiting chopper. Blown about by the raging downforce from the Merlin's rotors, Munroe boarded along with Sloan, and he found himself racking his mind for an answer to the biggest question still on his mind. What the hell did a Nazi serial killer have to do with him or his family?

"Looks like we're on our own. That's fine by me," Munroe yelled above the noise as the sliding side door was pulled closed and the helicopter began lifting into the air.

"Then you're in the right place, Ethan. They don't call us the Disavowed for nothing."

Chapter 20

The crystal mini chandeliers hanging above sparkled their brilliance down upon the two men striding their way along the long corridor, neither of them saying a word, their boot heels leaving small indentations upon the ruby carpet running its length. There were no paintings or pictures hanging from the white painted walls, and as the two men reached the doorway at the end they stopped. The first grasped the oval brass doorknob with his white-glove-covered hand and twisted it. He gently pushed open the door and then stood by its side, his back stiff and his chin raised up into the air. "Mr Bauer for you, gentlemen."

Wearing a Cranbourne tweed jacket, waistcoat, brown corduroys and red-tinted leather brogues, Hans Bauer made his way inside and raised his right arm into the air powerfully. "Heil Hitler," he said, before returning the arm to his side and staring at the six men seated before him. The room had the air of a decadent private library; it was set on two levels, with the higher one providing a walkway above the central room and allowing access to the dark lacquered bookcases lining it. Down below an overly large round mahogany table sat on anthracite-coloured carpet, and behind it a lit fireplace crackled away next to a large expansive window overlooking an icy mountain range.

"Please, Hans, take your seat. We've been waiting for you."

With a sharp nod, Bauer moved to the nearest seat as the man who had announced him pulled the chair back with his white-gloved hands and then gently pushed it forward as he sat down.

Upon the table, and in front of each seat, an engraved lightning bolt stretched towards the middle where they all met at a circle. Within this the centre displayed a triangle containing a maze, leading to its central point, and the image of a sun radiating light.

"Has our test site been taken care of?" the old man who'd told him to sit asked, tapping the top of the table with his fingers.

"The village of Cândido Godói has been sanitised, gentlemen, and all the test subjects have been removed from the equation. I saw to it myself."

The old man looked unsure about the information. "By taken out of the equation, do you mean completely? No trace?"

"I mean, sir, their bodies have been burnt to cinders. There is nothing but ashes, and certainly no way for any blood tests to be carried out. But we still have a small issue at hand."

The old man said nothing but instead raised his nose upwards in anticipation of the admission as Bauer explained further.

"The authorities turned up sooner than was expected, and we've not been able to take care of Dr Ferreira's... lab. The good news is they haven't found it yet, and once you have dismissed me from this meeting I will be going there to take care of it personally."

Bauer's assurance was met with a satisfied nod from the old man and he began moving on to the next order of business, in doing so showing the faith he had in his subordinate.

"That's exactly what I wanted to know. Going forward we cannot afford to leave any trails in our wake." The old man looked happy at the news, but the anxious look now appearing on Bauer's face caused his pleased demeanour to evaporate in a flash. "What is it?"

"Hanks is compromised, and I believe dead." This information gained a raised eyebrow from a few of the seated hosts, but not from the old man.

"What do you mean 'believe'?" the old man asked, with no hint of anger in his voice.

"Icarus tracked him to one of our safehouses and accosted him while I was on the video call. He, as you already know, is not a happy boy."

A younger man sat to Hans's left let out an amused snort. "I'm not surprised, considering we tried to have him killed."

The old man turned his head and stared at him warningly. As the younger man's smirk dissolved, Bauer was addressed once more. "Which safehouse?"

"I'm afraid it was a secure line and I don't know... yet. There are a few dozen it could have been, but I have our people checking each one. We'll find Hanks, dead or alive, but I very much doubt Icarus will still be there."

The old man's eyes dipped towards the surface of the table as he considered his response, and then with a swift breath he returned his gaze to Bauer. "Let's not worry too much about our boy. There's not much he can do except cause trouble for himself. And besides, things are progressing very well, despite a few bumps along the way.

There is, however, a more troubling issue to deal with, and it is one I want you to focus on."

"And what would that be, sir?"

"Ethan Munroe. We all agree he's a dead end, but it would be impractical for us if Icarus was to meet him face to face. It could cause additional problems we would prefer to avoid."

Bauer looked unbothered by the notion and he replied with a sober nod as the old man continued.

"I am more concerned with Kessler's slip of judgement, which is why I called you here in person."

The old man clicked his fingers and the white-gloved and black-suited announcer disappeared from where he had entered, closing the door behind him. "Kessler is a good man, and one of the old guard, but his mention of the Parliament bomb was most out of character and cost us a few additional cabinet ministers, I would wager. If Munroe had managed to get the word out sooner it could have cost us dearly. I think it's time for him to retire from the front line of our operations. I want you to set him up somewhere nice, no expense spared. It's the least we can do for such a valued old friend who's done so much for us over the years."

Bauer was already nodding as behind him the door opened and the newest guest was announced.

"Mr Kessler, gentlemen."

Tobias Kessler entered the room confidently, his eyes blackened from his car crash, and he raised his right hand in the air as his left hung motionless in the sling supporting it. "Heil Hitler," he yelled dramatically, taking great pride in the action.

"Thank you for coming, Tobias. How are the injuries?"

"Fine, sir. I was lucky. They are only minor."

The old man looked pleased by the reply. "I'm glad to hear that. Very glad indeed… but not so much with how you handled Ethan Munroe."

Some of the confidence drained from Kessler's face, and he looked nothing short of embarrassed. It visibly irked the older man.

"Don't tell me you feel an affinity with this man Munroe, as Icarus does!"

"No, sir," Kessler replied, his response coming quickly. "I thought I might have been able to turn him. That was my only goal."

The old man was now looking stunned and he closed his eyes and shook his head. "This Munroe is nothing to us. What if he had managed to tell them about the Parliament bomb in time!"

Kessler's embarrassment quickly turned into shame and his head drooped as he held his hands together respectfully. "It was foolish, sir. Please forgive me."

The old man stared at him with mistrust for a moment before leaning back in his padded black leather chair. "I forgive you, Tobias. But *we* believe it is best if you step down from your position. Time is catching up with you, my old friend, and over the years you've done enough for our cause. That is until Project Icarus is fully realised, and then you will be welcomed back with the honours you so richly deserve."

There was grave disappointment in Kessler's expression, but he dutifully nodded and once again raised his right arm. "Heil Hitler." He then paused, keeping his arm outstretched as he stared directly at the old man across the table. "And Heil Reich Führer Bormann."

A proud grin spread across Bormann's face, and he nodded at the acknowledgement. As Kessler stood there stoutly, proudly displaying his Nazi salute, a thin garrotte wire was swiftly dropped over his head and then tightened around his neck.

Kessler looked horrified as Bauer tightened his grip on the handles, and as the trickles of blood running down his neck were absorbed by his top collar, he slowly descended to the floor. The wire was cutting deeper and deeper, but throughout he never lowered his saluting arm or broke his stare with Reich Führer Bormann, until his body gave out and he collapsed to the floor.

"Thank you, Hans," Bormann said as Bauer uncoiled the garotte wire and wiped it down with a white handkerchief. "Please ensure the body is buried somewhere nice, no expense spared, and see that he has a good view from which to watch eternity pass him by."

"Yes, sir." Bauer headed for the door to retrieve the body bag he'd prepared in his car.

"Let's also tie up the last few loose ends on the Operation Icarus side please," Bormann called out as the other members of the circle now began to leave their seats, having observed the spectacle they'd come for. "If you can't get rid of Icarus, then damn well make sure that you get rid of Munroe."

Chapter 21

The scent of burnt embers and cooked meat hung in the air as a noxious testimony to the terrible events that had occurred the previous day, and as Munroe approached the scorched remains of the small church it smelt familiar. It was not the first time he had experienced such a uniquely foul odour. While conducting operations in Afghanistan his unit had come across a small village that the Taliban had deemed to be working with American forces. Under the cover of night they had rounded up the twenty or so residents and summarily executed them before dragging their bodies into a pile. Doused with gasoline they had been set alight, and by the time Munroe and his team passed through there was nothing left except a mound of smoking bones and a smell he would never forget. It was this same smell he now sniffed in the air, and it was becoming more potent the closer to the church he got. The blackened stone walls had given way, bringing down the roof, and the once-heavy timber frames were nothing more than ash and charcoal which largely hid the charred bodies that lay beneath.

"How many, Mr Silva?" Munroe asked, glancing over at the man by his side, who was still surveying the remnants of such a terrible tragedy.

"Who the hell knows, but our records indicate there were up to one hundred people living at this commune and all the houses are empty, so I'd say most of them."

At just under six foot Detective Carlos Silva was an intimidating presence, and with his deep husky voice and belligerent temperament Munroe had found himself liking the man instantly upon meeting him. He'd slept the entire flight to Brazil – Sloan had done likewise – and on arriving at São Paulo airport they had been greeted by a contingent from the Brazilian army, who were not happy to see them. Whether it was political, or just worries raised after the attack on Parliament, they had been instructed that one of them was to wait with the C-130 Hercules if the other was to continue. Sloan had not been happy, but even after a phone call to McCitrick the order had stood, and after an intense quarrel between them she had reluctantly agreed to remain with the aircraft. A rented private Learjet had taken Munroe the last few hours to Santa Rosa airport in the deep southern Brazilian forests, and there the uncordial Detective Silva had been waiting for him on the tarmac.

"This is a favour for McCitrick. Don't expect any pleasantry bullshit, Mr Munroe," were the first words out of Silva's mouth, the man clearly not happy at the request he was fulfilling. "Leaving the bodies of woman and children under burnt rubble for over twenty-four hours, just so you can turn up and nose around, is not agreeable to me."

Munroe empathised, and once they had made the ten-minute drive in Silva's white Chevrolet Onix, he had finally realised what, apart from the obvious, had the man so riled up. A detachment of army guards had been posted in jeeps around the church, and having to sit there and wait without beginning the retrieval of bodies had them all on edge. It was with this in mind that Munroe now moved quickly, and with a purely professional and dispassionate mindset.

"You mentioned the marking. Where?"

Silva made his way across the charred debris to the nearest corner of the church, careful in his stepping and followed with the same diligence by Munroe, until he reached a single black forearm sticking up through the ash, the fingers stretched out as if reaching for the sky. He lowered down onto his haunches and pointed to it as Munroe joined him.

"Just there."

It was impossible to even tell if the limb was still connected to a body under all the rubble, and it appeared as if a light tap would cause it to crumble.

Munroe craned his head downwards and squinted at the small marking still visible, its colour offset from the rest of the burnt skin. The fire had destroyed most of it, but he could tell what it was, a maze within a pyramid, identical to the one Kessler had shown him back in Bordeaux, tattooed on his inside arm.

Daedalus.

"Whoever did it must have forced the whole commune inside before setting the place on fire. It would take many men to round them up like this," Silva said, briefly looking around at the devastation of the former church. "You came a long way to see this, Mr Munroe. I hope it helps."

"On its own? No."

"Then perhaps this might." Silva ushered him back out of the church with a flick of his finger, studiously retracing his steps back to what once was the entrance to the church, and then back out to the main street. "When my men arrived they found a couple of kids hanging around." Silva clicked his fingers at one of the military guards standing in the doorway of a small house on the opposite side of the street, who swiftly disappeared inside. "They're from a village a few miles from here, Cândido Godói. They saw the smoke yesterday and were doing some exploring when we arrived."

"You've had them in custody here for twenty-four hours?" Munroe asked, surprised their parents hadn't already raised the alarm for two children missing for over a day.

Silva waved off the idea and shook his head, looking almost offended. "Don't be ridiculous, Mr Munroe, this may be South America but we're not a dictatorship. I had them brought back before I picked you up at the airport, but what they told us may interest you."

The guard now emerged from the doorway and behind him two boys were led out, but it wasn't the anxious, wide-eyed looks on their faces that caught Munroe's attention, it was their appearance. The children had blonde hair, blue eyes and light skin, and with short, cropped hair they were identical. Wearing matching navy-blue shorts and Manchester United tops the only difference was their height, one being about an inch taller, but they were without doubt twins.

"This is Jose and this is Luiz, they speak English," Silva announced, pointing to the smaller of the two. "Tell this man what you saw, boys."

The two kids were looking no less nervous having been introduced, and Munroe knelt down on one knee and smiled at them both. "Hello boys, my name is Ethan, and I'd very much like to know what you saw. Would that be OK?"

The two boys glanced at each other uneasily as Munroe attempted to soothe their nerves, so he pointed to the Manchester United crest embroidered on their shirts. "Great team. I've seen them play at Old Trafford."

The mention of the club's home ground brought a sparkle of interest from both boys, and the smaller one let slip a smile as Munroe nodded in appreciation.

"You're not in any trouble, guys. I'm just trying to find out what you saw, and then we'll get you back to your mum and dad. Sound good?"

A few moments of silence followed, and then the taller one began to talk, any angst in his demeanour evaporating.

"The men were all standing around the bonfire and then they left."

"Did you see their faces?" Munroe asked, not wanting to dwell on what the two young boys believed to be nothing more than a deliberate fire.

"No," the boy replied as the smaller one butted in, now seemingly happy to chat away.

"They were wearing army clothes like that," the boy said, pointing to the guard, who looked unimpressed by the comparison. "We saw where they went. It was to the doctor's shop."

"The doctor?"

"He's a travelling doctor, but he doesn't come to our village anymore, only here. He helped our mum when she was sick. We told the policeman... can we go now?"

Before Munroe could ask anything else, Silva motioned over to the guard. "Take them home and thank the parents for their cooperation."

Munroe followed the detective's lead. "Thanks, boys."

Both men waited in silence until the children were led over to one of the military jeeps.

"You brought them back to tell me that!" Munroe said, staring over at Silva, who brushed it off with a snort.

"I wanted you to see them with your own eyes. The blonde hair and blue eyes. You must have heard the stories of Cândido Godói?"

"I think I missed that one."

Silva turned and began making his way back to the white Chevrolet. "Had all the major newspapers down here twenty years ago. Cândido Godói has the highest rate of twins in the world. Blonde-haired, blue-eyed twins. The villagers had a local doctor who'd been offering his services since the fifties, working as a paediatrician. He was involved in most of the pregnancies up until the late sixties. When they were shown a picture of the man they all agreed it was the same person."

"Who was it?" Munroe asked, already getting the scent of what he was about to hear.

"Josef Mengele, the escaped war criminal. The Nazis' own angel of death, who experimented on twins in the concentration camps, trying to create the perfect Aryan specimen, and a way for woman to birth twins to bulk up the Nazi war machine."

Munroe came to a stop at the vehicle's passenger side as Silva reached down and pulled open the driver's door before resting his forearms on top of the roof. "The one that got away. He died in 1979, but researchers only discovered his remains in '85."

Munroe looked stunned. He'd never heard of it, but then again he had never had an interest in escaped Nazis... until now. "They think he continued his work after the war at Cândido Godói?"

"That was the theory, but after all the press attention the whole village clammed up. They've spent decades trying to explain it away as anything other than the last experiments of Mengele. Christ, they even went as far as to say the twin rate is a result of inbreeding. Rather the village was known for incest than the remnants of the Third Reich's experiments. Can you blame them?"

Silva slid his hands off the roof and then dropped into his seat as Munroe opened his own door and did likewise. "So where's the doctor's shop the boys mentioned? That's where we're going, isn't it?"

Silva nodded and turned on the engine before dropping the Chevrolet into first gear and slowly began heading down the main street. "I had the boys take me to it yesterday, just a few miles from here. I've had guards placed outside it since then and believe me, it's not a shop."

"What is it then?"

"I'm not exactly sure. Our mutual friend McCitrick asked me not to go in until you arrived, and I've honoured that." Silva glanced over at him and smiled. "I know what you're thinking, and you're right. I'm extremely curious, but I owe John, and besides, he's got a sixth sense when it comes to people keeping their word. Something I know well from experience."

As the car made its way down the dusty red trail Munroe had to agree. He'd only known the man for a short time, but it was long enough to know the DS5 chief was a wily old bastard, and not a man to cross. "Any leads on who the doctor is?"

"That I do know." The car's front wheel hit a deep pothole in the road, roughly bouncing them both about as the detective cursed. "Fucking roads are shit out here. This whole area is so isolated."

"Good place to go unnoticed, though," Munroe noted as they hit another pothole, sending a heavy thud rippling through the vehicle's chassis. "Probably why the doctor chose it. So you were saying."

Silva navigated another dip and then returned to the question in hand. "The land is owned by a Dr Manuel Ferreira, all seven acres of it."

"Have you spoken to him yet?"

"No, and I'm not going to. His residence was found burnt to the ground a few days ago. Haven't found a body yet, but if it's there, we will."

Munroe said nothing, but the look on his face had Silva glancing at him irritably. "Things work slower down here in Brazil, Mr Munroe, but either way it appears that whoever has their hand in this is cutting all ties and attempting to erase whatever's been going on."

It took them no more than five minutes to reach their destination, but black storm clouds were already starting to gather overhead. As the white Chevrolet entered the open steel-gated driveway, Munroe could see why Silva had been sure it wasn't a shop. The entire front of the property was guarded by a six-foot-high border, made up of rusting corrugated sheets, denying a view from the dirt road, and as they entered the central driveway the brown wilted lawns on either side offered only a hint of the lush grounds that must have once been here. At the end stood an impressive multi-floored white stone building, and Munroe couldn't help but get the feeling of déjà vu. The building looked so out of place in this isolated Brazilian suburb, more like a Scottish castle without the turrets, the kind he had visited as a boy.

Parked out on the moss-stained gravel in front of the building's double front doors was a military jeep, and the two occupant soldiers were already getting out to greet them.

"Any problems?" Silva asked as Munroe joined him.

Both guards only shook their heads, looking bored with their assignment "No, sir. Nothing."

"Good. Stay here. We're going inside."

The first guard simply nodded his head and tapped his finger against the IMBEL IA2 machine gun hanging from the strap around his neck. Silva made his way up to the front door and with a light nudge of his fist pushed it open.

"It wasn't locked?" Munroe asked, and Silva shook his head.

"But I assure you no one has been inside yet."

With a wary nod, Munroe pulled out a small black Maglite torch from his coat pocket and clicked it on before cautiously making his way past Silva and into the gloomy abyss of the run-down building, his free hand resting on the gun still in his hip holster.

The dead leaves scattered across the white cracked marble flooring and water-stained walls suggested the abandonment of the building had occurred many years ago. The interior's prime had long since passed, and as Munroe moved his torch beam across the walls he came to a stop at a wide central staircase leading upwards to a small arched window, before it split off to both the left and right and then on to the upper floor. About halfway up, rubble from the desiccated ceiling above had collapsed, blocking entry, and as Munroe now scoped the walls with his torchlight he found only dark rectangular stains where oversized paintings had once hung.

"Cosy," Silva remarked as he appeared behind Munroe, shining his own torch across the dilapidated surroundings. "Whoever used to live here is long gone."

Munroe said nothing and moved further inside as outside the sound of thunder grumbled in the distance and a flash of lightning momentarily lit up the interior before plunging the room back into gloom. The usually sunny Brazilian weather was quickly becoming darkly overcast, and with only the small central staircase window for light the torches were more a necessity than a luxury.

The fleeting illumination had revealed something that caught Munroe's eye, and he trained his torchlight on an open doorway to the left of the staircase. Without a word he moved over to it as the scattered brown leaves crunched beneath his feet.

The door had collapsed inwards, and as Munroe craned his head past the rotted doorframe he shone his torch inside to reveal a set of peeling wooden steps leading downwards to a lower level.

"We'll start down here and work our way up, if we can get past that staircase," Munroe said, quietly now, drawing his gun from its holster as a purely precautionary measure.

Silva did likewise, and with a nod they began to move downwards into the depths of the lower level, the stale smell in the air becoming stronger with every step.

The descent was brief, the staircase short, and at the bottom it opened out into a central corridor off to the left. The once-fine green fabric wallpaper hung ripped and soiled with dark stains, but the thick red carpet looked remarkably untouched by the elements. As Munroe headed down the short narrow passageway he sniffed at the potent stale, musty odour hanging in the air.

At its end stood a single white metal door peppered with rust marks, and after a glance back at Silva Munroe reached for the handle and pushed his way inside. The door swung back effortlessly and even though the rest of place, so far, had been left to rot, Munroe noted that the door hinges had been kept well-oiled. With his gun raised to his chest, he ventured inside and explored the area before him with his torchlight.

The central room was large, with long dusty benches set against the walls and with a large table in the middle. It appeared to act as a reception area, as on either side of the room further corridors ran off, creating separate wings that disappeared into the darkness.

Munroe scanned his torchlight across the cracked white tiled walls and as Silva moved beside him he brought the beam to a rest on a white switch which the detective stepped over to and clicked upwards.

Above them strip lights flickered into life, and one by one the connecting corridors lit up in an incandescent yellow glow, revealing the level's true size. Each of the corridors must have run close to a hundred metres in each direction, and connecting doorways lined the walls leading off to adjoining areas.

"This place is huge," Silva remarked as Munroe made his way over to the left side corridor and stared down it.

"I'll take this one," he said before motioning to the opposite side. "You take that, and shout if you find anything."

For a man who exuded toughness, Silva briefly hesitated before offering a nod and then carefully made his way down the passage as Munroe began heading in the opposite direction. It was impossible to say at a glance what the purpose of this place was, but he noticed that beside some of the doors were large windows, and so he headed to the nearest one first.

The doors he passed all had black numbers stencilled on them, 'A1, B2, C1', and nothing more than that, just reference numbers. As he reached the first window he looked in and felt an unsettling chill run through him of the type he'd not experienced in a while. Rows of desks bolted together sat before a metal counter at the far end of the room, and it was their size that caught his attention. They were for children.

On the walls hung posters one would expect to see in a classroom, except these didn't show images of the solar system or farmyard animals. Instead they showed images of the human anatomy, pressure points, and on one was a diagram of a person slitting a man's throat from ear to ear, with dotted lines indicating the perfect entry point. In that moment Munroe knew exactly what he was looking at, and it unnerved him. This was a training ground, a place to indoctrinate young minds. A place to produce killers to serve their masters, and he had no doubt Icarus had at one time graced these halls... this was his home.

Munroe now gazed up at the symbol emblazoned on the wall behind the teacher's desk, and it only confirmed what he already knew. The artwork had peeled in some places but he could still make it out. It was a symbol he was becoming all too familiar with. A maze, contained within a triangle leading to a central point, a black sun emanating its dark rays outwards.

Daedalus, the master race at play.

"Munroe." Silva's voice echoed down the corridor and he snapped out of his trance immediately and headed back to the main reception area. As he passed the other doors he could only imagine how huge this operation was in scope, and given its size how many kids had been here over the years. The notion of what must have happened here had him feeling twitchy. Of course the idea of kids being trained to be killers from birth was obviously unsettling, but there was something more to it, like a feeling of helplessness. Something he couldn't put his finger on.

"Munroe," Silva shouted for a second time, appearing from a doorway further up the opposite corridor. As Munroe reached him he could see the angry look of disgust on the detective's face. "You need to see this."

Silva stood back as Munroe looked up at the stencilling on the door, a single word.

Reorientation

Munroe entered the room swiftly before coming to an abrupt halt. Once again he felt a chill as he gazed down at the small metal chair in the middle of the room. Four weathered and cracked leather straps hung from slits in the metal where arms and legs could be secured and cables ran from the chair's sides into a wall socket. Above it a red ON/OFF switch had been placed. On one side was a desk, and a metal cage split the room down the middle from left to right. The cage was further split into three compartments, the outer ones large, sandwiching the central one between them, which was much smaller. About the size a small child could fit into. In both of the outer cages lay the desiccated bones of animals, judging by the skulls dogs of some breed, and the middle cage was empty except for a small bowl, maybe used for water or food.

Silva now stepped in behind him and they both stood there in silence for a moment.

"It's a form of conditioning. I've seen it before, but never used on children."

"You've seen or '*done*' it before!" Silva growled aggressively, but Munroe was already shaking his head sternly.

"I've never *done* it," he replied, almost spitting the words angrily, "but I've been told about it."

Munroe took a step over to the cages and flicked his finger towards them. "The subject is placed in the middle cage, with barely enough room to move, and starving dogs are placed in the outer cages and left, sometimes for days. Caught between dogs attempting to attack you on either side and keeping you pinned to where you sit, 24/7, can be excruciating. By the time they're let out, if they haven't lost their minds from fear they become fairly pliable, as you can imagine. Then the subject is placed on the chair and electrocuted over and over again, but there are certain compounds that can be administered which stop the subject from passing out."

Silva still had a look of disgust on his face, but he also looked confused. "What the hell is the point of that?"

"The Soviets tried it during the seventies and I heard some intelligence agencies played around with it. The basic premise is that passing out is, in a way, the body's method of preserving the mind. There's only so much pain a mind can handle... but, if you can't pass out, then the body deals with it in another way. The idea is that under the right circumstances the mind can fracture and create two personalities. It's seen in severely abused children who develop multiple personalities. Stronger personalities develop who can defend the original from the ongoing trauma. The mind's way of protecting the child's original personality."

Munroe felt sickened by what he was explaining but he compartmentalised it as he'd been trained to do. Silva sounded far more emotional, and not without reason.

"It's sick," he protested, as if it were Munroe's idea in the first place. "What good can come of it?"

Munroe took a final solemn look at the chair and then he turned to face the understandably troubled detective.

"To create people who wouldn't even know who they were… The perfect assassin, lying dormant until the right stimuli was given – the word, sentence or whatever they've been conditioned to respond to." Munroe walked past Silva and into the hallway and gazed over at the rows of doorways most likely hiding similar horrors. "And it looks like they managed it."

"Who are *they*?" Silva replied, and Munroe shot him a look of uncertainty. He couldn't tell the man about Daedalus and what they were, but Christ he wanted to. "I don't know."

"Bullshit, Munroe. They're the same people who torched the church, covering their tracks for a reason only you appear to know. Fucking McCitrick and his secrecy bullshit."

Munroe remained silent as Silva continued to unload. It was better to let the man get everything off his chest. "And if they took care of all those people in the church, why did they leave this place standing?"

It was a fair point, but Munroe didn't have an answer. "I honestly don't know, Detective. But I want to."

"Yeah," Silva spewed angrily, his cheeks darkening under the yellow glow of the strip lights above them. "Well, I would love to meet these sick bastards face to face."

Above them the lights suddenly blinked out as corridor by corridor the whole building descended into pitch darkness. Munroe immediately clicked on his torch and shone it upwards between them. He listened for any sounds but there was nothing. He turned his attention back to Silva and pulled his gun from his holster. "Careful what you wish for, Detective. I think you're about to get your chance."

Chapter 22

"Captain Munroe, it's a pleasure to meet you, even under these awkward circumstances."

The voice boomed through the corridors and Munroe immediately shone his torchlight upwards to its source: a flat, grated speaker, along with others equally spaced and set into the ceiling above them. "Despite the ideas running through your mind at this moment I can promise you that we have no wish to hurt you or Detective Silva. I only offer an introduction in the hopes we can talk. My name is Bauer, Hans Bauer, and if you will please come back outside I offer you the promise of protection and discussion on what you think you may have discovered."

Munroe glanced over at Silva, who shrugged his shoulders.

"He's not one of mine. I've never heard of him."

"Me neither," Munroe replied, turning his torch down to the floor between them, allowing them to be partially lit up from the reflection off the shiny white floor tiles. "But if they're the same ones who burnt down the church then he has no interest in talking. More like silencing. Could your two men upstairs be involved?"

Silva was already shaking his head. "Never. I know them personally."

"Then I'm sorry to say, Detective, that they are most likely incapacitated." Munroe didn't want to admit the likelihood that his colleagues were probably already dead but by the pained look on Silva's face he already understood the reality.

"Who the hell are these people, Mr Munroe?"

Munroe still couldn't tell the man, but he could tell him *what* they were. "They're trained killers. No compassion. No empathy... No fucking soul, if they are who I think they are, and they won't give us free passage out of here regardless of whether we talk to them or not. This Bauer and his goons up there are sick bastards. The kind of degenerates who pick pieces of sweetcorn out of poo as a hobby. Know what I mean?"

Silva looked confused by the unusual analogy and he shook his head. "Not really, Mr Munroe."

"Forget it, bad example," Munroe replied, putting aside his poor attempt at levity. "Suffice to say parley is not an option with these people. How many rounds do you have?"

Silva flicked open his revolver displaying the five chambered bullets it held and then tapped at a round metal quick changer holding a further five. "That's all... you?"

"Two magazines and the one I have loaded. Who knows if it's enough. We'll have to play it smart. I'm going up there to meet with this Bauer, and you cover me from the staircase. The moment he shows his face you shoot him in the head and we'll fight our way out from there."

By the shocked expression on Silva's face the idea of shooting a man in cold blood was not something he was happy about, and Munroe now clamped his hand onto the detective's shoulder. "I know it sounds cold, but all we'll get from these killers is torture and a slow death. Believe me, I know. We don't have much of an option, so after I've lulled him into a false sense of security you make sure you blow the back of his fucking head off. No misses. Understand?"

Silva was now wide-eyed, and to say the man looked uncomfortable was an understatement. He offered a jerky nod of his head as from the speaker above the voice of Hans Bauer crackled into life once again.

"Err, gentlemen. You might want to know that this is a two-way speaker system."

The revelation had Silva rolling his eyes and he gritted his teeth in angst as Munroe replied, "Well, our cards are on the table then, Mr Bauer, so you better come and get us."

There was silence for a moment, and then the suddenly the strip lights flickered back on and two black canisters dropped onto the floor of the reception area at the end of the corridor. Sparks flared outwards from their lids and dark plumes of smoke began to puff out from them, filling the area in a thick grey mist. Through it the hazy shapes of three men wearing gas masks began to emerge.

–

Up on the ground level the sound of shots echoed up the stairwell and into the main hallway as Hans Bauer, surrounded by eight armed guards, stood next to the main entrance and pressed his finger against a red speaker button contained inside a small hidden panel within the wall. "There is no way out of the basement, Mr Munroe. Please, for your own sake, stop resisting and let my men bring you upstairs. Despite what you may believe I have no interest in killing you. Consider it a professional courtesy between two warriors."

The sound of scuffling feet and coughing could be heard on the other end, and then Munroe's voice came across the speaker loud and clear.

"You're not a warrior, Bauer, and this place is vast. I doubt you have enough grenades to fill it completely with smoke. You should also know Detective Silva has just alerted his men and they're already on their way. Why don't you just clear out and we'll chalk this one up to experience."

Bauer smugly chuckled at the desperate ploy, and he pressed the speaker button once again. "Oh I doubt that, Mr Munroe, and even if they did arrive my men would ensure they never made it past the front gates."

There was a moment of silence and then Munroe came back on the line. "I'm sending one of your boys up alive, so don't shoot. Consider it a professional courtesy."

From the stairwell one of the guards wearing a navy-coloured flak jacket and body armour appeared and stumbled over to the other men, limping due to the gunshot wound to his shin. He pulled off his gas mask and dropped it to the floor, his face shining from the sweat and his teeth gritted together. "Bastards are holed up tightly. Those corridors are death traps, sir. If we had bulletproof shields we could take them easily."

"We don't have any, though, do we, idiot," Bauer growled, furious at, as he saw it, his men's incompetence. "Where are Delany and Josef?"

"Delany took one in the thigh and Josef is with him in the main reception room."

"And where are Munroe and his friend?"

"They're about halfway up corridor Z3. They're using the rooms for cover."

Another barrage of gunshots could now be heard and Munroe's voice came back on through the speaker.

"You're going to need more men, Hans. These two look like they've had enough."

Bauer looked furious and he pushed the injured man towards the main entrance. "Get yourself back to HQ and get cleaned up." He turned to the guard next to him. "Use the back entrance to the rear of the building. It leads to the lower level and the other end of corridor Z3, you know where it is. I'll stay here and cover the stairwell. Take the other half of the men. When you find them throw down a couple of flashbangs and we'll breach from this side. We'll sandwich the pricks."

The guard looked unsure of the order and he leant in closer to Bauer, not wanting the other men to hear. "Why don't we just blow the whole place up, sir? We were going to level the building anyway, we have the ordinance."

Bauer gazed back at him with an icy stare, not liking his orders questioned. "I want Munroe alive. What he knows could prove an asset to us."

"Yes, sir." Two more gas-masked guards appeared at the stairwell, one helping the other with a bloody wound in his thigh out through the main entrance. "And Detective Silva?"

Bauer watched the two wounded guards exit, looking furious. The death of his men was acceptable, and he had little if no compassion. Their type were nothing more than meat for the grinder, collateral damage, but the fact that Munroe and some two-bit cop were making them look foolish was what truly made his blood boil. "I don't give a fuck about Silva, but Munroe lives. Until we've had time to extract any information. Understand? I'll be waiting."

The guard nodded sternly and with a click of his fingers to summon the others he headed outside through the front entrance, and they began making their way around to the rear of the building. Bauer unclicked a radio from his belt and laid it next to the red speaker button. "I appreciate you not killing my men, Mr Munroe. But how are we going to get this resolved? You can't stay down there for ever."

"You could offer safe passage and we go our separate ways." Munroe's voice crackled over the speaker, his throat now sounding strained as he coughed loudly. "I'm sure we'll meet again."

The coughing drew a smile from Bauer. "Yes, the smoke will get you. It's eyewatering. But seeing as we could be here a while, why don't we chat, Mr Munroe."

"By all means," Munroe replied, stifling the cough he wanted to unload.

"Tobias Kessler told me about your little back and forth, and I must say your escape was impressive. Pity for you it was too late to make a difference back at the Houses of Parliament. Such an ancient institution, ripe for a change, wouldn't you agree?"

More sounds of coughing could now be heard and Munroe took a moment to clear his throat. "Just shy of a thousand years, Hans. It makes your boys' twelve years in power look rather pitiful, wouldn't you say? My AOL account lasted longer than that."

"Maybe so, but our second time will last a lot longer than that. That's where the name Daedalus comes from. We may have flown too close to the sun first time around, but this time those wings will never melt. That's what our symbol represents. A pyramid that, despite the passage of time, has remained the only man-made constant since the dawn of civilisation. Then the maze concealing the core, the all-seeing eye radiating its hidden power over all it surveys. And it would appear we have more in common than you think. We're both looking for Icarus, aren't we? I wonder who will get to him first."

Bauer released the speaker button just as a hushed voice came over the radio lying next to it.

"In position and ready to breach on your signal, sir."

Bauer picked up the radio. One of the guards passed him a gas mask, which he slipped on, and then he went to stand at the back of the line of men forming up at the top of the stairwell, each with one hand on the shoulder of the man in front, an M4 machine gun readied in the other.

"Breach," Bauer whispered into the radio, and seconds later the sound of flashbangs could be heard down below in the lower level as his group now zipped downstairs in unison with Bauer trailing at the rear.

The smoke from the previous smoke grenades had dispersed along the other corridors, leaving a mist which could be seen though easily, and as the line of guards piled into the reception area and forward down the corridor, Bauer saw the flashes of muzzle fire as he shouted into the radio, his voice muffled due to the gas mask.

"I want him alive." He barged his way past the guards to a room where the other unit had already entered as someone inside yelled "Clear!"

With smug satisfaction Bauer came to a halt and stared down at the two men splayed out on the floor before him, and for the first time gazed into the eyes of Captain Ethan Munroe and Detective Silva.

Only it wasn't them.

Delany and Josef, the two wounded guards, lay before him unconscious and with moist eyes due to the smoke. They had been stripped down to their briefs, and an array of shirts and clothes had been used to bind and gag them. On the floor between them sat an iPhone that had been put on loudspeaker.

"Sorry, Hans but we had to step out. Sure you understand." Munroe's voice boomed from the mobile's speaker. "You know, I thought you'd be brighter for a man in your position."

Bauer picked up the mobile and hurled it against the wall with such ferocity that the device shattered into pieces, and then he yelled at the top of his voice, "Find them."

–

Munroe hung up the call and passed the phone to Silva before accelerating the black Range Rover along the dirt road in the direction of the airport. "Make the call to your people. And you can take that off now."

"Who are those people?" Silva yelled in frustration, removing his mask as he tapped a number into the iPhone and placed it to his ear.

"Better you don't know," Munroe replied, swerving past a deep pothole, "but when we get to the airport you should contact your government immediately. These are not the kind of people you want on your doorstep."

From their position in the corridor in the depths of Dr Ferreira's school of re-education the three men with gas masks coming through the smoke had been easy targets. Then a change of clothes later, once the other guard had retreated back upstairs and after tying up and gagging the two guards, Munroe had simply left Silva's phone and called it using his, then walked up the stairs and out of the front door to the waiting Range Rover. No one, not even Bauer, had given them a glance, and seconds later they were driving out the front gate as they watched the team of guards heading to the rear of the house.

Silva had almost given the game away when they saw the dead Brazilian soldiers lying on the ground outside the building's entrance, each with a single gunshot to the head, but the detective had kept his anger in check. From what Munroe knew of Silva, the man would not be the kind of person to let it go, and even though he understood how he felt the very nature of Daedalus meant any investigation would lead nowhere.

"I'm sorry about your men," Munroe offered respectfully. "These people will pay, I promise."

"Easy for you to say, Mr Munroe. I'm still in the dark about all this, and they were colleagues of mine."

Silva cut the conversation short as his call was picked up and he started barking orders which sounded more like a cry for help. "It's Silva. Just listen. I'm five miles from Cândido Godói and heading for Santa Rosa airport on the south side. Approaching the main underpass. I need you to meet us en route. We're driving a black Range Rover. Leave two men at the church and bring everyone else now. Do it." Silva shouted his last sentence so loudly that he ended up spitting on the receiver of his phone and he wiped it off against his shirt before slipping the mobile into his trouser pocket. "It won't take them long to meet us, and Bauer and his cronies would have to be crazy to take on the Brazilian military."

Don't bet on it, Munroe thought to himself. He swerved off the dirt road and pulled onto the main road that would lead them to the small airport and the waiting jet, less than seven miles from their location. From there it would take a couple of hours to get back to Sloan and the waiting C-130, but apart from learning more about Daedalus and meeting Hans Bauer Munroe felt as if he was hitting a dead end. For Silva, though, it was the beginning. Knowing Daedalus, the investigation would hit the skids before it even started.

"I'm sorry, I really am, but I'm not at liberty to say anything. I will speak to McCitrick and explain what went on. And call me Ethan, will you?"

Silva sat there broodingly, and with his hands clenched he looked as if he were about to slam his fists down on the dashboard in frustration. Suddenly his expression blanked out as in the distance they heard a booming explosion. As it subsided Silva turned to stare at Munroe, a look of alarm on his face. "What the fuck was that?"

Munroe didn't have the chance to reply, because at that very moment he was distracted by a huge shadow that had crossed over the windscreen of the car.

The burst of fire from the Gatling gun ripped through the tarmac in front of them with ease, shredding the top layer like an erupting earthquake, and Munroe jabbed at the brakes as overhead a helicopter flew past and began to make an arching turn in the sky back towards them.

Munroe recognised the shape and lack of sound instantly. It was the same stealth helicopter he'd seen over Waterloo Bridge during Icarus's escape, and as it began making a sharp turn he had to admire the grease work that had gone into this aircraft. It came close to turning on a dime and the entire fuselage was contained within its grey metal frame, no exhaust visible.

Where did they get this thing?

Munroe slammed the accelerator down hard and began hurtling towards a small overpass just ahead of them, but the speed of the helicopter was tremendous, and as the sound of the on-board Gatling gun began to whir into action again it sent down a volley of destruction. The heavy ammunition tore up the road and then the concrete above them as Munroe came to a screeching halt directly underneath the underpass.

"We'll never outrun that," Silva shouted as a shroud of dust engulfed them, the passing rotors of the helicopter churning up the damage from off the road as it began to circle overhead.

Silva was right, and Munroe was already weighing up his options, or lack of them. There seemed to be only one option, and it was dependent on one thing.

"How long will it take your guys to reach us?"

"A few minutes, if that. We're only a couple of miles from the church's commune."

"And what firepower do they have?"

"Only what you saw, but the guns on the jeeps are 50mms. That helicopter looks armoured, but our guns will make one hell of a dent."

"Good," Munroe replied, exiting the car as above the stealth helicopter was already turning back towards the overpass. "Get out and hug the concrete. And stay down."

To Silva's credit he did exactly as he was told without hesitation as Munroe slipped the automatic gearstick in neutral and then pulled out his Maglite torch and jammed it between the top of the footwell and the accelerator, sending the engine into a high-pitched wail as the engine hit maximum revolutions. He then slapped the gearstick into drive and the vehicle sped off, its wheels flinging up dust in its wake, and Munroe jumped down to join Silva as overhead the helicopter saw its opportunity and skimmed past, quickly catching up to the black Range Rover.

Remarkably the car stayed on the road, maintaining a straight line for over a hundred metres, and it was only when the Gatling gun delivered its next barrage that the force of the bullets to the vehicle's roof caused it to swerve and career off into the nearest field. But it kept going for a short while further until finally it crossed into a ditch and slammed to a juddering halt as the bonnet crumpled and the vehicle's roof was hit by another round from the Gatling gun.

As Munroe watched the helicopter begin to descend for landing, Silva was already back on the mobile and speaking with his team.

"Do you see it? Yes, it's a fucking helicopter... engage it."

The stealth helicopter came within a few metres of landing as the small convoy of military jeeps appeared speeding down the opposite road towards it, and then it swiftly raised back up into the sky and was already turning as the first bullets hit its side.

The jeeps were too far away to deal any serious damage, and their shots were all over the place, but as they closed the gap and raced towards the wrecked Range Rover, the aircraft now picked up speed, staying low to the ground. Within moments it was just a dot on the horizon, and Munroe stood back up and watched the jeeps reaching their torn-up vehicle as Silva directed them to the underpass. With a wave from Munroe the military convoy turned towards them and Silva passed him back the phone.

"That was as close as I like to get, Ethan. I'll take the convoy back to Dr Ferreira's *school*, or whatever that place is, and find what we can."

Munroe was already shaking his head. "They'll already have gone, and I'll wager the building is being turned to rubble as we speak. That distant explosion we heard before the helicopter attacked. You can bet that was them."

Silva looked unconvinced. "Either way we're going back there."

Munroe was in agreement, and he began walking towards the jeep convoy approaching them when his iPhone began to ring. He didn't recognise the number but he tapped the green accept button and placed it to his ear. "Munroe."

"Ethan."

The voice sounded hoarse, but even with only his name spoken he recognised it immediately. He instinctively stared over at Silva, who was more interested in the first jeep that was pulling up to a full stop before them.

"Icarus."

Christ, the killer's timing was impeccable.

The line went silent for a moment and then Icarus began to speak. "Don't say anything, and don't bother trying to track this call. Just listen. It's time we met. I'm now in a position to tell you everything you want to know. Your family, Daedalus, everything. I offer you an invitation, but it is for you and you alone. And don't be foolish. If I see any authorities then you get nothing, and the only time you'll see me again is just before I slit your throat. I don't take deception well, my friend, but I think you already know that."

The line went silent but Munroe kept quiet, even though his first question was how the hell did this madman get his mobile number. But he restrained himself until Icarus began to speak again.

"Tell me, Ethan. When was the last time you visited New Orleans?"

Chapter 23

The excitement in the air was electric and infectious as preparations for the Mardi Gras parade ramped up along Bourbon Street in the French Quarter of New Orleans. Party revellers were already getting into the spirit, along with a multitude of colourful outfits whose owners were preparing for the three-day drinkathon. It was clear this year would be no less outrageous than the years before. Many were just sucking in the atmosphere, enjoying the calm before the storm, with a few groggy bar patrons sat in doorways, who had already got a head start on celebrations the night before. By the smiles gracing everyone's faces it was clear that they all planned to squeeze every last drop of fun from the occasion, with the exception of one, who was making his way down the street quickly, with his Chicago Cubs baseball hat pulled firmly down over his face.

Michael Hanks was a man who knew how to blend into a crowd, and anyone who saw him wouldn't have batted an eyelid at the man, but as the revellers and tourists alike sucked in the vibrant ambience of New Orleans, gearing up for the wild night ahead, he had far more serious things on his mind.

Hanks came to a stop outside Dr Bute's House of Voodoo and glanced in through the window to the unpleasant mix of skulls and dark trinkets. He could already smell the heavy scent of opium joss sticks and as he entered the smell only got stronger.

The shop was empty of customers and as he made his way across to the counter he found the clutter claustrophobic. There was not a single bare space inside with every corner of the shop filled with the kind of crap, eclectic useless pieces of spiritual garbage that tourists happily passed over their hard-earned cash for, to gain a small slice of New Orleans mystery.

"Jesus, *Dr Bute*, you trying to poison customers or sell to them?" Hanks said, wafting his hand back and forth at the swirls of blue smoke hanging in the air.

Dr Bute stood behind the counter looking stoic with a white frilly shirt, black waistcoat and strings of black pearly beads dangling from around his neck. "You're back then," he said in a thick Jamaican accent, leaning back against the glass cupboards, stacked full of black candles, home-made oils, gris-gris bags and all centred around a pathetic-looking stuffed white chicken that had seen better days. "'Ow was the business trip, Michael?"

"Fine, just fine," Hanks said, swiping away a dried-out bat carcass hanging above him by a piece of thin nylon. "When you said you were going to rearrange the shop front I didn't know you meant make it shittier than it already was."

Dr Bute raised his long finger and waved it warningly. "You'd be wise not to insult the spirits in this place, Michael. It's bad juju, bombaclaat."

"Shut up, Ralph," Hanks replied, pointing his finger at Dr Bute, "and I keep telling you, voodoo's Haitian, not Jamaican, you prick. Get the accent right, you sound like an idiot."

Dr Bute's whole cool, laid-back demeanour evaporated and he stood up straight. "Screw you, Mike," he replied in a thick New York accent.

Hanks was already heading for the draped multi-coloured beads covering the back stairwell. "I won't be long." He disappeared up the stairs as Dr Bute flicked the bird after him. "You never are," he replied, resuming his Jamaican inflection. "Pasty rassclaat."

Dr Bute's House of Voodoo was just a front, one of many safehouses used for Daedalus operations, and like the others the hired shopkeeper had no real idea of its actual purpose.

Hanks produced a Yale key from his pocket and slipped it into the lock of the heavy metal door. With a turn it creaked open and he headed inside before flipping the wall light switch. It was a typical back office housing an old wooden desk, with scenic pictures of New Orleans hanging from the lime-green painted walls. Hanks locked the door behind him and sat down at the desk before unlocking one of the side drawers and then pressing his finger against a small indentation inside it. A compartment rose upwards from the centre of the desk's surface, revealing a monitor and keypad, which Hanks began to tap on. One password later and a thin metal strut unfolded automatically from the monitor's casing into a retina scanner which Hanks dutifully rested his face against. After a dull beam of light passed across his pupil the monitor lit up and the scanner retracted and folded back to its original position.

Hanks leant back in his chair thoughtfully. The coming conversation could determine his future, whether long and illustrious or short and unrealised.

Hanks tapped his passcode into the blinking cursor box and after stretching his shoulders he waited.

Then he waited some more.

Five minutes passed until the image of a man popped onto the screen, and Hanks felt his body stiffen as Hans Bauer began to speak.

"I got your message, Michael. I assume you're back stateside? Where?"

Bauer's voice was calm, almost jovial in an unnerving way, and Hanks gave a swift nod. "One of our outposts, sir, but it's a secure line. I just arrived and tracking squads are on the ground looking for Icarus as requested."

"What news?"

"No contact as yet, sir, but it's early days."

"But we don't have days, Michael. We need this put to a stop now."

"I agree, sir, and we will have him back on a leash. I promise you that. I already have the teams—"

"I'm sure you do," Bauer interrupted, his eyes becoming cold and ungiving, "but what I would like to know is how he got away from you after we spent so much political capital on scooping him away from the UK police."

This was the part that Hanks had been dreading, but he raised his chin upwards confidently in near defiance. "We trained him well, perhaps too well, sir. It was a miscalculation on my part in trusting Davies to carry out Icarus's interrogation. The idiot didn't give him the respect he needed and our boy Icarus took advantage of that fact. He killed him and escaped before I returned. Davies was a poor choice, but I take full responsibility for putting my trust in him."

Bauer stared silently at him and Hanks knew to now keep his mouth shut. There was little to explain except that he'd screwed up, and he banked on his previous operational record redeeming him.

Bauer continued to stare for a few more uncomfortable seconds before leaning closer to the screen. "There can be no more fuck-ups, otherwise... well, you know what happens to those who betray our life's work, brethren or not."

Hanks felt a wave of relief crash over him. He was being given a second chance, and it would not be wasted. "I understand, sir, and thank you. Your faith in me won't be squandered."

Bauer sat back from the screen, his eyes still intently displaying menace. "I hope not, for your sake. You don't want me knocking at your door, Michael."

Hanks only nodded respectfully as he now sought to move the conversation along. "And how goes the operation?"

"Operation Icarus is on course after some readjustments. The action we took in Parliament has opened just the opportunity we expected. Because of Ambassador Breams's termination of the German Chancellor, and now the glorious takedown of Parliament, we have forged a new path to our destination." Bauer now smiled, showing the whites of his teeth. "High command is pleased."

The very mention had Hanks sitting up proudly, but it was short-lived. "But I've not mentioned your recent indiscretion, and I suggest you ensure I can keep it that way. Find Icarus, and use every one of our networks if need be. The moment you lay eyes on that wild animal you let me know. I want regular updates in the coming hours."

Over the top of the monitor something stirred, and the metal door to the office swung open slowly on the weight of its frame. Hanks's mouth dropped open.

He'd not even heard the lock being picked.

Stood in the doorway, wearing a bright flowery Mardi Gras T-shirt, and pointing a 9mm Glock directly at Hanks, was Icarus. He raised his finger to his lips and then moved over to the side of the monitor, out of view, and directed Hanks's eyes back down to the screen as Bauer continued delivering his orders.

"I won't have Icarus self-destructing and ruining the same plans he helped create. The Core feels we have no option. He's too dangerous and knows too much to be allowed to roam freely... Are you paying attention?"

Icarus slammed the butt of his gun into Hanks's skull, sending him off the seat and to the ground before taking his place in the chair and staring into the eyes of Bauer. "Hello, Hans."

Bauer looked momentarily shocked, his mouth opening slightly, but he immediately slipped back into character as Icarus continued to speak.

"High command feels they have no option, Hans? Interesting way to put it, when they chose the option to have me killed."

Bauer looked unrattled and he was already shaking his head. "That's not true, David."

Icarus snorted at the remark. "Only you could deliver a lie steeped in such bullshit and keep a straight face. And my name is Icarus. It's a testament to all the others you had no 'option' but to kill."

"There was no option, my friend, they were nothing like you. And you are nothing like them. Not until you decided to kill those two MI6 agents."

Icarus dismissed the notion with a limp flick of his wrist and he rolled his eyes sarcastically. "They weren't government spooks, Hans, they were DS5. Fair game as far as I could see."

Bauer was looking frustrated, but his tone of voice was calm. "Either way, it was a poor decision. But it doesn't matter anymore. Were back on track, and all I ask is that you come back to us, *Icarus*. It's time to come home and be a part of the future... our future."

Icarus stared at the screen blankly and then stretched out his arm and hovered his finger above the keyboard's return button. "I appreciate the offer, you back-stabbing Judas, but I have my own agenda now. And it doesn't include you."

Icarus tapped on the keypad and the monitor went blank as he now turned to Hanks's unconscious body. "But it does include you."

He hauled the man up off the floor and dumped him back into the seat before ripping the long power cord from the monitor and then binding Hanks's hands to the chair securely, whereupon he delivered a couple of sharp slaps to the man's face until Hanks groggily opened his eyes.

"I'm afraid I'm not going to be able to offer you the same professional courtesy you once offered me, Mikey boy."

Hanks said nothing, his eyes still glazing due to the blow, and he watched as Icarus stood over him, a cold unsettling smile spreading across his face. "I have some hours to kill, if you don't mind the pun, and I'm sure we can find something to keep us both occupied.

Hanks's eyes now widened in fear as Icarus pulled a Sheffield knife from his pocket and unfolded it delicately between his fingers. "So, Michael. Where should we begin?"

Chapter 24

The golden light of the rising sun seeped across the city skyline like a welcome guest, washing away the darkness of the night before, and illuminating the face of the man standing by the side of the road. He closed his eyes and allowed the warmth to fill every pore in his skin, before slowly breathing in a lungful of the crisp, moist air and relishing the sweet smell of fresh dew. His senses felt heightened, and in that moment the sound of birds chirping the arrival of a new day gently vibrated in his ears.

The man slowly opened his eyes and looked across the road, his vision blurry at first, to the Ford Sierra and the glint of sunlight reflecting off its white paint. The windows were dark but as his vision became focused they lightened and he raised his hands and waved to the blonde woman sitting in the driver's seat, as behind her a small girl with blonde braided hair flicked her tiny palms back and forth, desperate to get his attention.

The man slowly waved back, and now the little girl's eyes widened excitedly in acknowledgement, and she pressed a furry white unicorn up to the window and waved its hoof before shrieking in laughter as the woman glanced back at him with a loving smile.

The man lowered his hand and took a single step forward, but then hesitated as the little girl's face began to contort and her smile now transformed into a look of terror and she screamed. Behind her flames began creeping forward until they lapped up the side of the window, and although the man attempted to leap forward he found his feet fixed to the pavement. With his arm raised outwards a single word screamed from the girl's mouth before her face was consumed in a burst of flames.

"*Daddy!*"

"Ethan!" A voice called out from the gloom. "Munroe!"

Munroe's eyes flipped open to see Sloan leaning towards him.

"You all right?" she asked, and after few moments to get his bearings he acknowledged her with a grunt and then sat up as he rubbed his eyes.

"Sounded like you were having a nightmare," she said, and then reached into her trouser pocket and pushed something into his face. "Stick of gum?" Sloan asked, holding out the yellow strip of Juicy Fruit pinched between her fingers.

"I don't know. I never remember my dreams," Munroe replied, taking the piece, unwrapping it and folding it in to his mouth.

"Personally I prefer Hubba Bubba, but it's all we've got," she said before returning her attention to the disassembly of her silenced M9A3 handgun which both of them had received as part of McCitrick's care package on board the C-130 Hercules. Except for the two pilots, they were the only passengers on the cargo hauler and apart from another inflight refuelling a few hours ago the trip had been as uneventful as expected. Munroe's discovery back in Brazil had left him feeling troubled. Even though he was able to put the horrors of what those children must have gone through to one side, to compartmentalise the knowledge, it had left him with a sour feeling in his bones. It had also given him a conflicting viewpoint of Icarus. This in itself was unsettling given everything the man had done, but nonetheless he was caught between empathy for the child the killer had been, and the psychotic depraved killer the man had become. Jax, on the other hand, appeared more pissed off that she had not been involved in his Brazilian excursion, and although she had made no vocal complaints he could tell she felt left out of the loop. Perhaps it made her feel out of control, and that was the feeling that those in their position abhorred the most.

Munroe had left Silva to check out Dr Ferreira's 'school' building alone, and although he had heard nothing back as yet he figured no news would be good news. Daedalus had a good track record of cleaning up after themselves and despite allowing their escape he guessed this was not the last time he would cross paths with Hans Bauer.

Bauer.

He'd only just met him and Munroe already despised the man. Self-righteous, trustworthy as a snake, and an honest-to-God modern-day Nazi to boot. The man was a turd, pure and simple, but they did have one thing in common.

They both wanted Icarus.

Had Bauer let slip that Daedalus were also looking for him by mistake, or had his ego told him they would never live to tell anyone about it? Either way it gave some context to Icarus's actions, and with no one to turn to he had made a call to Munroe. But *why* still wasn't clear, although his invite to New Orleans could soon fill the gaps. Or get Munroe killed.

He'd already contacted McCitrick and debriefed him on the situation and the section head had agreed that they should go alone. Such was the DS5 ethos, but more importantly they couldn't afford to scare him off, and with the three kings now waging full-out war on Daedalus it was a lead they could not screw up.

"If he wants you then let's give the man what he wants." McCitrick had said bluntly. His only stipulation was that Jax back him up.

Munroe looked over at Sloan, and he was glad to have her at his side. Upon take-off the conversation had been light and he had dozed off as Sloan had set about disassembling and then reassembling her Beretta multiple times. Some people might have seen it as nervous repetition, but he saw it for what it was... focus.

Munroe chewed on the gum and attempted to remember the dream he had been having. Although it had already faded from his mind he knew it had not been pleasant. He snapped back into reality and focused on his colleague and her continuing obsession with the firearm. She was doing it to pass the time, but he couldn't help think it was more of a cathartic affair for the captain.

"I think it's in perfect working order," Munroe said, loosening the tight muscles in his shoulders with a stretch.

"Thanks, Ethan, but I knew that after the first time."

Jaqueline Sloan was an interesting soul and, despite the mostly cold demeanour, Munroe liked her. She spoke little but always seemed ready to go at a moment's notice, from what he had seen of her so far. What he did know about her, which was not a lot, was that her grasp of situations was solid, and she was able to think outside the box. Just what a unit like DS5 needed. She was, though, a tough nut to crack when it came to personal information. It was understandably an important trait given the clandestine and secretive nature of the Disavowed, which she wore with pride, but it wasn't the reason she had remained so quiet, and Munroe knew it. Before falling asleep he'd been conducting something of a test to see if she would crack first under the boredom of the flight and disclose some, any, personal information, but it seemed she was staying true to her word. She was a woman that kept to what she said, and expected the same from others. After so many hours of near silence he decided to end the deadlock. "So, do you finally fancy telling me about yourself?"

Sloan slid the firing pin spring back into the Beretta's slide and then looked up at him blankly.

"I don't fancy saying anything. Like I told you back on the *Elizabeth*, you first."

Munroe noted a slight curving at the corner of her mouth and he could tell she felt she'd won the waiting game, and he was now happy to oblige her. "Fair enough," he said, settling into his seat. "I spent most of my life in the military, and most of those years embedded with special forces. The SAS was always the pinnacle of my dreams as a kid. The excitement, danger, and knowing what you do has meaning. That's the thing with growing up as an orphan, you have a need to belong from a young age. To something… to anything. For some people it develops into anger, resentment at not having the usual parental bond, but for me I wanted to seek out my place in the world, and I did. The military gave me that home."

Sloan stopped assembling her handgun; she was now watching him intently as Munroe continued, and there was no hint of sadness in his voice, only a matter-of-fact confidence in the decisions he had made.

"For any grunt in the forces the belief in serving for Queen and country is only a half truth. The deeper reason is they do it for their family and those they love, that's the driving factor. They play out the most rudimentary of human traits. To protect our families. But for me my family became the country and all she stands for."

"That's a very mature and philosophical way to look at it," Sloan noted, delivering the sentence with a friendly sarcasm.

"*That's* the hostage negotiator in me. Negotiating is a battle of wits with potentially deadly consequences, but it wasn't an art I'd fully realised when still in the forces. I met my wife while serving with the SAS. She was working with the Red Cross in Afghanistan. Our paths crossed and a year later we were married. Nine months after that and our daughter was born."

"What were their names?"

"My wife's name was Natalie, and our daughter Lucy."

"Lucy's a pretty name. Good choice," Sloan replied, continuing her reassembling of the Beretta. "So what happened?"

Munroe hesitated, and though Sloan noticed the change in him she didn't say anything until he began to talk again.

"Do you remember the bombing in Edinburgh town centre a few years ago?"

"IRA?"

"Yes," he replied bluntly. "More accurately the 'Real IRA' as they call themselves. The group that formed after the peace process. Extremists are only afraid of one thing in this life, and that's peace."

Sloan said nothing but she gave a solemn nod in agreement as Munroe continued.

"Parked car full of explosives. Killed eight civilians, including my wife and little girl."

"Christ, Ethan. I'm sorry."

"Went to get fish and chips for us all and the bomb went off as I was heading back to the car. The blast knocked me out cold and I woke up in a hospital bed to a policeman telling me what I'd lost."

Munroe appeared to become momentarily lost in the story, the pain still raw despite the years past, but he then cleared his throat with a cough and was back in control. "Spent a couple of days in hospital and after the funeral I threw myself back into my work. I hoped it would give me something to focus on, and it did for a while, but I had an incident that convinced me I wasn't cut out for that type of stuff anymore, and I was granted an honourable discharge."

"It was the incident part I was curious about. McCitrick was tight-lipped about that. What happened?"

That Sloan had skipped over the tragedy of his family told Munroe one of two things. She was either colder than he had taken her for, or smart enough not to want him dwelling on such things. Munroe was sure it was the latter.

"My team were tasked with gathering intel from a small Afghan village in Helmand Province. Usual seek and reap. We were embedded with a Royal Marine unit at the time and after a series of contacts from the Taliban we made it inside, but not before we lost two soldiers along the way. That's the problem with that kind of warfare, you never know who's a civilian and who's the enemy. We ended up interrogating a man after finding a buried arms cache and it was clear he didn't know anything. Guy was shit-scared and just trying to protect his family, but a couple of the marines were pretty riled up and convinced otherwise."

Munroe paused momentarily and then shook his head. "You can train a soldier to deal with most anything, but dealing with seeing your friends blown apart is not one of them. As you can imagine, things got out of hand, and they went off the deep end. One of them placed a gun to the head of the man's daughter and threatened to shoot her if he didn't tell them what they wanted to hear."

Munroe glanced down at the floor pensively and visualised in his mind what had come next. "First time in my career that I snapped. The soldier was wrong to do it, war or no war, but all I could see was the fear on that girl's face. She was terrified, and in that moment her expression was somehow... so familiar."

Sloan now put down the Beretta and leant towards him humbly with her hands together. "She reminded you of Lucy."

"She really did. I'm not sure why, but her face and that look of fear still haunts me to this day."

"What did you do?" Sloan asked, and Munroe gazed up at her and blankly.

"I shot him."

The admission hung in the air like a bad smell, and Sloan stared at him with curiosity. There was no malice or disgust in her expression, but rather one of sombre understanding as Munroe sought to set the record straight.

"He wasn't killed, although after a gunshot to the knee he won't be appearing on *Strictly* any time soon."

It was strange that the captain showed little change in her demeanour upon hearing the man had survived, but Munroe didn't put any weight in her reaction, or lack thereof, and he finished off his story as matter-of-factly as he could.

"I was arrested on the spot and brought up on charges, but the top brass took mercy on me and after some legal wrangling gave me an honourable discharge."

"How did you manage that?" Sloan asked, now looking more surprised than shocked.

"With all the special operations I was involved in I think they decided it was better to let me go silently than open any potential can of worms, and so off I went. You know the rest."

They both sat there silently for a few moments and then Sloan nodded softly. "Can't say I blame you, Ethan, and given what you'd been through, and then seeing a trained marine putting a gun to a little girl's head..." she let her breath release through her lips with a whistle. "That bastard should have been court-martialled himself. That's no way for a soldier to act, I don't care how dire the circumstances are."

The comment relaxed Munroe. He felt the same way, but actually hearing it from someone else's lips was reaffirming. "So, Captain," he said, flipping the question back on her. "What's your story?"

Sloan finished assembling the last piece of her gun and she slapped in the magazine and placed it down next to her. Whatever her story was, it was still a fresh scar for her and Munroe waited patiently until she began to speak.

"Born in Wiltshire to a nice family. Good parents but broke, and I joined the military to get a college education. Did my basic at Sandhurst before moving into army intelligence and then counterintelligence. I crossed paths with McCitrick and he saw something in me. Shortly after he brought me into DS5."

Sloan's history was brief, too brief, and Munroe could tell she'd left out huge chunks of it. "Seems nice and tidy. What really happened?"

There was no hint of emotion in her eyes but she stared at him for a few moments and then with a deep breath began to speak. "I was deployed to Iraq in 2015 and my team and I were tasked with providing intel on the continuing insurgence. We all knew Iran was sponsoring most of it, but we had intel on a deal to buy uranium from a Western seller. They may have been causing chaos in Iraq, but nuclear ambition has always been their goal, and where better to trade than within the fog of war? Through our network of informants we managed to nail down a time and date of the sale and a special operations team was sent in to retrieve both buyer and seller, along with the material. I went with them."

Munroe looked unsure of the last part. "That's unusual. An intelligence officer going in with the operations team."

"Usually, yes. But we weren't sure exactly what we were dealing with. My informant insisted I be the one to meet him, and only then would he provide the exact location of the sale. We were dealing with a tight time-frame and my superior gave the OK. Turned out to be an ambush, and all six of the operations team were killed. I was taken hostage and interrogated for three days."

Munroe had more than a few questions but he let them lie, allowing Sloan to explain in her own time.

"I didn't know it then, but the seller was a Daedalus operative, and he wanted to know everything we knew about the sale." Sloan's eyes drooped downwards and then she stared up at him, her eyes dulled. "When male soldiers are captured on the battlefield they can expect torture. But when it's a woman, the word torture takes on a different meaning. Let's just say after three days of that bullshit it's unlikely I'll ever be able to have children."

Munroe wanted to wince at the idea but his expression remained static. This was not a woman who desired pity. "That's tough."

"That's war," she replied, showing no distress whatsoever. "On the third day, having not given up a single piece of intel except my name and rank, I used my feminine abilities on one of the guards, just long enough to take the AK-47 from him, and then I fought my out and managed to make it back to base. A little worse for wear, but I survived, and it was in the hospital that McCitrick visited me with an offer. I've been working for DS5 ever since, all of five years, and I won't quit until Daedalus is taken apart, piece by little piece."

To have gone through all that and still have the strength to escape was an impressive feat, and Munroe could understand why McCitrick had taken an interest in the young captain. The Daedalus connection had no doubt cemented it. "What happened to the operative, you couldn't have known he was Daedalus at the time?"

"No, I only found out after McCitrick gave me the same speech he probably gave you, but that blonde-haired, blue-eyed bastard did die screaming. Being shot in the balls tends to produce that kind of reaction."

Now Munroe did wince, but Sloan appeared to take it as a questioning of her actions. "When I got out of hospital, and on McCitrick's induction, I made a promise to him and myself that I would never again take a life without good reason."

"Sounded like a good reason to me," Munroe said, but Sloan shook her head. "I didn't have to kill the man, that was my choice, out of revenge, and it's not one I would make again."

"But it's understandable."

"Yes, it is. But as DS5 we have free rein to do what we need to do, and by any and all means necessary. Our moral decisions and those we make in the field have to be above reproach. Without that we're just common gangsters, flouting the law. Power corrupts, Ethan, and people in our position are no different. The way you handled yourself back at Brest airport was all I needed to see. You could have killed that man but you didn't, because there was no need to, and that's something you understand. It's why I gave McCitrick my approval to bring you in."

"*You* approved *me*?"

"Absolutely. Every member of DS5 has to give approval for any new agent. Get one 'no' and you won't get in. We're a bit like the mafia like that," she said with a wink.

Considering what a tight-knit group it was Munroe could see the sense in it, Cosa Nostra aside, and he smiled. "Then thank you, Jax."

"Don't thank me just yet. Now you've got to prove yourself."

At the far end of the cargo area the cockpit door opened and the co-pilot, wearing a grey military boiler suit, appeared. "We'll be descending in a moment. Touchdown at New Orleans airport within the next five minutes. We've made good time. Strong tailwind. Buckle yourself in."

Both Munroe and Sloan were already in the process when a deafening boom sounded outside the plane, sending shockwaves rippling through the main fuselage. The co-pilot was thrown forward, landing face first on the cargo floor, knocking him out cold as Munroe gripped the belt buckle for stability. Sloan was also clinging to her seat as the cabin was filled with a sudden rush of air and both their ears popped as the entire aircraft depressurised. As Munroe pulled himself up to the small portal window he caught the shimmering glow of a rocket trail, and that's when another explosion sounded off the portside wing, and with it the engines groaned and they were levitated into the air as the whole aircraft suddenly began to dive.

Chapter 25

The hissing sound of a high-pressure air escaping the aircraft was matched only by the gust of wind forcing itself through the open cockpit door and into the main cargo bay where Munroe and Sloan were clinging to their flapping seat buckles. The initial nosedive had eased but they were still descending rapidly. Munroe had no idea what height they were at but without oxygen they would soon pass out, and he pulled open the nearest metal flip door located on the fuselage and pulled out two portable masks, one of which he thrust into Sloan's hand. With the mask slipped over his nose and mouth Munroe was already on his feet and using the thick cargo netting secured against the wall to pull himself forward. He passed Sloan, who'd had the same idea, and they quickly began to propel themselves along when after a few seconds gravity returned fully and the C-130 began to level out.

Munroe immediately headed for the cockpit as Sloan checked on the pilot, who was still out cold. He pulled back the half open door to find the other pilot wearing a full-face mask and struggling with the yoke as air rushed through the broken side window.

"What happened?" he yelled above the roaring wind and the pilot looked back at him and gave a sharp nod in the direction of the left wing.

"We're being fired at," he shouted. "I'm trying to put the flames out."

Munroe craned his neck and looked out of the shattered cockpit window to see one of the two engines on fire, and as the pilot pulled a yellow lever jutting out from the panel above him the flame disappeared in a puff of smoke.

Munroe dropped into the co-pilot seat and pulled out the full-face oxygen face mask from underneath. He pulled the straps over the back of his neck and used the internal mic. "Who's firing?"

The pilot was adjusting the trim as he attempted to keep the plane level and he was oversteering to account for the lost engine. "Two ground missiles, coming from the Louisiana coast. Countermeasures flares drew them off but the second was close enough to damage the far port engine."

Sloan now appeared in the cockpit doorway and she steadied herself against Munroe's seat. She said nothing but Munroe pointed over to the smoking propeller and she understood straightaway.

"Can we make the airport?" Munroe yelled above the thunderous sound of swirling wind still surging into the cockpit.

"It'll be an emergency landing, but we can make it. As long as we don't get another incoming..."

Warning alarms lit up the cockpit and as Munroe looked out of the side window he could see the thin trail of a rocket burner heading straight towards them. The pilot instinctively began to lurch the aircraft steeply to the left as the yellow hue of flared countermeasures popped from the back of the fuselage in the direction of the incoming missile. The whole C-130 was shaking as the stress of the manoeuvre pushed its frame to the limits and Munroe reached back and grabbed on to Sloan's coat sleeve, offering support as the missile exploded into the countermeasures off the port side, sending shrapnel slicing through the cockpit. Metal debris blew out the remaining windows and disintegrated both HUD displays, also catching the pilot in the chest, sending blood splattering across the dashboard and causing him to lurch forward limply against the yoke, sending the aircraft into a steep freefall once again.

Munroe grabbed the co-pilot's yoke and pulled back on it and as he regained control, bringing the plane level. Sloan was already unbuckling the pilot and dragging him back into the cargo bay. Munroe wasn't sure if the man was alive; the crimson wound across his chest looked deep, and he unbuckled his seatbelt and took the pilot's as Sloan now returned to the cockpit and slid into the seat next to him, putting on the oxygen mask as she did so.

"Who the hell's firing at us?"

"Don't know, but it's ground-based," Munroe replied as the pressure of the oncoming wind seeping through the open windows pushed him back into his seat.

"Jesus, Ethan. Someone doesn't want us reaching New Orleans."

Munroe didn't reply; instead he was searching ahead for Louis Armstrong airport, and to his relief he found the landing strip lights directly ahead. They were still some miles out but with three engines functioning he could get them down.

"Can you land this?" Sloan yelled, and he gave her a firm nod.

"I've flown a C-130 before."

"Yeah, but have you landed one?"

His pause did not exude the confidence Sloan had hoped for.

"I'll get her down so long as we're not fired upon again."

He'd barely finished the sentence when the red emergency light lit up the dashboard and after a glance at the radar Munroe rolled the aircraft into a steep turn as the fuselage was lit up again by the automated flares popping into the air with their heated signatures attracting the incoming projectile.

"Hold on, this is going to be close."

The missile was again tempted by the flares and a bright flash lit up the cockpit with the explosion, but this time the shrapnel slammed into the nearest port propeller, and the shockwave rattled the whole plane so violently that it felt as if the whole aircraft would tear itself apart.

Munroe stared over at the nearest engine and he could tell the bent propellers were only being spun by force of the oncoming wind. They were now down to just two, on the right side, and the whole aircraft began to yaw downwards, shaking violently. As Munroe fought against the yoke he jammed his foot hard on the opposite rudder pedal and attempted to straighten his line of flight. With only one side having thrust he had to offset the nose of the plane at an angle so the remaining propellers had enough directed thrust to keep the aircraft moving forward, but the wind shear was testing the aircraft to its limits, the vibrations intensifying with every passing second.

They were now less than three miles out from the approaching runway, and down below the dense sprawl of New Orleans radiated its bright, welcoming glow. There wasn't time to head back out to the coast, and if they went down here the damage would be immense. A C-130 crashing full speed into the streets, during the Mardi Gras celebrations, would be nothing short of catastrophic, and Munroe pressed his thumb down on the yoke's mic button. "New Orleans international tower, this…"

Shit, he didn't even know the call sign.

"This is the C-130 military cargo plane approaching the main runway from the south east. Both port side propellers have failed. Emergency landing requested." Of course it wasn't a request but a demand, and as he waited for a response he yelled out to Sloan. "We need to slow her down, we're coming in too fast. See that grey switch between us?" He motioned with his chin but Sloan already had her hand on it. She clearly had more knowledge of aircraft than he'd realised.

"Extend the flaps, one stage only."

As Munroe continued his struggle with the yoke, Sloan engaged the flaps, and with a heavy buffeting to the wings the plane began to reduce in speed. With only two functioning propellers they couldn't slow too much or they'd stall and drop from the sky like a dead weight. For Munroe, judging the correct speed was nothing more than an educated guess and a feel for the aircraft, and he knew he would have to bring it down faster than he should do. Despite this dead reckoning he wasn't even sure where the landing gear was located.

There was still no answer from the tower and Munroe figured the radio had been damaged during one of the blasts.

"There it is." He nodded to the central panel and the landing gear handle as the runway loomed closer, less than a mile away. "Drop the wheels," he yelled, and Sloan pulled the handle and the sound of hydraulics hissed below them as the landing gears locked into place.

There was no need to say 'hang on'. They shared a simple glance and Sloan grabbed the sides of her seat as Munroe descended towards the matt black tarmac, fighting the yoke with all his strength.

They soared over the airport fencing and within metres of touching down he released some of the pressure on the yoke and the nose flipped back to its centre line, but his timing was slightly off. As the C-130's wheels slammed down onto the tarmac the entire aircraft wobbled and began to tip to one side. Munroe was already countering with the rudder pedals and he felt the plane's centre of gravity shifting, and then it stabilised and dropped back down onto all wheels with a heavy crunch. He slammed the brake pedals hard, too hard at first, almost causing the aircraft to careen off the runway, but then he lightened the pressure and the speed began to drop, knot by knot.

The sound of metal screeching against tarmac told him one of the wheels had crumpled during the initial touchdown, but the rudder pedals were still operational, and by the time they neared the end of the runway he was down to a comfortable roll, and he used the momentum to guide the plane along the nearest taxiway and then off onto a large patch of grass. He could think of better places to park, but at least they were clear of any incoming commercial flights, and as the wheels ground to a full stop he allowed himself to exhale deeply. To his right Sloan was doing the same, and as they both looked at each other she coolly nodded her appreciation.

"Welcome to New Orleans," he announced, his breathing heavy. Without even a reply Sloan was unbuckling and heading back into the cargo hold to check on the two pilots. Munroe should have joined her immediately, but as he stared out of the broken cockpit window and watched the convoy of emergency fire trucks and ambulances heading in their direction he found himself momentarily preoccupied. No, uneasy. But not because of the controlled adrenalin spike he could feel running through his veins. It had been a close call after all, but that wasn't it. What was making him uneasy was the 'how'. How did Daedalus, if it had been Daedalus, know where they were? Firing rockets at a UK military aircraft over an American city was insane enough, but how did they know their location?

His conclusion was the unsettling part, and he rubbed his forehead and then sat back in his seat. There were only a select few who knew where he and Sloan had been heading... and they were all DS5.

Chapter 26

Mardi Gras was already in full swing as Munroe and Sloan made their way down Bourbon Street and through the bustling crowds of revellers, all making the most of the organised chaos playing out on the streets of New Orleans. With every surge of the crowd Munroe stiffened and silently cursed the tightness in his neck which he'd managed to receive when making his 'gentle' touchdown at New Orleans airport over an hour earlier. The landing, as it turned out, had proved to be the easy part. After bringing the C-130 to an ungracious stop they'd been detained immediately. The safe landing of a British military aircraft after being attacked mid-air was one thing, but when one of the airport police had caught sight of Sloan's Beretta hanging from its holster there was instant suspicion. The whole airport was in partial lockdown in response to the terrorist attack in London and nerves were already heightened. Add that to a missile attack above the city and the authorities were understandably suspicious of anything out of the ordinary, and a woman and man wearing civilian clothes, each armed with silenced firearms, were not something to be glossed over lightly. They had been handcuffed soon after and it was not until Homeland Security had turned up, which was quickly, that Sloan had been allowed to make a phone call. One call to DS5's US section head Colonel Sinclair and they'd been released without any complaint. Munroe had no idea what the colonel had said, but it showed the real power DS5 had over law enforcement when necessary. The justice system in the US wasn't like the UK's, it was far more internalised, with each department always vying for jurisdiction. Given what must have been perceived as a terrorist attempt over the skies of Louisiana, their quick release had been all the more remarkable. They were even allowed to take their handguns with them. From there a waiting helicopter had flown them to a small private helipad just a stone's throw from Bourbon Street, in doing so bypassing the congested Louisiana roads. Sloan had been right, McCitrick was a master organiser, and despite the emergency landing and detention, it had taken a fraction of the time that a taxi drive would have.

The bars were overflowing, as was the alcohol, and there was hardly a person in sight not decorated in throws of multi-coloured bead necklaces. The media had been full of doubt as to whether the yearly event would still go ahead after the attack on London but after much lobbying from all sides of the political spectrum, all played out on TV, the decision had been made to commence with the celebrations. It did, however, mean that the police presence was heavy, and even though the atmosphere was exhilarating one could feel an almost tangible sense of underlying apprehension emanating from every uniformed lawman on the streets.

Despite the unease, Munroe had been draped with five necklaces, had multiple gold plastic doubloons thrown at him and a half empty plastic cup of beer thrust into his hand. Sloan hadn't fared much better, with the added ask that she lift her top off by a bystander who had come extremely close to receiving a broken wrist for his request.

"This is it," Munroe said as he reached the store front of Dr Bute's House of Voodoo and stared up at the skull-shaped wooden sign hanging above it. He gave the door a gentle push but it was locked tight. Sloan moved to his side, pushing back at the weight of the crowd which nudged them both backwards and forward in waves.

"It's locked," he said, turning the door handle again just to be sure.

"Let's try the back," Sloan suggested, and with a nod from Munroe they began to slowly push past the rows of people clogging the sidewalk, looking for a point of access that would lead them to the back of the shop buildings. After some hustling they reached the street corner and after a pleasant smile to a uniformed cop manning it they both headed down the road, relieved to see it mostly empty due to all the fun being had on the main street. There is an art to moving cautiously but not looking like you're moving cautiously, and as Sloan took the lead Munroe never took his eyes off the rooftops. Icarus knew they were coming, shit, he'd invited them, and as Sloan pulled up next to a narrow alleyway and peered around the corner Munroe expected to be ambushed at any moment. The good news was nothing had happened yet, but as he followed Sloan down the tight corridor and towards the darkened rear side of Dr Bute's House of Voodoo, the lack of any lighting had him feeling exposed.

"Hold up," he whispered, moving in front of Sloan. "Let me go to the back door first. I don't want him taking pot shots at us from the window."

It seemed unlikely that this would happen. Icarus, if he was telling the truth, wanted to talk with him, but Munroe wasn't taking any chances. How had the psychopath put it when it came to his own actions? *'Conflicted.'*

Sloan nodded and drew her weapon, covering the top windows as Munroe slunk past the arched opening to the rear yard and then up to the back door. Satisfied they were clear he motioned for Sloan to join him. By the time she did Munroe was already preparing the set of lockpicks as Sloan hugged the wall, her silenced Beretta still drawn.

Munroe slipped the first pick into the Yale lock, but then he paused before pulling it back out and trying the handle.

Icarus had invited them.

His guess was correct, and as the door swung open Munroe retrieved his own silenced Beretta from his waist holster and raised its handle closely to his chest before glancing over at Sloan, who took the lead and headed inside.

It was commonplace to see special forces hugging their pistols to their chests on TV shows, but the reality had nothing to do with trying to look cool on camera. When clearing an interior with tight corners, an outstretched pistol could be grabbed at by anyone hiding around them.

The narrow back hallway had a small restroom leading off to one side and as Sloan moved to clear it, Munroe continued past her to the open doorway, giving him access to the front of the building.

The odour of burnt opium joss sticks clung to the air, smelling like the aftermath of a party from the night before, and as he poked his head and barrel around the corner to survey the shop front crammed with trinkets and voodoo souvenirs, he could see the swell of bouncing shadows of outside partygoers against the closed blinds.

Sloan was now at his back and with a nod they both filtered into the room on opposite sides. As Munroe came around the till counter he saw the body of a black man in a white shirt and beads sprawled out on the floor beneath him. On either side of the corpse lay two more bodies, a man and a woman, both with blonde hair and wearing jeans and T-shirts, all three of them sharing similar deep cuts across their throats, from ear to ear.

For Munroe the deep knife wounds meant no checking of a pulse was warranted, and as Sloan joined him they both turned and brought their guns to bear on the only remaining unknown area of the shop, the dangling multi-coloured draped beads leading to a stairwell.

Sloan flicked her finger towards the opening and covered Munroe from the corner of the counter while he moved over to it, each of his footsteps delicately placed in total silence. With one hand he slipped his fingers between the centre beads and slowly pushed them to one side and while he moved up on to the first step Sloan took over and held the beaded drape in place before following him closely.

The steps were solid, and with no creaking it was easy to navigate silently. Upon reaching the top, Munroe waited for Sloan to position herself beside him and then he lightly gripped the doorknob and slowly turned it.

It wasn't locked, and instead of storming into the darkened room Munroe allowed the door to swing open on its oiled hinges. The only light came from a closed window on the right wall, opening up onto a fire exit and casting a thin shard across a wooden desk. As he approached something twitched from behind it.

"Don't move," Munroe ordered sharply, and he rushed inside to take a position on the right side of the room as Sloan moved to the opposite wall. Apart from the shuffling sound of movement Munroe could make out a faded silhouette, someone standing face front and pressed flat against the wall.

Sloan was having a tougher time seeing through the pitch black and with Munroe holding his gun on the murky shape she reached back and slid her free hand along the wall until she found the light switch.

The bulb above flicked on and as its brown rectangular lampshade directed light across the desk, Munroe found himself staring at the shifting body of Michael Hanks. His eyes rolled in and out of consciousness and his complexion, a near paper white, was understandable, considering his wounds and the amount of blood he had lost. Both his arms were stretched out above his head and each palm had sturdy metal spikes thrust through them, attaching him firmly to the wood frame behind the plasterboard, along with nylon rope ensuring he remained in place. Brown metal coat hangers had been clipped and straightened to fashion foot-long pins which had then been inserted into certain parts of his body, above the knees and elbows, and four of them dug deep into areas of his chest and groin. Around his neck a Motorola radio hung from a piece of thin knotted brown packaging string which had been tied in a bow, and as Sloan shot Munroe a look of disgust the walkie-talkie crackled into life.

"Welcome, Ethan. I knew you'd come."

Munroe edged to the window and looked outside but seeing only empty rooftops he ventured closer to Hanks. With Sloan still covering him he placed his gun back in his holster and lightly slid his fingers around the string hanging from Hanks's neck. As far as he could tell, there was no booby trap, but to be sure he motioned for Sloan to throw him something and, without any need for further instruction, she retrieved her flip knife and threw it over to him.

Munroe caught it and then clicked it open before setting about delicately cutting the fibrous brown string in half. Then he pulled the Motorola away and pressed its side button. "Hello, Icarus."

Although only semi-conscious, the very name caused Hanks to convulse momentarily and his muscles contorted in a twitching mass. The man was terrified, but it only took a few moments of squirming and, likely due to the immense pain, he quickly passed out and slumped, the spikes and bindings the only thing keeping him from dropping to the floor.

"Ignore my voodoo doll, he's just an acquaintance of mine whom I owed some of the same hospitality he recently showed me. You can't blame me for getting creative, Ethan. I've been here awaiting your arrival for hours."

"You could have just tied him up," Munroe replied as he looked at Sloan who lowered her Beretta and joined him beside the wall, remaining out of view from the window.

"Perhaps I did go a little overboard, but it seemed suitable given we are in Dr Bute's House of Voodoo. I'm not one for boredom, and you know what they say about idle hands. What you're looking at is tradecraft. Each one of those pins placed in just the right position so as to cause maximum pain without damaging any of the organs. So long as they're fed, watered and infection is kept at bay the patient may survive indefinitely, experiencing the excruciating pain only the most delicate nerve clusters can induce."

Munroe leant over to Sloan and whispered, "He must be close. Why don't you take a look outside while I keep him talking?"

Sloan nodded and then she hugged the wall and ducked out into the stairwell, keeping out of the window's line of sight.

"He must have committed a terrible crime. It takes time to perform what you've done, and I saw you didn't afford the same attention to the three people downstairs."

"The shop owner was just collateral, I'm afraid. You may or may not believe me when I say that I don't enjoy killing people without a reason… of course, there are times when I don't feel like I have a choice. As for the two Daedalus goons, it was only a matter of time before they showed up. I'm wanted on both sides, as you probably know."

The mere mention of Daedalus gave Munroe an insight into what Icarus already thought he knew about him, and he now played into it. "Daedalus's goons. I saw the blonde hair and it was dark, but I assume they had blue eyes as well."

"You'd be correct in that assumption, but they weren't built for this kind of work. Not like you and me, Ethan."

There was a strange wavering in Icarus's voice, a Jekyll and Hyde quality. Some sentences were said with almost pained emotion, while others were spoken with little if any, and given what Munroe had learnt at Ferreira's 'school' in Brazil it all made sense. "Icarus, may I speak to David?"

There was now nothing but static on the Motorola and Munroe waited for a few seconds before trying again. "I met with Tobias Kessler. He told me about your training. In fact he said you were his best student."

Still there came no reply. Munroe decided to throw caution to the wind and take a punt. Since first meeting Icarus the man had shown opposing behaviours. He wanted to meet with Munroe, then kill Munroe. He'd wanted him to find his house, yet he set booby traps for him, and now he'd invited him all the way to this location in New Orleans and all the man wanted to talk about was his tradecraft and murder credentials. It appeared that Ferreira's experiment of fracturing the psyche to create the perfect assassin had been a success... partially.

"I know what happened to you, David. I've seen the school in Brazil where you grew up. I know the experiments they did on you. To do that to a child is unforgivable. I can't imagine what you've been through – and to do things that you were compelled to do as if you had no free will..."

Of course Munroe only half believed what he was saying. The man was a vicious killer, and too dangerous to not spend his life behind bars or in a psychiatric ward, but all that being said, Icarus was just as much a victim as any of the other people Daedalus had tightened their grip around. "You asked me to come here for a reason. Something you need to tell me about, and here I am, willing and waiting. If you despise Daedalus as much as I think you do, then come with me. The enemy of my enemy is my friend, David. Haven't you suffered enough?"

He waited for over ten seconds, and just when he was about to try again he heard a faint sound. It was difficult to hear over the noise of the street party outside but it grew louder until it was unmistakable. It was the sound of crying. Icarus was crying, and then in an instant it cut off and the cold, monotone voice was back.

"I brought you here to show you something, but I'm not a fool, Ethan. You'll have me wrapped up in chains or put a bullet in my head the moment you lay eyes on me, so... I'm going to show you something, after which I'm hoping you'll join me in my quest."

"And that would be?" Munroe asked, even though his gut was telling him he didn't really want to know, and he felt apprehensive as Icarus gave him his answer.

"I want Daedalus destroyed, and all those associated with it."

"I thought you were part of Daedalus. Even without the blonde hair and blue eyes."

There was a pause, and then Icarus came back on the line, sounding annoyed by the observation. "Dyed hair and contacts are part of the trade, Ethan. We're all pretending we're something were not, aren't we?"

"I suppose we are." He took another peek out of the window but still couldn't see anyone there. "But I'm here now, at your request, and I have nothing to pretend about."

"Oh, that's not true, Ethan. You're the most dangerous pretender of all. Someone who doesn't even know he's pretending... but I do understand why you accepted my invitation. Your family, or dead family, I should say."

The gentle poke had no effect on Munroe and he replied calmly, "You seem to know more about it than I do, so I'm asking. What can you tell me?"

There was another pause, and when Icarus came back on the line any playfulness in his voice had vanished. "I'm offering you a chance to know the truth. About your family. So why don't I show you why you're here, and we can get on with it. On the table before you is a monitor.

I want you to take a look. And watch out for Mr Hanks, you don't want to get blood on your clothes."

Munroe looked over at the unconscious body of Hanks and then carefully moved around the table to face the dimly lit monitor screen.

"What you are looking at is Daedalus's private communications platform. Only a select few have total access to it, and Mr Hanks is one of them. It's why I followed him back here to New Orleans. It's a closed system, but as you can see you now have access to it. Don't worry, they have no idea we're even logged on, I've seen to that."

On the screen was nothing but a search engine window, and Munroe rested his hands against the protruding keyboard as Icarus began to deliver his instructions.

"The search window will take you directly to Daedalus's database. I want you to type in the name of your wife and your daughter."

Munroe said nothing but did as he was instructed. He typed in the name 'Natalie Munroe' and gently tapped the return key.

The monitor went blank and then a single document flashed onto the screen and Munroe began to read it, his own lips muttering the words, line by line.

Captain Ethan Munroe (29) sanctioned for termination.

Assets: Real Irish Republican Army (RIRA)

Action: Clandestine shadow operation DA1731. Section Chief Hans Bauer. Approved by High Command.

Result A: Target survived

Collateral: Wife Natalie Munroe (29), Lucy Munroe (4). Additional 5 civilians dead.

Result B: Filed as terrorist attack. Daedalus involvement unknown by authorities.

Review: It has been determined that any additional actions would bring unwarranted scrutiny to the organisation. File stored but open for revisiting further actions at a later date.

Section Chief
Hans Bauer

Munroe's hand slipped off the keyboard and he placed both his palms on either side of the desk. With his shoulders hunched he swallowed deeply. Instead of feeling anger or emotion he only felt numbness throughout his body.

"Bauer." He had questioned the familiarity of the man's tone in Brazil, but now he realised the killer had known him all along. "They were trying to kill me," he said in a whisper, and the words 'collateral' blazed in his mind as to why his own wife and child had died. It was because of him.

"I'm sorry, Ethan," Icarus said, his voice crackling over the radio, his soft tone of voice having now returned. "I had nothing to do with it. But I did tell you that once your eyes were opened you wouldn't want to stop me... you'd join me."

Joining Icarus was the furthest thing from Munroe's mind and he picked up the Motorola and held it close to his lips. But then he hesitated. He'd noticed something while Icarus had been speaking, and he chose not to reply as the sound of trumpets blared out from the mini parade passing the shop front. He waited in silence and then the Motorola crackled back into life.

"Ethan?" Icarus asked, and at that moment Munroe now knew exactly where the killer was, because above the sound of Icarus's voice the same loud trumpets rang out, and he looked up at the ceiling.

The son of a bitch was on the roof above him.

Chapter 27

Munroe slid open the office window and stepped gingerly out onto the fire escape, before making his way up the single flight to the roof. He covered the walkie-talkie with his jacket in an attempt to dampen the sounds of celebration and cheering and spoke into it. "We need to meet," he said as he stealthily crept up the steps, pulling out his silenced Beretta with his free hand, "face to face."

"If we meet face to face, Ethan, then one of us is going to get hurt. And it won't be me, so let me tell you how it's going to work."

Munroe was already at the roof, and as he peered over the brickwork to see a man wearing a knee-length over-coat crouched next to a large silver air-conditioning unit, Icarus continued with his list of requirements.

"I'm going to provide you with an address. An address to the place where it all began. The birthplace of Project Icarus. And once your little band of Disavowed have taken it I'll be in touch with more information. That's how we will play our game."

Munroe had heard enough and he now raised off his haunches so his body was above the brick roofline and aimed his gun directly at Icarus's silhouette. "Icarus! Don't move. Time to play the game my way."

The silhouette turned towards him and the flash of the first fireworks overhead lit up his face. Munroe could now see it was definitely him, still wearing his black contacts and with his hair still dyed brown. At first the killer looked stunned, but a smile began to creep across his face and he let the Motorola tumble to the rooftop and nodded, seemingly happy to see Munroe in the flesh.

"Can't do that, Ethan. It's either my way or no way."

Munroe remained still. Icarus was definitely armed, and the roof's brickwork could provide cover if needed. As he considered clipping the killer in the shoulder with a single round, another volley of fireworks exploded over-head and it was now that Icarus made his move. He leapt past the air-conditioning unit as Munroe lunged upwards and out onto the rooftop to see Icarus jumping the gap to the adjoining building. He could have taken a shot but it wouldn't have been accurate, and he needed the killer alive or this whole thing would be another dead end.

Munroe took chase, following over to the next rooftop and then down the long drop onto the next building. He rolled upon impact and using the momentum leapt back into a full stride as Icarus dove off the edge and down into the crowds of partygoers below.

Munroe reached the edge, jammed the gun back in its concealed holster, jumped down himself and joined the crowd as he caught sight of Icarus some metres ahead, frantically making his way past the sea of people.

It was like trudging through quicksand, and as he barged ahead the flickers of Icarus became less and less frequent until he'd lost him completely as bodies swamped his vision. Munroe pushed his way towards the centre of the street and slammed up against a pirate ship float with a large plastic harlequin head perched upon it. He pulled himself up onto it and scanned the crowd ahead. The ship's occupants, a band of creepy-looking clowns, approached him with raised hands, unhappy with the stowaway, as a young lady wearing a skimpy silver dress and unbothered by his arrival began dumping beaded necklaces over his head. It would only be a matter of time before one of the many police caught sight of him, and Munroe shoved the red-nosed freaks aside and ran the length of the ship, where he leapt onto the next float full of female cabaret dancers wearing high heels and oversized sparkling head-dresses. He was met with the same welcome, and as he ignored the hard slaps being thrown at his chest, courtesy of the float's furious occupants, he scanned the crowd down below.

The key to tracking someone in a crowd is to look for the commotion which usually surrounds the person scrambling to get away, but as Munroe looked across the hundreds of people all crammed together, each one causing their own celebratory commotion, he struggled to see Icarus. In fact the only person he did notice was the policeman up on the sidewalk who was now angrily demanding he come down off the float, his finger jabbing downwards to the road below.

Munroe continued his sweep as more slaps from the entertainers rained down on him, and then he saw what he was looking for. A man in a brown, knee-length overcoat, and the only face in the hordes of people not smiling or yelling fervently.

Icarus glanced back at him as he reached the junction of the road and then disappeared around a corner as Munroe ran to the far edge of the float and jumped down to give chase. Behind him the policeman's calls for him to stop were drowned out by the raucous crowd.

By the time he had barged his way back to the kerb the crowd was thinning out, and he reached the junction and flew around it to catch sight of Icarus sprinting down the main road and then down an alleyway on the opposite side. Munroe gave chase, and as he darted through the heavy traffic crawling down the main street at a snail's pace, an overzealous white Cadillac DeVille clipped him, sending him tumbling across the bonnet and landing on the other side with a thud.

The impact was minor, and without even looking back Munroe hauled himself to his feet and took off again, over and then through the same opening Icarus had disappeared down. He raced down the alleyway and came to a screeching halt at the iron sign arched across the black gates, which read LAFAYETTE CEMETERY NO 1.

The sounds of celebrations were still in the air but the noise had faded, and as he focused all his attention on his hearing he heard the faint sound of shoes scraping upon stone. He looked over at the cemetery gates and noticed the left-hand side swinging back and forth slightly. Munroe quickly stepped over to the metal gates and then with his gun drawn at his side, he stepped over the threshold and began to make his way deeper in to the dark, dank confines of Lafayette Cemetery.

For a cemetery the place was impressive, with rows of old tombs and family mausoleums, and except for a sign that read NO SOLICITING IN THE CEMETERY, which must mean that soliciting was a problem here, it appeared the kind of respectful resting place one would expect. The whole plot must have contained thousands of interred graves, and it did briefly cross his mind that it was the perfect place for a man like Icarus to seek refuge, even only temporarily.

Munroe moved from left to right, attempting to look straight down each row for any sight of movement, but there was none. If the place did get visitors then tonight they were all in the throes of Mardi Gras back on the main streets. As he came to the end of the first row he heard a footstep. It was barely audible above the background noise but he heard it, and he now began heading in the same direction, towards a gathering of stone mausoleums. The once stately white residences of families past were certainly no Taj Mahal, but their cracked paint on weathered stone provided a link to the city's gothic past, and as Munroe reached the centre of them he froze. He was very attuned to the feeling of being watched and it was this feeling that now tugged at Munroe's senses, and he felt the hairs on the back of his neck stand up.

"Hello, Ethan." A familiar voice called softly, and Munroe slowly brought his Beretta to bear on the silhouette of a man leaning against the furthest mausoleum, also holding a gun aimed directly at him. "Let's not do anything foolish."

Munroe watched as Icarus took a step forward so his face was visible in the shard of light from the nearby streets, and he remained calm, holding his aim. "It's over. You're coming in with me, and I guarantee your safety. You're going to tell me everything, and then we'll go from there. I'll listen to everything you have to say. You have my word."

Icarus responded with a nasal chuckle. "Things like this are never over, and you are far from having the upper hand. You're good, Ethan. But today is not yours to be had."

"So, what are you going to do… David?"

Icarus's real name drew a smile from the killer. "Good, we should be on a first name basis. Whether you realise it or not, we're the same, you and I."

Any suggested connection was lost on Munroe, but when a gun is being pointed at your chest you play along, and he did just that. "You've spent a lot of time and effort bringing us to this moment, David. And you're right, I don't know why. But I can tell you what I do know: I know about Daedalus. I know that you *were* working for them. I know that you killed two DS5 agents and a lot of other innocent people, and I know they've turned on you."

Icarus continued to point the gun at him, but the mention of innocent people had him shaking his head. "No one is innocent, Ethan. And what's the point of being given skills if you can't use them? I was bred to be an assassin and gain information using torture. I did everything Daedalus asked of me, and despite all that they have done to me I still believe in the cause... a Fourth Reich... a pure bloodline."

It almost sounded like the beginning of an apology. "I saw what you did to the people I found in your house. I saw your torture room, your wet room. And the mutilation of their bodies after death? That wasn't the work of an assassin. That was the work of someone who relished the act of killing and defiling a corpse."

Munroe realised he was getting a bit close to the bone as Icarus now used his free hand to roughly press at his forehead, as if his skull was causing him pain, and then he suddenly stopped, his demeanour calm once again.

"I'm not proud of everything I've done, Ethan, but much of it was necessary. It's what I was bred to do. But now Daedalus have their new models, with go-faster stripes, and all my brothers and sisters were deemed unworthy and retired. But not me... I was the one who got away, and I will now repay them in kind. With your help, I will bring down what they most hold dear. Project Icarus itself."

Icarus once again rubbed at his forehead, his eyes momentarily rolling back in their sockets. Munroe considered taking a shot, but instead he held fast and asked the only questions at that moment that mattered to him.

"What is Project Icarus? And why did Daedalus want me dead?"

The two questions had the killer focusing once more, and he shook his head, suddenly looking solemn. Tears were beginning to flow from his eyes when something zipped into his neck, and as he slapped at the irritation, Munroe heard the sound of compressed air and he felt a stinging thud in his own shoulder. Before him Icarus's legs began to crumple, and as he collapsed to the ground Munroe reached up and plucked whatever had hit him from his skin. As his vision began to blur he found himself looking at a red-tipped syringe dart. The surge of dizziness was overwhelming, and he sank slowly to the floor, the gun slipping from his hand and all senses deserting his body until every muscle became numb. Munroe's knees thumped down onto the gravel path below him, and then as darkness consumed his mind and vision he felt the gravel hit his face.

Chapter 28

Munroe awoke to the thunderous sound of flutes, bassoons, trumpets and trombones all woven together above the heavy beating of a drum. The music was recognisable even within a few notes, and his entire body pulsated rhythmically as the vibrations of Ludwig van Beethoven's Fifth Symphony rippled through him, wave after wave. A blindfold had been tightened around his head, covering his eyes, and he could feel the taut knot digging into the back of his skull. His head was throbbing from whatever drugs had been used to knock him out, and the deafening, brash cacophony pounded at his head, each note assaulting his senses, blow after blow.

"Hello!" he shouted loudly, but his voice was lost within the music as he tried to recall his last moments of consciousness. Images of the body impaled on the wall like a voodoo doll, and then giving chase after Icarus began flooding back to him, and finally he visualised the last thing he had seen, the killer dropping to the ground before him. It had not been Icarus who had brought him here. So who had?

Munroe attempted to move his hands but they were secured behind him, and the backrest of the chair he was sitting on was jutting into his biceps painfully. He shifted up and down, trying to gauge the texture, and determined the chair was plastic, which did him no good. Wooden chairs could be broken, but plastic not so much.

Munroe turned his attention to his ankles, only to find they had each been bound to the chair's legs. The restraints weren't digging into his skin, which suggested perhaps duct tape. Also not good, offering little if any wriggle room.

Munroe scraped his head against his shoulder in the hope of catching the blindfold and sliding it up his forehead, but the binding on his wrists was too tight, allowing hardly any movement in his upper body.

Shit. He wasn't going anywhere.

Above the vociferous noise of Beethoven's Fifth he could make out another sound, like a humming, which then gave way to the booming of trumpets before he heard it again. The sound came and went intermittently. It was sporadic, with no discernible timing to it, and Munroe now realised it was a voice, yelling, but it was impossible to determine the words. He began shouting back and the hum stopped suddenly before starting up again. Now he was sure there was someone else in here with him. Wherever 'here' was.

Although practically pointless there was not much else he could do, and Munroe found himself screaming back. It was on his second yell that something hard and narrow jabbed into his chest, inducing a short burst of coughing. He was still recoiling from the blow when the same object slapped him sharply across the left side of his head and he fell into silence, his muscles tensing in apprehension of the next strike.

Munroe sat, his body taut and primed, as the music began to fade out slowly until it became nothing more than pleasant background noise. He could now hear voices, but there was no clarity to the words. Then suddenly he felt hot breath in his ear, and the few words that came with it: "Welcome home, Ethan," and the blindfold was ripped from his head.

The light was blinding, and Munroe slowly opened his eyes, now getting his first sight of the man standing before him, wearing a tweed suit and holding a tanned bamboo cane with one frayed end.

"Good evening, Captain Munroe." The man took a step backwards, allowing a partial view of the room they were in. The walls, floor and ceiling were nothing more than smooth, grey concrete, and in the corners of the ceiling black mesh speakers had been attached by thick metal bolts. Overhead dangled a single light bulb exuding a stale yellow hue, and to his left was a green metal door lined with small metal rivets offering the only exit to the windowless room.

Munroe recognised the voice and face of the person standing smugly before him. He'd caught sight of him through the circular eyepiece of his gas mask while exiting Dr Ferreira's 'school' back in Brazil, but only now did he get a good look at the man who embodied modern-day Nazism, and had organised the death of his family. "Bauer."

Hans Bauer offered a smile, and bowed theatrically. He slicked his blonde hair back with his hand and gazed down at Munroe through cold, dark blue eyes. "It's a pleasure to finally meet you face to face, although I'm sure you don't feel the same. What you may not realise is that despite our little '*du tac au tac*' back in Brazil, our meeting has been a long time coming. You might have only recently met me but, I assure you, I've known you for many years." Bauer smiled conceitedly. "I have to congratulate you on the manner of your escape, by the way. Its ingenuity and daring was impressive, but somewhat slippery. Fleeing like a snake and slithering your way past my men was very unbecoming, but I would expect nothing less from a member of the Disavowed. They are, after all, the lowest form of life this planet has to offer. Shame…" Bauer placed the tip of his frayed bamboo rod down upon the floor like a walking stick. "You could have been so much more. But as the French say, '*C'est la vie.*'"

With the faces of his dead family suspended in his thoughts, Munroe could have jumped to his feet and snapped the man's neck without even a second thought, but given his current predicament, and the bindings chafing at his wrists, he remained calm and collected. "I may not know you, Hans, but I know what you are. You've got good taste in music, though, I'll give you that. The Nazis always did love their Germanic composers."

Bauer raised his chin upwards and nodded arrogantly. "What do you mean *did*? We still do. Beethoven is not high up on our collective top ten though. Most still favour Wagner or Bruckner. Many think Beethoven's deafness was a sign of genetic weakness, and it's true but you have to admit the man knew how to pump out a good tune. Still, purity of the species, is the name of the game. Survival of the fittest. It's hard to fault the laws of nature."

"World War Two, fifty million dead and the decimation of the German nation. I'd say that was a pretty big fault."

Munroe's summation brought a wide smile to Bauer's lips. "An idealist! I would have expected nothing less."

Bauer leant down and grasped Munroe by the chin before he turned it to one side, examining his features. "Strong bone structure. I like that. But polluted by the corruption of capitalism. Orphaned at four and with no

294

parents to guide you in the ways of the world. Indoctrinated by the nanny state and with no ties to bind you...
you don't even know who you are, Ethan. You're a man
with no past, and unfortunately no future."

Munroe jerked his chin away from Bauer's grip. "You
sound like your friend Icarus."

"Ah, Icarus. The thorn in my side. Just as his namesake
discovered, fly too close to the sun and you get your wings
burnt. Let's ask him, shall we."

Bauer took a step backwards, then moved over to one
side, and Munroe found himself staring directly at the
bloody and bruised face of Icarus. He was bound to a chair
on the opposite side of the room, but with no blindfold.
Instead he had a dirty piece of brown cloth stuffed in his
mouth.

"What about it, David. Anything to say?"

Icarus huffed against the gag as Bauer drew his hand
up to his own ear and cupped it theatrically. "I can't quite
hear you. Did you say you'll kill me?"

The man glanced back at Munroe and rolled his eyes
indifferently. "It's usually the kind of thing he says, but I
don't think he'll get the chance. Do you?"

The man brushed away his jacket and pulled out a grey
Luger from his waist holster. He then calmly strode over
and placed the gun to Icarus's head. "You've done great
things for us, David, great things... But not lately."

Munroe watched as Bauer pulled the trigger and
Icarus's entire body twitched as the click of the Luger's
hammer hitting an empty chamber echoed around the
room.

"You're not getting off that easy, David, despite what
our superiors may have instructed me to do. They would
have you put down like a rabid dog, but I won't do that. At

the very least you should see the conclusion of the thing that has preoccupied you these last few months."

Bauer ambled his way back to Munroe and presented the gun in the open palm of his hand. "It's an antique Luger. Second World War, owned by my father. Good weapon, and worthy of both your deaths, but I do believe in granting final wishes. I know that yours is information about your family, and poor David's over there, no matter how misguided, is to see that you get it."

As Bauer stared into Munroe's eyes he saw only furious anger, and he had a sudden realisation. "You know it was me. Don't you?" He glanced back at Icarus and wagged his finger. "David!" Bauer said with comical disappointment. "Is that what you were using Hanks's terminal for? So much for your vow of secrecy to your Daedalus family."

"Yes, I know it was you," Munroe growled, letting his game face slip as Bauer turned back towards him. "I saw your debrief. You tried to kill me and my family suffered for your failure. Why?"

Bauer said nothing at first, and instead stared down at Munroe coldly with his lips pursed together tightly. After a few more moments of consideration he reached over and banged his fist on the green metal door. Within moments two men with blonde hair and blue eyes, wearing combat armour and armed with M4 carbines, entered the room. One cut Munroe free from his binding as the other covered him with his weapon. Munroe's hands were then zip-tied in front of him and the guards heaved Icarus from his chair as Bauer pointed his finger at the killer.

"No funny stuff, David. Despite what I've told you there is still hope for you yet. But that is up to you." Bauer reached up and grasped the corner of the gag in Icarus's mouth and then looked over at Munroe. "What do you think, Ethan. Can our little assassin here behave himself?"

Without waiting for an answer, Bauer pulled the brown cloth away and Icarus instantly began shouting.

"You piece of shit, Hans, I'll cut your fucking head off…"

The gag was immediately jammed back into his mouth. "No, doesn't look like it." Bauer gave Icarus a gentle slap on his cheek and shook his head. "You don't do yourself any favours, David, but regardless, I will honour both of your last wishes. I'm just too kind. That's my problem." He spoke with an infuriating arrogance as one of the guards looped his arm around Munroe's, and with the other holding a gun at Icarus's back both men were roughly led out of the cell and into the adjoining room. Bauer closed the door behind them before joining them.

"Welcome to Blackstar." Bauer raised his arm in a melodramatic arc across the open plan room before him and then smiled as he saw the puzzlement on Munroe face. "It's one of the many jewels in our crown, and a place not many get to see the inside of."

Munroe stared out across the vast warehouse-sized space. On first impression it looked like nothing more than an open plan office, with the exception of the nine masked guards lining the walls. The floor, as far as he could see, was laid with grey lino tiles, paving walkways past low partitioned rooms which provided open cubicles, allowing visibility at all times. Halogen lights embedded in each of the square marble-coloured ceiling tiles lit the whole place up in an aesthetically pleasing way and metres from them stood a varnished wood reception desk which, although unmanned, provided a welcome point for guests. In many of the cubicles sat Apple computers on work desks, and lining both sides of the space were large Perspex windows looking into what appeared to be separate meeting rooms. It was impressively designed, in such a way that almost every square metre of space could be seen from the welcome desk, creating no blind spots.

"Blackstar…" Munroe knew the name well, but he was struggling to comprehend the connection to Daedalus. "The military contractor?"

Bauer raised his eyebrow, taking pride in this reveal as Munroe now realised how far Daedalus's grubby talons reached. Blackstar not only provided the US military with aircraft, vehicles and equipment, but were on the cutting edge of that technology. Along with a few other titanic companies like Lockheed and Northrop their customers included most of the Western governments, among others, and when people spoke of the military–industrial complex it was Blackstar in part they referred to. Christ, much of the equipment that Munroe had used during his time in the special forces had been made by these guys.

"Daedalus is Blackstar?" Munroe said, stunned at what he was hearing, but Bauer was already shaking his head.

"Blackstar is just a part, a cog in our organisation. A big one, but still just a cog." He smiled proudly as Munroe looked on in shock and, as the barrel in his back pushed him forward and past the reception desk, Bauer took great zeal in explaining further. "At the end of the war, German scientists were decades ahead of those in any other country on the planet. Their scientists were so prized by the Allies that any they could get their hands on were given full immunity for any perceived discretions during the war and brought and pressed to the bosom of the budding military–industrial complex.

Regardless of their Nazi affiliation or so-called 'crimes against humanity' they were integrated into the new future of the modern world, but although they changed their employers, many never changed their masters. World history knows it as Operation Paperclip, but to Daedalus it was the future of the Reich, and a means to an end. With an almost endless bankroll confiscated from Europe we were in the perfect position to get our feet in on the military ground floor, as it were, and Blackstar was the result."

With Icarus's handcuffs being held tightly by one of the guards, both he and Munroe were led past the office space and on towards the back of the warehouse until they reached a transparent, bulletproof door, if the signs were to be trusted. Bauer pulled a card from his pocket and slid it over the glowing pad. The door clicked open and automatically swung back and both Munroe and Icarus were ushered through into a plain white room with rows of cages bolted to the wall, filled with grey plastic cylinders.

"It's here that we store all Blackstar's R&D records, the culmination of decades of dedicated research. All our original designs and patents are kept here," Bauer said, motioning to the cages, all secured by digital locks. "We don't keep a full archive digitally. It may sound like a backwards step given the security technology available, but believe me, nothing is more secure than a bombproof room surrounded by guards. You might like to know that the original plans for the stealth helicopter you managed to evade are contained within these cages. Just another product of the cutting-edge technology we work on here at Blackstar."

"Good luck trying to sell it. If you offer up one of those then every government in the Western world is going to know you were involved in Icarus's breakout on Waterloo Bridge," Munroe said, but Bauer was already one step ahead of him, and he shook his head.

"We already have the intelligence services believing it was built by the Chinese. As for why they would use it in such a way, that is not our problem, but I will tell you what will happen next. The US government will approach us, wanting to keep up the weapons race with China, and offer a contract to anyone who can build such a prototype. We'll hold back on the specs for a few years and then, before anyone else does, we'll offer them the finished product. It should prove highly lucrative for Blackstar. When it comes to cutting-edge technology, the military are happy to ignore certain truths. So long as they are the ones, and only ones, to own it."

Bauer now took another key card from his other pocket and slid it across what looked like a section of white painted wall. "Now, let's take a short ride, shall we."

Munroe felt the tiles beneath him begin to vibrate, and the entire floor of the room began to descend.

"I guess you're not a real Nazi unless you have your own personal bunker." His guard jabbed the barrel of his gun into his back and his remark received an unimpressed look from Bauer.

"Very droll, Ethan. But what I'm about to show you is the result of decades of painstaking work, a promise the Führer made to the German people."

"Oh, I wouldn't call slavery, murder and the total collapse of Germany a promise, Hans," Munroe replied, happy to call out the sheer arrogance of the man, "more like an affliction, or a shitty virus."

The guard once more slammed his carbine into Munroe's back as Bauer shook his head in dismay. "I think you're referring to your own government, Ethan. No, it was a promise, and one that will be kept. Project Icarus, and the ushering in of a one-thousand-year Reich."

Chapter 29

The elevator jolted to a stop and as two thick metal doors slid back Munroe was shoved out onto a grated metal walkway as Icarus, still gagged but remarkably subdued given his previous outburst, joined him, under the care of the guard. Bauer moved to the opposite railing and waved them on and down a short length of metal steps to the level below. He waited until they'd all joined him and then placed his hand on Munroe's shoulder. "Take a look, Ethan. This is where the magic happens."

What Munroe saw produced the same feeling he had experienced upon seeing Dr Ferreira's 'school' back in Brazil, and even though the sight itself looked harmless enough, what it represented was anything but. It was a hospital. An underground hospital, with three floors. The whole area was devoid of any personnel, but from the shiny tiled floors to the corridors and rooms, to the oxygen access points and even to the red emergency lights above each doorway, Munroe could have been in any modern hospital in America.

"You look puzzled, Ethan, but use your imagination and think about it while I tell you a story. A story our friend Icarus wants you to hear, and one he knows all too well."

They were taken for a walk through the wards as Bauer began to impart a tale that, although Munroe had not realised it yet, was what had led him to this place.

"The school where we first met, in Brazil, was run by a scientist of ours, a Dr Manuel Ferreira. He was Daedalus through and through. Not because he was born into it but because he chose and believed in it. You see, the good doctor was a genius of psychiatry, but he was only following in the footsteps of a true titan. One of our first, and the creator of what would later become Project Icarus."

Bauer stopped at a small glass-faced refrigerator and gently opened it. "He was a man with the fascination and dedication to see his dreams realised and," Bauer continued, retrieving a small test tube filled with what looked like blood, which he held up in his fingers and inspected, "that was to create the perfect human specimen, the perfect human soldier. We know him as 'The Father', but you would recognise him by a different name... Josef Mengele."

"The Angel of Death," Munroe replied loathingly; the nickname seemed to genuinely offend Bauer.

"That's just a tacky label that stuck, gifted by people who had no understanding of the great accomplishments he sought to, and did, achieve."

"Your 'Father' was a child murderer, Hans. He experimented on and tortured hundreds, thousands of people."

Bauer looked unfazed by the accusation. "That was mainly confined to the concentration camps. His work acted as a catalyst for greater things, and in this case the end does justify the means."

Josef Mengele, a Nazi medical officer in the Waffen-SS, was a man less concerned with treatment and instead focused on pain and suffering. His obsession with creating a master race of blonde-haired, blue-eyed Aryans was well known in the history books, and his experiments on camp inmates were about as vile as one could imagine. Forced breeding between twins, the freezing to death of patients just to see how the human body reacted and far worse. His obsession with inducing twins in every German pregnancy to quickly fill the Nazis' sagging military ranks towards the end of the war was as infamous as it was heartless. He was also considered to be behind the inception of the Lebensborn breeding camps, where blonde-haired, blue-eyed children were kidnapped from all over the conquered nations of the Reich and used as stock for the Nazis' desired conquest of the world. It had failed, but not before Mengele escaped. Munroe thought back to his conversation with Silva. Mengele had died in 1979 somewhere within the depths of Brazil, escaping the justice he so richly deserved. Munroe had heard the stories, but since learning of Daedalus's existence they had taken on a whole new dimension.

"You've been creating a master race," Munroe said, glancing over at his blonde-haired, blue-eyed chaperones. Bauer shook his head.

"No, Ethan. You make it sound like some crass sci-fi movie. It's so much more than that. After the war Herr Mengele continued his work in Brazil, funded by us of course, but he only got so far before his death. Before his demise he was able, through specific breeding, to create the perfect human specimen with the attributes so valued by us. But it came with the realisation that the shell is only part of the equation in creating the perfect soldier, and then the perfect assassin. This is where Dr Ferreira became so essential to our work, with his experimentation into multiple personalities and the fracturing of the psyche." Bauer now motioned to Munroe's chaperones. "These men here are a direct result of that work, the creation of the perfect Aryan soldier. The Führer would have been proud, but although they are a result of perfect breeding, they never went through Dr Ferreira's programme. Of course this work, though essential, paled in comparison to what we have achieved since. Upon Herr Mengele's death we began a new programme, and in the modern age the breakthroughs in science and genetics gave us the ability to lay the foundations that would eventually become Project Icarus. Unfortunately we had to cut ties with Dr Ferreira's work, which until very recently he was still committed to. The village of Cândido Godói was a perfect testing ground for Herr Mengele's work, but with all the press attention it received after his death we had Dr Ferreira move to another facility very close by, and for decades no one ever suspected. His work at one of the local communes proved a valuable source of research until he had achieved all he could. We let him continue his work but, I'm afraid, that all had to come to an end when our attack on Parliament was carried out. We knew that little caper of ours would set DS5 ablaze and frothing at the mouths for answers, and so we had to tie up any loose ends."

Bauer sniffed the air and laughed. "When a predator gains your scent, the only true course of action is to cover one's tracks. It was very sad, a true waste, a whole village of his lab rats having to be wiped out, not even knowing that they had been at the centre of our research. Still, trails have to be dusted, and we can't have any leading to us, can we?"

The image of the burning church and the arm marked with the symbol of Daedalus now made perfect, if sick, sense. Those people had been corralled into the church and burnt alive not just for who they were... but *what* they were. Experimented on without their knowledge and marked like concentration camp victims, they had then been disposed of to conceal any tracks leading towards Daedalus's greater goal, and that was the question now on Munroe's lips.

"Why did you blow up Parliament?" he asked, sounding calm, not wanting to interrupt Bauer's continuing admissions, but he was met with a deep guttural laugh.

"Now that is well beyond your pay grade, Ethan. Just consider yourself fortunate I'm granting you information on Project Icarus."

Bauer rolled the vial containing the red liquid between his fingers before placing it back in the refrigerator and closing the door. "So, getting back to the point, let me ask you. What makes a good soldier, Ethan? Strength, stamina, reaction time, obedience... These are mainly physical qualities, and they can be produced through good breeding, just like we breed dogs for desirable traits. But what makes a good leader, what produces men with drive and charisma, what makes them stand out at such a young age, these natural born trailblazers?"

Bauer tapped his forefinger against his lips in wonderment. "These genetic traits are hidden to us, locked away in the human genome and far more difficult to reproduce. Project Icarus was begun to not only create the perfect Aryan warriors and assassins, but the world leaders of tomorrow. Can you imagine if we could identify, within the DNA double helix, those traits that the greatest leaders in world history all possessed? And once bred, to be then indoctrinated into the true ideology, the right ideology, the Nazi ideology. Anyone holding that power of creation would hold the keys to a kingdom, and the ability to reshape it in their image. Would they not?"

Munroe now knew what Bauer was getting at, but it seemed the stuff of science fiction. Designer babies were within humanity's grasp, but designer leaders? "You're talking about politicians. Humans genetically engineered to be the perfect leaders. Bullshitters, scam artists, con men with the intelligence and charisma to pull it off and win people over."

"Well, that's a rather base way to put it, but something like that, yes," Bauer replied, looking disheartened by Munroe's assessment. "Have you ever wondered why some men can walk into a crowded room and people are just drawn to them? Why is that? Why some have the ability to manipulate others with a single look or stare. It makes no physical sense unless, subconsciously or otherwise, people are drawn to these individuals because of what they possess on a genetic level. The Führer had it, many world leaders have it. What is that 'thing' that makes them stand out, which gives them an ability to seduce the masses? Well, through Project Icarus we discovered these mysteries, learnt how to rewire DNA in just the right way. And we have been refining the process ever since. It takes a while for humans to grow, but the more you produce the higher the likelihood of getting winners. Don't forget, Ethan, we're only animals. We respond to a vast array of unseen stimuli, and what we have found is that genetics plays a huge part in this. The age-old question of nature over nurture has been revealed, by us, and it seems that nature is far more influential than previously believed. If you ask someone what it is about *that* person, why am I drawn to them, why do I have such an instant connection with them, the answers are usually physical in nature. Their eyes, the way they smile, how they carry themselves… But what if it was far deeper than that? Deep below the skin, something in their genetic code. You can't tell me that you've never seen someone and just known they were special. They just had 'it'. We do it all the time, but never consider why that is."

Bauer's hypothesis sounded crazy, but who knew how long they had been experimenting on humans. Those trials could have put them decades ahead of the current understanding of genetics. Human experimentation was morally deplorable, although sadly its use could increase understanding and yield results far beyond what other methods allowed, and considering the lack of scruples these Nazis had it seemed more than plausible they could have made such a breakthrough. A breakthrough about what it was to be human, and how to manipulate that knowledge to their own ends.

There was, though, a big hole in Bauer's theory, and Munroe brought it up the instant he thought of it. "Are you seriously trying to tell me that Icarus," Munroe glanced back at the gagged killer and nodded towards him, "was bred to be a leader?"

His question received a shocked look from Bauer, and he wagged his head and laughed. "God no. David only took the name Icarus, he wasn't part of it. He was bred from Herr Mengele's initial work, to have all the qualities of a soldier. Faster reactions, stamina, strength, and with Dr Ferreira's contribution and his fracturing process, he and his brothers and sisters were bred and trained and brought up to be assassins for Daedalus. To pave the way for the leaders created by Project Icarus. But there was a difficult obstacle in our way, in the form of DS5. Churchill and Truman's charter has made it incredibly difficult to place our own produce within the political folds, which is why we changed tack and did the only thing we could. We targeted DS5 as well."

A sagging realisation now tugged at Munroe's stomach, and like a puzzle the pieces began sliding into place. The attack on their C-130, on a trip known only to a select few, and the ambush in New Orleans... How had they known he and Icarus would be there unless someone from DS5 had passed on Munroe's location? Who else knew?

He was still mulling over the possibilities as Bauer explained further and appearing to take great enjoyment in his own smugness.

"Infiltrating DS5 has proved tougher than any political hierarchy because of their hiring policy, their reliance on chance encounters. That is something which is extremely difficult to orchestrate."

Munroe said nothing, his mind was swirling with questions and calculations as to who the mole, or moles, at DS5 could be. Bauer saw the conflict in his eyes. "Not easy finding out you've been stabbed in the back, is it? But I think it may make what I'm about to tell you a lot easier to swallow. Please, follow me."

It wasn't as if Munroe had an option as the two guards nudged him forward and, along with Icarus, he was led by Bauer into a room located further up the corridor.

"Is this your office?" Munroe said with a sarcastic raising of his eyebrow, but Bauer gave a shake of his head as Icarus was also bundled inside by the guards.

"No, Ethan. This room contains the apex of our efforts. The culmination of all the decades of work we have carried out."

Bauer looked extremely proud as Munroe scanned the room. There was no desk, no computer, not even a chair, just empty space except for what hung from the walls. Dozens upon dozens of rows of large rectangular photos, and with a push from one of the guards Munroe walked over to the nearest ones and began to examine them, one by one. They looked like school photos, each picture containing around twenty children. It was a mix of girls and boys, with those at the front squatted on one knee as those in the rows behind stood proudly with folded arms. They couldn't have been more than ten years old. At the bottom a date had been printed in embossed gold type, starting in 1966, with each subsequent picture going up in two-year increments.

"The left and right walls are Herr Mengele's accomplishments," Bauer said, now taking a step towards the far wall, "but these are our crowning achievements. The accomplishments and fruits of Project Icarus."

There must have been over a hundred children on the far wall, but these were different. Whereas in the Mengele photos the children all had blonde hair and blue eyes, the ones on the Icarus wall were all different. Some had black hair, others red, some were blonde, but and if one counted all the photos in the room there must have been over four hundred young faces.

As Munroe gazed over them the reality of what Daedalus had achieved produced a tight knot in his stomach. "These are all genetically made kids, genetically purposed?" he said, and Bauer tapped the wall with his finger and smiled.

"Each one instilled with the genetic traits that best suited them for the role we have laid out. And each trained and serving the greater good. Our good."

While Munroe fathomed the incredible scope of Daedalus's endeavour Bauer continued to speak, his pride shining through in each word that was spoken by him.

"The war never ended, Ethan. It just took on a different form. They say that revenge is a dish best served cold, and I couldn't agree more. That isn't to say we've not had our setbacks. We came close to consolidating the world positions we needed back in the early noughties, but with 9/11 came a shift in political power and thinking. A whole generation of our candidates were lost to the political wilderness, but that was twenty years ago and now, with the landscape littered with identity politics and racial division, the time has never been riper to consolidate our power. The coming bondage of slavery will not be in physical chains but invisible ones, in the minds of free people."

An unpleasant feeling swirled in Munroe's stomach as Bauer now took great pleasure in disclosing his reasoning.

"War and conquest are driven by ideology. One group's wish to force its will and ideology upon another's. Whether it was the Mongols or the Romans, naked aggression has been the single most effective tool to achieve ideological domination of the human species. But that age-old truth crumbled with the advent of the atomic bomb. That single instant when critical mass was reached on the atomic level. From that moment on a world war could not ever happen again, not without destroying everyone and everything in the process. Conventional domination of the world ceased to be possible, and a new path needed to be forged. A path not cut on the battlefield but within the minds of those that believe themselves to be free. Take a look around you, Ethan. The notion of free speech and the rights of the individual is being slowly replaced with that of the group identity. The focus is now on the differences between us, and not those things we share in common. The technology of communication and social media is seeing to that, and the culmination of Project Icarus seeks to nurture those beliefs. Whether the public know it or not, the greatest political minds of our times have placed us on a course for something they believe to be for the good of humanity, a single world government where war is no more and the peoples of the world are united as one. Under this climate people are willing to give up more and more rights for the greater good, and when all is said and done, our leaders, the fruits of Project Icarus, will be at the top of it. And the best bit of all is they won't realise what's happening until it's already happened. It's just as the Führer imagined, a world order of national socialism working its way down from the top, all the way through society to the most basic but crucial levels. And with the common break-up of the of the nuclear family, something we can't take credit for unfortunately but which we will exploit, it allows children to be exposed to the state at an ever earlier age. A state that we will control. Winning hearts and minds has always been the key to long-lasting subjugation, and you know how its's done? We realised it with the inception of the Hitler Youth back in the Thirties, when an entire generation was indoctrinated into national socialism."

Bauer leant close to Munroe, and then he spoke in almost a whisper, as if telling a secret. "Morality. Teach a few generations that what they have been taught is morally right, and they will justify their actions for the rest of their lives. Human beings struggle to flat-out lie to themselves, it's not part of their condition. But to justify one's beliefs is far more acceptable in one's mind, no matter how illogical the reasoning might be. The Hitler Youth were taught that survival of the fittest was not only morally right but the natural order of things, and they went to their deaths still defending such ideas. And so it is happening with the younger generations of today. All they need is a little guidance from world leadership and like that," Bauer snapped his fingers, "the education systems of yesterday become the re-education camps of tomorrow."

Bauer now glared menacingly, and Munroe could see in his eyes the gaze of a true believer.

"So why tell me all this, Hans. Why Icarus's fascination with me and my family? He appeared to have focused on me long before I crossed paths with DS5."

As Icarus attempted to speak his muffled words were ignored by Bauer, who stood up straight and slipped his arm under Munroe's, and under the watchful eyes of the two guards he guided him over to the doorway, stopping beside a single photo frame offset from all the others, containing a group of much younger children, maybe three or four years old. They were all sitting next to individual nurses all dressed in the same white aprons and caps. "As I mentioned, we've had our setbacks. Not all our experiments turned out as they should have."

Bauer pointed to a child just off centre. "That is David, or Icarus, as he rechristened himself. It was taken back at Dr Ferreira's school in Brazil where these children were brought up. Where they lived and were educated for the first twelve years of their lives. It is the class of 1990, and the last of Herr Mengele's batch. All the children were gifted with the best genes we could provide, bestowing on them all the reflexes, stamina, strength and mental acuity genetics could afford them. They were bred from some of our best German stock, from a multitude of donors, and they were trained as assassins from a young age. I believe you met Tobias Kessler during your travels. He was one of the most competent tutors we've ever had, and the lessons and training he oversaw allowed these boys and girls to develop into highly proficient killers, as you've seen for yourself in David. But unfortunately, there was a problem with this batch. It wasn't on the genetics side of things but rather with Dr Ferreira's contribution. His process of fracturing the mind was a master stroke. Creating individuals whose programmed assassination training could be turned on and off at will through certain stimuli. We had great successes, but it was at a price. The older the subjects got the harder it became to separate the personalities. As such they became liabilities, and were all terminated with the exception of Icarus, who appeared to be the only one under our supervision that remained unaffected."

Bauer now looked over at Icarus, who only stared blankly. To Munroe the man looked broken, all the anger in his eyes evaporated.

"That was until six months ago, when he went on his unsanctioned murder spree, including two DS5 operatives embedded within MI6," Bauer finished, his face full of disdain for the gagged man before him.

The way Bauer called them 'batches' did not sit well with Munroe, but the Nazi was right about one thing. Icarus had descended into uncontrollable psychosis.

"Understandably he never forgave us for terminating his 'classmates', or brothers and sisters, as he saw them."

Bauer now pointed to the photo. "Tell me, Ethan. Does anything in this photo stand out to you?"

Munroe began to examine each of the children individually and he was quick to notice the odd one out. "That one's got black hair, and all the others have blonde."

"Well noticed," Bauer replied in an overly sarcastically tone. "In those days the idea of the perfect Aryan specimen had not yet taken a back seat to the more important need for anonymity, as was later created in subjects of Project Icarus. The child was not like the others. He showed similar abilities, so far as anyone could tell, but due to his undesirable features and young age the fracturing process was never performed on him. It would have been a waste of time, and soon after he was designated for termination. Unfortunately the nurse you see next to him had grown rather attached. Such a weak characteristic for anyone within the folds of Daedalus. She absconded with the child, but my predecessors caught up with her soon afterwards. She died never revealing the location of the child."

Bauer now tapped the golden embossed 1990 label at the bottom of the photo. "When this photo was taken these children were all four years old which means they were born in 1986... Tell me, Ethan. What year were you born?"

Munroe's breathing began to tighten and a nervous tingling rippled across his skin. "1986," he said, in nothing more than a shocked whisper. If what Bauer was alluding to was true, Icarus's fascination made complete sense. Munroe felt sick to his core.

Bauer smiled as one of the guards moved closer with his M4 raised, in anticipation of a reaction from their captive. "You weren't born, Ethan. You were manufactured. And you've exceeded all our expectations."

Chapter 30

"Bullshit. I know when I'm being played, Hans." His reply was aggressive, but the gnawing feeling in the pit of his stomach told him there was truth to all this. "You expect me to believe that it's pure coincidence that the one that got away from you just happened to turn up on your doorstep after all these years?"

"It's not a coincidence at all. If it wasn't for Icarus you never would have been drawn to us. I will admit your induction into DS5 was a surprise, but after that it was only a matter of time before our paths crossed."

"And how do you even know I'm with DS5?"

The question produced an odd, quizzical look from Bauer. "I already told you, we infiltrated DS5 some years ago. I think you're allowing your emotions to overwhelm you. You're not thinking straight."

Emotions no, anger yes.

"Who?" Munroe demanded, wishing to focus his attention back on the mole rather than the painful truth being revealed to him.

"Do you really want to know?"

"No! That's why I'm asking you," Munroe replied sarcastically, and Bauer leant forward and whispered a name in his ear before standing back up straight and taking a moment to enjoy the shocked expression.

"And in a way, you're the other one."

Munroe's face was now seething. Not because he was being toyed with, but because it could be true.

Was he really the result of a Nazi experiment to create a super soldier?

The ridiculous label caused him to relax slightly. This was all too crazy, and he reined in his anger as Bauer changed the subject.

"There is another truth that I feel you should know, and this one's going to sting." Bauer lifted his hands in the air with his palms open faced. "You wanted to know about the deaths of your family, and on this matter, I can provide some clarity. I heard the little conversation you had with Icarus back at Dr Bute's. We had the room bugged. Of course I know you saw my written debrief, but allow me to give you all the details you so want. From the beginning."

With his teeth gritted and struggling to contain his anger Munroe descended into silence, allowing Bauer to take the trip down memory lane. A trip the Nazi appeared excited for.

"You were stolen from us some time ago, that is true, but we rediscovered you a number of years ago purely by accident. When you entered the Special Air Service a blood sample was taken from you, as is standard practice. What you may not know is that these samples are checked by the military for genetic abnormalities, anything that could negatively affect a soldier's health. Your data was, as with others, placed on a governmental database. It is this database that we gained access to through our military contacts, and you can imagine our surprise when one of our scientists noticed our own handiwork."

Munroe looked wholly unconvinced. "Why would you do that?"

"Simple. Genetics is our speciality, and we're always looking for unique blends that may aid us in our work. We also have access to the databases of many health organisations and departments around the world. The NHS and WHO are but two. It's the only way to get genetic information from a broad range of the global populace. Many companies trade in personal information in the modern age, and we're no different. My superiors' initial idea was to just leave you alone. You had no idea who you were, and we were happy to leave it that way... that is, until you decided to marry and have a child."

Bauer shook his head in disappointment. "A *Jewish* wife! You can't really have expected us to stand by as your genome was polluted by a Zionist."

That Munroe's wife had been Jewish had never even entered his mind. Christ, he'd even considered converting at one point, and along with the anger he felt a cold sadness wash over him as Bauer callously made his point.

"The intention had been for you all to be killed in that bomb blast. My debrief stating your family as collateral was correct. You were the main target, but fate allowed you to dodge that bullet. Still, at least the abomination that was your child did not survive. That would have been unacceptable. As for you, Ethan, you are a survivor through and through. Just as we bred you to be. But you do seem to have an angel watching over you... an angel that has brought you to us."

Without warning Munroe dove forward and head-butted Bauer right at the base of his nose, hearing the bone crack, and as Bauer fell back against the wall one of the guards gripped him in a headlock from behind and restrained him tightly.

"You're dead, Bauer. And I'm taking Daedalus down with you." He fought wildly against the guard's grip as Bauer stood back up, his nose wrinkling at the pain. "Of course you will, Ethan, that's the spirit." He laughed sarcastically. "You're a killer at heart. Everything we made you to be."

The grip around Munroe's neck tightened and as he struggled Bauer pulled a white handkerchief from his pocket and used it to absorb the trickle of blood oozing from his nose. "Of course, you should know we're not alike, you and I. You were bred, whereas I am of pure stock." Bauer expelled a deep laugh. "Do you know who I am, Ethan? I am the direct descendent of Reinhard Heydrich, of pure Germanic blood. The person Hitler described as 'the man with an iron heart,' and whose righteous actions led to the concentration camps until he was gunned down by Serbian cowards. I have taken on his mantle, I have become death incarnate to all who would oppose a thousand-year Reich."

Munroe watched as Bauer changed from a mild-mannered man to a raving psychopath within the blink of an eye. He spat his words and his hair fell down across his face from the neatly slicked-back hairstyle he'd had moments earlier, his eyes widening feverishly. "Under Reich Führer Bormann we will cleanse the world of the rats who have infested its sacred soil for far too long and, when the time comes, we will march across their broken, shattered corpses and piss on their graves as the world bows down to our will. You thought we caused the world pain last time around? You ain't seen nothing yet."

Bauer slammed his fist into Munroe's gut before taking a step backwards, slicking back his hair again and composing himself, although his eyes still bulged with rage. "You will die a painful death, Ethan Munroe. You have my word on that. Perhaps you'll be eaten alive by rats, and as they sink their teeth into your soft, tender eyeballs you will think of me, slowly torturing to death anyone and everyone you ever cared about."

Bauer reached under his tweed jacket and pulled out a silver-coloured dagger with an ebony wood grip and now held the tip to Munroe's throat. "This was my father's SS dagger, and do you know what the inscription reads?"

There was no way Munroe could tell with the blade so close to his throat and he shook his head slowly.

"It reads '*Meine Ehre Heisst Treue*'. It means 'My Honour is my Loyalty,' and I will enjoy probing the softer parts of your body with it, Ethan. My loyalty to the Fourth Reich is beyond reproach, and I will do what I must to ensure its survival. Remember Herr Kessler? A great man, a man of the Reich. I slit his throat with a garotte wire for making one simple mistake, and he was a friend. That's loyalty to my cause. Just imagine what I will do to you before this night is over."

The mention of Kessler had Munroe staring at him wide-eyed and Bauer now grinned. "Does that surprise you, Ethan? That I would kill one of my own?"

"It's not a surprise, no. I was just thinking about how that old man manged to tag me with a tracker. There's just no way to escape you bastards, is there?"

"There's nowhere anyone can hide, Ethan. Daedalus is everywhere. We can track anyone."

"Well, that's good to know," Munroe replied, now swivelling his wrist against the zip tie binding it and motioning to the small cut in his forearm and the little bump protruding from it. The final parting gift from

McCitrick's care package, which Sloan had administered to him back on the C-130. "Because so can we."

From somewhere above the sound of an enormous explosion rocked the walls, and as Bauer reeled in surprise Munroe thrust his head back, catching the guard restraining him square on the nose, and the man lost his grip. Munroe slapped the dagger from Bauer's hands, sending it across the room before landing a kick to the Nazi's chest, throwing him backwards.

Behind Munroe, Icarus had also seized the moment and jammed his knee into his guard's groin. As the man bent forward in pain, Icarus brought up his knee and slammed it into his face, laying him out cold.

A second explosion now erupted from somewhere up on the ground floor, and as Munroe struggled with his guard Bauer did something unexpected. He didn't fight or hold his ground but instead ran for the doorway and disappeared through it. With no time to lose, Munroe slid his bound arms around the guard's neck and tensed before swivelling his shoulders powerfully. Hearing the neck snap, he dropped the body to the floor and made a dive for the SS dagger nearby. The sharp blade cut through the plastic with ease and as he turned to the open doorway he found Icarus standing in front of it with his bound hands held out before him.

If Bauer got to the elevator before he did then he'd be stuck down here until DS5 reached him, and so making a split decision he stepped over to Icarus and placed the knife against his plastic bindings. "Can I trust you?"

There was uncertainty in the Icarus's eyes, and it didn't look like even he knew the answer. "I think so," came his reply, and Munroe hesitated before cutting through the bindings.

"Good enough." He grabbed one of the M4s and tossed the dagger to the killer. "No guns. Now follow me."

Munroe was already out of the door and running down the hospital corridor before Icarus replied, but he did glance back to see him sticking to the request, holding only the dagger as they both charged back towards the elevator.

As they approached the grated metal stairs another series of explosions went off overhead but they were smaller this time, possibly grenades. DS5 were making one hell of an entrance, and Munroe was thankful. As he reached the first step of the stairwell, though, he was pushed aside by Icarus, who leapt past him and up towards the elevator as the sound of doors sliding open could be heard.

The barge caused Munroe to stumble, his knee slamming against the steps, and he paused for a moment in pain before striding up the stairs just in time to see Icarus disappear into the waiting elevator. There were the sounds of a struggle and as Munroe finally reached the opening with his M4 pointing inside he saw Bauer in the process of slamming Icarus's head against the wall, now raising the SS dagger to the killer's throat.

"Don't move or I'll slit his throat," Bauer yelled, but Munroe ignored the threat, and keeping his carbine raised he entered the elevator.

"Not another step, Ethan." Bauer's tone of voice was more measured this time, keeping his own head hidden behind Icarus's as best he could.

The doors slid shut and the elevator began to slowly ascend upwards, the commotion of gunfire above becoming ever louder.

"Shoot him, Ethan," Icarus ordered, without any hint of emotion. "Shoot him now."

"Shut up, you idiot," Bauer spat, with only one eye visible as he hid behind the killer.

The thought had crossed Munroe's mind, but given everything he had learnt about Icarus he was inclined not to take the chance. The Daedalus assassin was unstable and he needed to be locked up, but at that moment Munroe couldn't help but think a psychiatric ward was more suitable than a grave.

"There's nowhere to go, Hans. If you walk out of this elevator you'll likely be shot."

"Oh, I doubt that Ethan. I'm worth far more alive to DS5 than dead. I'm still holding all the cards, so here's what we're going to do. When we reach the ground floor, David and I are going to walk out of here. Considering the gunfire up there I would surmise that my men are holding their ground. We will part ways, and then the real game begins. You have learnt more about Daedalus than anyone else has in a long time, and that will be your reward. In fact it might even sway your buddies at DS5 not to have you sanctioned, given the truth of the origin of your birth. I doubt they will take kindly to having someone like you within their ranks."

Before Munroe could answer, the elevator floor raised back into the room and with a slight jolt Bauer was already moving towards the security door leading back into the main facility. His free hand appeared and he threw Munroe the key card. "Open the door, and you go first."

Munroe paused for a moment, but then he reached down, picked up the card and, carbine still held high, moved over to the door and swiped the card. The door automatically swung open and the whole room was flooded with the sound of gunfire as Munroe looked over to see two familiar figures. Sloan and Colonel Remus were hunkered down on the opposite wall twenty metres away. They were flanked by a small squad of US Marines who had taken cover inside the open cubicles and were already pressing their advance upon the group of Daedalus guards, who were huddled up at the far end, next to the welcome desk and clearly making a last stand.

From behind, Bauer was already slipping past with Icarus still in his grip, moving backwards with incredible speed to a set of fire escape stairs leading upwards, at a guess to the roof.

Help his squad, or go after Bauer.

Munroe hesitated, but then saw Sloan glance back at him and briefly smile as bullets thudded around her, stopping her from moving out of cover. She looked over at the man being dragged by knifepoint up the stairs and then flicked her finger in that direction before focusing back on the firefight.

Munroe turned and chased after Bauer as some of the Daedalus guards further up now noticed him and began sending a barrage of bullets his way. The wall plaster above him exploded into plumes of chalky dust as he leapt towards the stairwell and then upwards as more rounds exploded off the metal railings. As he reached the top the door was only just closing and he kicked it open to see Bauer, with Icarus still in tow, heading across the roof towards the same stealth helicopter he had seen back in London and Brazil. The rotors were already spinning and two guards standing next to the aircraft began shooting at Munroe, who dove to one side and sought refuge behind a large air-conditioning unit.

Bullets rattled the metal frame and then there was a pause, and as Munroe peeked out from behind, it all went to hell. He watched as Icarus grabbed the dagger pressed against his neck and pulled it downwards in an attempt to wrestle the weapon from Bauer's grip. As he did so the guard on the left turned and put a single shot in Icarus's, chest sending him down onto his knees, but having retrieved the dagger.

Munroe seized his chance and took aim at the shooter, landing a shot to the face, dropping him to the roof instantly. But in doing so he opened himself up to the other guard who had him in his sights.

As Munroe stared at the barrel aimed directly at him, time suddenly slowed, and even as he swung his gun towards the man he knew he was caught cold, with no hope.

Then the glint of something silver streaked across his line of sight before embedding itself square in the guard's chest. *The dagger.*

It gave Munroe time to squeeze off two rounds, which slammed the guard backwards down hard onto the rooftop. He turned to see Icarus, his arm still outstretched from the knife-throw, collapse in a heap. Behind him Bauer was mere metres from the helicopter and Munroe dropped to one knee, aimed and pulled the trigger.

The bullet shattered Bauer's left kneecap, causing him to tumble into a faceplant against the hard tar-coated rooftop, and he let out a high-pitched scream. It was a solid shot, especially as, and only now did Munroe realise, one of the guard's bullets had caught him in the shoulder, but he could hardly feel the wound, the adrenalin fuelling his focus.

Beyond Icarus's motionless body Bauer was now crawling to the helicopter, his face turning pasty and white, sweat already beading his brow at the shock such a painful wound had caused. But it was a futile attempt, and Munroe began firing at the helicopter cockpit. He knew the bullets wouldn't penetrate, but that wasn't the point. The shots ricocheted off the canopy but it was enough to warn the pilot off, and the helicopter pulled up into the air and reared off to one side. As Bauer yelled after it, clutching his shattered knee, the aircraft silently slunk off into the night sky.

Munroe approached Bauer with his gun raised. Bauer was fumbling for the Luger stuffed in his waist, and rolled onto his back, aiming it at Munroe. A single round into the Nazi's wrist sent the Luger scraping along the tar roof and out of reach.

Down below the sound of gunfire had stopped and Munroe figured he didn't have long before an audience arrived. He stopped a few feet away from Bauer and held the muzzle directly at the man's face. He said nothing as he mulled over his next move, and it was Bauer's whining that pulled him from his trance-like state.

"Kill me, Ethan," he spat through clenched teeth, the pain in his knee agonising. "I won't be taken alive. Pull the trigger and do what you do. What we bred you to do."

Munroe did nothing, and with his gun still raised he stood there in silence as Bauer attempted to goad him.

"I'll tell them everything. What you are. They'll never accept you. You'll be an outcast. They'll probably kill you themselves."

Munroe thought about it for a moment, images of the smiling faces of his family passing through his mind, and then he lowered his gun. "I'm not what you think I am. I'll take my chances."

With that he strode over and slammed the butt of his carbine across Bauer's head, dropping him unconscious, before quickly jogging back over to the body of Icarus. As he got closer he realised the killer was still alive… just. Munroe rolled him onto his back and immediately began pressing his hand against the wound, but he knew it was pointless and so did Icarus.

"Stay with me, David." Blood poured from Icarus's mouth, and even though no words were spoken Munroe knew exactly what his eyes were telling him, and he turned his attention to the quivering hand now being offered.

No one wanted to die alone.

Munroe gently clasped his hand around Icarus's, and the two men stared at each other for a few moments. He could not be forgiven for the things he had done, the pain he had caused his victims. But for what it was worth, in that moment, Munroe felt only pity for the person Daedalus had created, for the innocent boy he had once been.

With one final widening of his eyes Icarus's hand went limp, and slipped from Munroe's grasp.

From behind him, he heard the sound of the roof door being hurled open. He turned to see Sloan and Colonel Remus exiting, and while scanning the area for any hostiles they made their way over to him.

"Is he alive?" Remus asked, pointing his gun at Icarus.

"No, he's gone," Munroe replied as Sloan moved over to Bauer.

"How about him?"

"Took a nasty one to the kneecap but, yeah, he's alive."

"Good." Remus pulled a white zip tie from his pocket and set about securing Bauer's hands.

"You OK?" Sloan asked, and Munroe nodded.

"Where the hell are we?" he asked, the dark landscape beyond giving no clue to their location.

"Just outside Houston, Texas. You were out for hours but we followed you at a distance. You were never out of our sight, but you won't believe who owns this complex."

Munroe couldn't believe they had taken him so far, hundreds of miles from New Orleans. "Blackstar." Sloan raised her eyebrows at this response, and then smiled before tapping him on the shoulder. "I'm looking forward to your debrief, Ethan." She said and then reached over and slid her finger across the bump on his forearm. "The tracker worked, then."

Munroe nodded and got to his feet. "She did her job. I felt it click just before you breached, just like you said it would."

While sticking him with the tracker on the flight over Sloan had droned on about how the small pellet beneath their skin could not only track but emit a single pulse as a warning. She had repeated it multiple times not because she believed Munroe to be slow, but because she had found the technology so impressive. In truth, it was just a small metal ball that vibrated when activated, but it had worked, just as she said it would if either of them ran into any problems. And problems were just what Munroe had found.

Kneeling next to Bauer, Colonel Remus made sure the zip tie was secure and then he stood back up and joined them. "Good work, son. I'm hoping this place is a Daedalus goldmine. We should get a lot of…"

"Remus," Munroe said, cutting him off abruptly. "There's something important you need to know. About me. And if DS5 are OK with it, then we have to make a trip to London. ASAP."

Remus looked concerned, but he skipped over whatever Munroe wanted to tell him and went straight for the trip. "What's in London?"

Munroe glanced back at Bauer, who was still sleeping like a baby, and then took a deep breath. "The mole in DS5. And you're not going to like it."

Chapter 31

It was turning out to be a cold evening as Munroe pulled the collar of his black overcoat up around his neck. There was a chill in the air, and as he looked across the City of London from the rooftop of the old War Office building on the edge of the Thames, he knew it was about to get a lot colder. For over a century the building had been the centre of army operations for the British Empire until its offices had been relocated to the Ministry of Defence in 1968, the building just across the road. On the opposite side of that was Number 10 Downing Street, and only one building past that sat the Treasury offices, whose lights never went out. Death and taxes, the only two things one could be certain of in life. What was left of Parliament may have been the public face of government, but these few blocks of land were where the real power lay, the mandarins of Whitehall running their hive of workers and maintaining the circus that was modern-day politics.

Behind him he heard the creaking of a fire door, and after one last look over the landscape he turned around to see John McCitrick making his way over to him, followed by Home Secretary Jacob Ryan close on his heels.

"Ethan." McCitrick greeted him and came to a stop along with Ryan, who wasn't looking happy.

"Can someone please tell me why we're meeting on the roof of the old War Office?" Ryan asked, and McCitrick shook his head.

"As I told you, sir. I didn't call the meeting. Captain Munroe did."

Munroe offered only a nod and then stood there silently as Ryan raised his shoulders. "Well, I don't want to rush you, Captain. I believe we owe you and DS5 our thanks, but I need to prepare my speech for tomorrow. Hunting Nazis is just a small part of my remit."

"I heard, sir. Congratulations." Munroe replied, referring to the Home Secretary's step up in the political chain. After the footage of Ryan saving the young girl's life during the attack on Parliament had gone viral, and with most of the cabinet dead, the Secretary had been propelled by public opinion as the one to lead his party. He was already being hailed in the press as the only choice to fill the post of the Prime Minister, and although a general election would follow in the coming months, the Home Secretary would be confirmed within twenty-four hours after his party's committee had voted for him. The top job could not go unfilled, especially during a national crisis.

"Thank you, Ethan," Ryan replied, now turning his attention to McCitrick. "I may not be the UK's section head of DS5 for much longer, but I promise, you will always have my support whenever it is needed."

"That will be much appreciated, Minister," McCitrick replied, offering a respectful nod.

"Actually, DS5 is the reason I called this meeting, sir. I think we've found our mole."

Munroe addressed them both, and his sentence hung in the air like a bad smell. Ryan's eyes widened in surprise.

"Mole! What mole?" Ryan turned to McCitrick, whose blank expression gave nothing away. "John. You never mentioned anything about a mole in DS5. Are we talking Daedalus?"

"I'm afraid so, sir," Munroe replied, as McCitrick remained silent, still void of any emotion. "I heard it from the horse's mouth, as it were. A man named Hans Bauer, a high-level Daedalus operative I came across while I was in the States. He whispered it to me, only because he was sure I was about to be executed. You might call it a parting gift."

That McCitrick wasn't saying anything had Ryan staring at him suspiciously. "John, what's going on?"

"What's going on, sir, is that we've been betrayed," Munroe said, still staring at McCitrick. "From within the heart of the organisation. I couldn't figure out how they managed to always stay one step ahead of us. Such a quick rescue of Icarus was possible, given the local police were involved, but it was being drugged by Tobias Kessler during my visit that set off the first alarm bells. I doubt even a man like that has a sleeping drug on hand for any occasion, and his muscle, Gustav, was already waiting for me. How was that possible, unless they knew I was coming?"

"In our line of work coincidences do happen, Ethan," McCitrick said, finally breaking his silence, but Munroe shook his head.

"Maybe, McCitrick. But not in our business. Then there was the missile attack on board the C-130. How did Daedalus know our flight plan? Only a select few knew about it, and what you may not know is that the weapons used to fire at us were found. Remus told me on the flight over. Stroke of luck really. A police car was passing when they were fired. They went to investigate, there was a shoot-out and the people responsible manged to escape... but in the chaos they left the portable FIM-92 Stinger missile launcher and it was taken into evidence. Evidence we managed to access courtesy of Colonel Sinclair. Whomever Daedalus got to fire them did a sloppy job, because they still had their serial numbers. Those particular launchers were made by the US but supplied to a private contractor, and you know who footed the bill? The Ministry of Defence. In fact, it was the same department McCitrick works from."

McCitrick was still poker-faced, and he continued to listen in silence as Ryan now took a step back from the DS5 man, shaking his head in disbelief.

"And it was strange to run into Hans Bauer over in Brazil when the only people who knew about the trip were myself, Sloan and you, McCitrick. And, of course, the name that Bauer whispered in to my ear." In a flash, Munroe, pulled the SIG Sauer P320 from his holster and pointed it directly at McCitrick. "It's over, John. You were part of Project Icarus from the beginning."

Munroe motioned to Ryan as he kept his aim dead centre upon McCitrick's chest. "Minister Ryan, would you be so good as to relieve Mr McCitrick of his firearm, please?"

Ryan was looking completely shocked at the accusation, but he stepped forward and pulled the gun from its holster and then stood back as Munroe held his stance.

"You're making a big mistake," McCitrick said as next to him Ryan seethed.

"Jesus, John. After all these years. Right in our backyard. The people that have died... Parliament, for Christ's sake. I don't know what to say." Ryan tapped the gun against his thigh mindfully. "I guess Project Icarus didn't breed you as well as they thought."

Munroe now lowered his gun and he turned his attention to Ryan, who was looking wholly disappointed. "I never mentioned what Project Icarus *was*, sir."

"…What?"

"The breeding programme, sir. You haven't been briefed yet."

Without missing a beat Ryan pointed to McCitrick. "John told me on the way over."

"That's odd, sir, because I've not told him either."

Ryan was now looking unnerved as Munroe pulled out a piece of card from his pocket with his free hand and looked at it. "The name Bauer whispered in my ear wasn't McCitrick's… It was yours."

Ryan stood stunned, and with his whole face scrunched up he began to refute the accusation. "Oh, please. Just more subterfuge, Ethan. Daedalus would love nothing more than to turn us against each other."

Munroe nodded solemnly and looked at the card in his hand before returning Ryan's empathetic stare. "That's very true, but photos are worth a thousand words."

Munroe now turned the card so Ryan could see it. "That's you as a boy, isn't it, sir. We compared it to the ones we have on file, and it looks to be a match."

Ryan's shoulders sagged slightly and his lips parted in sheer astonishment as he stared at the photo.

"I took it from Bauer's 'Hall of Fame'. It's old, but it is definitely you."

Ryan was now breathing heavily, but he continued to shake his head furiously, his anger getting the better of him. "This is outrageous. I'm not a Daedalus mole!"

Munroe lowered his gaze to the weapon in Ryan's hand, which was raised slightly towards him. "Then why are you pointing that gun at me?" he asked calmly. "You *are* pointing it at me, sir. Aren't you?"

There was silence between the three men as the barrel of Ryan's gun wavered slightly, and then he raised it up, pointing it directly at Munroe's chest. "Well, I suppose there's no need for any more bullshit. In fact I rather prefer it this way. You're meant to be dead, Captain Munroe." Ryan glanced at the gun still in Munroe's hand. "Drop it on the floor, and don't be foolish, Captain. You're fast, but you're not that fast."

Munroe slowly bent his knees and dropped the gun to the floor as Ryan now glanced over at McCitrick. "And you, the great mole hunter John McCitrick. You couldn't sniff out a turd if it was right under your nose. You even bought my act in Parliament, which, if I do say so myself, was a sterling piece of work."

Ryan was looking pretty pleased with himself and he sucked in a deep breath and expelled it with pleasure. "No one would ever expect the Home Secretary to place a Semtex device directly under the PM's seat; they never check my bag upon entering. Privileges of the office. Security is far more concerned with checking the public than an MP at the centre of power. I simply walked in earlier that morning, stating government business, and placed the package before returning a few hours later, a little late I might add," Ryan raised his eyebrow, arrogantly enjoying telling his story, "and caused the blast by a remote detonation device in my pocket. I will admit I might have cut it a bit close, but it made for excellent media coverage, and the resuscitation of the young girl… well, who could have scripted that!"

McCitrick looked repulsed and he glared at Ryan with disgust. "A lot of good people died, Jacob, and the damage you've done will take the country years to recover from."

The sentiment was lost on Ryan and he winced at the idea. "Recover! You idiot, John. We're only just beginning. We're the future."

"You're a fucking Nazi, Jacob. The lowest form of scum humanity has ever served up."

Suddenly Ryan's cavalier attitude evaporated and he snarled in contempt at McCitrick's labelling.

"My colleagues and I were bred and educated to be what the Nazis only aspired to be. They came close, but coming second doesn't amount to shit in the game of global power."

"And what is that exactly?" Munroe asked, noting the familiar sudden change in demeanour that he had also seen in Hans Bauer. "You were born to do one thing, and one thing only. Create the fertile conditions for those who will really be in power if Daedalus gets its way. The Fourth Reich is a powerful idea, and pure bloodlines will always supersede those that are bred to do their bidding. Your buddy Hans Bauer taught me that. In fact he seemed to see Project Icarus as meat for the grinder. A means to an end."

"Oh, please. Bauer's had his time. You've seen to that, Captain, and those old fools with their bloodlines will be the first to peter out in the political landscape to come." Ryan's eyes squinted and he shook his head slowly. "I don't think you understand, either of you. I, and others like me, were born to rule. It's in our DNA. You can call it the Fourth Reich, national socialism, whatever, it doesn't matter. I and many like me see this for what it is. It's about power. It's about dominance. It's about a world

336

that can barely control itself through democratic means. Humans have always needed a master to guide them and tell them what to do in their lives. It is Daedalus who will answer the call. And what a beautiful future it will be. There is nothing you can do to stop it. Once the wheels of oppression begin rolling it is near impossible to turn back the tide. Besides, you're too late. In under twenty-four hours' time I will be visiting Buckingham Palace to have my premiership confirmed, officially. So, what are you going to do? Half the politicians have been wiped out and even if you did tell the British people, which you can't, they would never believe you. A Nazi spy for the Fourth Reich?" Ryan expelled a confident and bellowing laugh. "No, I think not. So, here's what's going to happen. I am going to shoot you, Ethan. Then I'm going to shoot you, John. My team will clean up the mess and then, gentlemen, tomorrow morning, I will meet with the Queen to be confirmed as Prime Minister of the United Kingdom and in the coming days and weeks I will use my considerable power to take apart DS5, piece by piece. They will be labelled as a rogue operation and classed as a terrorist group. The plan has been in place for a long time, and I will use its greatest strength against itself: its clandestine anonymity. The leaders of the US and France have no idea you even exist, and by the time I've finished they will believe you are traitors to their own governments. I will enjoy watching your compatriots burn. It's true what they say, a person's greatest strength is their greatest weakness, and I will take *great* satisfaction in your own secretive and shadowy cover being used against you."

Ryan straightened his arm, preparing to shoot. "Any last words, Captain? I would ask John here, but it will be the same old self-righteous bullshit he always comes out with."

"There are a couple of things, sir. Ambassador Breams. Did he go through the same mind-fracturing process as Icarus?"

"Bauer really told you a lot, didn't he?" Ryan replied, sounding surprised as he cocked the gun. "It took a lot of work to get him into that position, and all he needed was a sentence to click him into gear. His key sentence was a good one, a Walt Disney quote actually: 'all our dreams can come true, if we have the courage to pursue them.'"

Munroe looked unimpressed and immediately moved on to his next question. "And why did he shoot the Chancellor? Presumably it was to open the position for a Daedalus operative? Much like yourself."

Ryan shook his head. "No, the new Chancellor is not part of Daedalus. I would know if she was. Whatever high command have planned, it goes far deeper than that. Why do you care?"

Munroe now smiled politely. "No reason. I just don't like loose ends. No stone unturned. Well, that's all I have, and If you're going to shoot... aim high."

"Thank you, Ethan, I will." Ryan gave one last triumphant grin, and pulled the trigger, but there was no muzzle flash, no recoil. Instead there followed only the sound of a dull metallic click and Munroe turned his head, offering a view of the small white earpiece hidden in his ear canal. Ryan's eyes widened, but as he opened his mouth to speak, the back of his head exploded in a puffy red mist and he dropped to his knees before collapsing to the floor with a thud.

Munroe now looked over to the building opposite to see Colonel Remus already sliding the Mk 21 modular sniper rifle back into its case. "Solid shot, Colonel." He removed his earpiece and looked over at McCitrick, who was staring blankly at the still twitching corpse of Home Secretary Jacob Ryan.

"In the next hour Minister Ryan will be involved in a tragic car accident. His head will be so badly crushed that no trace of a gunshot wound will be found. We will ensure that any photos or paper trails to his links with Daedalus are destroyed and he will go down in history as a great man who stepped up to the plate after the attack on Parliament. Nothing more, nothing less."

McCitrick bent down and picked up his gun, which he then passed over to Munroe. "I want the firing pin back in my firearm within the hour, Ethan."

"I'll do it for you right now." Munroe holstered his own gun, retrieved a small piece of metal from his pocket, and then set about reassembling McCitrick's weapon. "Have you made a decision on my own situation? My connection with Project Icarus?"

McCitrick watched in silence as Munroe quickly replaced the firing pin. Once down he passed it over to the DS5 section head, who continued to stare at him. It appeared his boss was making his mind up there and then and Munroe held the gaze, never once breaking eye contact until McCitrick delivered a nasal snort. "A son cannot be held accountable for his father's actions. Whomever they may be."

It was a relief to hear, and Munroe offered a small nod of his head.

"Every member of DS5 knows, and they're all fine with it. So nothing's changed. Besides, we feel that having a super soldier on our side could be most beneficial."

Munroe winced at the title. "Could you please never use that term again?"

McCitrick actually let slip a vague smile at his embarrassment. "Very well, Ethan. But your teammates will take the piss out of you relentlessly for the foreseeable future."

"I can deal with that."

McCitrick nodded grimly, and then turned his attention back to the body of Jacob Ryan. "It's a damn shame. I always liked the man, but the havoc he's caused... Shocking."

Munroe offered a conciliatory nod. "It's concerning that Daedalus were able to install someone so high up the political ladder. If they could get the Home Secretary, then who else could they have?"

"Exactly." McCitrick held out his hand and Munroe shook it firmly. "That's what we're going to find out, and I suspect this is only the beginning. Now get going. Sloan's downstairs waiting for you. We have work to do, but I want you to take the night off. You deserve a few hours of R&R. We've got our foot in through Daedalus's door, and Bauer may not sing like a bird at first but given some time he should yield results. We are now on the offensive. Consider what happened over the past few days the end of the beginning. We're just getting started. Lots of work to be done. We still don't know why Ambassador Breams killed Chancellor Schenk but, suffice to say, we shall be keeping a very close eye on the new German Chancellor, regardless of what Ryan had to say."

"I might have some thoughts on that, sir. It will all be in my report," Munroe said.

McCitrick offered a nod. "Off you go then. And don't let me down, Ethan... Oh, and you can call me John from now on... unless you piss me off. In which case it's sir."

Chapter 32

Peter Devon was already waiting by the gates of Strawberry Field children's home as Munroe pulled up in his black BMW 330e. He switched off the engine and glanced over at Sloan, who was sprawled out in the passenger seat wearing a pair of black tinted Ray Ban sunglasses which she had perched on the tip of her nose. She had offered to make the trip with him and he'd accepted. They'd be spending a lot of time together in the future and even given the past few days he still was only just getting to know her. He'd figured they'd talk during the trip. As it turned out she'd hardly said a word and Munroe had finally conceded that she really wasn't one for small talk, but he was confident that would change... Perhaps. How long it would take, though, was anyone's guess. "I'll be waiting," was all she said, and Munroe nodded and exited the car before slowly making his way over to join the old orphanage overseer.

"She still looks magnificent," Devon said as Munroe neared, never taking his eyes off the building. "It's a shame they shut her down. We did a lot of good in this place."

"A fair amount of mystery as well, Peter," Munroe replied, joining him at the red spiked gates leading up the leafy drive to the building itself.

Devon passed over the comment and instead continued to stare. "There's a coffee shop in there now and they offer tours to die-hard Beatles fans. The Salvation Army opened a section for children with learning difficulties, but it's not the home it used to be."

Munroe stood alongside the old man and looked over to see a tear in the corner of Devon's eyes. "Things never are as you get older, Peter. But without you I can't imagine how we all would have turned out. Criminals most likely. We all did well by you."

The compliment made Devon smile. "But did I do well by you, Ethan? After your call last night I got to thinking. Did I make the right decision by never telling you how you arrived at Strawberry Field?"

"Well, what did you conclude?" Munroe asked as both men continued staring up at the old orphanage building.

"I concluded that I did, but I still regret it."

Devon turned to face him, the teardrop still swelling within the corner of his eye. "When children arrived at Strawberry I never wanted to cause them more pain than they had already experienced, and you were no different, Ethan. I remember the day you came to me well, and the young lady who brought you. She was adamant about not being your mother, but I thought at the time she just couldn't bring herself to admit it. Leaving her own child in the care of strangers couldn't have been an easy thing to live with, and I never questioned her intentions... until now."

After leaving McCitrick on the rooftop of the old War Office building Sloan had driven Munroe to pick his car up, still parked near the house where he'd first met Icarus. Police tape still covered the door and the investigation of the hostage situation was still open. It would not stay open for long if McCitrick had anything to do with it, and his name was already being scrubbed from the files. Munroe had dropped off Sloan, not at her home but instead a local pub, which said more about her than her lack of talking ever could, and then headed home and immediately called the head of hostage negotiation and his soon-to-be ex-boss, Mike Regis. There wasn't much he could divulge, and his work colleague had still been understandably unhappy at Munroe's actions back on Waterloo Bridge – and also the fact that his car had been a complete write-off, shot to hell with the engine destroyed. All Munroe had been able to say was that it was governmental business. But the fact that there would be no investigation into the man Munroe had shot had gotten right under Regis's skin. The man was a straight shooter, no grey areas, only black and white, and the whole thing stank to him of a cover-up, a flaunting of the justice system. He was right, too. He was also not happy when Munroe had handed in his notice, effective immediately, without even a reason. It had been the final straw. Regis had left him with the parting words, "Look after yourself, Ethan. It's what you're good at," before hanging up on him.

Munroe couldn't be angry, he'd have felt the same way if the roles had been reversed, but he knew at some point he would try to rekindle the friendship. Somehow.

His second call had been to Peter Devon. Firstly to apologise for leaving the Coppa Club so abruptly a few nights back, which the orphanage overseer had been more than understanding of, but also to confront him about his arrival at Strawberry Field. Of course he couldn't explain how or what he knew, but the mere mention of the woman who had dropped him off that fateful night had caused Devon to ashamedly explain. Munroe now knew she was the Daedalus nurse who had taken pity on the four-year-old who was destined to be terminated, but for Devon she had been just another mother unable to cope. This was all his friend would say over the phone, and his request for Munroe to make the four-hour drive up to Liverpool the next morning had been accepted.

After all these years it was only now that Munroe discovered that Devon still lived within a stone's throw of the old orphanage, and to him it made sense. To Devon the children who passed though these gates were family, and the building itself had become part of the clan. Buildings were funny like that, they became a conduit for memories, a tangible representation of all the lives they'd once contained. It was this reminiscing, Munroe figured, that was causing the old man to get sentimental, and he gave him a firm slap on the shoulder. "Jesus, Peter, enough with the waterworks. Don't go soft on me now."

The usual banter had Peter wiping away the tear and he grunted a laugh. "You wish, Ethan. But I do feel bad for not telling you the truth."

"Well go on, old man. Get it off your chest."

Peter composed himself and then he was back, although he looked perturbed, and as Munroe listened he was surprised by how bad the man felt at holding back this small yet important piece of personal history. It felt strange, because Munroe actually knew more than he did. And that Peter believed the woman to be Munroe's biological mother was an untruth that he would not refute. The truth was far too messy, and now tied up under the official secrets act, as all Daedalus information was.

"When your mother dropped you off, Ethan, she refused to give her name. I did try, but in vain. She only wanted to make sure that you were taken care of, and that no mention of her was ever to be made. It was a promise

I had intended not to keep, but about a week later I saw this in the papers."

Devon held a newspaper cutting in his hand and unfolded it before passing it over to Munroe.

WOMAN SLAIN IN HESWALL, the headline read, and next to it the picture of the same nurse Munroe had seen back at Bauer's office. The writing underneath read: 'Mary Cane of no fixed abode', and the article went on to report that the battered body had been found dumped by the roadside and that the police were asking for any eyewitnesses to come forward.

"She didn't go far, Heswall is just a short trip from here," Devon said, tapping the page with his finger. "After I saw this I thought it best to just let things lie, but now... well now, I'm not sure if I did the right thing."

Munroe stared at the article for a few moments longer before handing the cutting back. "You did the right thing, Peter. I'm good with it."

With an accepting nod, Devon took back the piece of paper and slid it into his trouser pocket. His shoulders sagged in relief and he expelled a short breath. "Thank you. It's been weighing at the back of my mind these past years."

"Not anymore," Munroe replied, smiling as Devon raised a finger into the air as he always did when about to add something to a conversation.

"You should know that it was her that named you. She told me your name and blood type but that was all. Your name is, and always has been, Ethan Munroe."

The extra bit of information made Munroe smile. "Thanks, Peter, good to know. And I've always known you had my back. Now, I'm afraid I need to get going."

Devon raised his eyebrows at the quick change of conversation, but then he glanced over to Sloan who, with her sunglasses on, leaning comfortably in the front passenger seat, looked as though she was fast asleep. "New lady friend, Ethan? Good for you."

"No, she's just a work colleague," Munroe was quick to correct. "She works in our admin department."

Now wasn't the time to tell Peter he was giving up his career as a hostage negotiator. He would spin that tale another time.

"Well, how about a fry-up before you go. There's a small cafe nearby that does a full heart-clogging spread, bacon, eggs, mushrooms, sausages, baked beans and a grease-packed side order of fried bread... Tempt you?"

Both he and Sloan had a meeting with McCitrick later that afternoon at the Ministry of Defence, but they had time. "Why not?"

Munroe walked over to the car as Sloan wound down the window. "Jax, this is Peter Devon. He was in charge of Strawberry Field when I was a boy, and... he's family."

Sloan reached out and shook Devon's hand. "You poor man. He must have been a nightmare."

"You have no idea," Devon replied, climbing into the back seat as Munroe got in and started up the car. "He was a constant bed-wetter. In fact that was one of the more pleasant things about him."

Sloan let out a deep chuckle as Munroe shook his head in dismay. "Don't make me dump you by the side of the road, old man."

Munroe put the BMW into first gear and took off at speed, leaving the sight of Strawberry Field's red gates in his rear-view mirror as he headed into an uncertain and secretive future. The summer was approaching but with the threat of Daedalus on the horizon it could prove to be bitterly cold. Frankly, he couldn't wait.

Epilogue

The old man tapped at the black keypad and then waited as his sliver monitor flickered brightly and the image of a middle-aged woman appeared on the screen. "Do we have a problem?" she asked politely, but with a stern resolve in her voice. "Ryan's car crash is all over the news."

The old man appeared in complete control, exuding authority, and he shook his head. "No, my dear. There is more than one way to skin a cat, and everything is proceeding as we expected."

The woman looked doubtful. "Ryan's death was *not* expected. How do we proceed? The timing is crucial, and this throws everything up in the air."

The old man looked surprised by the woman's lack of faith, and he raised one of his decrepit fingers in front of him and wagged it slowly. "Home Secretary Jacob Ryan was an unfortunate casualty of war, and although unexpected, it was not without a modicum of forewarning. As a result, we were not incapable of preparation. You may rest easy knowing those preparations are now in place."

The old man's vagueness did little to quench the woman's concerns and she was already shaking her head. "With respect, sir, his position was vital if we are to move to the next stage, and as of this moment I can't see that changing."

"The change is already being implemented as we speak, and we have many more hands to play. If you remember correctly, it was you who had hit a brick wall until we had Ambassador Breams make a breakthrough for you. Isn't that right?"

The woman now sat back in her chair, and although there was still much concern in her expression she nodded. "And I am grateful, as you know, but after the collateral of the attack on Parliament I am troubled by the options left to us. This is the first time in over twenty years we have had the chess pieces laid out in the right places, and there is only so much carnage we can cause before the media and the public take an interest in us. Our high profile is becoming unsustainable. And the mess with Icarus only appears to be galvanising DS5, hardening their resolve. Perhaps we should pull back and regroup."

The suggestion received a furious look from the old man and he slammed his hand down on the table before him. "Insurrection is a dangerous game. We are all expendable in our efforts to forge a new Reich. Don't ever forget that. Neither will we accept cowardice." He leant towards the screen and his eyes tightened. "You, like the rest of us, are in too deep to turn back now, and neither will I allow it. We are within grasp of fulfilling our goals and I won't allow your jittering nerves to fuck things up. We wouldn't want the tragedy of your predecessor repeating itself."

The warning had a notably calming effect on the woman and she relaxed in her chair. "Very well, but I ask that you tell me what your plans are, because we are running out of time."

"Don't worry, we have more than enough time, and even as we speak the wheels are turning, as you will see in the coming days. As for DS5, they are already dead in the water... You will see to that. Have some faith, Colonel Sinclair."

Colonel Anne Sinclair, US section head of DS5, sat back in her chair, looking uneasy, but she nodded. "Yes, Reich Führer Bormann. You have my unwavering support and loyalty."

Bormann looked pleased by the display and he smiled as she added, "Your father would be proud of his son. As we all are." Sinclair raised her right arm high up in the air. "Heil the coming of the Fourth Reich."

Acknowledgements

To Kit Nevile my editor for all his hours of help and advice in writing this book, both conventional and unorthodox. Couldn't have got there without you.

To Tom Marshall for giving me his time and insight into the man who would become Ethan Munroe.

To Michael, Iain, Nick and everyone at Canelo Publishing.

And as always Alison.

Praise for *Trigger Mortis*

'A humdinger of a Bond story, so cunningly crafted and thrill-ingly paced that 007's creator would have been happy to have owned it . . . The book is the best Bond movie you'll ever see without actually having to see the movie'

Simon Schama, *Financial Times*

'*Trigger Mortis* is a blast. Set two weeks after the end of the novel *Goldfinger* in 1957, it has a superb plot based around the early space race and features the return of the best Bond girl of them all, Pussy Galore'

Mail on Sunday

'Fleming fans certainly won't be disappointed. *Trigger Mortis* contains all the adrenaline you'd expect from a Bond novel with bags of humour, international jet-setting and a compel-ling cast of inventively named characters. It is, one suspects, a novel Fleming would be proud to have in the 007 canon'

Sunday Express

'Almost too good'   *Evening Standard*

'Horowitz is doing something both clever and audacious . . . a clever and enjoyable pastiche, which manages to press many of the buttons that were the purview of 007's creator'

Independent

'There is a delicate line separating imitation from parody and Horowitz stays on the right side of it to perfection'

Daily Express

Anthony Horowitz is one of the UK's most prolific and successful writers. His novels *The House of Silk* and *Moriarty* were *Sunday Times* Top Ten bestsellers and sold in more than thirty-five countries around the world. His bestselling Alex Rider series for children has sold more than nineteen million copies worldwide.

As a TV screenwriter he created both *Midsomer Murders* and the BAFTA-winning *Foyle's War*; other TV work includes *Poirot* and the widely acclaimed mini-series *Collision* and *Injustice*. Anthony has recently joined the board of the Old Vic and regularly contributes to a wide variety of national newspapers and magazines. In January 2014 he was awarded an OBE for his services to literature. Anthony Horowitz lives in London.

www.anthonyhorowitz.com

@AnthonyHorowitz